Moonlight and Vines

*M*oonlight and *V*ines

A Newford Collection

Charles de Lint

A TOM DOHERTY ASSOCIATES BOOK
NEW YORK

MOONLIGHT AND VINES

Copyright © 1999 by Charles de Lint

This book is printed on acid-free paper.

Edited by Terri Windling
Designed by Nancy Resnick

Grateful acknowledgments are made to: Kiya Heartwood for the use of lines from her song "Robert's Waltz" from the Wishing Chair album *Singing With the Red Wolves* (Terrakin Records). Copyright © 1996 by Kiya Heartwood, Outlaw Hill Publishing. Lyrics reprinted by permission. For more information about Kiya, her band Wishing Chair, or Terrakin Records, call 1-800-ROADDOG, or E-mail terrakin@aol.com.

A Tor Book
Published by Tom Doherty Associates, Inc.
175 Fifth Avenue
New York, NY 10010

Tor Books on the World Wide Web:
http://www.tor.com

Tor® is a registered trademark of Tom Doherty Associates, Inc.

Library of Congress Cataloging-in-Publication Data

De Lint, Charles
    Moonlight and vines : a Newford collection / Charles de Lint.—1st ed.
        p.   cm.
    "A Tom Doherty Associates book."
    ISBN 0-312-86518-X (alk. paper)
    1. City and town life—North America—Fiction.   2. Newford (Imaginary place)—Fiction.   3. Fantastic fiction, Canadian.
I. Title.
PR9199.3.D357M67   1999
813'.54—dc21   98-44610
                                                                          CIP

First Edition: January 1999

Printed in the United States of America

0 9 8 7 6 5 4 3

for all those
who seek light
in the darkness

for all those
who shine light
into the darkness

Contents

Author's Note

—

I've said it before, but it bears repeating: No creative endeavor takes place in a vacuum. I've been very lucky in having incredibly supportive people in my life to help in the existence of these stories, be it in terms of the nuts and bolts of editing and the like, or on more elusive, inspirational levels. To name them all would be an impossible task, but I do want to mention at least a few:

First my wife MaryAnn, for fine-tuning the words, for asking the "What if?" behind the genesis of many of the fictional elements, and for making the writing process so much less lonely;

My longtime editor Terri Windling, and all the wonderful folks at Tor Books and at my Canadian distributor H. B. Fenn, but particularly Patrick Nielsen Hayden, Jenna Felice, Andy LeCount, Suzanne Hallsworth, and of course, Tom Doherty and Harold Fenn. Short-story collections aren't exactly the bread and butter of the publishing industry these days, but the interest and support they have shown for my previous collections, *Dreams Underfoot* and *The Ivory and the Horn*, are what helped to make them the successes that they are;

Friends such as Rodger Turner, Lisa Wilkins, Pat Caven, Andrew and Alice Vachss, Charles Saunders, Charles Vess, Karen Shaffer, Bruce McEwen, and Paul Brandon who are there to commiserate when I get whiny, and cheer me on when things are going well;

The individual editors who first commissioned these stories: Anne McCaffrey, Elizabeth Ann Scarborough, Poppy Z. Brite, Peter Crowther, Katharine Kerr, Richard Gilliam, Martin H. Greenberg, Edward E.

Kramer, John DeChancie, Darrell Schweitzer, Neil Gaiman, Shawna McCarthy, Joe Lansdale, David Copperfield, Janet Berliner, Peter S. Beagle, Lawrence Schimel, Ed Gorman, James O'Barr, Bruce D. Arthurs, John Helfers, and Grant Watson;

And last, though certainly not least, my readers without whom these stories would only be soliloquies. From meeting many of you at various readings, signings, and other events, as well as the large amount of mail that arrives daily in my physical and virtual mailboxes, it's readily obvious that I'm blessed with a loyal readership made up of those for whom taking the moment for a random act of kindness is as natural as breathing. Your continued support is greatly appreciated.

If you are on the Internet, come visit my home page. The URL (address) is http://www.cyberus.ca/~cdl.

—Charles de Lint
Ottawa, Spring 1998

Sweetgrass & City Streets

Bushes and briar,
thunder and fire.

In the ceremony
that is night,
the concrete forest
can be anywhere,
anywhen.

In the wail of a siren
rising up from the distance,
I hear a heartbeat,
a drumbeat,
a dancebeat.

I hear my own
heart
fire
beat.

I hear chanting.

Eagle feather, crow's caw
Coyote song, cat's paw
Ya-ha-hey, hip hop rapping
Fiddle jig, drumbeat tapping

Once a
Once a
Once upon a time . . .

I smell the sweet smoke
of smudge sticks,
of tobacco,
of sweetgrass on the corner
where cultures collide
and wisdoms meet.

And in that moment of grace,
where tales branch,
bud to leaf,
where moonlight
mingles with streetlight,
I see old spirits in new skins,
bearing beadwork,
carrying spare change and charms,
walking dreams,
walking large.

They whisper.
They whisper to each other
with the sound of talking drums,
finger pads brushing taut hides.
They whisper,
their voices carrying,
deliberately,
like distant thunder,
approaching.

Bushes and briar . . .

—Wendelessen

Saskia

The music in my heart I bore
Long after it was heard no more.
—*Wordsworth*

1

I envy the music lovers hear.

I see them walking hand in hand, standing close to each other in a queue at a theater or subway station, heads touching while they sit on a park bench, and I ache to hear the song that plays between them: The stirring chords of romance's first bloom, the stately airs that whisper between a couple long in love. You can see it in the way they look at each other, the shared glances, the touch of a hand on an elbow, the smile that can only be so sweet for the one you love. You can almost hear it, if you listen close. Almost, but not quite, because the music belongs to them and all you can have of it is a vague echo that rises up from the bittersweet murmur and shuffle of your own memories, ragged shadows stirring restlessly, called to mind by some forgotten incident, remembered only in the late night, the early morning. Or in the happiness of others.

My own happinesses have been few and short-lived, through no choice of my own. That lack of a lasting relationship is the only thing I share with my brother besides a childhood neither of us cares to dwell upon. We always seem to fall in love with women that circumstance steals from us, we chase after ghosts and spirits and are left holding only memories and dreams. It's not that we want what we can't have; it's that we've held all we could want and then had to watch it slip away.

2

"The only thing exotic about Saskia," Aaran tells me, "is her name."

But there's more going on behind those sea-blue eyes of hers than he can see. What no one seems to realize is that she's always paying attention. She listens to you when you talk instead of waiting impatiently for her own turn to hold forth. She sees what's going on at the periphery of things, the whispers and shadows and pale might-bes that most of us only come upon in dreams.

The first time I see her, I can't look away from her.

The first time I see her, she won't even look at me—probably because of the company I'm keeping. I stand at the far end of the club, wineglass in hand, no longer paying attention to the retro-Beat standing on the stage declaiming her verses in a voice that's suddenly strident where earlier I thought it was bold. I'm not the only one Saskia distracts from the reading. She's pretty and blonde with a figure that holds your gaze even when you're trying to be polite and look away.

"Silicone," Jenny informs me. "Even her lips. And besides, her forehead's way too high. Or maybe it's just that her head's too long."

Aaran nods in agreement.

Nobody seems to like her. Men look at her, but they keep their distance. Women arch their eyebrows cattily and smile behind their hands as they whisper to each other about her. No one engages her in conversation. They treat her so strangely that I find myself studying her even more closely, wondering what it is that I'm missing. She seems so normal. Attractive, yes, but then there are any number of attractive women in the room and none of them is being ostracized. If she's had implants, she's not the first to do so, and neither that nor the size of her forehead—which I don't think is too large at all—seems to have any bearing on the reaction she seems to garner.

"She's a poseur," Aaran tries to explain. "A pretender."

"Of what?" I ask.

"Of everything. Nothing about her is the way it seems. She's supposed to be a poet. Supposed to be published, but have you ever heard of her?"

I shake my head, but what Aaran is saying doesn't mean much in this context. There are any number of fine writers that I've never heard of and—judging from what I know of Aaran's actual reading habits—the figure is even more dramatic for him.

"And then there's the way she leads you on," he goes on. "Leaning close like you're the most important person in the world, but turning a cold shoulder the moment any sort of intimacy arises."

So she turned you down? I want to ask, but I keep the question to myself, waiting for him to explain what he means.

"She's just so full of herself," Jenny says when Aaran falls silent. "The way she dresses, the way she looks down at everybody."

Saskia is wearing faded jeans, black combat boots, a short white cotton blouse that leaves a few inches of her midriff bare, and a plaid vest. Her only jewelry is a small silver Celtic cross that hangs from a chain at the base of her throat. I look at my companions, both of them overdressed in comparison. Jenny in silk blouse and skirt, heels, a clutch purse, hair piled up at the back of her head in a loose bun. Nose ring, bracelets, two earrings per ear, a ring for almost every finger. Aaran in chinos and a dark sports jacket over a white shirt, goatee, hair short on top and sides, pulled into a tiny ponytail in back. One ear double-pierced like Jenny's, the other virgin. Pinky ring on each hand.

I didn't come with either of them. Aaran's the book editor for *The Daily Journal* and Jenny's a feature writer for *In the City*, Newford's little too-cool-to-not-be-hip weekly arts-and-entertainment paper. They have many of the personality traits they attribute to Saskia and the only reason I'm standing here with them is that it's impolitic for a writer to make enemies with the press. I don't seek out their company—frankly, I don't care at all for their company—but I try to make nice when it's unavoidable. It drives my brother Geordie crazy that I can do this. But maybe that's why I can make a comfortable living, following my muse, while all too often he still has to busk on the streets to make his rent. It's not that I don't have convictions, or that I won't defend them. I save my battles for things that have meaning instead of tilting at every mild irritation that comes my way. You can fritter away your whole life with those kinds of windmills.

"So no one likes her?" I ask my companions.

"Why should they?" Jenny replies. "I mean, beyond the obvious, and that's got to wear thin once she opens her mouth."

I don't know what to reply to that, so I say, "I wonder why she comes around, then."

"Why don't you ask her yourself?" Aaran says with the same little smirk I see in too many of his reviews.

I'm thinking of doing just that, but when I look back across the club, she's no longer there. So I return my attention to the woman on the stage. She's onto a new poem now, one in which she dreams about a butcher's shop and I'm not sure if she really does, or if it's supposed to be a metaphor. Truth is, I'm not really listening to her anymore. Instead I'm thinking of Saskia and the way Aaran and Jenny have been sneering at her—physically and verbally—from the moment she walked in. I'm thinking that anyone who can call up such animosity from these two has got to have something going for her.

The poet on stage dreams of cleavers and government-approved steaks. That night I dream of Saskia and when I wake up in the morning the events of last night's reading in the club and my dream are all mixed up together. It takes the first coffee of the morning for me to sort them all out.

3

I have a friend who owns a bookstore just outside of the city and knows everything you'd ever want to know about literature, high-brow and low. She's the one who first turned me onto Michael Hannan and Jeanette Winterson. The first time I read Barry Lopez was because Holly sent me a copy of *River Notes*. We don't get together as much as either of us would like, but we've been corresponding for years—most lately by e-mail—and talk on the phone at least once a week. She's in love with books, and knows how to share that love so that when she tells you about a certain writer or book's merit, you immediately want to read it for yourself. More importantly, she's usually dead on the money. Holly's the only reason I still look at the Saturday book pages in *The Daily Journal* since Aaran took them over.

With her expertise in mind, I call Holly up after breakfast to see if she knows anything about Saskia and her poetry.

"What's her last name?" Holly asks.

I can picture her sitting at the big old rolltop desk that doubles as a sales counter in her store, a small figure in jeans and a sweater, long, dark red hair pulled back from her forehead with a pair of bobby pins, hazel eyes always bright with interest. You could come in looking for *Les Mis-*

érables or a nurse romance and she'd treat you with the same courtesy and respect. The store is crammed with books, literally, floor to ceiling. They gather like driftwood in tall stacks at the ends of bookcases, all around and upon her desk, in boxes and bags, filling the front window display except for the small cleared area where her Jack Russell terrier, Snippet, lies watching the street when she's not ensconced on Holly's lap. The sign painted onto the window, Gothic lettering, paint flaking, simply reads, HOLLY RUE, USED BOOKS.

I think about what she's just asked me and realize I don't know.

"Well, Saskia's unusual enough," Holly tells me. "Hang on while I go online."

Holly and some friends have been creating this huge database they call the Wordwood somewhere out in the Net, assuring themselves that the Information Highway will remember the old technologies—books and printing presses were marvels of technological import in their day, after all—at the same time as it embraces the new. I don't know how many of them are involved in the project, but they've been working on it for years. The Net connects them from every part of the world, each participant adding book titles, authors, bios, publishing histories, reviews, cross-references and whatever else they might think is pertinent to this amazing forest of information they've cultivated.

I tried logging on once when I was out visiting Holly and lost an afternoon glued to the screen, following some arcane trail that started with a short story by Sherman Alexie that I was trying to track down and ended up in a thicket of dissertations on Shakespeare's identity. Holly laughed at me when I finally came up for air. "The Wordwood's like that," she tells me. "One of these days I'm going to go in there and forget to come back." The way she talks about the place it's as though she actually visits it.

"Got something," she tells me. "Her last name's Madding, but she only uses her given name for a byline. We've got three titles listed—hey, wait a minute. I think I have one of these." I hear her get up from her chair and go looking for it, roam-phone in hand, because she's still talking to me. "Yeah, here it is. It's called *Mirrors* and it's her, let me see, second collection." More shuffling noises as she makes her way back to the desk and looks through the book. "You want me to read one to you? They're all pretty short."

"Sure."

"Okay. Here, I'll just do the first one, 'Tarot.'"

What she said:
You turn from me
as I turn
*   from the cards*
refusing to face
what we see.

Holly's got this amazing speaking voice, rough and resonant, like it's been strained through years of whiskey and cigarettes, though she doesn't smoke or drink. It gives the poem an edge that I'm not sure would be there if I'd just taken the words from the page.

"Nice," I say. "It sneaks up on you, doesn't it?"

"Mmm. There's a lot of sadness in those few lines. Oh, this is cool."

The word's just come back in fashion, but Holly never gave it up. She's been known to say "far out" as well.

"What's that?" I ask.

"I was looking back at the Wordwood and I see she's involved with *Street Times*. She does some editorial work for them."

That is interesting. *Street Times* is a thin little paper produced for street people to sell in lieu of asking for spare change. You see them selling it on half the corners downtown. The vendors pay something like fifty cents an issue and whatever you give them above that is what they earn. Most of the material is produced by the street people themselves—little articles, cartoons, photographs, free classifieds. Every issue they run a profile of one of the vendors, seriously heartbreaking stories. Jilly and some of her friends do free art for it occasionally and I remember Geordie played at a benefit to raise the money to set the whole thing up a couple of years ago.

"I wonder who entered this stuff on her," Holly asks.

The question's rhetorical. Considering how many people are involved in building and maintaining the Wordwood, it could be anybody.

"So you want me to keep this book for you?" she goes on.

"Sure."

I'm too intrigued to even ask the price.

"Should I put it in the mail or are you actually going to visit me for a change? It's been months."

"Five weeks, if you're counting," I say.

"Who's counting?"

"I'll be by later today if I can catch a ride with someone."

"There are buses that come out this far," she says with a smile in her voice.

"If you don't mind walking the last couple of miles."

"That's right, I forgot. You're an artiste and need to be chauffeured. So is she cute?"

Sometimes Holly's abrupt changes of topic throw me. You'd think I'd get used to it, hanging around with Jilly who can be worse, but I never do. Conversations between her and Holly are bewildering for common folk to follow.

"What do you mean, cute?" I ask.

"Oh, come on. You're calling up, looking for books by someone whose last name you don't even know and then—and this is the real giveaway—you don't even ask how much the book is. She's got to be cute."

"Maybe I'm just stimulated by her, intellectually."

I can almost see her shake her head. "Uh-uh. It's a guy thing, Christy. I know I've called you an honorary woman in the past, but you're still a guy. A single guy, yet."

So I tell her about last night.

4

It starts with a heartbeat, rhythm laid down, *one*-two, *one*-two, deep in your chest. It's not the pulse of everyday life but something that runs more profound, a dreaming cadence, a secret drumming that you can't share at first, not with anyone and especially not with her. The melody and chordal patterns might come later, when you've first made contact, when you discover that you haven't made an utter fool of yourself and she might actually reciprocate what you feel, adding her own harmonies to the score tattooed across your heart.

For now, all you can do is repeat her name like a mantra.

Saskia Madding. Saskia Madding. Saskia . . .

For now, it's all unrequited. New Age washes of sound when you think of her, great swelling chords if you happen to catch her going about her business. There, across the street, walking briskly in a light rain, skin glistening, hair feathered with moisture. There, squeezing melons at a fruit vendor's stall, laughing at something the man's said, standing with one hip jutted out, leaning over the front of the stall. There, leafing through a magazine in a smoke shop, a brief glimpse of her on the other side of the glass before you force yourself to walk by.

The music thunders in your chest. Nothing with structure. Nothing that can be transcribed or scored. But it leaves you helpless before its tumultuous presence, desperate to breathe.

5

I've read *Mirrors* a half-dozen times since Sue drove me by Holly's to pick it up. I've got Holly doing book searches for the other two collections. I've been by Angel's walk-in on Grasso Street and gone through her back issues of *Street Times*. I've even got my own modem hooked up—the one the professor gave me that's been languishing unused in a drawer of my desk for the past few months—entering the Wordwood myself to see if I can find some trace of her that Holly might have missed. A bio. A review. Anything.

In short, I've become obsessed with Saskia Madding.

I couldn't meet her now if I wanted to because I've become too desperate and there's nothing quite so pathetic or off-putting as the scent of desperation. It clings to you like a second skin, a nimbus of melancholy and pathos that, contrary to the Romantics with their marble skin and pining eyes, adds nothing to your attractiveness. You might as well have "Avoid me, I'm so hopeless" stenciled on your brow.

"The problem," Holly tells me the next time we're talking on the phone, "is that you're treating her no better than Aaran or Jenny do. No, hear me out," she says when I try to protest. "They've got their misconceptions concerning her and you're blithely creating your own."

"Not so blithely," I say.

"But still."

"But still what?"

"Don't you think it's time you stopped acting like some half-assed teenager, tripping over his own tongue, and just talked to her?"

"And say what?" I ask. "The last time I saw her was at that launch for Wendy's new book, but before I could think of something to say to her, Aaran showed up at my elbow and might as well have been surgically implanted he stayed so close to me. She probably thinks we're friends and I told you how he feels about her. I don't doubt that she knows, too, so what's she going to think of me?"

"You don't have to put up with him," Holly says.

"I know. He was on about her half the night again until I finally told him to just shut up."

"Good for you."

"Yeah, Geordie'd be proud, too. Wait'll Aaran reviews my next book."

"Does that bother you?" Holly asked.

"Not really. What bothers me is that I can't get her out of my head, but I can't even find the few ounces of courage I need to go up to her. Instead I just keep seeing her everywhere I go. I feel like I'm being haunted, except I'm the one playing the stalker and I'm not even doing it on purpose. She's probably seen me as often as I've seen her and thinks I'm seriously twisted."

"A dozen pieces of advice come to mind," Holly says, "but they'd all sound trite."

"Try one on me anyway. I need all the help I can get."

Sitting there in my apartment, receiver cradled against my ear, I can picture Holly at her desk in the bookshop. The image is so clear I can almost see her shrug.

"Just go up to her," Holly tells me. "Ask her if she wants to go for a coffee or something. The worst she can do is say no."

6

I love the poems in *Mirrors*. They're as simple as haiku and just as resonant. No easy task, I know. Every so often I turn from prose to verse, but under my direction the words stumble and flail about on the page and never really sing. I sit there and stare at them and I can't fix them. Give me a pageful of the crappiest prose and some time and I can whip it into shape, no problem. But I don't know where to begin with poetry. I know when it doesn't work. I even know what makes it work in someone else's lines. But I'm hopeless when it comes to trying to write it myself.

Saskia's poems are filled with love and sadness, explorations of social consciousness, profound declarations and simple lyric delights. The same small verse can make me smile and weep, all at the same time. But the one that haunts me the most, the one I return to, again and again, is "Puppet."

> *The puppet thinks:*
> *It's not so much*
> *what they make me do*
> *as their hands inside me.*

In what shadows did those words grow? And why wasn't I there to help her?

That makes me laugh. I can't even get up the nerve to approach her and I expect to protect her from the dangers of the world?

7

In the end it's my brother Geordie, of all people, who introduces her to me. We're sitting on the patio of The Rusty Lion on a Sunday afternoon, trying to do the familial thing that neither of us is much good at, but at least we try. Jilly always says the family we choose for ourselves is more important than the one we were born into; that people have to earn our respect and trust, not have it handed to them simply because of genetics. Well, blood ties aside, I'd still want Geordie as my brother, and I think he'd want me, but we've got so much weird history between us that our good intentions don't always play out the way we'd like them to. Every time we get together I tell myself I'm not going to rag him, I'm not going to be the know-it-all big brother, I'm not going to tell him how to live his life, or even suggest that I know better. Trouble is, we know each other too well, know exactly which buttons to push to get under each other's skin and we can't seem to stop doing so. Bad habits are the hardest to break.

We immediately start off on a bad foot when he orders a beer and I hear myself asking if he doesn't think a few minutes past noon is a little early for alcohol. So he orders a whiskey on the side, just to spite me, and says, "If you're going to have a cigarette, could you at least not blow the smoke in my face?" We're sitting there glowering at each other and that's when Saskia comes walking by, looking like she stepped out of an Alma-Tadema painting for all that she's wearing jeans and a baggy blue sweater that perfectly matches her eyes.

Geordie's face brightens. "Hey, Sass," he says. "How's it going?"

I've had this mantra going through my head for weeks now—*Saskia*

Madding, Saskia Madding—and all of a sudden I have to readjust my thinking. Her friends call her "Sass"? And how'd Geordie become one of them?

She smiles back at my brother. "Taking the day off?" she asks.

I have to give Geordie this: He works hard. He may play in a half-dozen bands and meet his rent and utilities by busking on street corners, but lazy he's not. Suddenly I want to tell him how I blew Aaran off the other night and didn't care what it might mean about how I'd get reviewed in the *Journal* in the future. I want to know if he's ever talked to Saskia about me, and if he has, what he's said. I want to ask Saskia about "Puppet" and a half-dozen other poems from *Mirror*. Instead, I sit there like a lump with a foolish grin. Words are my stock and trade, but they've all been swallowed by the dust that fills my throat. I find myself wiping the back of my hand across my brow, trying to erase the "Avoid me" I know is written there. Meanwhile, Geordie's completely at his ease, joking with her, asking her if she wants to join us. I wonder what their relationship is and this insane feeling of jealousy rears up inside me. Then Saskia's on the patio, joining us. Geordie's introducing us. My throat's still full of dust and I wish I'd ordered a beer as well instead of my caffè latte.

"So that's who you are," Saskia says as she sits down in the chair between Geordie's and my own. "I keep seeing you around the neighborhood."

"He's the original bad penny," Geordie says.

A part of me feels as though I should be angry with him for saying that. I wonder does he really mean it, have we drifted that far apart? But another part of me feels this sudden absurd affection for him for being here to introduce Saskia and me to each other. Against the rhythm of my pulse, I hear the first strains of melody, and in that instant, everything is right with the world. The desperate feeling in my chest vanishes. My throat's still dry, but the dust is gone. My features feel a little stiff, but my smile is natural.

"I've seen you, too," I find myself saying. "I've been wanting to meet you ever since I read *Mirrors*."

Her eyebrows arch with curiosity. "You've actually read it?" she asks.

"A number of times. I've tried to find your other two collections, but so far I haven't had any luck."

Saskia laughs. "I don't believe this. Newford's own Jan Harold Brunvand not only knows my work, but likes it, too?"

It never occurred to me that she might have read any of my books.

"Okay," Geordie says. "Now that we've got the mutual admirations out of the way, let's just try to enjoy the afternoon without getting into a book-by-book rundown of everything the two of you have written."

He seems as relaxed as I am, but I'm not surprised. We always do better in other people's company. It's not that we feel as though we have to put on good behavior. For some reason we simply don't pick at each other when anybody else is around. He also reads voraciously and loves to talk about books—that's probably the one thing we really have in common beyond the accident of our birth—so I know he's kidding us. I wish we could always be this comfortable with each other.

We both love books, only I'm the one that writes them. We both love music, only he's the musician. That makes us something of a rarity in our family. It wasn't that our parents didn't care for culture; it's just that they didn't have time for it. Didn't have time for us, either. I'm not sure why they had children in the first place and I really don't know why they had three of us. You'd think they'd have realized that they weren't cut out to be parents after our older brother Paddy was born.

The only thing they asked of us was that we be invisible which was like an invitation to get in trouble because we soon learned it was the only way we'd get any attention. None of us did well in school. We all had "attitude problems" which expanded into more serious run-ins with authority outside of school. The police were forever bringing us home for everything from shoplifting (Geordie) and spray-painting obscenities on an underpass (me) to the more serious trouble that Paddy got in which eventually resulted in him pulling ten-to-fifteen in a federal pen.

None of us talked to each other, so I don't know for sure why it was that Paddy hung himself in his cell after serving a couple of years hard time. But I can guess. It's hard to be alone, but that's all we ever knew how to be. Walled off from each other and anybody else who might come into our lives. Geordie and I made a real effort to straighten ourselves out after what happened to Paddy and tried to find the kind of connection with other people that we couldn't get at home. Geordie does better than I. He makes friends pretty easily, but I don't know how deep most of those friendships go. Sometimes I think it's just another kind wall. Not as old or tall as the one that stands between us, but it's there all the same.

8

Holly looks up in surprise when I walk into her shop the next day.

"What?" she asks. "Two visits in the same month? You sure you haven't gotten me mixed up with a certain blonde poet?"

"Who?" I reply innocently. "You mean Wendy?"

"You should be so lucky."

She accepts the coffee and poppyseed muffin I picked up for her on my walk from the bus stop and graciously makes room for me on her visitor's chair by the simple expediency of sweeping all the books piled up on it into her arms and stacking them in a tottery pile beside the chair. Naturally they fall over as soon as I sit down.

"You know the rules," she says. "If you can't treat the merchandise with respect—"

"I'm not buying them," I tell her. "I don't care how damaged they are."

Holly pops the lid from her coffee and takes an appreciative sip before starting in on the muffin. She no sooner unwraps it, than Snippet is on her lap, looking mournfully at every bite until I take a doggie bone out of my pocket and bribe her back onto the floor with it. I know enough to come prepared.

Holly doesn't ask what I'm doing here and for a long time I don't get into it. We finish our muffins, we drink our coffee. Snippet finishes her bone then returns to Holly's lap to look for muffin crumbs. Time goes by, a comfortable passage of minutes, silence that's filled with companionship, a quiet space of time untouched by a need to braid words into a conversation. We've done this before. There've been times we've spent the whole afternoon together and not needed to talk or even react to each other's presence. Sometimes just being with a friend is enough. I've never been able to tell Holly how much I appreciate her being a part of my life, but I think she knows all the same.

After a while I tell her about finally meeting Saskia yesterday, how Geordie introduced us, how I'm going to be seeing her tonight.

"So you're deliriously happy," Holly says, "and you've come by to rub it in on a poor woman who hasn't had a date in two months."

Holly smiles, but I don't need to be told she's teasing me.

"Something like that," I say.

She nods. "So what's the real reason you're here?"

"I logged onto the Wordwood last night and something really weird happened to me," I tell her. "I wasn't really thinking about what I was doing and started to type a question to myself—the way I do when I'm writing and I don't want to stop and check a fact—and the program answered me."

Holly makes an encouraging noise in the back of her throat to let me know she's paying attention, but that's it. I can't believe she's being this blasé and figure she hasn't really understood me.

"Holly," I say. "I didn't type something like 'Go Emily Carr' and wait for the program to take me to whatever references it has on her. I entered a question—misspelled a couple of words, too—and before I had a chance to go on, the answer appeared on my screen."

She shrugs. "That kind of thing happens all the time in the Wordwood."

"What? There's somebody sitting at their keyboard somewhere, scanning whoever else happens to be online and responding to their questions?"

Holly shakes her head. "The program wasn't set up for two-way dialogues between users. It's just a database."

"So who answered me?"

"I don't know." I hear a nervousness in the laugh she offers me. "It just happens."

"And you're not the least curious about it?"

"It's hard to explain," Holly says. "It's like the program's gone AI, kind of taken on a life of its own, and none of us quite knows how to deal with it, so we've sort of been ignoring it."

"But this has got to be a real technological breakthrough."

"I suppose."

I can't figure out why she's not as excited about it as I am. I don't keep up on all the scientific journals, but I've read enough to know that no one's managed to produce a real artificial intelligence program yet—something indistinguishable from a real person, except it hasn't got a body, it's just living out there in the Net somewhere.

"There's something you're not telling me," I say.

Holly gives me a reluctant nod. "None of us has been entering data into the program for months," she admits.

"What are you saying?"

"I'm saying it's getting the information on its own. The Wordwood's so comprehensive now that we couldn't have entered all the information it now holds even if each of us had spent all our time keying it in, twenty-four hours a day, seven days a week. And the really weird thing is, it's not on the hard drive of our server anymore. It's just . . . out there, somewhere."

I give her a blank look, still not understanding why she's not excited about this, why she hasn't trumpeted their accomplishment to the world.

"The Wordwood's everything we hoped it would be and more," she explains when I ask. "It's efficient beyond anything we could have hoped for."

"And?"

"And we're afraid of screwing around with it, or talking it up, for fear that it'll go away."

"It."

I suddenly find myself reduced to one-word responses and I don't know why.

"The program," Holly says. "The entity that's taken up residence in the Wordwood, whatever it is. It's like a piece of magic, our own guardian angel of books and literature. Nobody wants to take the chance of losing it—not now. It's become indispensable."

"Holly—"

"Did you recognize its voice?" she asks. I shake my head.

"Some of the others using the program recognize its speech patterns, the cadence of its language, as belonging to people they once knew—or still know, but rarely see anymore."

I finally manage a whole sentence. "You mean it's mimicking these people?"

"No. It's more like it really is these people—or at least it is them when you happen to be talking to it. When I'm online with the Wordwood, I hear my grandmother's voice in the way it responds to me. Sometimes . . ." She hesitates, then goes on. "Sometimes it's like I'm actually sitting in a forest somewhere with Gran, talking about books."

I love a good mystery and this has all the makings of the best kind of urban myth.

"How long has this been going on?" I ask.

"About two years."

It's not until much later that I realize this is around the same time Saskia first arrived in Newford.

9

Spirits and ghosts.

My last serious relationship was with a woman who wasn't so much flesh and blood as a spirit borrowing her cloak of humanity. Her name was Tally. Tallulah. The essence of the city, made manifest for the nights we stole from its darker corners, the hours in which we made light between us when everything else lay in shadows. She left because she had to be hard, she had to be tough to survive, the way the city is now. Loving me, she couldn't meet the spite and meanness with like intent. She couldn't survive.

She's out there still. Somewhere. I don't see her, but I can still feel her presence sometimes. On certain nights.

The last time Geordie got serious about a woman, she turned into a ghost.

My therapist would have a heyday with this material, but I've never come right out and told her about any of it. I couch the truths I give her with the same thin veneer of plausibility that I slip onto the facts of some of my stories. I know how weird that sounds, considering what I write, but I've seen things that are real—that I know are true—but they're so outrageous, the only way I can write about them is to start with "Once upon a time." Truth masquerading as lies, but then it's all artifice, isn't it? Language, conversation, stories. All of it. Since Babel fell, words can no longer convey our intent. Not the way that music can.

And the music I hear now . . .

I can't get enough of it. Long, slow chords that resonate deep in my chest for hours after Saskia and I have been together, tempered only by the fear that she's too deeply cloaked in mystery and that, like Tally, that mystery will one day take her away.

I don't mean the mystery that we are to each other, small islands of flesh and bone that are yet great with thought, lumbering like behemoths through dark waters, occasionally interacting with one another, but rarely understanding the encounter. No, I sense that Saskia is part of a deeper mystery, the kind that catwalks over the marrow of our spines, the kind that wakes awe deep in our chests and makes our ribs reverberate with their sacred tones. The kind that we may experience, but only briefly. The kind that resonates so deeply as much because of its brevity. Because our mortal frailty was not meant to hold such music for more than a whisper of time. A few days. A few weeks at most.

In short, I imagine Saskia as Geordie's ghost, as my Tallying spirit, a mystery that will hold me for a brief time, fill me with her inescapable music, then leave me holding only memories, chasing echoes.

I try to tell Geordie about it one day, but all he says is that I'm merely exaggerating what all new lovers feel, blowing my insecurities way out of proportion.

"Like you're suddenly an expert," I say, frustrated. "When was the last time you were even on a date?"

I regret the words as soon as they're out of my mouth—long before the hurt look comes into my brother's eyes. It was a cheap shot. Neither of us has to be reminded of his deficiencies, least of all by each other.

"I'm sorry," I tell him.

He knows it's true. He knows I mean it. But it doesn't change the fact that we're walking wounded, both of us, we've always been walking wounded, we've just learned how to hide it better than most. It's not simply the ghosts and spirits; it's the emotional baggage we've had to carry around with us ever since we were kids. Don't feel sorry for us. But don't pretend you understand, either.

"I know you miss Tally," Geordie says to me. "But—"

"Saskia's not Tally," I say.

Geordie nods.

"So what are you trying to tell me?" I have to ask.

"Just remember that," he says. "Take people as they are instead of always trying to second-guess them. Have some faith in her."

He smiles as he uses the word. We both know all about faith, how belief in something is a commodity that requires a coin that we usually find too dear to pay.

"What about music?" I ask suddenly, changing the subject as abruptly as Jilly or Holly might, but it doesn't faze Geordie. He and Jilly see so much of each other that he's obviously used to it by now.

"What about it?" he says.

"Where does it come from?"

Now he gives me a blank look.

"I mean, where does it originate for you?" I say. "When you write a tune, how do you hear it? Where does it come from?"

Geordie taps his ear. "I just hear them. Faintly at first. There's always music going on in my ear, but every once in a while a tune becomes insistent and won't go away until I work it out or write it down."

"So you have something like a soundtrack going on inside your head all the time?"

"No," he says. "It's not like that. I guess the tunes are always there, a kind of background to whatever else I'm doing, but I have to pay attention to them to bring one of them out from the rest. And it's not as though I can't ignore them. I can. But if I do ignore them for too long, they just go away. Like when I don't play my fiddle or whistle for awhile. The music kind of dries up inside me and all I know is that I'm missing something, but I don't always know what. That's why I can't do the regular nine-to-five—I'm away from the music too long and I end up carrying around this desert inside. I'd rather be broke but with a forest of tunes in my head."

I can't remember the last time Geordie talked to me like this, exposing such a private piece of himself at such length.

"For me it's like a soundtrack," I tell him. "I can't write a tune, but I hear this music all the time, especially when I'm with somebody."

Geordie smiles. "So what do you hear when you're with me?"

"Sad tunes," I tell him. "Adagios. A bittersweet music on bowed cellos and piano that seems to hold a great promise that never quite had the chance to break through."

Geordie's smile falters. He wants to think I'm kidding him, but he can tell I've given him an honest answer. One thing we've never been able to do is lie to each other. To ourselves, yes, but never to each other.

"I guess we should try harder," he says.

"We do try, Geordie. Look at us, we're here, talking to each other, aren't we? Have been for years. When was the last time you saw anybody else in our family? Our problem isn't a lack of trying, it's getting past all the crap we've let get in the way."

He doesn't say anything for a long time, but his gaze holds mine for longer than I can ever remember him doing.

"And Saskia?" he asks finally.

"I can't even begin to describe that music," I tell him.

10

Until I met Saskia, the most curious person I knew was Jilly. Everything interests Jilly—no object, no event, no person is exempt—but she's particularly taken by the unusual, the same as I. I know the reason I started chasing down urban legends and the like was because it was a way for me to escape from what was happening in my home life at the time, a chance for me to feel like I was a part of something. I don't know what her excuse is. She and Geordie have exchanged war stories, but conversations between Jilly and me invariably center around the latest curiosity we've happened to stumble across.

Saskia's inquisitiveness is more like Jilly's than mine—only multiplied a hundredfold. She wants to see and hear and taste everything. Whenever we eat out, it has to be at a different ethnic restaurant from the one before. I've seen her try every kind of coffee in a café, every kind of beer in a tavern, every kind of pastry in a bakery—not all in one day, of course. She simply keeps going back until she's had the chance to sample them all.

She's entranced with music and while she has very definite likes (opera, hip hop and flamenco) and dislikes (anything by Chopin—go figure), she approaches it in the same way she does food and drink: She wants to sample it all. Ditto live theater, films, TV, how and where we make love—everything except for books. The odd thing is that while she's incredibly knowledgeable with the background of just about everything she experiences, she savors each experience as though coming upon it for the first time. It can be disconcerting, this juxtaposing of familiarity and ignorance, but I like it. It's like being in the company of a friend with a particularly up-to-date edition of *Brewer's Phrase and Fable* in the back of her head.

What's less easy to accept is the negative reaction she garners from most people. Even complete strangers seem to go out of their way to be rude or impolite to her. Needless to say, it infuriates me, though it doesn't seem to bother Saskia at all. Or at least not so she ever lets on. Who knows how she really feels about it? It's not exactly the kind of question I feel comfortable bringing up this early in our relationship. What if she's never noticed it?

I ask Holly about it when I drop by the store, almost a month to the day I made my last visit. This time I come bearing fresh slices of banana bread with the usual coffees and doggie bone for Snippet.

"So now you've met her," I say. Saskia and I ran into Holly at the opening for a new show by Sophie last night and went for drinks afterward. "What do you think?"

Holly takes a sip of coffee to wash down the last of her banana bread and smiles. "I think she's lovely."

"Me, too." I pause for a moment, then ask, "Did you notice anything unusual about her?"

Holly hesitates. "Well, she seems to know an awful lot about brandies for someone who says she's never had one before."

"Besides that."

Holly shakes her head.

"The way other people reacted to her in the bar?" I prompt.

Holly strokes the fur on Snippet's shoulders—the dog, having hopped up on Holly's lap when she finished her own treat, is now looking for possible holdouts in the folds of Holly's skirt. Holly glances at her computer screen. I recognize the Wordwood menu.

"A lot of people feel uncomfortable around magic," she says finally. "You must've noticed this by now. The way some people will review your work, going into it with a negative attitude simply because of its content. Or the way they start to fidget and look uneasy if the conversation turns to the inexplicable."

"Of course," I say. "But I'm not sure I'm getting your point."

"It's Saskia," Holly says. "She's magic."

"Magic." I'm back to one-word echoes again.

Holly nods. "Her being magic is what antagonizes them. They recognize it in her, but they don't want to believe it, they can't believe it, so they lash out at her in defense. Humanity's whole unfortunate history is one long account of how we attack what we don't understand, what's strange to us. And what's stranger than magic?"

"How is she magic?" I want to know.

"It's like . . . well, does she remind you of anyone? Not the way she looks, though that seems familiar, too, but the way she talks. The cadence of her voice."

I shake my head.

"Well, she reminds me of Gran."

I'm starting to get a bad feeling about this as I realize that after one brief meeting, Holly's picked up on something that I should have seen from the start.

"Your grandmother," I say.

"Mm-hmm."

This time I'm the one who glances at the Wordwood menu on her computer screen. I turn back to Holly, but she won't quite meet my gaze.

"What exactly are you saying?" I ask.

"Maybe you should ask her about the Wordwood," Holly says.

That's when I realize that Saskia does remind me of someone—not in what she's saying, but in how she says it. She reminds me of Tally.

11

I feel like the person in the folk tale who calls the cat by its true name which makes it leave. Like the shoemaker putting out clothes for the brownies. Like the seventh bride with Bluebeard's key in hand, approaching the forbidden door.

I can hear, in the joyful music that arcs between Saskia and myself, the first faint strains of sadness, a bittersweet whisper of strings, a foreshadowing of the lament to come. If this were a film, I'm at the point where I'd want to shout up at the screen, "Don't screw it up! Leave well enough alone." But I can't stop myself. I have to know. Even understanding the price one must pay when unmasking faerie, I have to know.

So, heart in throat, I ask Saskia that night, where did she live before she moved to Newford, where is she from, expecting I'm not sure what, but not that a merry laugh would start in her eyes and spread across her face. Not that she'd put her hand tenderly against my cheek, look long into my eyes and then lean forward to kiss my mouth. I can taste the good humor on her lips.

"I thought you knew," she says. "I lived in the forest."

"The Wordwood."

She nods. "A forest of words and names and stories. I love it there, but I had to know more. I had to experience firsthand what I could only read about in the forest. I knew what the sun was supposed to feel like. I knew about rain and how it must feel against your face. I could imagine what food tasted like and drink and music and love. But reading about something's not the same as doing it, is it?"

I shake my head.

"So I chose a shape from a magazine picture that I thought would be pleasing and came across to be here."

How? I want to ask, but I realize it's irrelevant. Mysteries are what they are. If they could be explained, they would lose their resonance.

"Do you miss it at all?" I end up asking.

Saskia shakes her head. "No. I . . . ." She hesitates, looking for a way to explain herself clearly. "Part of me's still there," she settles on. "That's why I"—she laughs again—"seem to know so much. I just 'look' it up in the forest."

"When I put it all together," I tell her, "I didn't know what to think. I guess I still don't know."

"You think I'm going to leave you," she says. "You think I'm going back and when I do, I'll leave you behind."

I don't trust myself to speak. All I can do is nod. I can feel a deep chord welling up in my chest, building, building, to a crescendo. A tsunami of swelling, thrumming sound.

The merriment flees her eyes and she leans close to me again, so close I'm breathing her breathing. She looks so serious. The deep sea blue of her eyes starts to swallow me.

"The only way I'll leave you," she says, "is if you send me away."

The tsunami breaks over me as I hold her close.

12

Geordie doesn't usually come over to where I live unless it's to help me move, which I seem to do about once a year. So he gets to see the old place twice, the new place once, until I move again. The image he carries in his head of where I live must consist of empty apartments, bare walls and rugless floors, the furniture in odd arrangements, preparing to leave or having just arrived. And then there're all the boxes of books and papers and what-have-yous. Sometimes I think I just live out of boxes.

But we're in my study this evening and I'm not in the middle of a move, neither coming nor going, although there still are a half-dozen boxes of books in one corner, left over from the previous move. Geordie's standing by my desk, reading a poem called "Arabesque" that's taped to the wall beside my computer.

> *The artist closed her book,*
> *returning it to the shelf*
> *that stored the other*
> *stories of her life.*
> *When she looked up,*
> *there were no riddles*
> *   in her gaze;*
> *only knowing.*

Don't make of us
more than what we are,
she said.
We hold no great secret
except this:
We know that
all endeavor is art
when rendered
with conviction.
The simple beauty
   of the everyday
strikes chords
as stirring as
oil on canvas,
finger on string,
the bourée in
perfect demi-pointe.

The difference is
we consider it art.

The difference is
we consider
art.

When it consumes us,
what consumes us,
is art:
an invisible city
we visit with our dreams

   Returning,
we are laden down with
the baggage of
our journeys,
and somewhere,
in a steamer trunk
or a carry-on,
we carry souvenirs:
signposts,

> *guidebooks,*
> *messages from beyond.*
>
> *Some are merely*
> *more opaque*
> *than others.*

Geordie stands there, whiskey in hand, and reads it through a couple of times, before coming back to join me on the other side of the room. I have two club chairs there with a reading lamp and a table set between them. Geordie places his whiskey glass on the table and sits down.

"Did you write that?" he asks.

I shake my head. "No, it's one of Saskia's. I couldn't write a piece of verse if my life depended on it."

I've got a roast in the oven, with potatoes baking in a circle around it. Saskia was making a salad, but she ran out to the market to get some lemons just before Geordie arrived.

"I like it," Geordie says. "Especially that bit about art being like an invisible city from which we bring things back. It reminds me of Sophie's serial dreams."

Saskia moved in a couple of months ago, setting up her own study in what was my spare bedroom. It's a bright, airy room, with a thick Oriental carpet on the floor, tons of pillows, a shelf filled with knickknacks running along one wall and all sorts of artwork on the others. She writes at a small mahogany desk by the window that stands so short it won't take a chair. She sits on one of the pillows when she writes at it. There aren't any books in the room, but then she doesn't need them. She's got her own reference library in her head, or wherever it is that she connects with the Wordwood.

Now that I know, about that forest of words, how she grew up in the shelter of its storied trees, she doesn't remind me of Tally anymore. I can't remember how she ever did, though Holly still hears her Gran, and I suppose other people hear who they expect to hear. I don't know how, exactly, she crossed over from the Wordwood in the first place, but the longer she stays here, in this world, the more she becomes a part of it and the less she rattles people. Which is a good thing since it means no more unwarranted frowns and catty remarks directed her way.

"You guys seem pretty happy," Geordie says.

I smile. "We are. Who'd have thought I'd ever settle down?"

Ever since Saskia moved in, we've had Geordie over for dinner at least once every couple of weeks. But this is the first time we've been alone in the apartment.

"You know," I say, "there are things we never talk about. About back when."

I don't have to explain "back when" to him. Back when we lived at home. Back when Paddy was still alive. Back when we hid from each other as much as from our parents. Back when we shut each other out because that was the only way we knew how to deal with people, the only way we knew to relate to anybody. Stand back. Give me room.

"You don't have to say anything," Geordie tells me.

"But I do," I say. "I want to explain something. You know how sometimes you want something so badly, all you can do is drive it away? You keep looking for the weak link so that you can point at it and say, there it is. I knew this couldn't work out. I knew this was too good to be true."

He looks a little confused. "You're talking about what you went through with Saskia now, aren't you?"

"I went through that with Saskia," I agree. "But she was patient and waited me out instead of walking away."

"What's that got to do with us?" Geordie wants to know.

"I just want you to know that I'm not simply going through the motions here. That it's not only Saskia who wants to see you. I want to see you, too. I should have been there for you when we were kids. I was your older brother. I shouldn't have let you grow up alone the way I did."

"But we *were* just kids."

I nod. "But you had to resent me for not being the big brother you needed. I know I sure as hell resented Paddy. It's taken me a long time to work through that, but now that I finally have, it's way too late to tell him. I don't want the same thing to lie there between us."

"I never hated you," Geordie says. "I just didn't understand why things had to be the way they were."

"I know. But we've had that lying between us for all these years, the knowing that we weren't there for each other then and maybe we won't be there for each other in the future, some time when it really matters. It's the same self-fulfilling prophecy. You don't trust something to be true, so you push it to the point when it isn't true."

"That'll never happen," Geordie says, but I can see it's something he wants to believe, not something he really believes.

"We can't let it happen," I say. "So that's why I'm telling you now what Saskia said to me: The only way I'll leave you, is if you send me away."

13

I don't envy the music others hear anymore; I'm too filled with my own now, the strains that connect me to Saskia and my brother and the other people I love in my life. I'm not saying my world's suddenly become perfect. I've still got my ups and downs. You should see the review that *The Daily Journal* gave my last book—Aaran Block at his vitriolic worst. But whenever things get bad, all I do is slow down. I stop and listen to the music and then I can't help but appreciate what I do have.

It's funny what a difference a positive attitude can have. When you go out of your way to be nice to people, or do something positive for those who can't always help themselves the way Saskia does with her editorial work on *Street Times*, it comes back to you. I don't mean you gain something personally. It's just that the world becomes a little bit of a better place, the music becomes a little more upbeat, and how can you not gain something from that?

See, when you get down to the basics of it, everything's just molecules vibrating. Which is what music is, what sound is—vibrations in the air. So we're all part of that music and the worthier it is, the more voices we can add to it, the better off we all are.

Sure beats the silence that's threatening to swallow us otherwise.

14

"Tell me a story," Saskia says that night after Geordie's gone home.

I turn my face toward her and she snuggles close so that my mouth is right beside her ear.

"Once upon a time," I say, "there was a boy who lost his ability to sing and the only person who could find it for him lived in a forest of words, but he didn't meet her until he was much, much older. . . ."

In This Soul of a Woman

If I were a man, I can't imagine it would have turned out this way. I will say no more except what I have in my mind and that is that you will find the spirit of Caesar in this soul of a woman.

—from the letters of Artemisia Gentileschi (1593–c.1652)

1

"Eddie wants to see you."

"What's he want?" Nita asked. "Another blow job?"

"Probably. I think he's tired of the new girl."

"Well, fuck Eddie. And fuck you, too."

"Christ, Nita. You on the rag or what? I'm just passing along a message."

Nita didn't turn to look at Jennifer. She stared instead at her reflection in the mirror, trying to find even one familiar feature under the makeup. Even her eyes were wrong, surrounded by a thick crust of black eye shadow, the irises hidden behind tinted red contacts. From beyond the dressing room came the thumping bass line of whatever David Lee Roth song Candy used in her act. That meant she had ten minutes before she was up again. Lilith, Mistress of the Night. Black leather and lace over Gothic-pale skin, the only spots of color being the red of her eyes, her lips, and the lining of her cape. Nita's gaze dropped from her reflection to the nine-foot-long whip that lay coiled like a snake on the table in front of her.

"Fuck this," she said.

The dressing room smelled of cigarettes and beer and cheap perfume which just about summed up her life. She swept her arm across the top of the table and sent everything flying. Whip and makeup containers. A glass, half full of whiskey. Cigarettes, lighter, and the ashtray with butts spilling out of it. A small bottle filled with uppers. The crash of breaking glass was loud in the confined quarters of the dressing room.

Jennifer shook her head. "I'm not cleaning that shit up," she said.

Nita looked up from the mess she'd made. The rush of utter freedom she'd felt clearing the table top had vanished almost as quickly as it had come.

"So who asked you to?" she asked.

Jennifer pulled a chair over from one of the other tables and sat down beside her. "You want to talk about it?"

Nita bit back a sharp retort. Jennifer wasn't her friend—she didn't have any friends—but unlike ninety-nine-point-nine percent of the world, Jennifer had always treated her decently. Nita looked away, wishing she hadn't sent her shot of whiskey flying off the table with everything else.

"Last time I was up, my ex's old man was in the audience," she said.

"So?"

"So the only way I could keep my visitation rights with Amanda was by promising I'd get a straight job."

Jennifer nodded, understanding. "The old bad influence line."

"Like she's old enough to know or even care what her old lady does for a living." Nita was really missing that drink now. "It's so fucking un- fair. I mean, it's okay for this freak to come into a strip joint with his bud- dies and have himself a good time, but my working here's the bad influence. Like we even want to be here."

"I don't mind that much," Jennifer said. "It beats hooking."

"You know what I mean. He's going to run straight to a judge and have them pull my visiting rights."

"That sucks," Jennifer agreed. She leaned forward and gave Nita a quick hug. "But you gotta hang in there, Nita. At least we've got jobs."

"I know."

"And you'd better go see Eddie or maybe you won't even have that."

Nita shook her head. "I can't do it. I can't even go out on the stage again tonight."

"But . . ." Jennifer began, then she sighed. "Never mind. We'll figure out a way to cover for you."

"And Eddie?"

Jennifer stood up and tugged down on the hem of her miniskirt. "That's one you're going to owe me, girl."

2

When Nita stepped out the back door of the Chic Cheeks in her street clothes all that remained of her stage persona was the shock of jet-black hair that fell halfway down her back in a cascade of natural curls. She was wearing faded blue jeans that were tucked into cowboy boots. The jeans had a hole in the left knee through which showed the black fabric of her body stocking. Overtop of it was a checked flannel shirt, buttoned halfway up, the tails hanging loose. Her purse was a small khaki knapsack that she'd picked up at the Army Surplus over on Yoors Street. Her stage makeup was washed off and all she wore now was a hint of eye shadow and a dab of lipstick.

She knew she looked about as different from Lilith in her leathers and lace as could be imagined, so Nita was surprised to be recognized when she stepped out into the alleyway behind the club.

"Lilith?"

Nita paused to light a cigarette, studying the woman through a wreath of blue-grey smoke. The stranger was dressed the way Nita knew the club's customers imagined the dancers dressed offstage: short, spike-heeled boots; black stockings and miniskirt; a jean vest open enough to show more than a hint of a black lace bra. She wore less makeup than Nita had on at the moment, but then her fine-boned features didn't need it. Her hair was so blonde it was almost white. It was cut punky and seemed to glow in the light cast from a nearby streetlamp.

"Who wants to know?" Nita finally asked.

"Does it matter?"

Nita shrugged and took another drag from her cigarette.

"I saw you dancing," the woman went on. "You're really something." Now she got it.

"Look," Nita said. "I don't date customers and—no offense—but I don't swing your way. You should go back inside and ask for Candy. She's always looking to make a little something on the side and I don't think she much cares what you've got between your legs, just so long as you can pay."

"I'm not looking for a hooker."

"So what are you looking for?"

"Someone to talk to. I recognized a kindred soul in you."

The way she said it made Nita sigh. She'd heard this about a hundred times before.

"Everybody thinks we're dancing just for them," she said, "but you know, we're not even thinking about you sitting out there. We're just trying to get through the night."

"So you don't feel a thing?"

"Okay, so maybe I get a little buzz from the attention, but it doesn't mean I want to fuck you."

"I told you. That's not what I'm looking for."

"Yeah, yeah. I know." Nita ground her cigarette out under the heel of her boot. "You just want to talk. Well, you picked the wrong person. I'm not having a good night and to tell you the truth, I'm not all that interesting anyway. All the guys figure women with my job are going to be special—you know, real exotic or something—but as soon as we go out on a date with somebody they figure out pretty quick that we're just as boring and fucked up as anybody else."

"But when you're on the stage," the woman said, "it's different then, isn't it? You feed on what they give you."

Nita gave her an odd look. "What're you getting at?"

"Why don't we go for a drink somewhere and talk about it?" the woman said. She looked around the alleyway. "There's got to be better places than this to have a conversation."

Nita hesitated for a moment, then shrugged. "Sure. Why not? It's not like I've got anything else to do. Where'd you have in mind?"

"Why don't we simply walk until we happen upon a place that appeals to us?"

Nita lit another cigarette before she fell in step with the woman.

"My name's not Lilith," she said.

"I know." The woman stopped and turned to face her. "That's my grandmother's name."

Like people couldn't share the same name, Nita thought. Weird.

"She used to call me Imogen," the woman added.

She offered her hand, so Nita shook it and introduced herself. Imogen's grip was strong, her skin surprisingly cool and smooth to the touch. Shaking hands with her was like holding onto a hand made of porcelain. Imogen switched her grip on Nita's hand, shifting from her right to her left, and set off down the alleyway again. Nita started to pull free, but then decided she liked the feel of that smooth cool skin against her own and let it slide.

"What does 'Nita' mean?" Imogen asked.

"I don't know. Who says it's supposed to mean anything?"

"All names mean something."

"So what does your name mean?"

" 'Granddaughter.' "

Nita laughed.

"What do you find so humorous?"

Nita flicked her cigarette against the nearest wall which it struck in a shower of sparks. "Sounds to me like your grandmother just found a fancy way of not giving you a name."

"Perhaps she had to," Imogen said. "After all, names have power."

"Now what's that supposed to mean?" Nita asked.

Imogen didn't answer. She came to an abrupt halt and then Nita saw what had distracted her. They'd been walking toward the far entrance of the alley and were now only a half-dozen yards from its mouth. Just ahead lay the bright lights of Palm Street. Unfortunately, blocking their way were three men. Two Anglos and a Hispanic. Not yet falling-down drunk, but well on the way. Palm Street was as busy as ever but Nita knew that in this part of the city, at this time of night, she and Imogen might as well have been on the other side of the world for all the help they could expect to get from the steady stream of pedestrians by the mouth of the alley.

"Mmm-mmm. Looking good," one of the three men said.

"But the thing is," added one of his companions, "I've just got to know. When you're fucking each other, which one's pretending to be the guy?"

Drunken laughter erupted from all three of them.

Imogen let go of Nita's hand. She was probably scared, Nita thought. Nita didn't blame her. She'd be scared herself if it wasn't for the fact that she'd come to a point in her life where she just didn't give a shit anymore.

Reaching into one of the front pockets of her jeans, she pulled out a switchblade. When she thumbed the button on the side of the handle, it opened with an evil-sounding *snick*.

"Oh, *conchita*," the Hispanic said, shaking his head in mock sorrow. "We were just going to have some fun with you, but now there's got to be some pain."

He stepped forward, the Anglos flanking him, one on either side. Before Nita could decide which of them was going to get the knife, Imogen moved to meet them. What happened next didn't seem to make any sense at all. It looked to Nita that Imogen picked up the first by his face, thumb on one temple, fingers on the other, and simply pitched him over her shoulder, back behind them, deeper into the alley. The second she took out with a blow to the throat that dropped him on the spot. The third tried to bolt, but she grabbed his arm and wrenched it up behind his back until Nita heard the bone snap. He was still screaming from the pain when Imogen grabbed his head and snapped his neck with a sudden twist.

Imogen held the dead man for a long moment, staring into his face as though she wanted to memorize his features, then she let him fall to the pavement. Nita stared at the body, at the way it lay so still on the ground in front of them. Her gaze went to the other two assailants. They lay just as unmoving. One moment there had been three half-drunk men about to assault them and in the next they were all dead.

"What—" Nita had to clear her throat. "What the fuck did you do to them?"

Imogen didn't even seem to be breathing hard. "It's a . . . a kind of judo," she said.

Nita looked at her companion, but it was hard to make out her features in the poor light. She seemed to be smiling, her teeth flashing as white as did her hair. Nita slowly closed up her knife and stowed it back in her jeans.

"Judo," Nita repeated slowly.

Imogen nodded. "Come on," she said, offering Nita her hand again.

Nita hesitated. She lit a cigarette with trembling fingers and took a long drag before she eased her way around the dead man at her feet to take Imogen's hand. The porcelain coolness calmed her, quieting the rapid drum of her pulse.

"Let's get that drink," Imogen said.

"Yeah," Nita said. "I think I could really use a shot right about now."

3

They ended up in Fajita Joe's, a Mexican bar on Palm Street with a terrace overlooking Fitzhenry Park. The place catered primarily to yuppies and normally Nita wouldn't have been caught dead in it, but by the time they were walking by its front door she would have gone in anywhere just to get a drink to steady her jangled nerves. They took a table on the terrace at Imogen's insistence—"I like to feel the night air," she explained. Nita gulped her first shot and immediately ordered a second whiskey, double, on the rocks. With another cigarette lit and the whiskey to sip, she finally started to relax.

"So tell me about yourself," Imogen said.

Nita shook her head. "There's nothing to tell. I'm just a loser—same as you've got to be if the only way you can find someone to have a drink with you is by hanging out around back of a strip club." Then she thought of the three men in the alley. " 'Course, the way you took out those freaks . . . those moves weren't the moves of any loser."

"Forget about them," Imogen said. "Tell me why you're so sad."

Nita shook her head. "I'm not sad," she said, lighting up another cigarette. "I'm just fucked up. The only thing I'm good at is running away. When the going gets tough, I'm gone. My whole life, that's the way I deal with the shit."

"And the dancing doesn't help?"

"Give me a break. That's not dancing—it's shaking your ass in a meat market. Maybe some of the girls've convinced themselves they're in show business, but I'm not that far out of touch with reality."

"But you still get something from it, don't you?"

Nita butted out her cigarette. "I'll tell you the truth, I always wanted to be up on a stage, but I can't sing and I can't play a guitar and the only way I can dance is doing a bump 'n' grind. When you've got no talent, your options get limited real fast."

"Everyone has a talent."

"Yeah, well, mine's for fucking up. I work with women who are dancing to put themselves through college, single mothers who're feeding their families, a writer who's supporting herself until she can sell her first book. The only reason I'm dancing is that I couldn't make that kind of money doing anything else except hooking and I'm not that hard up yet."

"Perhaps you've set your sights too high," Imogen said. "It's hard to attain goals when they seem utterly beyond your reach. You might consider concentrating on smaller successes and then work your way up from them."

"Yeah? Like what?"

Imogen shrugged. "Breathing's a talent."

"Oh, right. And so's waking up in the morning."

"Feel this," Imogen said.

She caught Nita's wrist and started to bring it toward her chest.

"Hey!" Nita said, embarrassed. "I told you I'm not like that."

She was sure everybody on the terrace was staring at them, but when she tried to pull free, she couldn't move her hand. She might as well have been trying to move the building under them. Imogen brought Nita's palm through the open front of her jean vest and laid it against the cool smooth skin between her breasts. In the light cast from the terrace lanterns, her eyes gleamed like a cat's caught in a car's headbeams.

"What do you feel?" Imogen asked.

"Look, why don't you . . ."

Just get out of my face, was what Nita was going to say, except as her palm remained on Imogen's skin, she suddenly realized—

"You . . . you're not breathing," she said.

Imogen released Nita's wrist. Nita rubbed at the welt that the grip of Imogen's fingers had left on her skin.

"I'm sorry," Imogen said. "I didn't mean to hurt you."

"How can you not breathe?"

Imogen smiled. "It's a talent I don't have," she said.

This was seriously strange, Nita thought. She was way, way out of her depth.

"So," she began. She had to stop to clear her throat. Her mouth felt as though it was coated with dry dust. She took a gulp of whiskey and fumbled another cigarette out of her package. "So what are you?" she finally managed.

Imogen shrugged. "Immortal. Undead."

That moment in the alley flashed in Nita's mind. The three men, dispatched so quickly and Imogen not even out of breath. The vise-like strength of her fingers. The weird gleam in her eyes. The cool touch of her skin. The fact that she really didn't breathe.

Nita tried to light her cigarette, but her hand shook too much. She flinched when Imogen reached out to steady it, but then accepted the help. She drew the smoke in deeply, held it, exhaled. Took another drag.

"Okay," she said. "So what do you want from me?"

"No more than I told you earlier: company."

"Company."

Imogen nodded. "When the sun rises this morning, I'm going to die. I just didn't want to die alone."

"You want me to die with you?"

"Not at all. I just want you to be there when I do. I've lived this hidden life of mine for too long. Nobody knows me. Nobody cares about me. I thought you'd understand."

"Understand what?"

"I just want to be remembered."

"This is too weird," Nita said. "I mean, you don't look sick or anything."

Like I'd know, Nita added to herself.

"I'm not sick. I'm tired." Imogen gave a small laugh that held no humor. "I'm always amazed at how humans strive so desperately to prolong their lives. If you only knew. . . ."

Nita thought about her own life and imagined it going on forever.

"I think I see where you're coming from," she said.

"It's not so bad at first—when you outlive your first set of friends and lovers. But it's harder the next time, and harder still each time after that, because you start anticipating the end, their deaths, from the first moment you meet them. So you stop having friends, you stop taking lovers, only to find it's no easier being alone."

"But aren't there . . . others like you around?" Nita asked.

"They're not exactly the sort of people I care to know. I'm not exactly the sort of person I care to know. We're monsters, Nita. We're not the romantic creatures of myth that your fictions perpetuate. We're parasites, surviving only by killing you."

She shook her head. "I look around and all I see is meat. All I smell is blood—some diseased, and not fit for consumption, it's true, but the rest . . ."

"So how do I smell?" Nita wanted to know.

Imogen smiled. "Very good—though not as good as you did when those men attacked us in the alley earlier. Adrenaline adds a spicy flavor to human scent, like a mix of jalapeños and chili."

The new turn their conversation had taken made Nita feel too much like a potential meal.

"If your life's so shitty," she asked, "why've you waited until now to put an end to it?"

"My existence is monstrous," Imogen told her. "But it's also seductive. We are so powerful. I hate what I am at the same time as I exult in my existence. Nothing can harm us but sunlight."

Nita shivered. "What about the rest of it?" she asked, thinking of the dozens of late-night movies she'd watched. "You know—the running water, the garlic, and the crosses?"

"Only sunlight."

"So tomorrow morning you're just going to sit in the sun?"

Imogen nodded. "And die. With you by my side to wish my spirit safe-journey and to remember me when I'm gone."

It was so odd. There was no question in Nita's mind but that Imogen was exactly what she said she was. The strange thing was how readily she accepted it. But accepting it and watching Imogen die were two different things. The endings of all those late-night movies went tumbling through her in all their grotesque glory.

"I don't know if I can do it," Nita said.

Imogen's eyebrows rose questioningly.

"I'm not real good with gross shit," Nita explained. "You know—what's going to happen to you when the sunlight touches you."

"Nothing will happen," Imogen assured her. "It's not like in the films. I'll simply stop living, that's all."

"Oh."

"Have you finished your drink?" Imogen asked. "I'd like to go for a last walk in the park."

4

Fitzhenry Park was probably the last place Nita would go for a walk at this time of night, but remembering how easily Imogen had dealt with their attackers in the alley behind the club, she felt safe enough doing so tonight. Walking hand in hand, they seemed to have the footpaths to themselves. As they got deeper inside the park, all sense of the city sur-rounding them vanished. They could have been a thousand miles away, a thousand years away from this time and place. The moon was still work-ing its way up to its first quarter—a silvery sickle hanging up among the stars that came and went from view depending on the foliage of the trees lining the path.

Nita kept stealing glances at her companion whenever there was enough light. She looked so normal. But that was how it always was, wasn't it? The faces people put on when they went out into the world could hide anything. All you ever knew about somebody was what he or she cared to show you. Nita normally didn't have much interest in any-one, but she found herself wanting to know everything she could about Imogen.

"You told me you live a hidden life," she said, "but the way you look seems to me would turn more heads than let you keep a low profile."

"I dress like this to attract my prey. Since I must feed, I prefer to do so on those the world can do better without."

Makes sense, Nita thought. She wondered if she should introduce Imogen to Eddie back at the club.

"How often do you have to . . . feed?" she asked.

"Too often." Imogen glanced at her. "The least we can get by on is once a week."

"Oh."

"I've been fasting," Imogen went on. "Preparing for tonight. I wanted to be as weak as possible when the moment comes."

If Imogen was weak at the moment, Nita couldn't imagine what she'd be like at full strength. She wasn't sure if she was being more observant, or if her companion had lowered her guard now that they were more familiar with each other's company, but Imogen radiated a power and charisma unlike anyone Nita had ever met before.

"You don't seem weak to me," she said.

Imogen came to a stop and drew Nita over to a nearby bench. When they sat down, she put a hand on Nita's shoulder and looked her directly in the face.

"It doesn't matter how weak or hurt we feel," she said, "we have to be strong in here." Her free hand rose up to touch her chest. "We have to project that strength or those around us will simply take advantage of us. We can take no pride in being a victim—we belittle not only ourselves, but all women, if we allow that to happen to us without protest. You must stand up for yourself. You must always stand up for yourself and your sisters. I want you to remember that as you go on with your life. Never give in, never give up."

"But you're giving up."

Imogen shook her head. "Don't equate the two. What I am doing is taking the next step on a journey that I should have completed three hundred years ago. I am not surrendering. I am hoping to kill the monster that I let myself become and finally moving on."

Imogen looked away then. She shifted her position slightly, settling her back against the bench. After a few moments, she leaned her head against Nita's.

"What do you think it's like when you die?" Nita asked. "Do you think everything's just over, or do we, you know, go on somewhere?"

"I think we go on."

"What'll you miss the most?"

Imogen shrugged. "What would you miss if you were in my position?"

"Nothing."

"Not even your daughter?"

Nita didn't even bother to ask how Imogen knew about Amanda.

"You've got to understand," she said. "I love her. And it makes me feel good to know that something I was a part of making isn't fucked up. But it makes me feel even better knowing that she's going to be raised properly. That she'll be given all the chances I never had. I didn't want her to grow up to be like me."

"But you still visit her."

Nita nodded. "But once she's old enough to understand what I am, I'll stop."

If not sooner. If John's old man didn't get the judge to revoke her visitation rights because of what he'd seen her doing tonight.

"It's getting late," Imogen said. She stood up, drawing Nita to her feet.

"Where're we going?"

"To my apartment."

5

To call it an apartment was a bit of a misnomer. It turned out that Imogen owned the penthouse on top of the Brighton Hotel, overlooking the harbor. The only time Nita had ever seen a place this fancy was in the movies. While Imogen went to get her a drink, she walked slowly around the immense living room, trailing her hand along the polished wood tables and the back of a chesterfield that could seat five people comfortably. There was even a baby grand in one corner. She finally ended up at the glass doors leading out onto a balcony where she saw two images superimposed over each other: a view of the lake and Wolf Island in the distance, and one of herself standing at the window with the living room behind her, Imogen walking toward her with a brandy glass in each hand.

Nita turned to accept the brandy. Imogen touched her glass against Nita's and then they both drank.

"Why'd you pick me?" Nita asked.

"The name on the flyer outside the club first caught my eye," Imogen said. "Then, when I began to study your life, I realized that we are much the same. I was like you, before the change—deadened by the ennui of my life, feeding on the admiration of those who courted my favor much the same as you do with those who come to watch you dance. It's not such a great leap from using their base interest as a kind of sustenance to taking it from their flesh and blood."

Nita couldn't think of anything to say in response to that so she took another sip of her brandy.

"I want you to have this when I'm gone," Imogen went on.

"Have what?"

Imogen made a languid movement with her arm that encompassed the penthouse. "This place. Everything I have. I've already made the arrangements for everything to be transferred into your name—barring unforeseen difficulties, the transaction will be completed tomorrow at noon."

"But—"

"I have amassed a considerable fortune over the years, Nita. I want it to go to you. It will give you a chance to make a new start with your life."

Nita shook her head. "I don't think it'd work out."

She'd won a thousand dollars in a lotto once. She'd planned to do all sorts of sensible things with it, from taking some development courses to better herself to simply saving it. Instead, she'd partied so hearty over the space of one weekend she'd almost put herself in the hospital. The only reason she hadn't ended up in emergency was that everybody else that weekend had been too wasted to help her. She still didn't know how she'd managed to survive.

"It'd just make me fuck up big-time," she said.

Imogen nodded—not so much in acceptance of what she was saying, Nita realized, as to indicate that she was listening.

"I have to admit that I haven't been entirely honest with you," Imogen said. "What we're about to embark upon when the sun rises could be very dangerous to you."

"I . . . don't understand."

"I won't die the instant the sunlights strikes me," Imogen said. "It will take a few minutes—enough time for the beast inside me to rise. If it can feed immediately and get out of the sun, it will survive."

"You mean you'd . . . eat me?"

"It's not something I would do, given a choice. But the survival instinct is very strong."

Nita knew about that. She'd tried to kill herself three times to date—deliberately, that is. Twice with pills, once with a razor blade. It was astonishing how much she'd wanted to survive, once it seemed she had no choice but to die.

"I will fight that need," Imogen told her. "It's why I've been fasting. To make the beast weak. But I can't guarantee your safety."

Nita filled in the silence that followed by lighting a cigarette.

"Understand," Imogen said, "it's not what I want. I don't normally have conversations with my meals any more than you would with a hamburger you're about to eat. I truly believe that it's time for me to put the monster to rest and go on. Long past time. But the beast doesn't agree."

"You've tried this before, haven't you?" Nita asked.

Imogen nodded.

"What happened?"

"I'm still here," Imogen said.

Nita shivered. She silently finished her cigarette, then butted it out in an ornate silver ashtray.

"I'll understand if you feel you must leave," Imogen said,

"You'd let me go—even with everything I now know?"

Imogen gave her a sad smile. "Who'd believe you?"

Nita lit another cigarette. She was surprised to see that her hands weren't even shaking.

"No," she said. "I'll do it. But not for the money or this place."

"It will still be in your name," Imogen said.

Unspoken between them lay the words: if you survive the dawn.

Nita shrugged. "Whatever."

Imogen hesitated, then it seemed she had to ask. "Is it that you care so little about your life?"

"No," Nita said. "No matter how bad shit gets, whenever it comes down to the crunch, I always surprise myself at how much I want to live."

"Then why will you see this through?"

Nita smiled. "Because of you. Because of what you said about us having to be strong and stand up for each other. I won't say I'm not scared, 'cause I am, but . . ." She turned to the glass doors that led out onto the balcony. "I guess it's time, huh? We better get to it before I bail on you."

She put down the glass and butted out her cigarette after taking a last drag. Imogen stepped forward. She brushed Nita's cheek with her lips, then hand in hand they went out onto the balcony to meet the dawn.

The Big Sky

We need Death to be a friend. It is best to have
a friend as a traveling companion when you
have so far to go together.

—*attributed to Jean Cocteau*

1

She was sitting in John's living room when he got home from the recording studio that night, comfortably ensconced on the sofa, legs stretched
out, ankles crossed, a book propped open on her lap which she was pretending to read. The fact that all the lights in the house had been off until
he turned them on didn't seem to faze her in the least. She continued her
pretense, as though she could see equally well in the light or dark and it
made no difference to her whether the lights were on or off. At least she
had the book turned right-side up, John noted.

"How did you get in?" he asked her.

She didn't seem to present any sort of a threat—beyond having gotten
into his locked house, of course—so he was more concerned with how
she'd been able to enter than for his own personal safety. At the sound of
his voice, she looked up in surprise. She laid the book down on her lap,
finger inserted between the pages to hold her place.

"You can see me?" she said.

"Jesus."

John shook his head. She certainly wasn't shy. He set his fiddlecase down by the door. Dropping his jacket down on top of it, he went into the living room and sat down in the chair across the coffee table from her.

"What do you think?" he went on. "Of course I can see you."

"But you're not supposed to be able to see me—unless it's time and that doesn't seem right. I mean, really. I'd know, if anybody, whether or not it was time."

She frowned, gaze fixed on him, but she didn't really appear to be studying him. It was more as though she was looking into some unimaginably far and unseen distance. Her eyes focused suddenly and he shifted uncomfortably under the weight of her attention.

"Oh, I see what happened," she said. "I'm so sorry."

John leaned forward, resting his hands on his knees. "Let's try this again. Who are you?"

"I'm your watcher. Everybody has one."

"My watcher."

She nodded. "We watch over you until your time has come, then if you can't find your own way, we take you on. They call us the little deaths, but I've never much cared for the sound of that, do you?"

John sighed. He settled back in his chair to study his unwanted guest. She was no one he knew, though she could easily have fit in with his crowd. He put her at about twenty-something, a slender five-two, pixy features made more fey by the crop of short blonde hair that stuck up from her head with all the unruliness of a badly-mowed lawn. She wore black combat boots; khaki trousers, baggy, with two or three pockets running up either leg; a white T-shirt that hugged her thin chest like a second skin. She had little in the way of jewelry—a small silver ring in her left nostril and another in the lobe of her left ear—and no makeup.

"Do you have a name?" he tried.

"Everybody's got a name."

John waited a few heartbeats. "And yours is?" he asked when no reply was forthcoming.

"I don't think I should tell you."

"Why not?"

"Well, once you give someone your name, it's like opening the door to all sorts of possibilities, isn't it? Any sort of relationship could develop from that, and it's just not a good idea for us to have an intimate relationship with our charges."

"I can assure you," John told her. "We're in no danger of having a relationship—intimate or otherwise."

"Oh," she said. She didn't look disappointed so much as annoyed. "Dakota," she added.

"I'm sorry?"

"You wanted to know my name."

John nodded. "That's right. I—oh, I get it. Your name's Dakota?"

"Bingo."

"And you've been . . . watching me?"

"Well, not just you. Except for when we're starting out, we look out after any number of people."

"I see," John said. "And how many people do you watch?"

She shrugged. "Oh, dozens."

That figured, John thought. It was the story of his life. He couldn't even get the undivided attention of some loonie stalker.

She swung her boots to the floor and set the book she was holding on the coffee table between them.

"Well, I guess we should get going," she said.

She stood up and gave him an expectant look, but John remained where he was sitting.

"It's a long way to the gates," she told him.

He didn't have a clue as to what she was talking about, but he was sure of one thing.

"I'm not going anywhere with you," he said.

"But you have to."

"Says who?"

She frowned at him. "You just do. It's obvious that you won't be able to find your way by yourself and if you stay here you're just going to start feeling more and more alienated and confused."

"Let me worry about that," John said.

"Look," she said. "We've gotten off on the wrong foot—my fault, I'm sure. I had no idea it was time for you to go already. I'd just come by to check on you before heading off to another appointment."

"Somebody else that you're *watching*?"

"Exactly," she replied, missing, or more probably, ignoring the sarcastic tone of his voice. "There's no way around this, you know. You need my help to get to the gates."

"What gates?"

She sighed. "You're really in denial about all of this, aren't you?"

"You were right about one thing," John told her. "I am feeling confused—but it's only about what you're doing here and how you got in."

"I don't have time for this."

"Me neither. So maybe you should go."

That earned him another frown.

"Fine," she said. "But don't wait too long to call me. If you change too much, I won't be able to find you and nobody else can help you."

"Because you're my personal watcher."

"No wonder you don't have many friends," she said. "You're really not a very nice person, are you?"

"I'm only like this with people who break into my house."

"But I didn't—oh, never mind. Just remember my name and don't wait too long to call me."

"Not that I'd want to," John said, "but I don't even have your number."

"Just call my name and I'll come," she said. "If it's not too late. Like I said, I might not be able to recognize you if you wait too long."

Though he was trying to take this all in stride, John couldn't help but start to feel a little creeped out at the way she was going on. He'd never realized that crazy people could seem so normal—except for what they were saying, of course.

"Goodbye," he told her.

She bit back whatever it was that she was going to say and gave him a brusque nod. For one moment, he half expected her to walk through a wall—the evening had taken that strange a turn—but she merely crossed the living room and let herself out the front door. John waited for a few moments, then rose and set the deadbolt. He walked through the house, checking the windows and back door, before finally going upstairs to his bedroom.

He thought he might have trouble getting to sleep—the woman's presence had raised far more questions than it had answered—but he was so tired from twelve straight hours in the studio that it was more a question of, could he get all his clothes off and crawl under the blankets before he faded right out? He had one strange moment: when he turned off the light, he made the mistake of looking directly at the bulb. His uninvited guest's features hung in the darkness along with a hundred dancing spots of light before he was able to blink them away. But the moment didn't last long and he was soon asleep.

2

He didn't realize that he'd forgotten to set his alarm last night until he woke up and gave the clock a bleary look. Eleven-fifteen. Christ, he was late.

He got up, shaved and took a quick shower. You'd think someone would have called him from the studio, he thought as he started to get dressed. He was doing session work on Darlene Flatt's first album and the recording had turned into a race to get the album finished before her money ran out. He had two solos up first thing this morning and he couldn't understand why no one had called to see where he was.

There was no time for breakfast—he didn't have much of an appetite at the moment anyway. He'd grab a coffee and a bagel at the deli around the corner from the studio. Tugging on his jeans, he carried his boots out into the living room and phoned the studio while he put them on. All he got was ringing at the other end.

"Come on," he muttered. "Somebody pick it up."

How could there be nobody there to answer?

It was as he was cradling the receiver that he saw the book lying on the coffee table, reminding him of last night's strange encounter. He picked the book up and looked at it, turning it over in his hands. There was something different about it this morning. Something wrong. And then he realized what it was. The color dust wrapper had gone monochrome. The book and . . . His gaze settled on his hand and he dropped the book in shock. He stared at his hand, turning it front to back, then looked wildly around the living room.

Oh, Jesus. Everything was black and white.

He'd been so bleary when he woke up that he hadn't noticed that the world had gone monochrome on him overnight. He'd had a vague impression of gloominess when he got up, but he hadn't really thought about it. He'd simply put it down to it being a particularly overcast day. But this . . . this . . .

It was impossible.

His gaze was drawn to the window. The light coming in was devoid of color where it touched his furniture and walls, but outside . . . He walked slowly to the window and stared at his lawn, the street beyond it, the houses across the way. Everything was the way it was supposed to be. The day was cloudless, the colors so vivid, the sunlight so bright it hurt his eyes. The richness of all that colour and light burned his retinas.

He stood there until tears formed in his eyes and he had to turn away. He covered his eyes with his hands until the pain faded. When he took his palms away, his hands were still leached of color. The living room was a thousand monochrome shades of black and white. Numbly, he walked to his front door and flung it open. The blast of color overloaded the sensory membranes of his eyes. He knelt down where he'd tossed his jacket last night and scrabbled about in its pockets until he found a pair of shades.

The sunglasses helped when he turned back to the open door. It still hurt to look at all that color, but the pain was much less than it had been. He shuffled out onto his porch, down the steps. He looked at what he could see of himself. Hands and arms. His legs. All monochrome. He was like a black and white cutout that someone had stuck onto a colored background.

I'm dreaming, he thought.

He could feel the start of a panic attack. It was like the slight nervousness that sometimes came when he stepped onto stage—the kind that came when he was backing up someone he'd never played with before—only increased a hundredfold. Sweat beaded on his temples and under his arms. It made his shirt clammy and stick to his back. His hands began to shake so much that he had to hug himself to make them stop.

He was dreaming, or he'd gone insane.

Movement caught his eye down the street and he recognized one of his neighbors. He stumbled in the man's direction.

"Bob!" he called. "Bob, you've got to help me." The man never even looked in his direction. John stepped directly in front of him on the sidewalk and Bob walked right into him, knocking him down. But Bob hadn't felt a thing, John realized. Hadn't seen him, hadn't felt the impact, was just walking on down the street as if John had simply ceased to exist for him.

John fled back into the house. He slammed the door, locked it. He pulled the curtains in the living room and started to pace, from the fireplace to the hallway, back again, back and forth, back and forth. At one point he caught sight of the book he'd dropped earlier. Slowly, he walked over to where it lay and picked it up. He remembered last night's visitor again. Her voice returned to him.

If you change too much . . .

This was all her fault, he thought.

He threw the book down and shouted her name.

"Yes?"

Her voice came from directly behind him and he started violently.

"Jesus," he said. "You could've given me a heart attack."

"It's a little late for that."

She was wearing the same clothes she'd worn last night except today there was a leather bomber's jacket on over her T-shirt and she wore a hat that was something like a derby except the brim was wider. There was one other difference. Like himself, like the rest of his house, she'd been leached of all color.

"What did you do to me?" he demanded.

She reached out and took his hand to lead him over to the sofa. He tried to pull free from her grip, but she was stronger than she looked.

"Sit down," she said, "and I'll try to explain."

Her voice was soothing and calm, the way one would talk to an upset child—or a madman. John was feeling a little bit like both at the moment, helpless as a child and out of his mind. But the lulling quality of her voice and the gentle manner of her touch helped still the wild drumming of his pulse.

"Look," he said. "I don't know what you've done to me—I don't know how you've done this to me or why—but I just want to get back to normal, okay? If I made you mad last night, I'm sorry, but you've got to understand. It was pretty weird to find you in my house the way I did."

"I know," she said. "I didn't realize you could see me at first, or I would have handled it differently myself. But you took me by surprise."

"I took *you* by surprise?"

"What do you remember of last night?" she asked.

"I came home and found you in my living room."

"No, before that."

"I was at High Lonesome Sounds—working on Darlene's album."

She nodded. "And what happened between when you left the studio and came home?"

"I . . . I don't remember."

"You were hit by a car," she said. "A drunk driver."

"No way," John said, shaking his head. "I'd remember something like that."

She took his hand. "You died instantly, John Narraway."

"I . . . I . . ."

He didn't want to believe her, but her words settled inside him with a finality that could only be the truth.

"It's not something that anyone could have foreseen," she went on. "You were supposed to live a lot longer—that's why I was so surprised that you could see me. It's never happened to me like that before."

John had stopped listening to her after she'd said, "You were supposed to live a lot longer." He clung to that phrase, hope rushing through him.

"So it was a mistake," he said.

Dakota nodded.

"So what happens now?" he asked.

"I'll take you to the gates."

"No, wait a minute. You just said it was a mistake. Can't you go back to whoever's in charge and explain that?"

"If there's anyone in charge," she said, "I've never met or heard of them."

"But—"

"I understand your confusion and your fear. Really I do. It comes from the suddenness of your death and my not being there to help you adjust. That's the whole reason I exist—to help people like you who are unwilling or too confused to go on by themselves. I wasn't ready to go myself when my time came."

"Well, I'm not ready either."

Dakota shook her head. "It's not the same thing. I wasn't ready to go because when I saw how much some people need help to reach the gates, I knew I had to stay and help them. It was like a calling. You just aren't willing to accept what happened to you."

"Well, Christ. Who would?"

"Most people. I've seen how their faces light up when they step through the gates. You can't imagine the joy in their eyes."

"Have you been through yourself?" John asked.

"No. But I've had glimpses of what lies beyond. You know how sometimes the sky just seems to be so big it goes on forever?"

John nodded.

"You stand there and look up," she went on, "and the stars seem so close you feel as though you could just reach up and touch them, but at the same time the sky itself is enormous and has no end. It's like that, except that you can feel your heart swelling inside you, big enough to fill the whole of that sky."

"If what's waiting beyond these gates is so wonderful," John wanted to know, "why haven't you gone through?"

"One day I will. I think about it more and more all the time. But what I'm doing now is important and I'm needed. There are never enough of us."

"Maybe I'll become a watcher instead—like you."

"It's not something one takes on lightly," Dakota said. "You can't just stop when you get tired of doing it. You have to see through all of your responsibilities first, make sure that all of your charges have gone on, that none are left behind to fend for themselves. You share the joys of your charges, but you share their sorrows, too. And the whole time you know them, you're aware of their death. You watch them plan, you watch their lives and the tangle of their relationships grow more complex as they grow older, but the whole time you're aware of their end."

"I could do that," John said.

Dakota shook her head. "You have always been sparing with your kindnesses. It's why your circle of friends is so small. You're not a bad person, John Narraway, but I don't think you have the generosity of spirit it requires to be a watcher."

The calm certainty with which she delivered her judgment irritated John.

"How would you know?" he said.

She gave him a sad smile. "Because I've been watching you ever since you were born."

"What? Every second of my life?"

"No. That comes only at first. It takes time to read a soul, to unravel the tangle of possibilities and learn when the time of death is due. After that it's a matter of checking in from time to time to make sure that the assessment one made still holds true."

John thought about the minutiae that made up the greater portion of everyone's life and slowly shook his head. And what if you picked a person who was really dull? Everybody had slow periods in their lives, but some people's whole lives were one numbed shuffle from birth to death.

And since you knew the whole time when the person was going to die . . . God, it'd be like spending your whole life in a doctor's waiting room. Boring and depressing.

"You don't get tired of it?" he asked.

"Not tired. A little sad, sometimes."

"Because everybody's got to die."

She shook her head. "No, because I see so much unhappiness and there's nothing I can do about it. Most of my charges never see me—they make their own way to the gates and beyond. I'm just there as a kind of insurance for those who can't do it by themselves and I'm only with them for such a little while. I miss talking to people on a regular basis. Sometimes I see some of the other watchers, but we're all so busy."

"It sounds horrible."

She shrugged. "I never think of it that way. I just think of those who need help and the looks on their faces when they step through the gates." She fell silent for a moment, then gave him a smile. "We should go now. I've got other commitments."

"What if I refuse to go? What happens then?"

"No one can force you, if that's what you mean."

John held up his hand. He looked around himself. Okay, it was weird, but he could live with it, couldn't he? Anything'd be better than to be dead—even a half-life.

"I know what you're thinking," she said. "And no, it's not because I'm reading your mind, because I can't."

"So what's going to happen to me?"

"I take it you're already experiencing some discomfort?"

John nodded. "I see everything in black and white—but only in the house. Outside, nothing's changed."

"That will grow more pronounced," she told him. "Eventually you won't be able to see color at all. You might lose the clarity of your vision as well so that everything will seem to be a blur. Your other senses will become less effective as well."

"But—"

"And you won't be able to interact with the world you've left behind. In time, the only people you'll be able to see are others like yourself—those too willful or disturbed to have gone on. They don't exactly make the best of companions, John Narraway, but then, by that point, you'll be so much like them, I don't suppose it will matter."

"But what about all the stories of ghosts and hauntings and the like?"

"Do you have a particularly strong bond with a certain place or person?" she asked. "Someone or something you couldn't possibly live without?"

John had to admit that he didn't, but he could tell that she already knew that.

"But I'll still be alive," he said, knowing even as he said the words that they made no real sense.

"If you want to call it that."

"Don't you miss life?"

Dakota shook her head. "I only miss happiness. Or maybe I should say, I miss the idea of happiness because I never had it when I was alive."

"What happened to you?" John wanted to know.

She gave him a long sad look. "I'm sorry, John Narraway, but I have to go. I will listen for you. Call me when you change your mind. Just don't wait too long—"

"Or you won't be able to recognize me. I know. You already told me that."

"Yes," she said. "I did."

This time she didn't use the door. One moment she was sitting with him on the sofa and the next she faded away like Carroll's Cheshire cat except with her it was her eyes that lingered the longest, those sad dark eyes that told him he was making a mistake, those eyes to which he refused to listen.

3

He didn't move from the sofa after Dakota left. While the sunlight drifted across the living room, turning his surroundings into a series of shifting chiaroscuro images, he simply sat there, his mind empty more often than it was chasing thoughts. He was sure he hadn't been immobile for more than a few hours, but when he finally stood up and walked to the window, it was early morning, the sun just rising. He'd lost a whole night and a day. Maybe more. He still had no appetite, but now he doubted that he ever would again. He didn't seem to need sleep, either. But it scared him that he could lose such a big chunk of time like that.

He turned back to the living room and switched on the television set to make sure that all he'd lost had been the one day. All he got on the screen was snow. White noise hissed from the speaker grill. Fine, he thought, remembering how he'd been unable to put a call through to the recording studio yesterday morning. So now the TV wouldn't work for him. So he couldn't interact with the everyday mechanics of the world anymore. Well, there were other ways to find out what he needed to know.

He picked up his fiddlecase out of habit, put on his jacket and left the house. He didn't need his shades once he got outside, but that was only because his whole street was now delineated in shades of black and white. He could see the color start up at the far ends of the block on either side. The sky was overcast above him, but it blued the further away from his house it got.

This sucked, he thought. But not so much that he was ready to call Dakota back.

He started downtown, putting on his sunglasses once he left the monochromic zone immediately surrounding his house. Walking proved to be more of a chore than he'd anticipated. He couldn't relax his attention for a moment or someone would walk into him. He always felt the impact while they continued on their way, as unaware of the encounter as his neighbor Bob had been.

He stopped at the first newsstand he came upon and found the day's date. Wednesday, he read on the masthead of *The Newford Star*. November tenth. He'd only lost a day. A day of what, though? He could remember nothing of the experience. Maybe that was what sleep would be like for him in this state—simply turning himself off the way fiction described vampires at their rest. He had to laugh at the thought. The undead. *He* was one of the undead now, though he certainly had no craving for blood.

He stopped laughing abruptly, suddenly aware of the hysterical quality that had crept into the sound. It wasn't that funny. He pressed up close against a building to keep out of the way of passing pedestrians and tried to quell the panic he could feel welling up inside his chest. Christ, it wasn't funny at all.

After a while he felt calm enough to go on. He had no particular destination in mind, but when he realized he was in the general vicinity of High Lonesome Sounds, he decided to stop by the studio. He kept waiting for some shock of recognition at every corner he came to, something that would whisper, this is where you died. This is where the one part of your life ended and the new part began. But the street corners all looked the same and he arrived at the recording studio without sensing that one had ever had more importance in his life than the next.

He had no difficulty gaining entrance to the studio. At least doors still worked for him. He wondered what his use of them looked like to others, doors opening and closing, seemingly of their own accord. He climbed the stairs to the second floor loft where the recording studio was situated and slipped into the control booth where he found Darlene and Tom Norton listening to a rough mix of one of the cuts from Darlene's album. Norton owned the studio and often served as both producer and sound engineer to the artists using his facilities. He turned as John quietly closed the door behind him but he looked right through John.

"It still needs a lead break," Norton said, returning his attention to Darlene.

"I know it does. But I don't want another fiddle. I want to leave John's backing tracks just as they are. It doesn't seem right to have somebody else play his break."

Thank you, Darlene, John thought.

He'd known Darlene Flatt for years, played backup with her on and off through the past decade and a half as she sang out her heart in far too many honky-tonks and bars. Her real name was Darlene Johnston, but by this point in her career everyone knew her by her stage name. Dolly Parton had always been her idol and when Darlene stepped on stage with her platinum wig and over-the-top rhinestone outfits, the resemblance between the two was uncanny. But Darlene had a deeper voice and now that she'd finally lost the wigs and stage gear, John thought she had a better shot at the big time. There was a long tradition of covering other people's material in country music, but nothing got tired more quickly than a tribute act so far as John was concerned.

She didn't look great today. There was a gaunt look about her features, hollows under her eyes. Someone mourned him, John realized.

"Why don't we have Greg play the break on his Dobro?" Darlene said. She sounded so tired, as though all she wanted to do was get through this.

"That could work," Norton said.

John stopped listening to them, his attention taken by the rough mix that was still playing in the control booth. It was terrible. All the instruments sounded tinny and flat, there was no bass to speak of, and Darlene's voice seemed to be mixed so far back you felt you had to lean forward to be able to hear it. He winced, listening to his own fiddle-playing.

"You've got a lot more problems here than what instrument to use on the break," he said.

But of course they couldn't hear him. So far as he could tell, they liked what they were hearing which seemed particularly odd, considering how long they'd both been in the business. What did they hear that he couldn't? But then he remembered what his mysterious visitor had told him. How his sight would continue to deteriorate. How . . .

Your other senses will become less effective as well.

John thought back to the walk from his house to the studio. He hadn't really been thinking of it at the time, but now that he did he realized that the normal sounds of the city had been muted. Everything. The traffic, the voices of passersby, the construction site he'd passed a couple of blocks away from the studio. When he concentrated on Darlene and Norton's conversation again, listening to the tonal quality of their voices rather than what they were saying, he heard a hollow echo that hadn't registered before.

He backed away from them and fumbled his way out into the sitting room on the other side of the door. There he took his fiddle out of his case. Tuning the instrument was horrible. Playing it was worse. There was nothing there anymore. No resonance. No depth. Only the same hollow echoing quality that he'd heard in Darlene and Norton's voices.

Slowly he laid his fiddle back into its case, loosened the frog on his bow and set it down on top of the instrument. When he finally made his way back down the stairs and out into the street, he left the fiddle behind. Outside, the street seemed overcast, its colors not yet leached away, but definitely faded. He looked up into a cloudless sky. He crossed the street and plucked a pretzel from the cart of a street vendor, took a bite even though he had no appetite. It tasted like sawdust and ashes. A bus pulled up at the curb where he was standing, let out a clutch of passengers, then pulled away again, leaving behind a cloud of noxious fumes. He could barely smell them.

It's just a phase, he told himself. He was simply adjusting to his new existence. All he had to do was get through it and things would get back to normal. They couldn't stay like this.

He kept telling himself that as he made his way back home, but he wasn't sure he believed it. He was dead, after all—that was the part of the equation that was impossible to ignore. Dakota had warned him that this was going to happen. But he wasn't ready to believe her either.

He just couldn't accept that the way things were for him now would be permanent.

4

He was right. Things didn't stay the same. They got worse. His senses continued to deteriorate. The familiar world faded away from around him until he found himself in a grey-toned city that he didn't always recognize. He stepped out of his house one day and couldn't find his way back. The air was oppressive, the sky seemed to press down on him. And there were no people. No living people. Only the other undead. They huddled in doorways and alleys, drifted through the empty buildings. They wouldn't look at him and he found himself turning his face away as well. They had nothing they could share with each other, only their despair, and of that they each had enough of their own.

He took to wandering aimlessly through the deserted streets, the high points of his day coming when he recognized the corner of a building, a stretch of street, that gargoyle peering down from an utterly unfamiliar building. He wasn't sure if he was in a different city, or if he was losing his memory of the one he knew. After a while it didn't seem to matter.

The blank periods came more and more often. Like the other undead, he would suddenly open his eyes to find himself curled up in a nest of newspapers and trash in some doorway, or huddled in the rotting bulk of a sofa in an abandoned building. And finally he couldn't take it anymore.

He stood in the middle of an empty street and lifted his face to grey skies that only seemed to be kept aloft by the roofs of the buildings.

"Dakota!" he cried. "Dakota!"

But he was far too late and she didn't come.

Don't wait too long to call me, she'd told him. *If you change too much, I won't be able to find you and nobody else can help you.*

He had no one to blame but himself. It was like she'd said. He'd changed too much and now, even if she could hear him, she wouldn't recognize him. He wasn't sure he'd even recognize himself. Still, he called her name again, called for her until the hollow echo that was his voice grew raw and weak. Finally he slumped there in the middle of the road, shoulders sagged, chin on his chest, and stared at the pavement.

"The name you were calling," a voice said. "Did it belong to one of those watchers?"

John looked up at the man who'd approached him so silently. He was a nondescript individual, the kind of man he'd have passed by on the street when he was alive and never looked at twice. Medium height, medium build. His only really distinguishing feature was the fervent glitter in his eyes.

"A watcher," John repeated, nodding in response to the man's question. "That's what she called herself."

"Damn 'em all to hell, I say," the man told him. He spat on the pavement. " 'Cept that'd put 'em on these same streets and Franklin T. Clark don't ever want to look into one of their stinkin' faces again—not unless I've got my hands around one of their necks. I'd teach 'em what it's like to be dead."

"I think they're dead, too," John said.

"That's what they'd like you to believe. But tell me this: If they're dead, how come they're not here like us? How come they get to hold onto a piece of life like we can't?"

"Because . . . because they're helping people."

Clark spat again. "Interferin's more like it." The dark light in his eyes seemed to deepen as he fixed his gaze on John. "Why were you calling her name?"

"I can't take this anymore."

"An' you think it's gonna be better where they want to take us?"

"How can it be worse?"

"They can take away who you are," Clark said. "They can *try*, but they'll never get Franklin T. Clark, I'll tell you that. They can kill me, they can dump me in this stinkin' place, but I'd rather rot here in hell than let 'em change me."

"Change you how?" John wanted to know.

"You go through those gates of theirs an' you end up part of a stew. Everythin' that makes you who you are, it gets stole away, mixed up with everybody else. You become a kind of fuel—that's all. Just fuel."

"Fuel for what?"

"For 'em to make more of us. There's no goddamn sense to it. It's just what they do."

"How do you know this?" John asked.

Clark shook his head. "You got to ask, you're not worth the time I'm wastin' on you."

He gave John a withering look, as though John was something

he'd stepped on that got stuck to the bottom of his shoe. And then he walked away.

John tracked the man's progress as he shuffled off down the street. When Clark was finally out of sight, he lifted his head again to stare up into the oppressive sky that hung so close to his face.

"Dakota," he whispered.

But she still didn't come.

5

The day he found the infant wailing in a heap of trash behind what had once been a restaurant made John wonder if there wasn't some merit in Clark's anger toward the watchers. The baby was a girl and she was no more than a few days old. She couldn't possibly have made the decision that had left her in this place—not by any stretch of the imagination. A swelling echo of Clark's rage rose up in him as he lifted the infant from the trash. He swaddled her in rags and cradled the tiny form in his arms.

"What am I going to do with you?" he asked.

The baby stopped crying, but she made no reply. How could she? She was so small, so helpless. Looking down at her, John knew what he had to do. Maybe Clark was right and the watchers were monsters, although he found that hard to reconcile with his memories of Dakota's empathy and sadness. But Clark was wrong about what lay beyond the gates. He had to be. It couldn't be worse than this place.

He set off then, still wandering aimlessly, but now he had a destination in mind, now he had something to look for. He wasn't doing it for himself, though he knew he'd step through the gates when they stood in front of him. He was doing it for the baby.

"I'm going to call you Dolly," he told the infant. "Darlene would've liked that. What do you think?"

He chucked the infant under her chin. Her only response was to stare up at him.

6

John figured he had it easier than most people who suddenly had an infant came into their lives. Dolly didn't need to eat and she didn't cry unless he set her down. She was only happy in his arms. She didn't soil the rags he'd wrapped her in. Sometimes she slept, but there was nothing restful about it. She'd be lying in his arms one minute, the next it was as though someone had thrown a switch and she'd been turned off. He'd been frantic the first time it happened, panicking until he realized that she was only experiencing what passed for sleep in this place.

He didn't let himself enter that blank state. The idea had crept into his mind as he wandered the streets with Dolly that to do so, to let himself turn off the way he and all the other undead did, would make it all that much more difficult for him to complete his task. The longer he denied it of himself, the more seductive the lure of that strange sleep became, but he stuck to his resolve. After a time, he was rewarded for maintaining his purposefulness. His vision sharpened; the world still appeared mono-chromatic, but at least it was all back in focus. He grew more clear-headed. He began to recognize more and more parts of the city. But the gates remained as elusive as Dakota had proved to be since the last time he'd seen her.

One day he came upon Clark again. He wasn't sure how long it had been since the last time he'd seen the man—a few weeks? A few months? It was difficult to tell time in the city as it had become because the light never changed. There was no day, no night, no comforting progression from one into the other. There was only the city, held in eternal twilight.

Clark was furious when he saw the infant in John's arms. He ranted and swore at John, threatened to beat him for interfering in what he saw as the child's right of choice. John stood his ground, holding Dolly.

"What are you so afraid of?" he asked when Clark paused to take a breath.

Clark stared at him, a look of growing horror spreading across his fea-tures until he turned and fled without replying. He hadn't needed to rely. John knew what Clark was afraid of. It was the same fear that kept them all in this desolate city: Death. Dying. They were all afraid. They were all trapped here by that fear. Except for John. He was still trapped like the others; the difference was that he was no longer afraid.

But if a fear of death was no longer to be found in his personal lexicon, despair remained. Time passed. Weeks, months. But he was no closer to finding these fabled gates than he'd been when he first found Dolly and took up the search. He walked through a city that grew more and more familiar. He recognized his own borough, his own street, his own house. He walked slowly up his walk and looked in through the window, but he didn't go in. He was too afraid of succumbing to the growing need to sit somewhere and close his eyes. It would be so easy to go inside, to stretch out on the couch, to let himself fall into the welcoming dark.

Instead he turned away, his path now leading toward the building that housed High Lonesome Sounds. He found it without any trouble, walked up its eerily silent stairwell, boots echoing with a hollow sound, a sound full of dust and broken hopes. At the top of the stairs, he turned to his right and stepped into the recording studio's lounge. The room was empty, except for an open fiddlecase in the middle of the floor, an instrument lying in it, a bow lying across the fiddle, horsehairs loose.

He shifted Dolly from the one arm to the crook of the other. Kneeling down, he slipped the bow into its holder in the lid of the case and shut the lid. He stared at the closed case for a long moment. He had no words to describe how much he'd missed it, how incomplete he'd felt without it. Sitting more comfortably on the floor, he fashioned a sling out of his jacket so that he could carry Dolly snuggled up against his chest and leave his arms free.

When he left the studio, he carried the fiddlecase with him. He went down the stairs, out onto the street. There were no cars, no pedestrians. Nothing had changed. He was still trapped in that reflection of the city he'd known when he was alive, the deserted streets and abandoned buildings peopled only by the undead. But something felt different. It wasn't just that he seemed more himself, more the way he'd been when he was still alive, carrying his fiddle once more. It was as though retrieving the instrument had put a sense of expectation in the air. The grey dismal streets, overhung by a brooding sky, were suddenly pregnant with possibilities.

He heard the footsteps before he saw the man: a tall, rangy individual, arriving from a side street at a brisk walk. Faded blue jeans, black sweatshirt with matching baseball cap. Flat-heeled cowboy boots. What set him apart from the undead was the purposeful set to his features. His gaze was turned outward, rather than inward.

"Hello!" John called after the stranger as the man began to cross the street. "Have you got a minute?"

The stranger paused in mid-step. He regarded John with surprise, but waited for John to cross the street and join him. John introduced himself and put out his hand. The man hesitated for a moment, then took John's hand.

"Bernard Gair," the man said in response. "Pleased, I'm sure." His look of surprise had shifted into one of vague puzzlement. "Have we met before . . . ?"

John shook his head. "No, but I do know one of your colleagues. She calls herself Dakota."

"The name doesn't ring a bell. But then there are so many of us—though never enough to do the job."

"That's what she told me. Look, I know how busy you must be so I won't keep you any longer. I just wanted to ask you if you could direct me to . . ."

John's voice trailed off as he realized he wasn't being listened to. Gair peered more closely at him.

"You're one of the lost, aren't you?" Gair said. "I'm surprised I can even see you. You're usually so . . . insubstantial. But there's something different about you."

"I'm looking for the gates," John told him.

"The gates."

Something in the way he repeated the words made John afraid that Gair wouldn't help him.

"It's not for me," he said quickly. "It's for her."

He drew back a fold of the sling's cloth to show Gair the sleeping infant nestled against his chest.

"I see," Gair said. "But does she want to go on?"

"I think she's a little young to be making that kind of decision for herself."

Gair shook his head. "Age makes no difference to a spirit's ability to decide such a thing. Infants can cling as tenaciously to life as do the elderly—often more so, since they have had so little time to experience it."

"I'm not asking you to make a judgment," John said. "I'm just asking for some directions. Let the kid decide for herself once she's at the gates and can look through."

Gair needed time to consider that before he finally gave a slow nod.

"That could be arranged," he allowed.

"If you could just give me directions," John said.

Gair pulled up the left sleeve of his sweatshirt so that he could check the time on his wristwatch.

"Let me take you instead," he said.

7

Even with directions, John couldn't have found the gates on his own. "The journey," Gair explained, "doesn't exercise distance so much as a state of mind." That was as good a description as any, John realized as he fell in step with his new companion, for it took them no time at all to circumvent familiar territory and step out onto a long boulevard. John felt a tugging in that part of his chest where his heart had once beaten as he looked down to the far end of the avenue. An immense archway stood there. Between its pillars the air shimmered like a heat mirage and called to him.

When Gair paused, John came to a reluctant halt beside him. Gair looked at his watch again.

"I'm sorry," he said, "but I have to leave you now. I have another appointment."

John found it hard to look at the man. His gaze kept being drawn back to the shimmering air inside the arch.

"I think I can find my way from here," he said.

Gair smiled. "I should think you could." He shook John's hand. "Godspeed," he murmured, then he faded away just as Dakota had faded from his living room what seemed like a thousand lifetimes ago.

Dolly stirred against John's chest as he continued on toward the gates. He rearranged her in the sling so that she, too, could look at the approaching gates, but she turned her face away and for the first time his holding her wasn't enough. She began to wail at the sight of the gates, her distress growing in volume the closer they got.

John slowed his pace, uncertain now. He thought of Clark's cursing at him, of Gair telling him that Dolly, for all her infancy, was old enough to make this decision on her own. He realized that they were both right. He couldn't force her to go through, to travel on. But what would he do if she refused? He couldn't simply leave her behind either.

The archway of the gates loomed over him now. The heat shimmer had changed into a warm golden light that washed out from between the pillars, dispelling all the shadows that had ever taken root in John's soul. But the infant in his arms wept more pitifully, howled until he covered her head with part of the cloth and let her burrow her face against his chest. She whimpered softly there until John thought his heart would break. With each step he took, the sounds she made grew more piteous.

He stood directly before the archway, bathed in its golden light. Through the pulsing glow, he could see the big sky Dakota had described. It went on forever. He could feel his heart swell to fill it. All he wanted to do was step through, to be done with the lies of the flesh, the lies that had told him, this one life was all, the lies that had tricked him into being trapped in the city of the undead.

But there was the infant to consider and he couldn't abandon her. Couldn't abandon her, but he couldn't explain it to her, that there was nothing to fear, that it was only light and an enormous sky. And peace. There were no words to capture the wonder that pulsed through his veins, that blossomed in his heart, swelled until his chest was full and he knew the light must be pouring out of his eyes and mouth.

Now he understood Dakota's sorrow. It would be heartbreaking to know what waited for those who turned their backs on this glory. It had nothing to do with gods or religions. There was no hierarchy of belief entailed. No one was denied admittance. It was simply the place one stepped through so that the journey could continue.

John cradled the sobbing infant, jigging her gently against his chest. He stared into the light. He stared into the endless sky.

"Dakota," he called softly.

"Hello, John Narraway."

He turned to find her standing beside him, her own solemn gaze drinking in the light that pulsed in the big sky between the gates and flowed over them. She smiled at him.

"I didn't think I'd see you again," she said. "And certainly not in this place. You did well to find it."

"I had help. One of your colleagues showed me the way."

"There's nothing wrong with accepting help sometimes."

"I know that now," John said. "I also understand how hard it is to offer help and have it refused."

Dakota stepped closer and drew the infant from the sling at John's chest.

"It is hard," she agreed, cradling Dolly. Her eyes still held the reflected light that came from between the gates, but they were sad once more as she studied the weeping infant. She sighed, adding, "But it's not something that can be forced."

John nodded. There was something about Dakota's voice, about the way she looked that distracted him, but he couldn't quite put his finger on it.

"I will take care of the little one," Dakota said. "There's no need for you to remain here."

"What will you do with her?"

"Whatever she wants."

"But she's so young."

The sadness deepened in Dakota's eyes. "I know."

There was so much empathy in her voice, in the way she held the infant, in her gaze. And then John realized what was different about her. Her voice wasn't hollow, it held resonance. She wasn't monochrome, but touched with color. There was only a hint, at first, like an old tinted photograph, but it was like looking at a rainbow for John. As it grew stronger he drank in the wonder of it. He wished she would speak again, just so that he could cherish the texture of her voice, but she remained silent, solemn gaze held by the infant in her arms.

"I find it hardest when they're so young," she finally said, looking up at him. "They don't communicate in words so it's impossible to ease their fears."

But words weren't the only way to communicate, John thought. He crouched down to lay his fiddlecase on the ground, took out his bow and tightened the hair. He ran his thumb across the fiddle strings to check the tuning, marveling anew at the richness of sound. He thought perhaps he'd missed that the most.

"What are you doing?" Dakota asked him.

John shook his head. It wasn't that he didn't want to explain it to her, but that he couldn't. Instead he slipped the fiddle under his chin, drew the bow across the strings, and used music to express what words couldn't. He turned to the gates, drank in the light and the immense wonder of the sky and distilled it into a simple melody, an air of grace and beauty. Warm generous notes spilled from the sound holes of his instrument, grew stronger and more resonant in the light of the gates, gained such presence that they could almost be seen, touched and held with more than the ear.

The infant in Dakota's arms fell silent and listened. She turned innocent eyes toward the gates and reached out for them. John slowly brought the melody to an end. He laid down his fiddle and bow and took the infant from Dakota, walked with her toward the light. When he was directly under the arch, the light seemed to flare and suddenly the weight was gone from his arms. He heard a joyous cry, but could see nothing for the light. His felt a beating in his chest as though he was alive once more, pulse drumming. He wanted to follow Dolly into the light more than he'd ever wanted anything before in his life, but he slowly turned his back on the light and stepped back onto the boulevard.

"John Narraway," Dakota said. "What are you doing?"

"I can't go through," he said. "Not yet. I have to help the others—like you do."

"But—"

"It's not because I don't want to go through anymore," John said. "It's . . ."

He didn't know how to explain it and not even fiddle music would help him now. All he could think of was the despair that had clung to him in the city of the undead, the same despair that possessed all those lost souls he'd left there, wandering forever through its deserted streets, huddling in its abandoned buildings, denying themselves the light. He knew that, like Dakota and Gair, he had to try to prevent others from making the same mistake. He knew it wouldn't be easy, he knew there would be times when it would be heartbreaking, but he could see no other course.

"I just want to help," he said. "I have to help. You told me before that there aren't enough of you and the fellow that brought me here said the same thing."

Dakota gave him a long considering look before she finally smiled. "You know," she said. "I think you do have the generosity of heart now."

John put away his fiddle. When he stood up, Dakota took his hand and they began to walk back down the boulevard, away from the gates.

"I'm going to miss that light," John said.

Dakota squeezed his hand. "Don't be silly," she said. "The light has always been inside us."

John glanced back. From this distance, the light was like a heat mirage again, shimmering between the pillars of the gates, but he could still feel its glow, see the flare of its wonder and the sky beyond it that went on forever. Something of it echoed in his chest and he knew Dakota was right.

"We carry it with us wherever we go," he said.

"Learn to play that on your fiddle, John Narraway," she said.

John returned her smile. "I will," he promised. "I surely will."

Birds

Isn't it wonderful? The world scans.
—*Nancy Willard, from "Looking for Mr. Ames"*

1

When her head is full of birds, anything is possible. She can understand the slow language of the trees, the song of running water, the whispering gossip of the wind. The conversation of the birds fills her until she doesn't even think to remember what it was like before she could understand them. But sooner or later, the birds go away, one by one, find new nests, new places to fly. It's not that they tire of her; it's simply not in their nature to tarry for too long.

But she misses them. Misses their company, the flutter of wings inside her head and their trilling conversations. Misses the possibilities. The magic.

To call them back she has to approach them as a bride. Dressed in white, with something old and something new, something borrowed and something blue. And a word. A new word, from another's dream. A word that has never been heard before.

2

Katja Faro was out later than she thought safe, at least for this part of town and at this time of night, the minute hand of her old-fashioned wristwatch steadily climbing up the last quarter of her watch face to count the hour. Three A.M. That late.

From early evening until the clubs close, Gracie Street is a jumbled clutter of people, looking for action, looking for gratification, or just out and about, hanging, gossiping with their friends. There's always something happening, from Lee Street all the way across to Williamson, but tag on a few more hours and clubland becomes a frontier. The lights advertising the various cafés, clubs, and bars begin to flicker and go out, their patrons and staff have all gone home, and the only people out on the streets are a few stragglers, such as Katja tonight, and the predators.

Purple combat boots scuffing on the pavement, Katja felt adrift on the empty street. It seemed like only moments ago she'd been secure in the middle of good conversation, laughter and espressos; then someone remarked on the time, the café was closing and suddenly she was out here, on the street, by herself, finding her own way home. She held her jean jacket closed at her throat—the buttons had come off, one by one, and she kept forgetting to replace them—and listened to the swish of her long flowered skirt, the sound of her boots on the pavement. Listened as well for other footsteps and prayed for a cab to come by.

She was paying so much attention to what might be lurking behind the shadowed mouths of the alleyways that she almost didn't notice the slight figure curled up in the doorway of the pawnshop on her right. The sight made her pause. She glanced up and down the street before crouching down in the doorway. The figure's features were in shadow, the small body outlined under what looked like a dirty white sheet, or a shawl. By its shape Katja could tell it wasn't a boy.

"Hey, are you okay?" she asked.

When there was no response, she touched the girl's shoulder and repeated her question. Large pale eyes flickered open, their gaze settling on Katja. The girl woke like a cat, immediately aware of everything around her. Her black hair hung about her face in a tangle. Unlike most street people, she had a sweet smell, like a field of clover, or a potpourri of dried rosehips and herbs, gathered in a glass bowl.

"What makes you think I'm not okay?" the girl asked.

Katja pushed the fall of her own dark hair back from her brow and settled back on her heels.

"Well, for one thing," she said, "you're lying here in a doorway, on a bed of what looks like old newspapers. It's not exactly the kind of place people pick to sleep in if they've got a choice."

She glanced up and down the street again as she spoke, still wary of her surroundings and their possible danger, still hoping to see a cab.

"I'm okay," the girl told her.

"Yeah, right."

"No, really."

Katja had to smile. She wasn't so old that she'd forgotten what it felt like to be in her late teens and immortal. Remembering, looking at this slight girl with her dark hair and strangely pale eyes, she got this odd urge to take in a stray the way that Angel and Jilly often did. She wasn't sure why. She liked to think that she had as much sympathy as the next person, but normally it was hard to muster much of it at this time of night. Normally she was thinking too much about what terrors the night might hold for her to consider playing the Good Samaritan. But this girl looked so young. . . .

"What's your name?" she asked.

"Teresa. Teresa Lewis."

Katja offered her hand as she introduced herself.

Teresa laughed. "Welcome to my home," she said and shook Katja's hand.

"This a regular squat?" Katja asked. Nervous as she was at being out so late, she couldn't imagine actually sleeping in a place like this on a regular basis.

"No," Teresa said. "I meant the street."

Katja sighed. Immortal. "Look. I don't have that big a place, but there's room on my couch if you want to crash."

Teresa gave her a considering look.

"Well, I know it's not the Harbor Ritz," Katja began.

"It's not that," Teresa told her. "It's just that you don't know me at all. I could be loco, for all you know. Get to your place and rob you. . . ."

"I've got a big family," Katja told her. "They'd track you down and take it out of your skin."

Teresa laughed again. It was like they were meeting at a party somewhere, Katja thought, drinks in hand, no worries, instead of on Gracie Street at three A.M.

"I'm serious," she said. "I've got the room."

Teresa's laughter trailed off. Her pale gaze settled on Katja's features.

"Do you believe in magic?" she asked.

"Say what?"

"Magic. Do you believe in it?"

Katja blinked. She waited for the punch line, but when it didn't come, she said, "Well, I'm not sure. My friend Jilly sure does—though maybe magic's not quite the right word. It's more like she believes there's more to this world than we can always see or understand. She sees things. . . ."

Katja caught herself. How did we get into this? she thought. She wanted to change the subject, she wanted to get off the street before some homeboys showed up with all the wrong ideas in mind, but the steady weight of Teresa's intense gaze wouldn't let her go.

"Anyway," Katja said, "I guess you could say Jilly does. Believes in magic, I mean. Sees things."

"But what about you? Have you seen things?"

Katja shook her head. "Only 'old, unhappy, far-off things, and battles long ago,' " she said. "Wordsworth," she added, placing the quote when Teresa raised her eyebrows in a question.

"Then I guess you couldn't understand," Teresa told her. "See, the reason I'm out here like this is that I'm looking for a word."

3

I can't sleep. I lie in bed for what feels like hours, staring up at the shadows cast on the ceiling from the streetlight outside my bedroom window. Finally I get up. I pull on a pair of leggings and a T-shirt and pad quietly across the room in my bare feet. I stand in the doorway and look at my guest. She's still sleeping, all curled up again, except her nest is made up of a spare set of my sheets and blankets now instead of old newspapers.

I wish it wasn't so early. I wish I could pick up the phone and talk to Jilly. I want to know if the strays she brings home tell stories as strange as mine told me on the way back to my apartment. I want to know if her strays can recognize the egret which is a deposed king. If they can understand the gossip of bees and what crows talk about when they gather in a murder. If they ever don the old-woman wisdom to be found in the rattle-and-cough cry of a lonesome gull and wear it like a cloak of story.

I want to know if Jilly's ever heard of bird-brides, because Teresa says that's what she is, what she usually is, until the birds fly away. To gather them back into her head takes a kind of a wedding ritual that's sealed with a dream-word. That's what she was doing out on Gracie Street when I found her: worn out from trying to get strangers to tell her a word that they'd only ever heard before in one of their dreams.

I don't have to tell you how helpful the people she met were. The ones that didn't ignore her or call her names just gave her spare change instead of the word she needs. But I can't say as I blame them. If she'd come up to me with her spiel I don't know how I'd have reacted. Not well, probably. Wouldn't have listened. Gets so you can't walk down a block some days without getting hit up for change, five or six times. I don't want to be cold; but when it comes down to it, I've only got so much myself.

I look away from my guest, my gaze resting on the phone for a moment, before I turn around and go back into my room. I don't bother undressing. I just lie there on my bed, looking up at the shadow play that's still being staged on my ceiling. I know what's keeping me awake: I can't decide if I've brought home some poor confused kid or a piece of magic. It's not the one or the other that's brought on my insomnia. It's that I'm seriously considering the fact that it might be one or the other.

4

"No, I have a place to live," Teresa said the next morning. They were sitting at the narrow table in Katja's kitchen that only barely seated the two of them comfortably, hands warming around mugs of freshly brewed coffee. "I live in a bachelor in an old house on Stanton Street."

Katja shook her head. "Then why were you sleeping in a doorway last night?"

"I don't know. I think because the people on Gracie Street in the evening seem to dream harder than people anywhere else."

"They're just more desperate to have a good time," Katja said.

"I suppose. Anyway, I was sure I'd find my word there and by the time I realized I wouldn't—at least last night—it was so late and I was just too tired to go home."

"But weren't you scared?"

Teresa regarded her with genuine surprise. "Of what?"

How to explain, Katja wondered. Obviously this girl sitting across from her in a borrowed T-shirt, with sleep still gathered in the corners of her eyes, was fearless, like Jilly. Where did you start enumerating the dangers for them? And why bother? Teresa probably wouldn't listen any more than Jilly ever did. Katja thought sometimes that people like them must have guardian angels watching out for them—and working overtime.

"I feel like I'm always scared," she said.

Teresa nodded. "I guess that's the way I feel, when the birds leave and all I have left in my head are empty nests and a few stray feathers. Kind of lonely, and scared that they'll never come back."

That wasn't the way Katja felt at all. Her fear lay in the headlines of newspapers and the sound-bites that helped fill newscasts. There was too much evil running loose—random, petty evil, it was true, but evil all the same. Ever-present and all around her so that you didn't know who to trust anymore. Sometimes it seemed as though everyone in the world was so much bigger and more capable than her. Too often, confronted with their confidence, she could only feel helpless.

"Where did you hear about this . . . this thing with the birds?" she said instead. "The way you can bring them back?"

Teresa shrugged. "I just always knew it."

"But you have all these details. . . ."

Borrowed from bridal folklore, Katja added to herself—all except for the word she had to get from somebody else's dream. The question she'd really wanted to ask was, *why* those particular details? What made their borrowed possibilities true? Katja didn't want to sound judgmental. The truth, she had to admit if she was honest with herself, wasn't so much that she believed her houseguest as that she didn't disbelieve her. Hadn't she woken up this morning searching the fading remnants of her dreams, looking for a new word that only existed beyond the gates of her sleeping mind?

Teresa was smiling at her. The wattage behind the expression seemed to light the room, banishing shadows and uncertainties, and Katja basked in its glow.

"I know what you're thinking," Teresa said. "They don't even sound all that original except for the missing word, do they? But I believe any of us can make things happen—even magical, impossible things. It's a matter of having faith in the private rituals we make up for ourselves."

"Rituals you make up . . . ?"

"Uh-huh. The rituals themselves aren't all that important on their own—though once you've decided on them, you have to stick to them, just like the old alchemists did. You have to follow them through."

"But if the rituals aren't that important," Katja asked, "then what's the point of them?"

"How they help you focus your will—your intent. That's what magic is, you know. It's having a strong enough sense of self and what's around you to not only envision it being different but to *make* it different."

"You really believe this, don't you?"

"Of course," Teresa said. "Don't you?"

"I don't know. You make it sound so logical."

"That's because it's true. Or maybe—" That smile of Teresa's returned, warming the room again. "—because I'm *willing* it to be true."

"So would your ritual work for me?"

"If you believe in it. But you should probably find your own—a set of circumstances that feels right for you." She paused for a moment, then added, "And you have to know what you're asking for. My birds are what got me through a lot of bad times. Listening to their conversations and soliloquies let me forget what was happening to me."

Katja leaned forward. She could see the rush of memories rising in Teresa, could see the pain they brought with them. She wanted to reach out and hold her in a comforting embrace—the same kind of embrace she'd needed so often but rarely got.

"What happened?" she asked, her voice soft.

"I don't want to remember," Teresa said. She gave Katja an apologetic look. "It's not that I can't, it's that I don't want to."

"You don't have to talk about it if you don't want to," Katja assured her. "Just because I'm putting you up, doesn't mean you have to explain yourself to me."

There was no sunshine in the smile that touched Teresa's features now. It was more like moonlight playing on wild rosebushes, the cool light glinting on thorns. Memories could impale you just like thorns. Katja knew that all too well.

"But I can't not remember," Teresa said. "That's what so sad. For all the good things in my life, I can't stop thinking of how much I hurt before the birds came."

5

I know about pain. I know about loneliness. Talking with Teresa, I realize that these are the first real conversations I've had with someone else in years.

I don't want to make it sound as though I don't have any friends, that I never talk to anyone—but sometimes it feels like that all the same. I always seem to be standing on the outside of a friendship, of conversations, never really engaged. Even last night, before I found Teresa sleeping in the doorway. I was out with a bunch of people. I was in the middle of any number of conversations and camaraderie. But I still went home alone. I listened to what was going on around me. I smiled some, laughed some, added a sentence here, another there, but it wasn't really me that was partaking of the company. The real me was one step removed, watching it happen. Like it seems I always am. Everybody I know seems to inhabit one landscape that they all share while I'm the only person standing in the landscape that's inside of me.

But today it's different. We're talking about weird, unlikely things, but I'm *there* with Teresa. I don't even know her; there are all sorts of people I've known for years, known way better, but not one of them seems to have looked inside me as truly as she does. This alchemy, this magic she's offering me, is opening a door inside me. It's making me remember. It's making me want to fill my head with birds so that I can forget.

That's the saddest thing, isn't it? Wanting to forget. Desiring amnesia. I think that's the only reason some people kill themselves. I know it's the only reason I've ever seriously considered suicide.

Consider the statistics: One out of every five women will be sexually traumatized by the time they reach their twenties. They might be raped, they might be a child preyed upon by a stranger, they might be abused by the very people who are supposed to be looking out for them.

But the thing that statistic doesn't tell you is how often it can happen to that one woman out of five. How it can happen to her over and over and over again, but on the statistical sheet, she's still only listed as one woman in five. That makes it sound so random, the event an extraordinary moment of evil when set against the rest of her life, rather than something that she might have faced every day of her childhood.

I'd give anything for a head full of birds. I'd give anything for the noise and clamor of their conversation to drown out the memories when they rise up inside of me.

6

Long after noon came and went the two women still sat across from each other at the kitchen table. If their conversation could have been seen as well as heard, the spill of words that passed between them would have flooded off the table to eddy around their ankles in ever-deepening pools. It would have made for profound, dark water that was only bearable because each of them came to understand that the other truly understood what they had gone through, and sharing the stories of their battered childhoods at least reminded them that they weren't alone in what they had undergone, even if it didn't make the burden easier to bear.

The coffee had gone cold in their mugs, but the hands across the table they held to comfort each other were warm, palm to palm. When they finally ran out of words, that contact helped maintain the bond of empathy that had grown up between them.

"I didn't have birds," Katja said after a long silence. "All I had was poetry."

"You wrote poems?"

Katja shook her head. "I became poetry. I inhabited poems. I filled them until their words were all I could hear inside my head." She tilted her head back and quoted one:

> Rough wind, that moanest loud
>   Grief too sad for song;
> Wild wind, when sullen cloud
>   Knells all the night long;
> Sad storm, whose tears are vain,
> Bare woods, whose branches strain,
> Deep caves and dreary main,—
>   Wail, for the world's wrong!

"That's so sad. What's it called?" Teresa asked.

" 'A dirge.' It's by Shelley. I always seemed to choose sad poems, but I only ever wanted them for how I'd get so full of words I wouldn't be able to remember anything else."

"Birds and words," Teresa said. Her smile came out again from behind the dark clouds of her memories. "We rhyme."

7

We wash Teresa's dress that afternoon. It wasn't very white anymore—not after her having grubbed about in it on Gracie Street all day and then worn it as a nightgown while she slept in a doorway—but it cleans up better than I think it will. I feel like we're in a detergent commercial when we take it out of the dryer. The dress seems to glow against my skin as I hand it over to her.

Her something old is a plastic Crackerjack ring that she's had since she was a kid. Her something new is her sneakers—a little scuffed and worse for the wear this afternoon, but still passably white. Her borrowed is a white leather clasp-purse that her landlady loaned her. Her blue is a small clutch of silk flowers: forget-me-nots tied up with a white ribbon that she plans to wear as a corsage.

All she needs is that missing word.

I don't have one for her, but I know someone who might. Jilly always likes to talk about things not quite of this world—things seen from the corner of the eye, or brought over from a dream. And whenever she talks about dreams, Sophie Etoile's name comes up because Jilly insists Sophie's part faerie and therefore a true dreamer. I don't know Sophie all that well, certainly not well enough to guess at her genealogy, improbable or not as the case may be. But she does have an otherworldly, Pre-Raphaelite air about her that makes Jilly's claims seem possible—at least they seem possible considering my present state of mind.

And there's no one else I can turn to, no one I can think of. I can't explain this desperation I feel toward Teresa, a kind of mothering/big sister complex. I just have to help her. And while I know that I may not be able to make myself forget, I think I can do it for her. Or at least I want to try.

So that's how we find ourselves knocking at the door of Sophie's studio later that afternoon. When Sophie answers the door, her curly brown hair tied back from her face and her painting smock as spotless as Jilly says it always is, I don't have to go into a long explanation as to what we're doing there or why we need this word. I just have to mention that Jilly's told me that she's a true dreamer and Sophie gets this smile on her face, like you do when you're thinking about a mischievous child who's too endearing to get angry at, and she thinks for a moment, then says a word that at least I've never heard before. I turn to Teresa to ask her if it's what she needs, but she's already got this beatific look on her face.

"Mmm," is all she can manage.

I thank Sophie, who's giving the pair of us a kind of puzzled smile, and lead Teresa back down the narrow stairs of Sophie's building and out onto the street. I wonder what I'm going to do with Teresa. She looks for all the world as though she's tripping. But just when I decide to take her home again, her eyes get a little more focused and she takes my hand.

"I have to . . . readjust to all of this," she says. "But I don't want to have us just walk out of each others' lives. Can I come and visit you tomorrow?"

"Sure," I tell her. I hesitate a moment, then have to ask, "Can you really hear them?"

"Listen," she says.

She draws my head close to hers until my ear is resting right up against her temple. I swear I hear a bird's chorus resonating inside her head, conducting through skin and bone, from her mind into my mind.

"I'll come by in the morning," she says, and then drifts off down the pavement.

All I can do is watch her go, that birdsong still echoing inside me.

8

Back in my own living room, I sit on the carpet. I can feel a foreign vibe in my apartment, a quivering in the air from Teresa having been there. Everything in the room carries the memory of her, the knowledge of her gaze, how she handled and examined them with her attention. My furniture, the posters and prints on my walls, my knickknacks, all seemed subtly changed, a little stiff from the awareness of her looking at them.

It takes a while for the room to settle down into its familiar habits. The fridge muttering to itself in the kitchen. The pictures in their frames letting out their stomachs and hanging slightly askew once more.

I take down a box of family photos from the hall closet and fan them out on the carpet in front of me. I look at the happy family they depict and try to see hints of the darkness that doesn't appear in the photos. There are too many smiles—mine, my mother's, my father's. I know real life was never the way these pictures pretend it was.

I sit there remembering my father's face—the last time I saw him. We were in the courtroom, waiting for him to be sentenced. He wouldn't look at me. My mother wouldn't look at me. I sat at the table with only a lawyer for support, only a stranger for family. That memory always makes me feel ashamed because even after all he'd done to me, I didn't feel any triumph. I felt only disloyalty. I felt only that I was the one who'd been bad, that what had happened to me had been my fault. I knew back then it was wrong to feel that way—just as I know now that it is—but I can't seem to help myself.

I squeeze my eyes shut, but the moment's locked in my brain, just like all those other memories from my childhood that put a lie to the photographs fanned out on the carpet around me. Words aren't going to blot them out for me today. There aren't enough poems in the world to do that. And even if I could gather birds into my head, I don't think they would work for me. But I remember what Teresa told me about rituals and magic.

It's having a strong enough sense of self and what's around you to not only envision it being different but to make *it different.*

I remember the echoing sound of the birds I heard gossiping in her head and I know that I can find peace, too. I just have to believe that I can. I just have to know what it is that I want and concentrate on having it, instead of what I've got. I have to find the ritual that'll make it work for me.

Instinctively, I realize it can't be too easy. Like Teresa's dream-word, the spell needs an element to complete it that requires some real effort on my part to attain it. But I know what the rest of the ritual will be—it comes into my head, full-blown, as if I've always known it but simply never stopped to access that knowledge before.

I pick up a picture of my father from the carpet and carefully tear his face into four pieces, sticking one piece in each of the front and back pockets of my jeans. I remember something I heard about salt, about it being used to cleanse, and add a handful of it to each pocket. I wrap the fingers of my left hand together with a black ribbon and tie the bow so that it lies across my knuckles. I lick my right forefinger and write my name on the bare skin of my stomach with saliva. Then I let my shirt fall back down to cover the invisible word and leave the apartment, looking for a person who, when asked to name a nineteenth-century poet, will mistakenly put together the given name of one with the surname of another.

From somewhere I hear a sound like Teresa's birds, singing their approval.

Passing

Great God! I'd rather be
A pagan suckled in a creed outworn;
So might I, standing on this pleasant lea,
Have glimpses that would make me less forlorn.
        —*William Wordsworth,*
            from "The World Is Too Much With Us"

1

The sword lies on the grass beside me, not so much a physical presence as an enchantment. I don't know how else to describe it. It's too big to be real. I can't imagine anyone being able to hold it comfortably, little say wield it. Looking at it is like looking through water, as though I'm lying at the bottom of a lake and everything's slightly in motion, edges blurring. I can see the dark metal of the sword's pommel and cross guard, the impossible length of the blade itself that seems to swallow the moonlight, the thong wrapped round and round the grip, its leather worn smooth and shiny in places.

I can almost believe it's alive.

Whenever I study it, time gets swallowed up. I lose snatches of the night, ten minutes, fifteen minutes, time I don't have to spare. I have to be finished before dawn. With an effort, I pull my gaze away and pick up the shovel once more. Hallowed ground. I don't know how deep the grave should be. Four feet? Six feet? I'm just going to keep digging until I feel I've got it right.

2

Lucy Grey was a columnist and features writer for *The Newford Sun*, which was how she first found herself involved with the city's gay community. Her editor, enamored with the most recent upsurge of interest in gay chic and all things androgynous, sent her down to the girl bars on Gracie Street to write an op-ed piece that grew into a Sunday feature. Steadfastly heterosexual in terms of who she'd actually sleep with, Lucy discovered she was gay in spirit, if not in practice. Sick of being harassed by guys, she could relax in the gay clubs, stepping it out and flirting with the other girls on the dance floor and never having to worry about how to go home alone at the end of the night.

Her new girlpals seemed to understand and she didn't think anybody considered her a tease until one night, sitting in a cubical of a washroom in Neon Sister, she overheard herself being discussed by two women who'd come in to touch up their makeup. They were unaware of her presence.

"I don't know," one of them said. "There's something about her that doesn't ring true. It's like after that piece she did in *The Sun*, now she's researching a book—looking at us from the inside, but not really one of us."

"Who, Lucy?" the other said.

Lucy recognized her friend Traci's voice. It was Traci who befriended her the first night she hit Gracie Street and guided her through the club scene.

"Of course Lucy. She's all look, but don't touch."

"Sounds more to me like you're miffed because she won't sleep with you."

"She doesn't sleep with anybody."

"So?"

"So she's like an emotional tourist, passing through. You know what happens when the straights start hanging out in one of our clubs."

It becomes a straight club, Lucy thought, having heard it all before. The difference, this time, was that the accusation was being directed at her and she wasn't so sure that it was unfair. She wasn't here just because she preferred the company of women, but to avoid men. It wasn't that she disliked men, but that her intimacy with them never seemed to go beyond the bedroom. She was neither bisexual nor experimenting. She was simply confused and taking refuge in a club scene where she could still have a social life.

"You're reading way too much into this," Traci said. "It's not like she's seriously coming on to anyone. It's just innocent flirting—everybody does it."

"So you don't want a piece of what she's got?"

Traci laughed. "I'd set up house with her in a minute." Sitting in the cubicle, Lucy found herself blushing furiously, especially when Traci added, "Long-term."

"What you're setting yourself up for is a broken heart."

"I don't think so," Traci said. "I try to keep everything in perspective. If she just wants to be friends, that's okay with me. And I kind of like her the way she is: social, but celibate."

That was a description Lucy embraced wholeheartedly after that night because it seemed to perfectly sum up who she was.

Until she met Nina.

3

It all starts out innocently enough. Nina shows up at the North Star one night, looking just as sweet and lost as Traci said I did the first time she saw me on Gracie Street, trying to work up the nerve to go into one of the clubs. She has her hair cut above her ears like Sadie Benning and she's wearing combat boots with her black jeans and white T-shirt, but she looks like a femme, and a shy one at that, so I take her under my wing.

Turns out she's married, but it's on the rocks. Maybe. There's no real intimacy in their relationship—tell me about it. Thinks her husband's getting some on the side, but she can't swear to it. She's not sure what she's doing here, she just wants a night out, but she doesn't want to play the usual games in the straight bars, so she comes here, but now that she's here, she's not sure what she's doing here.

I tell her to relax. We dance some. We have a few drinks. By the time she goes home she's flushing prettily and most of the shadows I saw haunting the backs of her eyes are gone.

We start to hang out together. In the clubs. Have lunch, dinner once. Not dates. We're just girlpals, except after a few weeks I find myself thinking about her all the time, fixating on her. Not jealous. Not wondering where she is, or who she's with. Just conversations we had running through my mind. Her face a familiar visitor to my mind's eye. Her trim body.

Is this how it starts? I wonder. There's no definition to what's growing inside me, no "I used to like men, now I'm infatuated with a woman." It's just this swelling desire to be with her. To touch her. To bask in her smile. To know she's thinking of me.

One night I'm driving her home and I don't know how it happens, but we pull up in front of her apartment building and I'm leaning toward her and then our heads come together, our lips, our tongues. It's like kissing a guy, only everything's softer. Sweeter, somehow. We're wrapped up against each other, hands fumbling, I'm caressing her hair, her neck, her shoulder—until suddenly she pulls away, breathless, like me, a surprised look of desire in her eyes, like me, but there's something else there, too. Not shame. No, it felt too good. But confusion, yes. And uncertainty, for sure.

"I'm sorry," I say. I know she's been passing, just like me. Gay in spirit. We've talked about it. Lots of times.

"Don't be," she says. "It felt nice."

I don't say anything. I'm on pins and needles, not understanding the intensity of these feelings I have for her, for another woman, not wanting to scare her off, but knowing I want more. Nice doesn't even begin to describe how it felt to me.

Nina sighs. "It's just . . . confusing."

This I understand.

"But it feels wrong?" I ask.

She nods. "Only not for the reason you're probably thinking. It's just . . . if I was sure Martin was cheating on me . . . that our marriage was over . . . I think it would be different. I wouldn't feel like *I* was betraying him. I could do whatever I wanted, couldn't I?"

"Do you still love him?"

"I don't know," Nina says. "If he's cheating on me again, the way I think he is . . ." She gives me a lost look that makes me want to just take her in my arms once more, but I stay on my own side of the front seat. "Maybe," she says in this small voice, her eyes so big and hopeful, "maybe you could find out for me . . . for us. . . ."

"What? Like follow him?"

Nina shakes her head. "No. I was thinking more like . . . you could try to seduce him. Then we'd *know*."

I don't like the way this is going at all, but there's a promise in Nina's eyes now, a promise that if I do this thing for her, she'll be mine. Not just for one night, but forever.

"You wouldn't actually have to *do* anything," she says. "You know, like sleep with him. We'd only have to take it far enough to see if he's cheating on me."

"I don't know," I tell her, doubt in my voice, but I can already feel myself giving in.

She nods slowly. "I guess it's a pretty stupid idea," she says. She looks away embarrassed. "God. I can't believe I even asked you to do something like that."

She leans forward and gives me a quick kiss, then draws back and starts to get out of the car.

"Wait a minute," I say, catching hold of her arm. She lets me tug her back in the car. "I didn't say I wouldn't do it. It's just . . . we'd need a good plan, wouldn't we? I mean, where would I even meet him in the first place?"

So we start to talk about it and before I know it, we've got the plan. She tells me where he goes after work for a drink on Fridays. We figure it'll be best if she goes away somewhere for the weekend. We work everything out, sitting there in the front seat of my car, arms around each other. We kiss again before she finally leaves, a long deep kiss that has my head swimming, my body aching to be naked against hers. I don't even consider second thoughts until I wake up alone in my own apartment the next morning and begin to realize what I've gotten myself into.

I remember the last thing she said before she got out of the car.

"If he *is* cheating on me . . . and he takes you to our apartment, could you do something for me before you leave?"

"What's that?"

"There's a sword hanging on the wall over the mantel. Could you take it with you back to your place?"

"A sword."

She nodded. "Because if it's over, I'm not ever going back to that place. I won't ever want to see him again. But . . ." She gave me a look that melted my heart. "The sword's the only thing I'd want to take away with me. It used to belong to my mother, you see. . . ."

I lie there in bed thinking about it until I have to get up to have a pee. When I'm washing my face at the basin, I study my reflection looking back at me, water dripping from her cheeks.

"Lucy," I say to her. "What have we gotten ourselves into this time?"

4

It was a quiet night at Neon Sister, but it was still early, going on to eleven. Lucy saw Traci sitting by herself in one of the booths beside the dance floor. She was easy to spot with her shoulder-length dreadlocks, her coffee-colored skin accentuated by the white of her T-shirt. Lucy waited a moment to make sure Traci was alone, then crossed the dance floor and slid into the booth beside her. She ordered a drink from the waitress, but wasn't in the mood to do more than sip from it after it arrived. There was always something about being in Traci's calm, dark-eyed presence that made Lucy want to open up to her. She didn't know what it was that usually stopped her, but tonight it wasn't there.

"I'm not really gay, you know," she said when the small talk between them died.

Traci smiled. "I know."

"You do?"

Traci nodded. "But you're not sure you're straight, either. You don't know who you are, do you?"

"I guess. Except now I'm starting to think maybe I am gay."

"Has this got something to do with Nina?"

"Is it that obvious?"

"We've all been there before, Lucy."

Lucy sighed. "So I think I'm ready to, you know, to find out who I really am, but I don't think Nina is."

"Welcome to that club as well."

Lucy took another sip of her drink and looked out at the dance floor. An hour had passed and the club was starting to fill up. She brought her gaze back to Traci.

"Were you ever in love with a guy?" she asked.

Traci hesitated for a moment, then gave a reluctant nod. "A long time ago."

"Does it feel any different—I mean, with a woman?"

"You mean inside?"

Lucy nodded.

"It doesn't feel different," Traci confirmed. She studied Lucy, her dark gaze more solemn than usual, before going on. "Straights always think it's hard for us to come out—to the world—but it's harder to come out to ourselves. Not because there's anything wrong with what we are, but because we're made to feel it's wrong. I used to think that with the strides in gay rights over the past few years, it wouldn't be like that anymore, but society still feeds us so much garbage that nothing much seems to have changed. You know what kept going around and around in my head when I was trying to figure myself out?"

Lucy shook her head.

"That old *The Children's Hour* with Shirley MacLaine from the sixties—the one where she finds out she's a lesbian and she kills herself. I was so ashamed of how I felt. Ashamed and confused."

"I don't feel ashamed," Lucy said.

"But you do feel confused."

Lucy nodded. "I don't know what to do."

"Well, here's my two cents: Don't be in a rush to work it out. Be honest—to yourself as well as to Nina—but take it slow."

"And if I lose her?"

"Then it was never meant to be." Traci gave her a wry smile. "Pretty lame, huh? But there's always a grain of truth—even in populist crap like that. You wanna dance?"

Lucy thought about the night she'd overheard Traci and another woman discussing her in the washroom, thought about what Traci had said about her, thought about what she herself was feeling for Nina. Didn't matter the combination of genders, she realized. Some things just didn't change. She gave Traci a smile.

"Sure," she said.

It was a slow dance. She and Traci had danced together many times before, but it felt different tonight. Tonight Lucy couldn't stop focusing on the fact that it was a woman's body moving so closely to hers, a woman's arms around her. But then ever since kissing Nina last night, everything had felt different.

"Gay or straight," Traci said, her voice soft in Lucy's ear, "the hurt feels the same."

Lucy nodded, then let her head rest against Traci's once more. They were comforting each other, Lucy realized, but while Traci was offering more, the dance was all that Lucy had to give.

5

So I go ahead and do it. I meet Martin in Huxley's, that yuppie bar across from Fitzhenry Park, and I flirt outrageously with him. Picking him up is so easy, I wish there was a prize for it. I'd collect big-time.

By the time we've had dinner, I've got enough on him to take back to Nina, but I'm curious now, about him, about where they live, and I can't seem to break it off. Next thing I know I'm in their apartment, the same one I sat outside of a few nights ago, necking with his wife in the front seat of my car. Now I'm here with him, sitting on their couch, watching him make us drinks at the wet bar in the corner of the living room.

He comes back with a drink in each hand and gives me one. We toast each other, take a sip. This is seriously good brandy. I like it. I like him, too—not a man-woman kind of thing, but he seems like a nice guy. Except he cheats on his wife—whom I'm trying to get into my own bed. It's time to go, I realize. Way past time to go. But then he floors me.

"So when did you meet Nina?" he asks.

I look at him, unable to hide my surprise. "How did you—" I break off before I get in too deep and take a steadying breath to try to regain my composure. It's not easy with that pale blue gaze of his wryly regarding me. Earlier, it reminded me of Traci, kind of solemn and funny, all at the same time, like hers, but now there's something unpleasant sitting in back of it—the same place the hurt sat in Nina's eyes the night I first met her.

"She's sent other people to get the sword, you know."

I've been trying to avoid looking at it all night but now I can't stop my gaze from going to it. I remember thinking how big it was when I first stepped into the living room and stole a glance at it. No way it was going to fit into my handbag. I'd given up the idea of walking out with it pretty quick.

"What story did she tell you?" Martin went on. "That it belonged to her grandmother and it's the only thing she's got left to remind her of the old bag?"

Not grandmother, I think. Mother. But I don't say anything. One of the things I've learned working on the paper: If you can keep quiet, nine out of ten times the person you're with will feel obliged to fill the silence. You'd be surprised the kinds of things they'll tell you.

"Or did she tell you about the family curse," he asks, "and how the sword has to be sheathed for it to end?"

I still say nothing.

"Or did she tell you the truth?"

This time he plays the waiting game until I finally ask, "So what is the truth?"

"Well, it's all subjective, isn't it?"

There's an undercurrent of weirdness happening here that tells me it's really time to go now. I take a good swig of the brandy to fortify myself, then pick up my jacket and slip it on.

"I don't mean to sound so vague," he says before I get up. "It's just that, no matter what she's told you, it's only a piece of the truth. That's what I mean about it all being subjective."

I find myself nodding. What he's saying is something I learned my first week at the paper: There's no one thing called truth; just one's individual take on it.

"We're not married," he says.

"Uh-huh. It's kind of late for that line, isn't it?"

"No, you don't get it. She's not even human. She's this . . . this *thing*."

His gaze shifts to the sword above the mantel, then returns to mine. I realize the unpleasant thing I see sitting in the back of his eyes is fear.

"What are you saying?" I ask.

"She really is under a curse, except it's nothing like what she probably told you."

"She didn't say anything about a curse—except for being married to you."

"The way things look," Martin says, "I deserve that. But we're really not married. I don't have a hold over her. It's the other way around. She scares the shit out of me."

I shake my head. Considering the size of him and the size of her, I find that hard to believe.

"I met her a few years ago," he explains. "At a party. I made her a promise, that I'd help her break the curse that's on her, but I didn't. I broke my promise and she's been haunting me ever since."

Curses. Haunting. It's like he's trying to tell me Nina's a ghost. I'm beginning to wish that I'd just let it play out in the restaurant and gone on to my own place. By myself. Too late for that now. He's still sitting there, looking at me all expectantly, and I have to admit that while I think it's all a load of crock, I can't seem to check my curiosity. It's a bad habit I bring home from the office. It's probably why I applied for the job in the first place.

"So what's this curse?" I ask.

"She's trapped in the shape of that sword," he says, pointing to the mantel.

"Oh, please."

Nina passing as gay I can buy—I've been doing it myself. But passing as human as well?

"Look. I know what it sounds like. But it's true. She promised me a year of companionship—good company, great sex, whatever I wanted— and at the end of that year I had to fulfill my part of the bargain, but I couldn't go through with it."

"Which was?"

The only thing I'm really interested in now is how far he'll take all of this.

"The sword once had a scabbard," Martin says. "When it was sheathed, she could stay in human form. But the scabbard got lost or stolen or something—there was something enchanted about it as well. It kept its bearer free from all hurt and harm. Anyway, the way things are now, she can only be human for short bits of time before she has to return into the sword."

I give him a noncommittal "Uh-huh."

"The bargain I made," he says, "was that I'd sheathe the sword for her at the end of the year, but I couldn't do it."

"Why not?"

"Because I have to sheathe it in myself."

I sit up straighter. "What? You mean impale yourself on it—a kind of *seppuku* like the samurai used to do in Japan?"

He doesn't answer me, but goes on instead. "See, for the curse to be broken, I have to believe that it'll work while I do it. And I have to want to do it—you know, be a willing sacrifice. I can't do either."

I look at him, I read his fear, and realize that he really believes all of this.

"So why don't you just get rid of the sword?" I ask, which seems reasonable enough to me.

"I'm scared to. I don't know what'll happen to me if I do."

I think of Nina. I think of this big guy being scared of her and I have to shake my head.

"So . . . has Nina threatened you?"

He shakes his head. "No, she just stands there by the mantel, or at the foot of my bed, and looks at me. Haunts me. She won't talk to me anymore, she doesn't do anything but stare at me. It's driving me crazy."

Well, something sure is, I want to say. Instead I consider the sword, hanging up there on the wall. I try to imagine Nina's—what? Spirit? Essence?—trapped in that long length of blade. I can't even work up the pretense of belief.

"So give it to me," I say.

He blinks in confusion, then shakes his head again. "No, I can't do that. Something horrible will happen to me if I do."

"I don't think so," I tell him. "Nina specifically asked me to take the sword with me when I left. You say she's sent other people to get it. Doesn't it seem obvious that all she wants is the sword? Give it to me and we'll all be out of your life. Nina. The sword. Me." Your sanity, I add to myself, though maybe a good shrink can help you get some of it back.

"I . . ."

He looks from me to the sword, torn. Then he comes to a decision. He gets up and fetches a blanket, wraps the sword in it and hands it to me.

"Look," I say, staggering a little under its weight. "What you really should do is—"

"Just go," he tells me.

He doesn't physically throw me out, but it's close. Truth is, he looks so freaked about what he's doing that I'm happy to put as much distance as I can between us. I end up hauling the sword down to the street to where I parked my car. It won't fit in the trunk, so I put it on the backseat. I look up at the window of the apartment above me. Martin's turned all the lights off.

It's weird, I think, sliding into the driver's seat. He seemed so normal when I first picked him up in Huxley's, but then he turned out to be loopier than anyone I've ever met on this side of the Zebrowski Institute's doors. It just goes to show you. No wonder Nina wanted to leave him.

I stop at that thought, the car still in neutral. Except that wasn't why she said she wanted to leave him. I look up at the darkened apartment again, this time through my windshield. Though now that I think about it, if I were in her position, I probably wouldn't want to tell the truth about why I was leaving my husband either.

I shake my head. What a mess. Putting the car into gear, I drive myself home. I have a column due for the Monday paper and I don't know what it's going to be about yet. Still, I know this much—it won't be about swords.

<h1 style="text-align:center">6</h1>

Nina really was out of town, so Lucy couldn't call her. "I don't want to lie to him," she'd told Lucy. "That'd make me just as bad as he is." What about Nina's lying to her? Lucy wondered, but she knew she was willing to give Nina the benefit of the doubt, seeing how nuts her husband was. Besides, even if Nina wasn't out of town, the only number Lucy had for her was the same as Martin's—she'd looked his up as she was making herself a coffee on Sunday morning.

She'd left the sword where she'd dropped it last night—wrapped in its blanket on the floor in her hallway, right beside the front door—and hadn't looked at it since. Didn't want to look at it. It wasn't that she believed any of Martin's very weird story about the sword and Nina, so much as that something about the weapon gave her the creeps. No, that wasn't quite right. It was more that thinking about it made her feel odd— as though the air had grown thicker, or the hardwood floor had gone slightly spongy underfoot. Better not to think of it.

Saturday, she did some grocery shopping, but she stayed in with a video on Saturday night. Sunday afternoon, she went in to the office and worked on Monday's column—deciding to do a piece on cheap sources for fashion accessories. She finished it quickly and then spent a couple of hours trying to straighten out the mess on her desk without making any real noticeable progress. It was the story of her life. Sunday night, Nina called.

As soon as she recognized Nina's voice, Lucy looked down the hall to where the sword still lay and thought of what Martin had told her.

"I've got the sword," she said without any preamble. "It's here at my place. Do you want to come by to pick it up?"

"And take it where?" Nina asked. "Back to Martin's and my apartment?"

"Oh. I never thought of that. I guess you need to find a place to live first."

She hesitated a moment, but before she could offer her own couch as a temporary measure, Nina was talking again.

"I can't believe he just gave it to you," she said. "Did he give you a hard time? Was . . . seducing him . . . was it horrible?"

"It didn't go that far."

"But still," Nina said. "It couldn't have been pleasant."

"More like strange."

"Strange how?"

Was there a new note in Nina's voice? Lucy wondered. A hint of— what? Tension?

"Well, he hit on me just like you said he would," she said. "He picked me up at Huxley's after work, took me out for dinner and then back to—" she almost said "his" "—your place."

"I guess I'm not surprised."

"Anyway, as soon as we got to the apartment, almost the first thing he asked me was when I'd met you. Nina, he told me you guys were never married. He told me all kinds of weird things."

There was a moment's silence on the line, then Nina asked, "Did you believe him?"

"The stuff he was telling me was so crazy that I don't know what to believe," Lucy said. "But I want to believe you."

"I'll tell you everything," Nina said. "But not now. I've just got a few things to do and then I'll come see you."

Lucy could tell that Nina was about to hang up.

"What sort of things?" she asked, just to keep Nina on the line.

Nina laughed. "Oh you know. I just have to straighten my affairs, say goodbye to Martin, that kind of thing."

Lucy found herself remembering Martin's fear. Crazy as he was, the fear had been real. Why he should be scared of Nina, Lucy couldn't begin to imagine, but he had been afraid.

"Listen," she said, "you're not going to—"

"I have to run," Nina broke in. "I'll call you soon."

"—do anything crazy," Lucy finished.

But she was talking to a dead line.

Lucy stared at the phone for a long moment before she finally cradled the receiver. A nervous prickle crept up her spine and the air seemed to thicken. She turned to look at the sword again. It was still where she'd left it, wrapped in Martin's blanket, lying on the floor.

There's no such thing as an enchanted sword, she told herself. She knew that. But ever since leaving Martin's place last night there'd been a niggling little doubt in the back of her mind, a kind of "What if?" that she hadn't been able to completely ignore or refute with logic. She couldn't shake the feeling that *something* was about to happen and whatever it was was connected to the sword and Martin. And to Nina.

She stood up quickly and fetched her car keys from the coffee table. Maybe it was stupid, worrying the way she was, but she had to know. Had to be sure that the boundaries of what could be and what could not still existed as they always had. She left so quickly, she was still buttoning up her jacket when she reached the street.

It took her fifteen minutes to get to the apartment where Nina and Martin lived. She parked at the curb across from the building and studied their place on the third floor. The windows were all dark. There was no one on the street except for a man at the far end of the block who was poking through a garbage can with a stick.

Lucy sat there for five minutes before she reluctantly pulled away. She cruised slowly through the neighborhood, looking for Nina's familiar trim figure. Eventually the only thing left to do was drive back to her own apartment and wait for Nina to call. She sat up in bed with the telephone on the quilt beside her leg, trying to read because she knew she wouldn't be able to sleep. After a while she phoned Traci, nervous the whole time that Nina was trying to get through while she was tying up the line. She told Traci everything, but it made no more sense to Traci than it did to her.

"Weird," Traci said at last.

"Am I blowing this way out of proportion?" Lucy wanted to know.

She could almost feel Traci's smile across the telephone line.

"Well, it is a bit much," Traci said. "All this business with the sword and Nina. But I've always been one to trust my intuition. If you feel there's something weird going on, then I'm willing to bet that there is— something on a more logical level than curses and hauntings, mind you."

"So what do I do?"

Traci sighed. "Just what you're doing: wait. What else can you do?"

"I know. It's just . . ."

"You want some company?" Traci asked.

What Lucy wanted was Nina. She wanted to know that Martin had nothing to fear from her, that Nina wasn't about to do something that was going to get her into serious trouble. But Traci couldn't help her with any of that.

"No," she told her friend. "I'll be okay."

"Call me tomorrow."

"I will."

Finally she drifted off with the lights on, sitting up against the headboard, the book still open on her lap. She dreamed that the sword lay on the other side of the bed, talking to her in a low murmuring voice that could have belonged to anybody. When she woke, she couldn't remember what it had told her.

7

By nine o'clock, Monday morning, I'm a mess. Punchy from the weird dreams and getting so little sleep. Sick with worry. Nina still hasn't called and I'm thinking the worst. It kind of surprises me that the worst I imagine isn't that she's done something to Martin, but that she doesn't want to see me anymore.

I'm already late for work. I consider phoning in sick, but I know I can't stay at home—I'm already bouncing off the walls—so I go in to the office. I know I can check my machine for messages from there and at least I'll be able to find something to keep me busy.

I have this habit of going over the police reports file when I first get in. It's kind of a gruesome practice, reading the list of break-ins, robberies, rapes, and the like that occurred the night before, but I can't seem to shake it. It's not even my beat; I usually get assigned the soft stories. I think maybe the reason I do it is that it's a way of validating that, okay, so the city's going down the tubes, but I'm still safe. I'm safe. The people I know and love are safe. This kind of horrible thing goes on, but it doesn't really touch me. It's fueled by the same impulse that makes us all slow down at accidents and follow the news. Sometimes I think we don't so much want to be informed as have our own security validated.

This morning there's a report of an apparent suicide on a street that sounds familiar. They don't give the victim's name, but the street's all I need. Shit. It's Martin. It says, Caucasian male did a jump from his third-story apartment window, but I know it's Martin. The coroner's still waiting for the autopsy report; the cops are pretty much ruling out foul play.

But I know better, don't I? Martin himself told me what'd happen if he got rid of the sword and he looked so terrified when I left his place Friday night.

But I still can't believe it of Nina. I can't believe all this crap he told me about her and the sword.

I've only been away from home for thirty-five minutes, but I immediately close the file and phone my apartment to check for messages. Nothing. Same as ten minutes ago—I called when I first got here.

There's nothing all day.

I try to stick it out, but in the end I have to leave work early. I start for home, but wind up driving by the apartment—looking for Nina, I tell myself, but of course she wouldn't be there, hanging around on the pavement where Martin hit. I know why I'm really doing this. Morbid curiosity. I look up at the windows, third floor. One of them's been boarded up.

I go home. Shower. Change. Then I hit the bars on Gracie Street, looking for Nina. The North Star. Neon Sister. Girljock. Skirts. No sign of her. I start to check out the hardcore places, the jack-and-jill-off scenes and clubs where the rougher trade hangs out. Still nothing. The last place I go into this blonde leatherette in a black push-up bra and hot pants smiles at me. I start to smile back, but then she makes a V with her fingers and flicks her tongue through them. I escape back up the stairs that let me into the place. I'm not sure what I am anymore—gay, straight, what—but one thing I know is I'm still not into casual sex.

Once outside, I lean against the front of the building, feeling just as lost as I did the night Traci took me under her wing. I don't know what to do anymore, where to turn. I start to look for a pay phone—I figure I can at least check my answering machine again—when someone grabs me by the arm. I yelp and pull free, but when I turn around, it's Nina I find standing beside me—not the blonde from the club I just left.

"Sorry," she says. "I didn't mean to make you jump like that."

She's smiling, but I can see she really means it. She leans forward and gives me a kiss on the lips. I don't know what to do, what to think. I'm so glad to see her, but so scared she had something to do with Martin's death. Not magic mumbo-jumbo, nothing like that. Just plain she couldn't take the shit from him anymore and it all got out of hand.

"Martin's dead," I say.

"I know. I was there."

My breath catches in my throat. "You . . . you didn't . . . ?"

I can't get it out, but she knows what I'm asking. She shakes her head. Taking my arm, she leads me off down the street.

"I think we have to talk," she tells me.

She leads me to my car, but I don't feel like I'm in any condition to drive. I start to go to the passenger's side.

"I can't drive," Nina tells me.

Right. So we sit there in my car, parked just off Gracie Street, looking out the windshield, not saying anything, not touching each other, just sitting there.

"What did he tell you about me?" Nina asks finally.

I look at her. Her face isn't much more than a silhouette in the illumination thrown by the streetlights outside. After a few moments, I clear my throat and start to talk, finishing with, "Is it true?"

"Mostly."

I don't know what to say. I want to think she's crazy but there's nothing about her that I associate with craziness.

"Where did you go after you called me?" I ask instead.

Nina hesitates, then says, "To the lake. To talk to my sister."

"Your sister?"

I hadn't stopped to think of it before, but of course she'd have family. We all do. But then Nina pulls that piece of normal all out of shape as well.

"She's one of the Ladies of the Lake," she says. "Bound to her sword, just like me. Just like all of us."

It's my turn to hesitate. Do I really want to feed this fantasy? But then I ask, "How many are you?"

"Seven of us—for seven swords. My oldest sister is bound to the one you'd know best: Excalibur."

I really have to struggle with what I'm hearing. I'd laugh, except Nina's so damn serious.

"But," I say. "When you're talking about a Lady of the Lake . . . you mean like in Tennyson? King Arthur and all that stuff?"

Nina nods. "The stories are pretty close, but they miss a lot."

I take a deep breath. "Okay. But that's in England. What would your sister be doing here? What are you doing here?"

"All lakes are aspects of the First Lake," Nina says. "Just as all forests remember the First Forest."

I can only look blankly at her.

Nina sighs. "As all men and women remember First Man and First Woman. And the fall from grace."

"You mean in Eden?"

Nina shakes her head. "Grace is what gives this world its worth, but there are always those who would steal it away, for the simple act of doing so. Grace shames a graceless people, so they strike out at it. Remember Martin told you about the scabbards that once protected our swords?"

"I guess. . . ."

"They had healing properties and when men realized that, they took the scabbards and broke them up, eliminating a little more of their grace and healing properties with each piece they took. That's why I'm in my present predicament. Of the seven of us, only two still have their swords, kept safe in their scabbards. Three more still retain ownership of their swords. Ailine—my sister—and I don't have even that. With our swords unsheathed, we've lost most of our freedom. We're bound into the metal for longer and longer periods of time. A time will come, I suppose, when we'll be trapped in the metal forever."

She studies me for a long moment, then sighs again. "You don't believe any of this, do you?"

I'm honest with her. "It's hard."

"Of course. It's easy to forget marvels when your whole life you're taught to ignore them."

"It's just—"

"Lucy," Nina says. "I'll make the same bargain with you that I made with Martin. I'll stay with you for a year, but then you must hold up your side."

I shake my head. I don't even have to think about it.

"But you wanted to sleep with me," Nina says. "You wanted my love."

"But not like this. Not bargaining for it like it's some kind of commodity. That's not love."

Nina looks away. "I see," she says, her gaze locked on something I can't see.

"Tell me what you'd want me to do," I say.

Nina's attention returns to me. "There's no point. You don't believe."

"Tell me anyway."

"You must take the sword inside yourself. You must do it willingly. And you must believe that by doing so, you are freeing me."

"I just stick it into myself?"

"Something like that," Nina says. "It would be clearer if you believed."

"And what would happen to me?" I ask. "Would I die?"

"We all die, sooner or later."

"I know that," I say, impatiently. "But would I die from doing this?"

Nina shakes her head. "No. But you'd be changed."

"Changed how?"

"I don't know. It's—" She hesitates, then plunges quickly on. "I've never heard of it being done before."

"Oh."

We look some more out the windshield. The street we're on is pretty empty, cars parked, but not much traffic, vehicular or pedestrian. Over on Gracie we can see the nightlife's still going strong. I want to ask her, Why didn't you tell me the truth before? but I already know. I don't believe her now so what difference would having heard it a few days earlier have made?

"Did you love Martin?" I ask instead. "I mean, at first."

"I'm not sure what love is."

I guess nobody really does, I think. Is what I'm feeling for Nina love? This feeling that's still swelling inside me, under the confusion and jumpiness—is it love? People die for love. It happens. But surely they *know* when they make the sacrifice?

"I really didn't kill him," she tells me. "I went to the apartment—I'm not sure why or what I meant to do—and let myself in. When he saw me, he went crazy. He looked terrified. When I took a step closer, he threw himself out the window—straight through the glass and all. He didn't say anything and he didn't give me a chance to speak either."

"He told me he was scared."

Nina nods. "But I don't know why. He had no reason to be scared of me. If I hadn't harmed him in the two years since he failed to keep his side of our bargain, why should he think that I'd hurt him now?"

I have no answer to that. Only Martin could explain it, but he'd taken the secret with him on his three-story plunge to the pavement below his window.

"I should go," Nina says then, but she makes no move to open the door.

"What about the sword?" I ask.

She turns to me. My eyes are adjusted enough to the vagaries of the lighting to see the expression on her face, but I can't figure it out. Sadness? My own feelings returned? Fear? Maybe a mix of the three.

"Would you do this for me?" she asks. "Would you bury the sword—in hallowed ground?"

"You mean like in a churchyard?"

She shakes her head. "It will need an older hallowing than that. There is a place where the river meets the lake."

I know where she's talking about. The City Commission keeps the lawns perfectly groomed around there, but there's this one spot right on the lake shore where a stand of old pines has been left to make a little wild acre. The trees there haven't been touched since the city was first founded, back in the eighteenth century.

"Bury the sword there," she tells me. "Tonight. Before the sun rises."

I nod. "What'll happen to you?"

"Ailine says it would let me sleep. Forever." She smiles, but it doesn't touch her eyes. "Or at least until someone digs it up again, I suppose."

"I . . . I'd do this other thing," I say, "but I'm too scared."

She nods, understanding. "And you don't believe."

She says it without recrimination. And she doesn't say anything at all about love, about how, to make the sacrifice willingly, I'd have to really love her. And she's right. I don't believe. And if I love her, I don't love her enough.

She leans across the seat and gives me a kiss. I remember the last time she did this. There was so much promise. In her kiss. In her eyes. Now she's only saying goodbye. I want to talk to her. I want to explain it all over again. But I just let her go. Out of the car. Down the street. Out of my life.

There's a huge emptiness inside me after she's gone. Maybe what hurts the most is the knowledge I hold that I can't let go—that I love her, but I don't love her enough. She asked too much of me, I tell myself, but I'm not sure if it's something I really believe or if I'm trying to convince myself that it's true to try and make myself feel better. It doesn't work.

I drive home to get the sword. I unwrap it, there in my hall, and hold it in my hands, trying to get some sense of Nina from it. But it's just metal. Eventually I wrap it up again and take it down to my car. I get a shovel from the toolshed behind the building. It belongs to the guy who lives on the ground floor, but I don't think he'll miss it. I'll have it back before he even knows it's gone.

And that's how I get here, digging a grave for a sword in hallowed ground. I can hear the lake against the shore, the wind sighing in the pines above. I can't hear the city at all, though it's all around me. Hallowed ground—hallowed by something older than what I was taught about in Sunday school, I guess. Truth is, I turned into an agnostic since those long-ago innocent days. I was just a girl then, didn't even know about sapphic impulses, little say think I might be feeling them.

It's easier to dig in amongst the roots of these pines than I would have thought possible, but it still takes me a long time to get the grave dug. I keep stopping to listen to the wind and the sound of the lake, the waves lapping against the shore. I keep stopping to look at the sword and the minutes leak away in little fugue states. I don't know where my mind goes. I just suddenly find myself blinking beside the grave, gaze locked on the long length of the sword. Thinking of Nina. Wanting to find the necessary belief and love to let me fill the emptiness I feel inside.

Finally it's getting on to the dawn. The grave's about four feet deep. It's enough. I'm just putting things off now. It's all so crazy—I *know* it's crazy—but I can't help but feel that it really is Nina I'm getting ready to lay in the hole and cover over with dirt.

I consider wrapping the sword back up again, but the blanket was Martin's and somehow it doesn't feel right. I pick the sword up and cradle it for a moment, as though I'm holding a child, a cold and still child with only one long limb. I touch the blade with a fingertip. It's not particularly sharp. I study the tip of the blade in the moonlight. You'd have to really throw yourself on it for it to pierce the skin and impale you.

I think maybe Nina's craziness is contagious. I find myself wishing I loved Nina enough to have done this thing for her, to believe, to trust, to be brave—crazy as it all is. I find myself sitting up, with the sword tip lying on my knees. I open my blouse and prop the sword up, lay the tip against my skin, between my breasts, just to see how it feels. I find myself leaning forward, putting pressure on the tip, looking down at where the metal presses against my skin.

I feel as though I've slipped into an altered state of consciousness. I look down to where the sword meets my skin and the point's gone, it's inside me, an inch, two inches. I don't feel anything. There's no pain. There's no blood. There's only this impossible moment like a miracle where the sword's slipping inside me, more and more of its length, the harder I push against it. I'm bent almost double now and still it keeps going inside me, inch after inch. It doesn't come out my back, it's just being swallowed by my body. Finally I reach out with my hands, close my fingers around each side of the hilt, and push it up inside me, all the rest of the way.

And pass out.

8

When I come to, the air's lighter. I can't see the sun yet, but I can feel its light seeping through the trees. I can still hear the lake and the wind in the pines above me, but I can hear the traffic from the city, too.

I sit up. I look at the grave and the shovel. I look at the blanket. I look for the sword, but it's gone. I lift my hands to my chest and feel the skin between my breasts. I remember the sword sliding into my chest last night, but the memory feels like a hallucinatory experience.

No, I tell myself. Believe. I hear Nina's voice in my mind, hear her telling me, *It's easy to forget marvels when your whole life you're taught to ignore them,* and tell myself: Don't invalidate a miracle because you've been taught they're not real. Trust yourself. Trust the experience. And Nina. Trust Nina.

But she's not here. My body might have swallowed the sword, impossibly sheathing the long length of its metal in my flesh, but she's not here.

My fingers feel a bump on my skin and I look down to see I've got a new birthmark, equidistant from each of my breasts. It looks like a cross. Or a sword, standing on its point. . . .

I feel so calm. It seems as though I should be either freaking out completely or delirious with wonder and awe, but there's only the calm. I sit there for a long time, running my finger across the bump of my new birthmark, then finally I button up my blouse. I fill the grave—this goes a lot quicker than digging it did—and cover up the raw dirt with pine needles. I wrap the shovel in my blanket and walk back to where I parked my car on Battersfield Road.

9

Traci has to know the whole story, of course, so I tell her everything. I don't know how much she believes, but crazy as it all sounds, she believes that I believe, and that's enough for her. I'm afraid of getting involved with her at first—afraid that I'm turning to her on the rebound from what I never quite had with Nina but certainly felt for her. But it doesn't work that way. Or if I am rebounding, it's in the right direction.

I remember Nina telling me that I'd be changed if I—I guess absorbed the sword is the best way to put it—but that she didn't know how. I do now. It's not a big thing. My world hasn't changed—though I guess my view of it has to some degree. What's happened is that I'm more decisive. I've taken control of my life. I'm not drifting anymore—either in my personal life or on the job. I don't go for the safe, soft stories anymore. One person can't do a whole lot about all the injustice in the world, but I'm making damn sure that people hear about it. That we all do what we can about it. I'm not looking for a Pulitzer; I just want to make sure that I leave things a little better behind me when I go.

Six months or so after Traci and I start living together, she turns to me one night and asks me why it didn't disappoint me that Nina never came back to me after I did what she asked.

"It's because I remember what she told me in that dream I had the night Martin died," I explain. "You know, when I dreamed the sword was lying on the bed beside me and talking to me? I didn't remember when I woke, but it came back to me a few days after I got back from the pine grove."

Traci gives me a poke with her finger. "So aren't you going to tell me?" she says when I've fallen silent.

I smile. "She said that if she was freed, she might not be able to come back. That really being human, instead of passing for one, might mean that she'd be starting her life all over again as an infant and she wouldn't remember what had gone before."

Now it's Traci's turn to fall silent. "Is that why you want us to have a kid?" she asks finally.

With modern medicine, anything's possible, right? Or at least something as basic as artificial insemination.

"I like to think she's waiting for us to get it together," I say.

"So you're planning on a girl."

"Feels right to me."

Traci reaches over and tracks the contour of my sword birthmark with a finger. "Think she'll have one of these?"

"Does it matter?" I ask.

"Doesn't matter at all," Traci says. She rolls over to embrace me. "And I guess it means we don't have to worry about what to name her either."

I snuggle in close. I love finally knowing who I am; loving and being loved for who I am. I just hope that wherever and whenever Nina is reborn, she'll be as lucky as I feel I am.

Held Safe by Moonlight and Vines

1

Lillie's in the graveyard again, looking for ghosts. She just can't stay away.

"I'm paying my respects," she says, but it doesn't make sense.

These days All Souls Cemetery's about as forgotten as the people buried in it. The land belongs to some big company now and they're just waiting for the paperwork to go through at city hall. One day soon they'll be moving what's left of the bodies, tearing down all those old-fashioned mausoleums and crypts and putting up something shiny and new. Who's going to miss it? Nobody goes there now except for the dealers with their little packets of oblivion and junkies looking for a fix.

The only people who care about the place are from the Crowsea Heritage Society. And Lillie. Everybody else just wants to see it go. Everybody else likes the idea of making a place gone wild safe again, never mind they don't put it quite that way. But that's what they're thinking. You can see it in the back of their eyes when they talk about it.

See, there's something that scares most people about the night, something that rises out of old memories, out of the genetic soup we all carry around inside us. Monsters in closets when we were kids and further back still, a long way, all the way back to the things waiting out there where the fire's light can't reach. It's not something anybody talks about, but I know that's what they see in All Souls because I can see it, too.

It's got nothing to do with the drug deals going down. People know a piece of the night is biding in there, thinking about them, and they can't wait to see it go. Even the dealers. You see them hanging around by the gates, money moves from one hand to the other, packets of folded paper follow suit, everything smooth, moves like magic—they're fearless, these guys. But they don't go any further in than they have to. Nobody does except for Lillie.

"There's been nobody buried there in fifty years," I tell her, but that just gets her back up. "All the more reason to give those old souls some respect," she says.

But that's not it. I know she's looking for ghosts. Thing is, I don't know why.

2

Alex's problem is he wants an answer for everything. All he ever does is go around asking questions. Never lets a thing lie. Always has to know what's going on and why. Can't understand that some things don't have reasons. Or that some people don't feel like explaining themselves. They just do what feels right. Get an idea in their head and follow it through and don't worry about what someone else is going to think or if anybody else understands.

In Alex's world there's only right and wrong, black and white. Me, I fall through the cracks of that world. In my head, it's all grey. In my head, it's all like walking in the twilight, a thousand shades of moonglow and dusky skies and shadow.

He thinks of me sitting here in the dark, all those old stone mausoleums standing around me, old and battered like the tenements leaning against each other on the streets where we grew up, and it spooks him. But All Souls comforts me, I don't know why. Half the trees inside are dead, the rest are dying. Most of the grass is yellow and brown and the only flowers in this place these days grow on weeds, except in one corner where a scraggly old rose bush keeps on trying, tough old bugger doesn't know enough to give up. The stone walls are crumbling down, the cast-iron gates haven't worked in years. There's a bunch of losers crowded around those gates, cutting deals, more nervous of what's here, inside, than of the man showing up and busting them. I come in over the wall and go deep, where the shadows hide me, and they never even know I'm here. Nobody does, except for Alex and he just doesn't understand.

I know what Alex sees when he looks at this place. I see it, too, at first, each time I come. But after a while, when I'm over the wall and inside, walking the narrow lanes in between the stones and tombs, uneven cobbles underfoot, the shadows lying thick everywhere I look, it gets different. I go someplace else. I don't hear the dealers, I don't see the junkies. The cemetery's gone, the city's gone, and me, I'm gone, too.

The only thing still with me are the walls, but they're different in that other place. Not so worn down. The stones have been fit together without mortar, each one cunningly placed against the other and solid. Those walls go up ten feet and you'd have to ram them with a bulldozer before they'd come down.

Inside, it's a garden. Sort of. A wild place. A tangle of bushes and briars, trees I've got no name for and vines hanging everywhere. A riot of flowers haunts the ground cover, pale blossoms that catch the moonlight and hold it in their petals.

The moonlight. That moon is so big in this place it feels like it could swallow the world. When I stand there in the wild garden and look up at it, I feel small, like I'm no bigger than the space of time between one moment and the next, but not the same way I feel small anywhere else. Where I come from there are millions of people living everywhere and each one of them's got his or her own world. It's so easy to lose a part of yourself in those worlds, to just find yourself getting sucked away until there's next to nothing left of who you are. But I don't have to be careful about that here. There aren't any of those millions of people here and that moon, it doesn't swallow up who I am, its golden light fills me up, reveling in what it knows me to be. I'm small in its light, sure, but the kind of small that can hold everything there is to be held. The moon's just bigger, that's all. Not more important than me, just different.

Those junkies don't know what they're missing, never getting any further inside the gates than the first guy in a jean vest with the right price.

3

Trouble is, Lillie doesn't understand danger. She's never had to go through the hard times some of us did, never really seen what people can do to each other when they're feeling desperate or just plain mean. She grew up poor, like everybody else in our neighborhood, but her family loved her and she didn't get knocked around the way those of us who didn't have her kind of parents did. She was safe at home; out on the streets, I always looked after her, made sure the hard cases left her alone.

I'm working as a bouncer at Chic Cheeks the night I hear she's been going to All Souls, so I head down there after my shift to check things out. It's a good thing I do. Some of the guys hanging around by the gates have gotten bored and happened to spot her, all alone in there and looking so pretty. Guess they decided they were going to have themselves a little fun. Bad move. But then they didn't expect me to come along.

I remember a teacher I had in junior high telling me one time how wood and stone make poor conductors. Well, they conduct pain pretty good, as those boys find out. I introduce one of them face-first to a tombstone and kind of make a mess of his nose, knock out a couple of teeth. His pals aren't chickenshit, I'll give them that much. I hear the *snickt* of their blades snapping open, so I drop the first guy. He makes some kind of gurgling noises when he hits the ground and rolls onto my boot. I push him away and then ignore him. He's too busy feeling his pain to cause me any immediate grief. I turn to his buddies, a little pissed off now, but we don't get into it.

"Oh Christ," one of them says, recognizing me.

"We didn't mean nothing, Al," the other one says.

They're putting their knives away, backing up.

"We knew she was one of your people, we never would've touched her. I swear it, man."

Guess I've got a bit of a rep. Nothing serious. I'm not some big shot. What it's got to do with is my old man.

Crazy Eddie is what they used to call him on the streets. Started running numbers for the bosses back when he was a kid, then moved into collections, which is where he got his name. You don't want to think it of your own flesh and blood, but the old man was a psycho. He'd do any crazed thing came to mind if you couldn't pay up. You're in for a few yards, you better cough it up, don't matter what you've got to do to get the money, because he'd as soon as cut your throat as collect the bread.

After a while the bosses started using him for hits, the kind where they're making a statement. Messy, crazy hits. He did that for years until he got into a situation he couldn't cut his way out of. Cops took him away in a bunch of little bags.

Man, I'll never forget that day. I was doing a short stretch in the county when I found out and I near laughed myself sick. I'd hated that old bastard for the way he'd treated ma, for what he did to my sister Juney. He used to kick the shit out of me on a regular basis, but I could deal with that. It was the things he did to them. . . . I knew one day I'd take him down, didn't matter he was my old man. I just hadn't got around to it yet. Hadn't figured out a way to let the bosses know it was personal, not some kind of criticism of their business.

Anyway, I'm not mean like the old man was, I'll tell you that straight-off, but I purely don't take crap from anybody. I don't have to get into it too much anymore. People take a look at me now and think, blood is blood. They see my old man's crazy eyes when they look in mine, and they find some other place to be than where I'm standing.

So I make the point with these boys that they don't want to mess with Lillie, and all it takes is a tap against a tombstone for them to get the message. I let them get their pal and take off, then I go to see what Lillie's doing.

It's the strangest thing. She's just standing there by one of those old stone mausoleums, swaying back and forth, looking off into the space between a couple of those stone crypts. I scratch my head, and take a closer look myself. She's mesmerized by something, but damned if I know what. I can hear her humming to herself, still doing that swaying thing, mostly with her upper body, back and forth, smiling that pretty smile of hers, short black hair standing up at attention the way it always does. I'm forever trying to talk her into growing it long, but she laughs at me whenever I do.

I guess I watch her for about an hour that night. I remember thinking she'd been sampling some of the dealers' wares until she suddenly snaps out of it. I fade back into the shadows at that point. Don't want her to think I've been spying on her. I'm just looking out for her, but she doesn't see it that way. She gets seriously pissed at me and I hate having Lillie mad at me.

She walks right by me, still humming to herself. I can see she's not stoned, just Lillie-strange. I watch her climb up some vines where one of the walls is broken and low, and then she's gone. I go out the front way, just to remind the boys what's what, and catch up with Lillie a few blocks away, casual-like. Don't ask her where she's been. Just say how-do, make sure she's okay without letting on I'm worried, and head back to my own place.

I don't know exactly when it is I realize she's looking for ghosts in there. It just comes to me one day, slips in sideways when I'm thinking about something else. I try talking to her about it from time to time but all she does is smile, the way only she can.

"You wouldn't understand," she says.

"Try me."

She shakes her head. "It's not something *to* understand," she says. "It's just something you do. The less you worry at it, the more it makes sense."

She's right. I don't understand.

4

There's a boy living in the garden. He reminds me a little of Alex. It's not that they look the same. This kid's all skin and bones, held together with wiry muscles. Naked and scruffy, crazy tangled hair full of burrs and twigs and stuff, peach-fuzz vying with a few actual beard hairs, dink hanging loose when he's not holding onto it—I guess you've got to do something with your hands when you don't have pockets. Alex, he's like a fridge with arms and legs. Big, strong, and loyal as all get-out. Not school-smart, but bright. You couldn't pick a couple of guys that looked less alike.

The reason they remind me of each other is that they're both a little feral. Wild things. Dangerous if you don't approach them right.

I get to the garden one night and the trees are full of grackles. They're feeding on berries and making a racket like I've never heard before. I know it's an unkindness of ravens and a murder of crows, but what do you call that many grackles all together? I'm walking around, peering up at them in the branches, smiling at the noise, when I see the boy sitting up in one of the trees, looking back down at me.

Neither of us says anything for a long time. There's just the racket of the birds playing against the silence we hold between us.

"Hey there," I say finally. "Is this your garden?"

"It's my castle."

I smile. "Doesn't look much like a castle."

"Got walls," he tells me.

"I suppose."

He looks a little put out. "It's a start."

"So when are you going to start building the rest?" I ask.

He looks at me, the way a child looks at you when you've said something stupid.

"Go away," he says.

I decide I can be as much of an asshole as he's being and play the why game with him.

"Why?" I ask.

"Because I don't like you."

"Why?"

"Because you're stupid."

"Why?"

"I don't know. Guess you were born that way."

"Why?"

"Have to ask your parents that."

"Why?"

"Because I don't know."

"Why?"

He finally catches on. Pulling a twig free from the branch he's sitting on, he throws it at me. I duck and it misses. When I look back up, he's gone. The noise of the grackles sounds like laughter now.

"Guess I deserve that," I say.

I don't see the boy for a few visits after that, but the next time I do, he pops up out of the thick weeds underfoot and almost gives me a heart attack.

"I could've just snuck up on you and killed you," he tells me. "Just like that."

He leans against a tree, one hand hanging down in between his legs like he's got a piece of treasure there.

"Why would you want to do that?" I ask.

His eyes narrow. "I don't want to play the why game again."

"I'm not. I really want to know."

"It's not a thing I do or don't want to do," he tells me. "I'm just saying I could. It was a piece of information, that's all."

There's something incongruous about the way he says this—innocent and scary, all at the same time. It reminds me of when I was a little girl, how it took me the longest time to admit that I could ever like a boy, they were all such assholes. All except Alex. I wouldn't have minded so much if he'd pulled my hair or pushed me on the schoolyard, but he never did.

He was always so sweet and polite to me and then after classes, he'd go out and beat up the guys that had been mean to me. I guess I was flattered, at first, but then I realized it wasn't a very nice thing to do. You have to understand, we're both still in grade school when this is going on. Things weren't the same back then the way they are for kids now. We sure never had to walk through metal detectors to get into the school.

Anyway, I asked him to stop and he did. At least so far as I know, he did. I wonder sometimes, though. Sometimes my boyfriends have the weirdest accidents—walking into doors and stuff like that.

5

This one time Lillie's going out with this college-type. Dave, his name is. Dave Taylor. Nice enough looking joe, I suppose, but he's not exactly the most faithful guy you'd ever meet. Happened to run into him getting a little on the side one night, so I walk up to his table and tell him I have to have a word with him, would his lady friend excuse us for a moment? He doesn't want to step outside, so I suggest to his lady friend that she go powder her nose, if she understands my meaning.

"So what the hell's this all about?" Dave asks when she's gone. He's blustering, trying to make up for the face he feels he lost in front of his girlfriend.

"I'm a friend of Lillie's," I tell him.

"Yeah? So?"

"So I don't like the idea of her getting hurt."

"Hey, what she doesn't know—"

"I'm not discussing this," I say. "I'm telling you."

The guy shakes his head. "Or what? I suppose you're going to go running to her and—"

I hit him once, a quick jab to the head that rocks him back in his seat. Doesn't even break the skin on my knuckles, but I can see he's hurting.

"I don't care who you go out with, or if you cheat on them," I say, keeping my voice conversational. "I just don't want you seeing Lillie any more."

He's holding a hand to his head where the skin's going all red. Looks a little scared like I'm going to hit him again, but I figure I've already made my point.

"Do we understand each other?" I ask him.

He gives me a quick nod. I start to leave, then pause for a moment. He gives me a worried look.

"And Dave," I say. "Let's not get stupid about this. No one's got to know we had this little talk, right?"

"What . . . whatever you say. . . ."

6

I wonder about Alex—worry about him, I guess you could say. He never seems to be happy or sad. He just is. It's not like he's cold, keeps it all bottled in or anything, and he's always got a smile for me, but there doesn't seem to be a whole lot of passion in his life. He doesn't talk much, and never about himself. That's another way he and the boy in the garden differ. The boy's always excited about something or other, always ready for any sort of mad escapade. And he loves to talk.

"Old castle rock," the boy tells me one time. His eyes are gleaming with excitement. "That's what these walls are made of. They were part of this castle on the other side and now they're here. There's going to be more of the castle coming, I just know there is. Towers and turrets and stables and stuff."

"When's the rest of it going to come?" I ask.

He shrugs his bony shoulders. "Dunno. Could be a long time. But I can wait."

"Where's it coming from?" I ask then.

"I told you. From the other side."

"The other side of what?"

He gives me that look again, the one that says *don't you know anything?*

"The other side of the walls," he says.

I've never looked over the walls—not from the garden. That's the first thing Alex would have done. He may not have passion in his life, but he's sure got purpose. He's always in the middle of something, always knows what's going on. Never finished high school, but he's smarter than most people I meet because he's never satisfied until he's got everything figured out. He's in the public library all the time, reading, studying stuff. Never does anything with what he knows, but he sure knows a lot.

I walk over to the nearest of those tall stone walls and the boy trails along behind me, joins me when I start to go up. It's an easier climb than you might think, plenty of finger- and toe-holds, and we scale it like a couple of monkeys, grinning at each other when we reach the top. It's flat up there, with lots of room on the rough stone to sit and look out, only there's nothing to see. Just fog, thick, the way it rolls into the city from the lake sometimes. It's like the world ends on the other side of these walls.

"It's always like this," the boy says.

I turn to look at him. My first impression was that he'd come in over the walls himself and I never learned anything different to contradict it, but now I'm not so sure anymore. I mean, I knew this garden was someplace else, someplace magical that you could only reach the way you get to Neverneverland—you have to really want to get there. You might stumble in the first time, but after that you have to be really determined to get back in. But I also thought the real world was still out there, on the other side of the garden's magic, held back only by the walls.

"Where did you come from?" I ask him.

He give me this look that manages to be fierce and sad, all at the same time.

"Same place as you," he says and touches a closed fist to his heart. "From the hurting world. This is the only place I can go where they can't get to me, where no one can hurt me."

I shake my head. "I didn't come here looking for sanctuary. I'm not running from anything."

"Then why are you here?"

I think of Alex and the way he's always talking about ghosts, but it's not that either. I never really think about it, I just come. Alex is the one with the need to have answers to every question. Not me. For me the experience has been enough of and by itself. But now that I think about it, now that I realize I want an answer, I find I don't have one.

"I don't know," I say.

"I thought you were like me," the boy says.

He sounded disappointed. Like I've disappointed him. He sounds angry, too. I want to say something to mollify him, but I can't find those words either. I reach out a hand, but he jerks away. He stands up, looks at me like I've turned into the enemy. I guess, in his eyes, I have. If I'm not with him, then I'm against him.

"I would never hurt you," I finally say. "I've never hurt anybody."

"That's what you think," he says.

Then he dives off the top of the wall, dives into the fog. I grab for him, but I'm not fast enough. I hold my breath, waiting to hear him hit the ground, but there's no sound. The fog swallows him and I'm alone on the top of the wall. I feel like I've missed something, something important. I feel like it was right there in front of me, all along, but now it's gone, dove off the wall with the boy and I've lost my chance to understand it.

The next time I come to the garden, everything's the same, but different. The boy's not here. I've come other times, lots of times, and he hasn't been here, but this time I feel he won't be back, won't ever be back, and I miss him. I don't know why. It's not like we had a whole lot in common. It's not like we had long, meaningful conversations, or were in love with each other or anything. I mean, he was just a kid, like a little brother, not a lover. But I miss him the way I've missed a lover when the relationship ends.

I feel guilty, too. Maybe this place isn't a sanctuary for me, but it was for him. A walled, wild garden, held safe by moonlight and vines. His castle. What if I've driven him away forever? Driven him back to what he called the hurting world.

I hate that idea most, the idea that I've stolen the one good thing he had in a life that didn't have anything else. But I don't know what to do about it, how to call him back. I'd trade my coming here for his in a moment, only how can I tell him that? I don't even know his name.

7

Lillie doesn't leave the graveyard this night. I watch her sitting there on the step of one of those old mausoleums, sitting there all hunched up, sitting there all night. Finally, dawn breaks in the east, swallows the graveyard's spookiness. It's just an old forgotten place now, fallen in on itself and waiting for the wreckers' ball. The night's gone and taken the promise of danger away with it. I go over to where Lillie is and sit down beside her on the steps. I touch her arm.

"Lillie?" I say. "Are you okay?"

She turns to look at me. I'm expecting her to be mad at me for being here. She's got to know I've been following her around again. But all she does is give me a sad look.

"Did you ever lose something you never knew you had?" she asks.

"I only ever wanted one thing," I tell her, "but I never had it to lose."

"I don't even know what it is that I've lost," she says. "I just know something's gone. I had a chance to have it, to hold it and cherish it, but I let it go."

The early morning sunlight's warm on my skin, but a shiver runs through me all the same. I think maybe she's talking about ghosts. Maybe there really are ghosts here. I get the crazy idea that maybe we're ghosts, that we died and don't remember it. Or maybe only one of us did.

"What was the one thing you wanted that you never got?" she asks.

It's something I would never tell her. I promised myself a long time ago that I'd never tell her because I knew she deserved better. But that crazy idea won't let go, that we're dead, or one of us is, and it makes me tell her.

"It's you," I say.

8

Did you ever hear someone tell you something you always knew but it never really registered until they put it into words? That's what happens to me when Alex tells me he loves me, that he's always loved me.

His voice trails off and I look at him, really look at him. He almost flinches under my gaze. I can tell he doesn't want to be here, that he wishes he'd never spoken, that he feels a hurt swelling up inside him that he would never have to experience if he'd kept his feelings to himself. He reminds me of the boy, the way the boy looked before he dove off the wall into the fog, not the anger, but the sadness.

"Why did you never say anything before this?" I finally ask.

"I couldn't," he says. "And anyway. Look at us, you and me. We grew up in the same neighborhood, sure, but . . ." He shrugs. "You deserve better than me."

I have to smile. This is so Alex. "Oh, right. And who decided that?"

Alex chooses not to answer me. "You were always different," he says instead. "You were always the first on the block with a new sound or a new look, but you weren't following trends. It's like they followed you. And you never lost that. Anyone looks at you and they can tell there's nothing holding you back. You can do anything, go anywhere. The future's wide open for you, always was, you know what I'm saying? The streets never took their toll on you."

Then why am I still living in Foxville? I want to ask him. How come my star didn't take me to some nice uptown digs? But I know what he's talking about. It's not really about where I can go as much as where I've been.

"I was lucky," I say. "My folks treated me decently."

"And you deserved it."

"Everybody deserves to be treated decently," I tell him.

"Well, sure."

We grew up in the same building before my parents could afford a larger apartment down the block. My mom used to feel sorry for Alex's mother and we'd go over to visit when Crazy Eddie wasn't home. I'd play with Alex and his little sister, our moms would pretend our lives were normal, that none of us were dirt poor, everybody dreaming of moving to the 'burbs. Some of our neighbors did, but most of us couldn't afford it and still can't. Of course the way things are going now, you're not any safer or happier in the 'burbs than you are in the inner city. And living here, at least we've got some history.

But we never thought about that kind of thing at the time because we were just kids. Older times, simpler times. I smile, remembering how Alex always treated me so nice, right from the first.

"And then, of course, I had you looking out for me, too," I say.

"You still do."

I hadn't really got around to thinking what he was doing here in All Souls at this time of the morning, but now it makes sense. I don't know how many times I've had to ask him not to follow me around. It gives some people the creeps, but I know Alex isn't some crazed stalker, fixated on me. He means well. He really is just looking out for me. But it's a weird feeling all the same. I honestly thought I'd got him to stop.

"You really don't have to be doing this," I tell him. "I mean, it was kind of sweet when we were kids and you kept me from being bullied in the playground, but it's not the same now."

"You know the reason the dealers leave you alone?" he asks.

I glance toward the iron gates at the other end of the graveyard, but there's no one there at the moment. The drug market's closed up for the morning.

"They never knew I was here," I say.

Alex shakes his head and that's enough. He doesn't have to explain. I know the reputation he has in the neighborhood. I feel a chill and I don't know if it's from the close call I had or the fact that I live in the kind of world where a woman can't go out by herself. Probably both.

"It's still not right," I say. "I appreciate your looking out for me, really I do, but it's not right, your following me around the way you do. You've got to get a life, Alex."

He hangs his head and I feel like I've just reprimanded a puppy dog for doing something it thought was really good.

"I know," he mumbles. He won't look at me. "I . . . I'm sorry, Lillie."

He gets up and starts to walk away. I look at his broad back and suddenly I'm thinking of the boy from the garden again. I'm seeing his sadness and anger, the way he dove off the wall into the fog and out of my life. I'm remembering what I said to him, that I would never hurt him, that I've never hurt anyone. And I remember what he said to me, just before he jumped.

That's what you think.

I'm not stupid. I know I'm not responsible for someone falling in love with me. I can't help if it they get hurt because maybe I don't love them back. But this isn't anyone. This is Alex. I've known him longer than maybe anyone I know. And if he's looked out for me, I've looked out for him, too. I stood up for him when people put him down. I visited him in the county jail when no one else did. I took him to the hospital that time the Creevy brothers left him for dead on the steps of his apartment building.

I know that for all his fierceness, he's a sweet guy. Dangerous, sure, but underneath that toughness there's no monster like his old man was. Given a different set of circumstances, a different neighborhood to grow up in, maybe, a different father, definitely, he could have made something of himself. But he didn't. And now I'm wondering if looking out for me was maybe part of what held him back. If I'd gotten myself out of the neighborhood, maybe he would have, too. Maybe we could both have been somebody.

But none of that's important right now. So maybe I'm not in love with Alex. So what? He's still my friend. He opened his heart to me and it's like I didn't even hear him.

"Alex!" I call after him.

He pauses and turns. There's nothing hopeful in the way he looks, there's not even curiosity. I get up from where I've been sitting and go to where he's standing.

"I've got to let this all sink in," I tell him. "You caught me off guard. I mean, I never even guessed you felt the way you do."

"I understand," he says.

"No, you don't. You're the best friend I ever had. I just never thought of us as a couple. Doesn't mean all of a sudden I hate you or something."

He shrugs. "I never should have said anything," he says.

I shake my head. "No. What you should have done is said something a lot sooner. The way I see it, your big problem is you keep everything all bottled up inside. You've got to let people know what you're thinking."

"That wouldn't change anything."

"How do you know? When I was a kid I had the hugest crush on you. And later, I kept expecting you to ask me out, but you never did. Got so's I just never thought of you in terms of boyfriend material."

"So what're you saying?"

I smile. "I don't know. You could ask me to go to a movie or something."

"Do you want to go to a movie?"

"Maybe. Let me buy you breakfast and we'll talk about it."

9

So I'm trying to do like Lillie says, talk about stuff that means something to me, or at least I do it with her. She asks me once what I'd like to do with my life, because she can't see much future in my being a bouncer for a strip joint for the rest of my life. I tell her I've always wanted to paint and instead of laughing, she goes out and buys me a little tin of watercolors and a pad of paper. I give it a go and she tells me I'm terrible, like I don't know it, but takes the first piece I do and hangs it on her fridge.

Another time I tell her about this castle I used to dream about when I was a kid, the most useless castle you could imagine, just these walls and a garden in them that's gone all wild, but when I was there, nobody could hurt me, nobody at all.

She gives me an odd look and says, "With old castle rock for the walls."

10

So I guess Alex was right. I must have been looking for ghosts in All Souls—or at least I found one. Except it wasn't the ghost of someone who'd died and been buried in there. It was the ghost of a kid, a kid that was still living somewhere in an enclosed wild garden, secreted deep in his grown-up mind, a kid fooling around in trees full of grackles, hidden from the hurting world, held safe by moonlight and vines.

But you know, hiding's not always the answer. Because the more Alex talks to me, the more he opens up, the more I see him the way I did when I was a little girl, when I'd daydream about how he and I were going to spend the rest of our lives together.

I guess we were both carrying around ghosts.

In the Pines

Life ain't all a dance.
—attributed to Dolly Parton

1

It's celebrity night at the Standish and we have us some line-up. There are two Elvises—a young one, with the swiveling hips and a perfect sneer, and a white-suited one, circa the Vegas years. A Buddy Holly who sounds right but could've lost fifty pounds if he really wanted to look the part. A Marilyn Monroe who has her boyfriend with her; he'll be wearing a JFK mask for her finale, when she sings "Happy Birthday" to him in a breathless voice. Lonesome George Clark has come out of semi-retirement to reprise his old Hank Williams show and then there's me, doing my Dolly Parton tribute for the first time in the three years since I gave it up and tried to make it on my own.

I don't really mind doing it. I've kind of missed Dolly, to tell you the truth, and it's all for a good cause—a benefit to raise money for the Crowsea Home for Battered Women—which is how they convinced me to do that old act of mine one more time.

I do a pretty good version of Dolly. I'm not as pretty as her, and I don't have her hair—hey, who does?—but I've got the figure while the wig, makeup and rhinestone dress take care of the rest. I can mimic her singing, though my natural voice is lower, and I sure as hell play the guitar better—I don't know who she's kidding with those fingernails of hers.

But in the end, the looks never mattered. It was always the songs. The first time I heard her sing them, I just plain fell in love. "Jolene." "Coat of Many Colors." "My Blue Tears." I planned to do a half hour of those old hits with a couple of mountain songs thrown in for good measure. The only one from my old act that I was dropping was "I Will Always Love You." Thanks to the success Whitney Houston had with it, people weren't going to be thinking Tennessee cabins and Dolly anymore when they heard it.

I'm slated to follow the fat Elvis—maybe they wanted to stick all the rhinestones together in one part of the show?—with Lonesome George finishing up after me. Since Lonesome George and I are sharing the same backup band, we're going to close the show with a duet on "Muleskinner Blues." The thought of it makes me smile and not just because I'll get to do a little bit of yodeling. With everything Dolly's done over the years, even she never got to sing with Hank Williams—senior, of course. Junior parties a little too hearty for my tastes.

So I'm standing there in the wings of the Standish, watching Marilyn slink and grind her way through a song—the girl is good—when I get this feeling that something is going to happen.

I'm kind of partial to premonitions. The last time I felt one this strong was the night John Narraway died. We were working late on my first album at Tommy Norton's High Lonesome Sounds and had finally called it quits sometime after midnight when the feeling hit me. It starts with a hum or a buzz, like I've got a fly or a bee caught in my ear, and then everything seems . . . oh, I don't know. Clearer somehow. Precise. Like I could look at Johnny's fiddle bow that night and see every one of those horsehairs, separate and on its own.

The trouble with these feelings is that while I know something's going to happen, I don't know what. I get a big feeling or a little one, but after that I'm on my own. Truth is, I never figure out what it's all about until after the fact, which doesn't make it exactly the most useful talent a girl can have. I don't even know if it's something good or something bad that's coming, just that it's coming. Real helpful, right?

So I'm standing there and Marilyn's brought her boyfriend out for the big finish to her act and I know something's going to happen, but I don't know what. I get real twitchy all through the fat Elvis's act and then it's time for me to go up and the buzzing's just swelling up so big inside me that I feel like I'm fit to burst with anticipation.

We open with "My Tennessee Mountain Home." It goes over pretty well and we kick straight into "Jolene" before the applause dies off. The third song we do is the first song I ever learned, that old mountain song, "In the Pines." I don't play it the same as most people I've heard do—I learned it from my Aunt Hickory, with this lonesome barred F# minor chord coming right in after the D that opens every line. I remember cursing for weeks before I could finally get my fingers around that damn chord and make it sound like it was supposed to.

So we're into the chorus now—

> *In the pines, in the pines,*
> *Where the sun never shines*
> *And the shiverin' cold winds blow.*

—and I'm looking out into the crowd and I can't see much, what with the spotlights in my eyes and all, but damned if I don't see her sitting there in the third row, my Aunt Hickory, big as life, grinning right back up at me, except she's dead, she's been dead fifteen years now, and it's all I can do to get through the chorus and let the band take an instrumental break.

2

The Aunt—that's what everybody in those parts called her, 'cept me, I guess. I don't know if it was because they didn't know her name, or because she made them feel uneasy, but nobody used the name that had been scratched onto her rusty mailbox, down on Dirt Creek Road. That just said Hickory Jones.

I loved the sound of her name. It had a ring to it like it was pulled straight out of one of those old mountain songs. Like Shady Groves. Or Tom Dooley.

She lived by her own self in a one-room log cabin, up the hill behind the Piney Woods Trailer Park, a tall, big-boned woman with angular features and her chestnut hair cropped close to her head. Half the boys in the park had hair longer than hers, slicked back and shiny. She dressed like a man in blue jeans and a flannel shirt, barefoot in the summer, big old workboots on those callused feet when the weather turned mean and the snows came.

She really was my aunt. She and Mama shared the same mother except Hickory had Kickaha blood, you could see it in the deep coppery color of her skin. Mama's father was white trash, same as mine, though that's an opinion I never shared out loud with anyone, not even Hickory. My daddy never needed much of a reason to give us kids a licking. Lord knows what he'd have done if we'd given him a real excuse.

I never could figure out what it was about Hickory that made people feel so damn twitchy around her. Mama said it was because of the way Hickory dressed.

"I know she's my sister," Mama would say, "but she looks like some no account hobo, tramping the rail lines. It's just ain't right. Man looks at her, he can't even tell she's got herself a pair of titties under that shirt."

Breasts were a big topic of conversation in Piney Woods when I was growing up and I remember wishing I had a big old shirt like Hickory's when my own chest began to swell and it seemed like it was never gonna stop. Mama acted like it was a real blessing, but I hated them. "You can't have too much of a good thing," she told me when she heard me complaining. "You just pray they keep growing a while longer, Darlene, 'cause if they do, you mark my words. You're gonna have your pick of a man."

Yeah, but what kind of a man? I wanted to know. It wasn't just the boys looking at me, or what they'd say; it was the men, too. Everybody staring down at my chest when they were talking to me, 'stead of looking me in the face. I could see them just itching to grab themselves a handful.

"You just shut your mouth, girl," Mama would say if I didn't let it go.

Hickory never told me to shut my mouth. But then I guess she didn't have to put up with me twenty-four hours a day, neither. She just stayed up by her cabin, growing her greens and potatoes in a little plot out back, running trap lines or taking to the hills with her squirrel gun for meat. Maybe once a month she'd head into town to pick up some coffee or flour, whatever the land couldn't provide for her. She'd walk the five miles in, then walk the whole way back, didn't matter how heavy that pack of hers might be or what the weather was like.

I guess that's really what people didn't like about her—just living the way she did, she showed she didn't need nobody, she could do it all on her own, and back then that was frowned upon for a woman. They thought she was queer—and I don't just mean tetched in the head, though they thought that, too. No, they told stories about how she'd sleep with other women, how she could raise the dead and was friends with the devil, and just about any other kind of foolish idea they could come up with.

'Course I wasn't supposed to go up to her cabin—none of us kids were, especially the girls—but I went anyways. Hickory played the five-string banjo and I'd go up and listen to her sing those old lonesome songs that nobody wanted to hear anymore. There was no polish to Hickory's singing, not like they put on music today, but she could hold a note long and true and she could play that banjo so sweet that it made you want to cry or laugh, depending on the mood of the tune.

See, Hickory's where I got started in music. First I'd go up just to listen and maybe sing along a little, though back then I had less polish in my voice than Hickory did. After a time I got an itching to play an instrument too and that's when Hickory took down this little old 1919 Martin guitar from where it hung on the rafters and when I'd sneak up to her cabin after that I'd play that guitar until my fingers ached and I'd be crying from how much they hurt, but I never gave up. Didn't get me nowhere, but I can say this much: whatever else's happened to me in this life, I never gave up the music. Not for anything, not for anyone.

And the pain went away.

"That's the thing," Hickory told me. "Doesn't matter how bad it gets, the pain goes away. Sometimes you got to die to stop hurting, but the hurting stops."

I guess the real reason nobody bothered her is that they were scared of her, scared of the big dark-skinned cousins who'd come down from the rez to visit her sometimes, scared of the simples and charms she could make, scared of what they saw in her eyes when she gave them that hard look of hers. Because Hickory didn't back down, not never, not for nobody.

3

I fully expect Hickory to be no more than an apparition. I'd look away, then back, and she'd be gone. I mean, what else could happen? She was long dead and I might believe in a lot of things, but ghosts aren't one of them.

But by the time the boys finish their break and it's time for me to step back up to the mike for another verse, there she is, still sitting in the third row, still grinning up at me. I'll tell you, I near choke right about then, all the words I ever knew to any song just up and fly away. There's a couple of ragged bars in the music where I don't know if I'll be finishing the song or not and I can feel the concern of the boys playing there on stage behind me. But Hickory she just gives me a look with those dark brown eyes of hers, that look she used to give me all those years ago when I'd run up so hard against the wall of a new chord or a particularly tricky line of melody that I just wanted to throw the guitar down and give it all up.

That look had always shamed me into going on and it does the same for me tonight. I shoot the boys an apologetic look, and lean right into the last verse like it never went away on me.

> *The longest train that I ever saw*
> *Was nineteen coaches long,*
> *And the only girl I ever loved*
> *She's on that train and gone.*

I don't know what anyone else is thinking when I sing those words, but looking at Hickory I know that, just like me, she isn't thinking of trains or girlfriends. Those old songs have a way of connecting you to something deeper than what they seem to be talking about, and that's what's happening for the two of us here. We're thinking of old losses and regrets, of all the things that might have been, but never were. We're thinking of the night lying thick in the pines around her cabin, lying thick under those heavy boughs even in the middle of the day, because just like the night hides in the day's shadows, there's lots of things that never go away. Things you don't ever want to go away. Sometimes when that wind blows through the pines, you shiver, but it's not from the cold.

4

I was fifteen when I left home. I showed up on Hickory's doorstep with a cardboard suitcase in one hand and that guitar she'd given me in the other, not heading for Nashville like I always thought I would, but planning to take the bus to Newford instead. A man who'd heard me sing at the roadhouse just down a ways from Piney Woods had offered me a job in a honky-tonk he owned in the city. I'm pretty sure he knew I was lying about my age, but he didn't seem to care any more than I did.

Hickory was rolling herself a cigarette when I arrived. She finished the job and lit a match on her thumbnail, looking at me in that considering way of hers as she got the cigarette going.

"That time already," she said finally, blowing out a blue-grey wreath of smoke on the heel of her words.

I nodded.

"Didn't think it'd come so soon," she told me. "Thought we had us another couple of years together, easy."

"I can't wait, Aunt Hickory. I got me a singing job in the city—a real singing job, in a honky-tonk."

"Uh-huh."

Hickory wasn't agreeing or disagreeing with me, just letting me know that she was listening but that she hadn't heard anything worthwhile hearing yet.

"I'll be making forty dollars a week, plus room and board."

"Where you gonna live?" Hickory asked, taking a drag from her cigarette. "In your boss's house?"

I shook my head. "No, ma'am. I'm going to have my own room, right upstairs of the honky-tonk."

"He know how old you are?"

"Sure," I said with a grin. "Eighteen."

"Give or take a few years."

I shrugged. "He's got no trouble with it."

"Well, what about your schooling?" Hickory asked. "You've been doing so well. I always thought you'd be the first one in the family to finish high school. I was looking forward to that—you know, to bragging about you and all."

I had to smile. Who was she going to brag to?

"Were you going to come to the graduation ceremony?" I asked instead.

"Was thinking on it."

"I'm going to be a singer, Aunt Hickory. All the schooling I'm ever going to need I learned from you."

Hickory sighed. She took a final drag from her cigarette then stubbed it out on the edge of her stair, storing the butt in her pocket.

"Tell me something," she said. "Are you running from something or running to something?"

"What difference does it make?"

"A big difference. Running away's only a partial solution. Sooner or later, whatever you're running from is going to catch up to you again. Comes a time you're going to have to face it, so it might as well be now. But running to something . . . well."

"Well, what?" I wanted to know when she didn't go on right away.

She fixed that dark gaze of hers on me. "I guess all I wanted to tell you, Darlene, is if you believe in what you're doing, then go at it and be willing to pay the price you have to pay."

I knew what she was trying to tell me. Playing a honky-tonk in New-ford was a big deal for a girl from the hills like me, but it wasn't what I was aiming for. It was just the first step and the rest of the road could be long and hard. I never knew just how long and hard. I was young and full of confidence, back then at the beginning of the sixties; invulnerable, like we all think we are when we're just on the other side of still being kids.

"But I want you to promise me one thing," Hickory added. "Don't you never do something that'll make you feel ashamed when you look back on it later."

"Why do you think I'm leaving now?" I asked her.

Hickory's eyes went hard. "I'm going to kill that daddy of yours."

"He's never tried to touch me again," I told her. "Not like he tried that one time, not like that. Just to give me a licking."

"Seems to me a man who likes to give out lickings so much ought to have the taste of one himself."

I don't know if Hickory was meaning to do it her own self, or if she was planning to put one of her cousins from the rez up to it, but I knew it'd cause her more trouble than it was worth.

"Leave 'im be," I told her. "I don't want Mama getting any more upset."

Hickory looked like she had words for Mama as well, but she bit them back. "You'll do better shut of the lot of them," was what she finally said. "But don't you forget your Aunt Hickory."

"I could never forget you."

"Yeah, that's what they all say. But then the time always comes when they get up and go and the next you know you never do hear from them again."

"I'll write."

"I'm gonna hold you to that, Darlene Johnston."

"I'm changing my name," I told her. "I'm gonna call myself Darlene Flatt."

I figured she'd like that, seeing how Flatt & Scruggs were pretty well her favorite pickers from the radio, but she just gave my chest a considering look and laughed.

"You hang onto that sense of humor," she told me. "Lord knows you're gonna need it in the city."

I hadn't thought about my new name like that, but I guess it shows you just how stubborn I can be, because I stuck with it.

5

I don't know how I make it through the rest of the set. Greg Timmins who's playing Dobro for me that night says except for that one glitch coming into the last verse of "In the Pines," he'd never heard me sing so well, but I don't remember it like that. I don't remember much about it at all except that I change my mind about not doing "I Will Always Love You" and use it to finish off the set. I sing the choruses to my Aunt Hickory, sitting there in the third row of the Standish, fifteen years after she up and died.

I can't leave, because I still have my duet with Lonesome George coming up, and besides, I can't very well go busting down into the theater itself, chasing after a ghost. So I slip into the washroom and soak some paper towels in cold water before holding them against the back of my neck. After a while I start to feel . . . if not better, at least more like myself. I go back to stand in the wings, watching Lonesome George and the boys play, checking the seats in the third row, one by one, but of course she's not there. There's some skinny old guy in a rumpled suit sitting where I saw her.

But the buzz is still there, humming away between my ears, sounding like a hundred flies chasing each other up and down a windowpane, and I wonder what's coming up next.

6

I never did get out of Newford, though it wasn't from want of trying. I just went from playing with housebands in the honky-tonks to other kinds of bands, sometimes fronting them with my Dolly show, sometimes being myself, playing guitar and singing backup. I didn't go back to Piney Woods to see my family, but I wrote Aunt Hickory faithfully, every two weeks, until the last letter came back marked, "Occupant deceased."

I went home then, but I was too late. The funeral was long over. I asked the pastor about it and he said there was just him and some folks from the rez at the service. I had a lot more I wanted to ask, but I soon figured out that the pastor didn't have the answers I was looking for, and they weren't to be found staring at the fresh-turned sod of the church-yard, so I thanked the pastor for his time and drove my rented car down Dirt Creek Road.

Nothing looked the same, but nothing seemed to have changed either. I guess the change was in me, at least that's how it felt until I got to the cabin. Hickory had been squatting on government land, so I suppose I shouldn't have been surprised to find the cabin in the state it was, the door kicked in, the windows all broke, anything that could be carried away long gone, everything else vandalized.

I stood in there on the those old worn pine floorboards for a long time, looking for some trace of Hickory I could maybe take away with me, waiting for some sign, but nothing happened. There was nothing left of her, not even that long-necked old Gibson banjo of hers. Her ghost didn't come walking up to me out of the pine woods. I guess it was about then that it sunk in she was really gone and I was never going to see her again, never going to get another one of those cranky letters of hers, never going to hear her sing another one of those old mountain songs or listen to her pick "Cotton-Eyed Joe" on the banjo.

I went outside and sat down on the step and I cried, not caring if my makeup ran, not caring who could hear or see me. But nobody was there anyway and nobody came. I looked out at those lonesome pines after a while, then I got into my rented car again and drove back to the city, pulling off to the side of the road every once in a while because my eyes got blurry and it was hard to stay on my own side of the dividing line.

7

After I finish my duet with Lonesome George, I just grab my bag and my guitar and I leave the theater. I don't even bother to change out of my stage gear, so it's Dolly stepping out into the snowy alley behind the

Standish, Dolly turning up the collar of her coat and feeling the sting of the wind-driven snow on her rouged cheeks, Dolly fighting that winter storm to get back to her little one-bedroom apartment that she shares with a cat named Earle and a goldfish named Maybelle.

I get to my building and unlock the front door. The warm air makes the chill I got walking home feel worse and a shiver goes right up my spine. All I'm thinking is to get upstairs, have myself a shot of Jack Daniel's, then crawl into my bed and hope that by the time I wake up the buzzing in my head'll be gone and things'll be back to normal.

I don't lead an exciting life, but I'm partial to a lack of excitement. Gets to a point where excitement's more trouble than it's worth and that includes men. Maybe especially men. I never had any luck with them. Oh, they come buzzing around, quick and fast as the bees I got humming in my head right now, but they just want a taste of the honey and then they're gone. I think it's better when they go. The ones that stay make for the kind of excitement that'll eventually have you wearing long sleeves and high collars and pants instead of skirts because you want to hide the bruises.

There's a light out on the stairs going up to my apartment but I can't even find the energy to curse the landlord about it. I just feel my way to the next landing and head on up the last flight of stairs and there's the door to my apartment. I set my guitar down long enough to work the three locks on this door, then shove the case in with my knee and close the door behind me. Home again.

I wait for Earle to come running up and complain that I left him alone all night—that's the nice thing about Maybelle; she just goes round and round in her bowl and doesn't make a sound, doesn't try to make me feel guilty. Only reason she comes to the side of the glass is to see if I'm going to drop some food into the water.

"Hey, Earle," I call. "You all playing hidey-cat on me?"

Oh that buzz in my head's rattling around something fierce now. I shuck my coat and let it fall on top of the guitar case and pull off my cowboy boots, one after the other, using my toes for a boot jack. I leave everything in the hall and walk into my living room, reaching behind me for the zipper of my rhinestone dress so that I can shuck it, too.

I guess I shouldn't be surprised to see Hickory sitting there on my sofa. What does surprise me is that she's got Earle up on her lap, lying there content as can be, purring up a storm as she scratches his ears.

But Hickory always did have a way with animals; dying didn't seem to have changed that much. I let my hand fall back to my side, zipper still done up.

"That really you, Aunt Hickory?" I say after a long moment of only being able to stand there and stare at her.

"Pretty much," she says. "At least what's left of me." She gives me that considering look of hers, eyes as dark as ever. "You don't seem much surprised to see me."

"I think I wore out being surprised 'round about now," I say.

It's true. You could've blown me over with a sneeze, back there in the Standish when I first saw her, but I find I'm adjusting to it real well. And the buzz is finally upped and gone. I think I'm feeling more relieved about that than anything else.

"You're looking a bit strollopy," she says.

Strollops. That's what they used to call the trashy women back around Piney Woods, strumpets and trollops. I haven't heard that word in years.

"And you're looking pretty healthy for a woman dead fifteen years."

Maybe the surprise of seeing her is gone, but I find I still need to sit me down because my legs are trembling something fierce right about now.

"What're you doing here, Aunt Hickory?" I ask from the other end of the sofa where I've sat down.

Hickory, she shrugs. "Don't rightly know. I can't seem to move on. I guess I've been waiting for you to settle down first."

"I'm about as settled down as I'm ever going to be."

"Maybe so." She gives Earle some attention, buying time, I figure, because when she finally looks back at me it's to ask, "You remember what I told you back when you first left the hills—about never doing something you'd be ashamed to look back on?"

"Sure I do. And I haven't never done anything like that neither."

"Well, maybe I put it wrong," Hickory says. "Maybe what I should have said was, make sure you can be proud of what you've done when you look back."

I don't get it and I tell her so.

"Now don't you get me wrong, Darlene. I know you're doing the best you can. But there comes a point, I'm thinking, when you got to take stock of how far your dreams can take you. I'm not saying you made a mistake, doing what you do, but lord, girl, you've been at this singing for twenty years now and where's it got you?"

It was like she was my conscience, coming round and talking like this, because that's something I've had to ask myself a whole pile of times and way too often since I first got here to the city.

"Not too damn far," I say.

"There's nothing wrong with admitting you made a mistake and moving on."

"You think I made a mistake, Aunt Hickory?"

She hesitates. "Not at first. But now . . . well, I don't rightly know. Seems to me you've put so much into this dream of yours that if it's not payback time yet, then maybe it is time to move on."

"And do what?"

"I don't know. Something."

"I don't know anything else—'cept maybe waiting tables and the like."

"I see that could be a problem," Hickory says.

I look at her for a long time. Those dark eyes look back, but she can't hold my gaze for long and she finally turns away. I'm thinking to myself, this looks like my Aunt Hickory, and the voice sounds like my Aunt Hickory, but the words I'm hearing aren't what the Hickory I know would be saying. That Hickory, she'd never back down, not for nobody, never call it quits on somebody else's say-so, and she'd never expect anybody else to be any different.

"I guess the one thing I never asked you," I say, "is why did you live up in that old cabin all on your ownsome for so many years?"

"I loved those pine woods."

"I know you did. But you didn't always live in 'em. You went away a time, didn't you?"

She nods. "That was before you was born."

"Where'd you go?"

"Nowhere special. I was just traveling. I . . ." She looks up and there's something in those dark eyes of hers that I've never seen before. "I had the same dream you did, Darlene. I wanted to be a singer so bad. I wanted to hear my voice coming back at me from the radio. I wanted to be up on that big stage at the Opry and see the crowd looking back at me, calling my name and loving me. But it never happened. I never got no further than playing the jukejoints and the honky-tonks and the road bars where the people are more interested in getting drunk and sticking their hands up your dress than they are in listening to you sing."

She sighed. "I got all used up, Darlene. I got to where I'd be playing on those dinky little stages and *I* didn't even care what I was singing about anymore. So finally I just took myself home. I was only thirty years old, but I was all used up. I didn't tell nobody where I'd been or what I'd done or how I'd failed. I didn't want to talk to any of them about any of that, didn't want to talk to them at all because I'd look at those Piney Woods people and I'd see the same damn faces that looked up at me when I was playing my heart out in the honky-tonks and they didn't care any more now than they did then.

"So I moved me up into the hills. Built that cabin of mine. Listened to the wind in the pines until I could finally start to sing and play and love the music again."

"You never told me any of this," I say.

"No, I didn't. Why should I? Was it going to make any difference to your dreams?"

I shook my head. "I guess not."

"When you took to that old guitar of mine the way you did, my heart near broke. I was so happy for you, but I was scared—oh, I was scared bad. But then I thought, maybe it'll be different for her. Maybe when she leaves the hills and starts singing, people are gonna listen. I wanted to spare you the hurt, I'll tell you that, Darlene, but I didn't want to risk stealing your chance at joy neither. But now . . ."

Her voice trails off.

"But now," I say, finishing what she left unsaid, "here I am anyway and I don't even have those pines to keep me company."

Hickory nods. "It ain't fair. I hear the music they play on the radio now and they don't have half the heart of the old mountain songs you and me sing. Why don't people want to hear them anymore?"

"Well, you know what Dolly says: Life ain't all a dance."

"Isn't that the sorry truth."

"But there's still people who want to hear the old songs," I say. "There's just not so many of them. I get worn out some days, trying like I've done all these years, but then I'll play a gig somewhere and the people are really listening and I think maybe it's not so important to be really big and popular and all. Maybe there's something to be said for pleasing just a few folks, if it means you get to stay true to what you want to do. I don't mean a body should stop aiming high, but maybe we shouldn't feel so bad when things don't work out the way we want 'em to. Maybe we should be grateful for what we got, for what we had."

"Like all those afternoons we spent playing music with only the pines to hear us."

I smile. "Those were the best times I ever had. I wouldn't change 'em for anything."

"Me, neither."

"And you know," I say. "There's people with a whole lot less. I'd like to be doing better than I am, but hell, at least I'm still making a living. Got me an album and I'm working on another, even if I do have to pay for it all myself."

Hickory gives me a long look and then just shakes her head. "You're really something, aren't you just?

"Nothing you didn't teach me to be."

"I been a damn fool," Hickory says. She sets Earle aside and stands up. "I can see that now."

"What're you doing?" I ask. But I know and I'm already standing myself.

"Come give your old aunt a hug," Hickory says.

There's a moment when I can feel her in my arms, solid as one of those pines growing up the hills where she first taught me to sing and play. I can smell woodsmoke and cigarette smoke on her, something like apple blossoms and the scent of those pines.

"You do me proud, girl," she whispers in my ear.

And then I'm holding only air. Standing there alone, all strolloped up in my wig and rhinestone dress, holding nothing but air.

8

I know I won't be able to sleep and there's no point in trying. I'm feeling so damn restless and sorry—not for myself, but for all the broken dreams that wear people down until there's nothing left of 'em but ashes and smoke. I'm not going to let that happen to me.

I end up sitting back on the sofa with my guitar on my lap—the same small-bodied Martin guitar my Aunt Hickory gave a dreamy-eyed girl all those years ago. I start to pick a few old tunes. "Over the Waterfall." "The Arkansas Traveler." Then the music drifts into something I never heard before and I realize I'm making up a melody. About as soon as I realize that, the words start slipping and sliding through my head and before I know it, I've got me a new song.

I look out the window of my little apartment. The wind's died down, but the snow's still coming, laying a soft blanket that takes the sharp edge off everything I can see. It's so quiet. Late night quiet. Drifting snow quiet. I get a pencil from the kitchen and I write out the words to that new song, write the chords in. I reread the last lines of the chorus:

> *But my Aunt Hickory loved me,*
> *and nothing else mattered*
> *nothing else mattered at all.*

There's room on the album for one more song. First thing in the morning I'm going to give Tommy Norton a call and book some time at High Lonesome Sounds. That's the nice thing about doing things your own way—you answer to yourself and no one else. If I want to hold off on pressing the CDs for my new album to add another song, I can. I can do any damn thing I want, so long as I keep true to myself and the music.

Maybe I'm never going to be the big star the little girl with the cardboard suitcase and guitar thought she'd be when she left the pine hills all those years ago and came looking for fame and fortune here in the big city. But maybe it doesn't matter. Maybe there's other rewards, smaller ones, but more lasting. Like knowing my Aunt Hickory loves me and she told me I do her proud.

Shining Nowhere but in the Dark

If we look at the path, we do not see the sky.
—*Native American saying*

Because I could not stop for Death—
He kindly stopped for me—
—*Emily Dickinson*

1

"Spare change?"

The crowd eddies by on either side of me as I pause. It seems point-less, doling out a quarter here, a quarter there, as if twenty-five cents can make that much of a difference in anyone's life, but I can't stop myself from doing it, because it does make a difference. It means we're at least paying attention to each other, acknowledging each other's presence.

Come lunch time, some people buy lottery tickets, others waste their money on junk food. Me, I usually brown-bag it. Then after I've eaten, I go out for a walk, making sure I have a handful of change in the pocket of my jacket.

So I turn to the girl, my hand already in my pocket, fingers sorting through the coins by feel. She has a raggedy Gothic look about her, from her pale skin and the unruly tangle of her short dark hair to the way her clothes hang from her skinny frame. I find myself wondering, is this all she has to wear or a fashion statement? These days it's hard to tell.

Scuffed workboots, torn jeans, black T-shirt, black cotton jacket. She has so many earrings in one ear that I'm surprised her head doesn't tilt in that direction. Her other lobe has only one small silver stud of an owl's head. Except for her blood-red lipstick, she's entirely monochrome.

She smiles as I drop a pair of quarters in her palm. "If this were a fairy tale," she says, "you'd have just guaranteed yourself some unexpected help later on in the story."

It's such a charming and unexpected line, I have to return her smile. "But first I suppose I'd have to stand on one foot and call your name three times while hopping in a circle."

"Something like that."

"Except I don't know your name."

She grins. "It's not supposed to be easy, is it? But maybe a random act of kindness is magic enough, in its own small way. Maybe I owe you now and I'll have to come to you if ever you need my help."

"That's not why I gave you the money."

"I know." She touches my arm, her fingers weightless on my skin and soft as a feather. "Thanks."

She pockets her fifty cents and turns away. "Spare change?" I hear as I start walking again.

Just before I fall asleep that night, I find myself thinking about fairy tales. I try to imagine myself in stories of old women and spoons that go adventuring and talking cats that repay a small kindness with a great kindness until I remember that I'm not a thirdborn child the way the central characters usually are in a fairy tale. That brings me wide awake again. Once upon a time I was the middle child; now I'm an orphan, without siblings. Thinking about family takes me to a place I try to never go, but it's too late now.

I lie awake for hours, watching the slow shadow of the streetlight outside my window as it crawls across my ceiling. Finally I get up and go to the window. I mean to pull the shade, but then I see someone standing out there on the street, under the streetlight, looking up at me.

He's dark-eyed, dark-haired, that ravened thatch an unruly nest of untamed locks standing up at attention around his head; alabaster skin—brow, cheeks, throat, hands, even his lips. He has a face like a knife, all sharp angles, and there's a Gothic look about him that reminds me of the girl panhandling earlier today. With him it's reinforced by the old-fashioned cut of his clothes—Heathcliff come off the moor, not exactly the way Brontë described him, but the way I imagined him, a figure of shadow and pale skin that haunted my sleep for weeks. I used to live in delicious dread of his appearing at the foot of my bed and sweeping me up into his arms and away. Where, I was never exactly sure. Before I got the chance to figure out where I might like a man like that to take me, my life was irrevocably changed and I didn't think about that kind of thing again for a very long time.

But that was over twenty years ago, when I was barely into my teens, and still had dreams. Right now I'm thirty-six, suffering from a familiar insomnia, and not at all happy to have acquired my very own stalker, no matter how handsome he might be. Bunching the open V of my nightgown closer to my throat with one hand, I step back, out of his line of sight, and sit down on the bed again. Safe, I think, only something makes me turn my head and that's when I see the spare-change girl from earlier today, sitting on the other side of my bed like an invited guest.

"Don't worry about him," she says. "He won't hurt you."

My heartbeat goes into overdrive. I start to ask how she got in here, but the words stick in my throat and a half second later I realize that I have to be dreaming. My pulse is still drumming way too fast, but I don't feel quite so nervous now. It's funny. Maybe I don't dream—or at least I don't remember my dreams—and I certainly can't remember ever knowing that I was dreaming *while* I was dreaming, but here I am, doing both. I wonder if I'll retain any of this tomorrow morning.

"Do you know him?" I find myself asking.

"He's my sister."

"He?"

She laughs. "Oh, I guess that sounds pretty confusing, doesn't it?"

Even for a dream, I think.

"We're . . . wyrds," she says. "Or at least that's what they used to call us."

"Weirds?"

I don't realize until later that we're using two entirely different words. She nods. "Exactly. As in the fates. Sometimes we were called muses, too, though I doubt anyone would do that today. There doesn't seem to be a whole lot of interest in muses anymore."

I give her a blank look. My hand goes to the night table and finds cigarettes, matches and ashtray. I have the usual twinge of regret as I light up, that familiar I-really-should-quit-one-of-these-days nag, but I ignore it.

Dropping the cigarette package and matches on the bed between us, I take a long drag, then tip the grey end of my cigarette into the middle of the ashtray.

"These days," she explains, "people don't really care about using the muscles of their own imaginations. I mean, why bother when the media can provide every thought or idea you'll ever need?"

"That's a bit cynical."

"But no less true."

I shrug. "And it doesn't explain what he's doing down there—or why you're in my bedroom, for that matter."

Or, come to think of it, what she was doing out on the street at noon, cadging spare change.

"My sister being down there is my fault," she says. "He saw me talking to you earlier today and when he realized that you don't dream at all, he had to have a closer look."

"I'm dreaming now."

"Are you?"

I better be, I think, but decide to change the subject.

"So you're fates," I say.

She nods again. "There are three of us—like in the stories. They got that much right."

I finally start to twig. "You mean like in the Greek myths?"

"Something like that."

I'm thinking, there are three of them in the stories, one to spin the threads of our lives, one to weave them, and one to cut them when you've reached the end of your thread. Spin, weave, cut. Birth, life, death. I steal a glance out the window and Heathcliff's still standing out there, looking up. He hasn't got a hooded cloak or a scythe, but I'm pretty sure I know which one of the three he is now. Snip, snip.

My cigarette's already at the filter. I stub it out and light another one. Even sucking smoke into my lungs the way I am, I can't believe my time has come. I'm not ready, but then who is? I've always subscribed to Woody Allen's philosophy: "I'm not afraid of dying," he's supposed to have said. "I just don't want to be there when it happens." Or I guess I just pretended I did. I feel guilty about being alive, but fear's a bigger emotion. I'm afraid of dying. Not because it means my life's over—what I've got is no big deal—but because of who I might meet when I do die and what they'll say to me.

"And . . . your other sister?" I ask.

"She's spinning."

I nod because it makes sense. The spare-change girl sitting on the edge of my bed is too much a part of the here and now, too full of vitality not to be the weaver. Life. I take a drag from my cigarette and sneak another look at her older sister, waiting for me down there on the street.

"Why does she look like a man?" I ask, thinking maybe I can postpone the inevitable if I can just keep her talking.

The girl shrugs. "He got disbelieved into looking the way he does. That sort of thing happens to us when people stop dreaming their own dreams. And no dreams at all makes it even worse."

I'm finding this way too confusing, even for a dream.

"Okay," I tell her. "So your sister's down there because I don't dream." I find that I don't want to let on that I know why she's really here—maybe because if I ignore it, it won't be real. "Why are you here?"

"Because it's my fault that he's here right now and I didn't want you to be upset. A lot of people find him unsettling."

Maybe the strangest thing about all of this is the way she keeps referring to her sister as "he."

"But sooner or later . . ." I begin.

"He would have come around to see you," she says, finishing when I let my voice trail off. "It just takes time, getting to everyone. You probably wouldn't have even known he was nearby, if you hadn't seen me earlier today."

One of the curses of fairyland, I think. Once you've had a glimpse of it, you can always see it, just there on the periphery of your vision. Or at least that's the way it goes in some of the old stories. I played Good Samaritan with fifty cents, and the next thing I know I've got two of the Greek fates hanging around.

I've finished my second cigarette even quicker than the first. I stub it out and light yet another one. I don't want to hold on to what she's telling me, but I can't let it go. Death's down there on the street, his gaze meeting mine every time I look out the window. Eternity seems to linger in his eyes and I can't read him at all. Is he bored, sad, amused?

"If he's busy," I say, turning back to the girl. "I can wait. Really. I'm in no hurry."

"That's not the way it works," she tells me. "Everybody has to dream, just as one day, everybody has to die."

2

Jenny Wray woke in a cold sweat. She sat up and stared frantically at the side of her bed, but of course there was no one there. She leaned forward so that she could see out the window and there was no one standing under the streetlight either. She started to reach for the cigarettes on her night table, then remembered that she'd given them up over ten years ago.

God, it had seemed so real. Death below, his younger sister in the room with her. The taste of the cigarette.

She sat up against the headboard, arms wrapped around her knees, reliving memories that had no business hanging on for so long, no business still being so clear. It was a long time before she could even think of trying to get back to sleep. Her visitors had been wrong about one thing, she thought as she stretched out once more.

"See," she murmured into her pillow. "I do dream."

Because what else could it have been?

"When we visit, we come like a dream," she heard someone reply. "But it's not the same. It's not the same thing at all."

She recognized the voice. It was the spare-change girl. She could picture her face without having to open her eyes, could imagine Death having joined her, standing at the foot of the bed now in all his Gothic trappings.

The idea of dreaming about them still being in the room with her gave her the creeps. Maybe if she pretended they weren't there, they'd simply go away. The skin prickled up and down her spine at the thought of their presence until she stole a glance through her eyelashes and saw she really was alone. When she finally drifted off, she wasn't sure if she was falling asleep, or dreaming she was falling asleep. The difference seemed important, but she was too tired to try to make sense of it now.

3

The dream wouldn't go away.

It followed Jenny through the day, clinging to the wool of her thoughts like a persistent burr until she knew she had to talk to someone about it. The trouble was, who? She was temping these days, only her second day at this particular office, so she couldn't approach one of her coworkers, and it wasn't the sort of topic that normally came up in conversations among her own small circle of acquaintances; she didn't have any real friends. It wasn't until she was leaving the office that she thought of someone who wouldn't think she was weird or laugh her off. So instead of taking the bus home, she caught a subway downtown.

It took her a little while to find the shop she was looking for. When she finally did and went inside, she stood in the doorway, momentarily distracted. The air in the shop was several shades darker than outside and redolent with the scent of incense. There were packets of herbs for sale and bins of candles; crystals displayed on swatches of dark velvet along with ornately-designed daggers and goblets; ceremonial hooded cloaks hanging along one wall and books crammed on shelves, many with the word *magic* or *magick* in the title, as well as any number of items that Jenny couldn't identify, or if she recognized the item, didn't know the use to which it would be put, presented as it was in this context.

Ash Enys, the young woman behind the counter, was the niece of a woman Jenny had met while sitting a booth at a craft show a few years before. She reminded Jenny of last night's dream, of the middle fate with her pale skin and punky hair. They shared the same monochrome wardrobe: black jeans, jacket and combat boots, white T-shirt, smudges of dark kohl around the eyes. Ash's lips even had the slash of blood-red lipstick, except the shade of hers ran more toward the purple spectrum. The only real difference was that the spare-change girl hadn't had a nose ring.

"Never thought I'd see you in here," Ash said with a smile when she recognized Jenny.

Jenny returned her smile. "Why not?"

"I don't know. Doesn't seem to be your style."

"So what is my style?"

"Uptown," Ash said. "No offense."

Jenny liked to dress well, not voguing, but definitely stylish. Today she was wearing patterned stockings, heels, a form-hugging short skirt, silk blouse. She didn't use much makeup, but the little she did was artfully applied. Her dark hair was a short pageboy with long bangs. Minimal jewelry—a stud and a dangling earring in one ear, the latter's match in the other, a plain silver band on the ring finger of her right hand.

"No offense taken," she said. "But everybody's got secrets."

They were alone in the store. Feeling bold, she tugged her blouse free from her skirt and lifted it so that Ash could see the small silver ring that pierced her navel. She got it one day when she wanted to prove to herself that she was brave. That hadn't happened. Bravery, she realized, had nothing to do with what one chose to do to one's self. But she did like the secret of it, the knowledge of its existence, hidden there under her clothes where no one else could see it.

"Cool," Ash said.

Jenny tucked the tails of her blouse back into her skirt.

"So what are you looking for here?" Ash asked.

"You." As Ash's eyebrows rose questioningly, Jenny went on to explain. "I remember Gwen telling me you'd gotten a job here and I had a question about, you know—" She waved her hand vaguely in the direction of a shelf full of books on dreaming. "Stuff like this. Dreams."

"I'm not exactly an expert," Ash said.

"Well, you're the closest to an expert that I know."

Ash smiled. "Uptown girl."

"That's me."

"So what do you want to know?"

"What does it mean when you dream about Death?"

"Yours or somebody else's?"

"I mean the personification of Death," Jenny said. "You know, a pale-faced guy, all in black."

"Did he ask you to play chess?"

Jenny smiled at the film reference, but shook her head. "He just stood in the street outside my apartment last night, watching me."

"Well, some people think dreams can be like premonitions—"

Jenny shivered.

"—while other people think that's bullshit."

"What do you think?"

Ash shrugged. "If I had a dream like yours, I'd definitely lean toward it being bullshit."

"No, seriously."

Ash leaned on the counter to look more closely at her. "This has really got you spooked, hasn't it?"

"No. Of course not. It's just . . ." Jenny sighed. There was no point in lying. "Yeah. I found it really creepy. Especially because, normally, I don't dream—or at least I never remember my dreams. But this one won't go away. It keeps popping back into my mind when I'm least expecting it."

"Well," Ash said, "symbolically, meeting Death isn't necessarily such a bad thing. I mean, Shiva is the god of both Dance and Death, and in the Tarot, the Death card is more often considered to be a symbol of transformation and spiritual rebirth. Even in Western culture we didn't always depict Death as the hooded skeleton with a scythe. The Greeks envisaged Death as the daughter of night and the sister of sleep." She cocked an eye at Jenny. "Maybe that's why Keats described himself as 'half in love with easeful Death.' They used to call sleep the little death, you know, so maybe when we die we step into a dream that never ends because we never wake up again."

Jenny stared at Ash, not really seeing her. She was remembering what the middle fate had told her about dreams and dreaming. When she finally focused her gaze she saw Ash wearing an apologetic look.

"I guess I'm not being much help, am I?" she said.

"She said the reason he'd come to see me is because I don't dream," Jenny told her.

"She?"

"The middle fate. That's what she said they were—wyrds. The fates— or at least two of them. She was the one who was actually in my room— Death was sort of hanging around on the street outside."

"This sounds like it was quite the dream."

"It was," Jenny said. "She looked a little bit like you."

Ash laughed. "Generic Goth, right? I guess I deserve that for my uptown-girl comments."

Jenny shrugged that off.

"So where does the girl come in?" Ash wanted to know.

"I don't know exactly," Jenny said. "The first time I saw her I was awake—she was panhandling near my office and I gave her some money. But then later I dreamed about her and that feels more true now than what I know for sure happened. She kept going on about muses and dreams and . . ." She let her voice trail off. "God, would you listen to me? I'm talking about it as though it actually happened, as though she really was in my bedroom."

"I've had dreams like that," Ash said. "Everybody does. It's like you wake up and you can't believe it didn't really happen. I know this guy who had a dream about cats Morris dancing. He really, really believed it had happened. He was so excited when he woke up, he wanted to tell everybody. I just happened to be the first person he saw that morning, so I saved him the embarrassment of trying to convince anybody else that it had been real."

Jenny was only half listening. "She said it wasn't a dream," she told Ash. "She said that they came like a dream, but it wasn't the same thing as a real dream. She was pretty emphatic about it."

"So what did they want?"

"That's what I was hoping you could tell me."

Ash lifted her hands, palms up. "The Goth strikes out," she said, "because I don't have a clue. I guess you'll have to ask them yourself if you dream about them again."

"I hope the opportunity never comes up," Jenny said.

4

But of course it does. Not that night, nor the next, but Friday, I no sooner put my head on the pillow, than I find myself in this club I've never been in before—at least I don't recognize the place. Dark, smoky, loud. The DJ's spinning "Le Bien, Le Mal" by Guru and MC Solaar. I remember the first time I heard the piece, I thought it was so weird hearing somebody rapping in French, but it's got a definite groove and the dance floor is happening, so I don't think I'm the only person who likes it.

There's a guy standing close beside me and I don't know if I'm with him, or if the crowd's just pushed together, but he lights my cigarette for me. The music's turned up past conversation volume which makes it hard to talk. He's nice-looking and I think maybe I'd like to dance, but then I see a familiar figure going up the stairs on the far side of the club and out the door. I think: It's Ash, but I know it's not. It's not any other generic Goth either. I tell the guy I've got to go, using sign language because the music's still seriously loud, and he just gives me a shrug. I guess I wasn't with him after all.

It takes me a while to make it across the club and up the stairs myself. By the time the cool air outside hits my face, there's no sign of the girl. I have that hum in my head—you know, the one that follows you home after a concert or a night of clubbing—and I figure I must have had enough loud music for one night, even though all I can remember is the last few minutes or so. I hail a cab and settle down in the back seat. We go about a half-dozen blocks before I turn to look out the window on my left and realize the girl's sitting beside me. Was she there all along, or did she simply materialize on the seat beside me? It doesn't really matter because that's when I figure out that I'm dreaming again.

"See," I say to her, "I told you I dream," but she shakes her head.

"And I told you," she says, "that we only seem like a dream. It's easier for you to deal with us that way."

"Who do you mean by 'us'?"

She shrugs. "People like me. Or my sisters."

One of whom's been disbelieved into looking like a guy and just happens to be Death. It's so strange, when you think about it. Death's got sisters. They never told us that, but then nobody has the real scoop on death, do they? There are all the light at the end of the tunnel stories, but those people come back, so who knows if their near-death experience really connected them into the secret, or if they simply imagined the light and the tunnel?

"So . . ." I clear my throat. "Where *is* your sister? Out taking a few lives?"

I don't feel nearly as cocky as I'm trying to sound.

She gives me a strange look. "More like living them," she says.

I've no idea what she's talking about, but I figure as long as I've got the ear of one of the fates, I might as well ask her a few questions, find out for sure what everybody else has to guess at.

"Why do we have to die?" I ask.

She shrugs. "What you really want to know is, 'Why do I have to die?' "

"I guess."

She doesn't answer me right away. Instead she says, "It's such a beautiful night, why don't we walk?"

When I agree, she taps the cabbie on the shoulder and tells him we'll get out here. He pulls over to the curb. She doesn't offer to pay, so I dig out my wallet, but he just shakes his head. Says we didn't go far enough to make it worthwhile. I don't argue. I just thank him the way my companion does and join her on the pavement, but it's the first time I ever saw a Newford cabbie turn down money.

The spare-change girl slips her arm in mine and we head off down the street. For some reason I don't feel weird, walking arm in arm with another woman like this. Maybe it's because it's such a beautiful night, one of those rare times when the lights of the city just can't drown out the starlight that's pouring down from the sky above. Maybe it's because I know I'm only dreaming.

"Why do you have to die?" she says, returning to our earlier conversation. "You might as well ask, why were you born? It's all part of the same mystery."

"But it's not a mystery to you, is it? Or at least it's not to your sister."

"Which one?"

"You know. The one who was standing outside my apartment the other night. He'd know, wouldn't he?"

"Perhaps," she says. "He's always had access to a lot of very potent imaginations. It wouldn't surprise me at all if he's run across the answer in one lifetime or another."

I know she doesn't mean he's immortal—though of course he is. She means all the lives he's taken.

"But you don't know," I say.

She shakes her head. "I think it's all part of a journey and what you're thinking of as the start and the end are just convenient markers along the way. You don't get the whole picture right away. Maybe you never do. Maybe it's like *tao* and it's only the journey itself that's important, what you do on it, how you grow, not where you come from or where you finally end up."

"I can't buy that," I tell her. I have an old pain aching in my chest, but I don't speak about it. It's not something I can speak about—that I even know how to speak about. But while I can't deal in specifics, the general injustice that crowds my head whenever I think about death and how people die is easy to verbalize.

"What about little kids?" I ask. "What about infants who die at birth? What do they get a chance to learn? Or what about all the terrible suffering that some people have to undergo while others just drift peacefully away in their sleep? If this isn't random, then, I'm sorry, but Death's one spiteful bastard."

She gets this sad look. "Death can't pick when you die, or how you die, just as no one can decide what you dream."

"You make it sound like the people who suffer *choose* to suffer. That a baby *chooses* to die when it does."

"You have so much anger in you."

"Well, excuse me," I tell her, "but I'm not like you and your sisters. I have to die."

And probably sooner than I want to, considering how my companion's older sister has taken this sudden interest in me. But that's not why I'm really angry. I think maybe she knows, only she doesn't call me on it.

"But is dying so bad?" she asks. "How else can you move on to what comes next, if you don't leave the baggage of this life behind? What comes next might well be more wonderful than anything you can even begin to imagine in this world."

"You don't know that."

"No," she admits. "I don't. Just as I don't know why some die in pain and others in their sleep. Why some die young and others in their old age. Why good people can suffer and evil ones prosper."

"Well, what about your sister?"

"What about him?"

"Doesn't *he* know? I mean, if anyone should know, it'd be him."

"My sister has many good qualities," she says, "but omniscience isn't among them."

"I just think if he's going to show up standing outside my apartment that he should at least have the decency to tell me where I'm headed next."

She shakes her head. "All he's concerned with is why you don't dream."

"Why should that bother him?"

"I told you. People not dreaming changes us. Every one who doesn't dream is like a little black hole. If it isn't tended to, it'll draw other dreamers into its net and soon there'll be vast numbers of you, abed and dreamless."

"Well, what does that matter? I mean, who really cares if we dream or not?"

"We do. He does."

I try to digest this. "So dreaming is important to him."

"Very much so."

"I was talking to someone recently," I tell her, "and they mentioned something about how people once called sleep the little death."

She nods her head. "I remember."

Like she was there, but I let it pass because she probably was.

"So maybe," I say, "dying is like going into a dream that never ends because you never wake up again."

This seems to interest her. "I like the idea of that," she says.

I feel like I'm on a roll now. "And maybe that's another reason why it's so important that I dream. Because if I don't dream, then I won't die."

She doesn't reply. Instead she says, more to herself than to me, "I wonder if that's the real reason John's been around for all these years."

"Excuse me?"

"John Buttadćus. It's like he just doesn't quite scan."

"What are you talking about?" I ask.

She blinks out of her reverie and gives me this irresistible smile that I can't help but return.

"What were you saying?" she asks.

I start to repeat what I've just said, until I realize she's gone back to what we were talking about before she spaced out on me.

"Does this mean that so long as I don't dream, I don't die?" I ask.

"I don't think there's been an appointment made for you yet," she tells me. "At least, not that anyone's told me."

"And we're not dreaming right now?"

She shakes her head.

"Well, I can sure live with that," I say and then I have to laugh at the double meaning of what I've just said.

I pause to light a cigarette. Our reflection in a store window catches my eye. She looks Gothic, I'm uptown, but the poor light and dark glass blend the differences. We could almost be sisters.

"Those are going to kill you," she says as I put away my lighter.

I blow a wreath of blue-grey smoke into the air between us.

"Is that inside information?" I ask.

She shakes her head.

"Because I quit years ago," I tell her. "And besides, I don't dream, remember? I'm going to live forever. I could probably take them up again if I wanted to."

I have this giddy feeling that I can't shake. I feel immortal, the way I did when I was a kid, when my life was still normal. That makes me almost fall into the trap of reliving the past, but I manage to sidestep the memories. I've had to live with them for almost as long as I can remember. Right now, I just want to hold onto this good feeling and never let it go.

I'm still smiling when I wake up the next morning, never mind that what I experienced last night had to be a dream. Except it wasn't—at least not according to Death's sister, the middle fate, and if anybody should know, it'd be her, right? So I'm safe from him—safe from what I know will be waiting for me when I die. Until I have a real dream. So I guess the big question is, how do I stop myself from inadvertently doing just that?

5

Saturday found Jenny back at The Occult Shop, but Ash didn't appear to be working this morning. In her place behind the counter was a tall, green-eyed woman who presented a look that was the direct opposite of Ash's Goth image. She wore a high-necked black dress over tights the same color and a pair of combat boots. The dress was unadorned except for a bone ankh broach pinned above her right breast. Her long blonde hair was gathered into a loose ponytail that hung down to the small of her back in a golden waterfall. She looked like she should be in a fashion magazine instead of working the counter here.

"Ash doesn't work Saturdays," the woman told Jenny when she asked. "Maybe I can help you. My name's Miranda."

The store was much busier than it had been the last time Jenny was here—too busy, she thought, for the kind of conversation that would ensue when she explained why she was here. And where would she even begin? Ash at least had the background.

"It's sort of personal," she explained, trying not very successfully to hide her disappointment.

"Well, you can usually find her over in the park on weekends," Miranda said.

"The park?"

"Fitzhenry Park. She's generally hanging somewhere around the War Memorial with Cassie or Bones."

Jenny had no idea who Cassie or Bones might be, or what they would look like, but she fastened onto Ash's possible whereabouts with a single-mindedness that surprised her and was almost out of the store before she remembered to thank Miranda for her help.

"No problem," Miranda replied, but she was speaking to a closed door.

6

Jenny found Ash sitting on the steps of the War Memorial with a man she decided had to be Bones. He was a Native American—probably from the Kickaha reservation north of the city. His skin had a dark coppery cast and his features were broad—the chin square, eyes widely set, nose flat. His hair was as long as Miranda's back in The Occult Shop, except he wore his in a single tight braid, with feathers and beads interlaced in the braiding. He looked to be in his early thirties and so far as Jenny was concerned he could have stepped into modern Newford right out of some forgotten moment in history, if it hadn't been for his clothing: faded jeans, torn at the knees, scuffed leather work boots, a white T-shirt with DON'T! BUY! THAI! written across the front.

"Hey, pretty lady," he called to her as she came near. "Medicine's right here—plenty powerful—if you got the wampum."

Before Jenny could answer, Ash elbowed him in the side.

"Enough with the talking Tonto already," Ash said. "She's a friend. Jenny, this is Bones; Bones, Jenny."

Bones gave Jenny a grin that made him look a little demented and she took an involuntary step back.

"He likes to act the fool," Ash explained, "but don't mind him. He's okay."

"I'm okay, you're okay," Bones said. "Pull up some stone, Jenny, and have yourself a seat."

Jenny gave him an uncertain smile. There was something about the way he looked at her—some dark light in his eyes—that reminded her of the eldest fate, standing outside her apartment the other night, except it didn't wake awe in her so much as nervousness. An uncomfortable feeling washed over her, a sense that in this man's presence, anything could happen. And probably would. She wasn't sure she was ready for another strange encounter—not when she still hadn't gotten over the one that had brought her here in the first place, looking for advice.

"What are those for?" she asked, pointing at a pile of tiny animal bones that lay on a square of beaded deerskin by Bones' feet. "Besides giving you your name, I mean."

She asked as much out of curiosity as to get him to stop regarding her so intently.

"It's the eyes, isn't it?" Ash said. "That and the grin."

Jenny looked up at her. "What?"

"She thinks you don't know what to make of me," Bones said.

"Well, I . . ."

"Bones always makes people feel a little strange when they first meet him," Ash said. "He says his real name translates into something like Crazy Dog. I say, whoever named him knew what they were doing."

Bones nodded, still grinning. "And these," he said, indicating the bones, "are my medicine wheel."

"Oh."

Ash laughed. "But you didn't come here to get your fortune read—did you?"

"No. I . . ." Jenny hesitated, feeling as intimidated with Bones's presence as she'd felt in The Occult Shop with all the people standing around. But she took a breath and plunged on. "Do you know a way to make sure that you don't dream?" she asked.

Ash shook her head. "No, that's a new one on me."

"It's just that I know you sell herbs and stuff to help people dream. . . ."

"Like a dream-catcher?"

"I guess. What's that?"

Ash described the spider-web like weaving of threads that went back and forth around a twig that had been bent into the rough shape of a circle, how the pattern, and the feathers, beads, shells, and the like woven into it, were supposed to draw good dreams to a sleeper.

Jenny nodded. "Yes, like that. Only something that'll do the opposite."

"You've got me."

"You don't like your dreams?" Bones asked.

"No, it's not that. I don't dream."

"So what's the problem?"

"I want to make sure it stays that way."

"Maybe you should go back to the beginning," Ash suggested, "so Bones knows what we're talking about."

"I . . ."

"Don't feel shy. He's a good listener and maybe he can help. He's gotten me out of a jam or two."

Jenny felt a flush coming on. "I don't know. I feel weird. . . ."

"Weird is good," Bones said. "Means you're not locked into what's here and now, but you're seeing a little further than most people do."

That was an understatement if Jenny had ever heard one. "Okay," she said with a sigh. "It started with a dream that wasn't a dream. . . ."

7

"So one of the fates is a guy," Bones said when Jenny finished relating her recent experiences.

"I think he's like Coyote," Ash said. "A shapeshifter—only the face he wears is the one you least expect."

Jenny looked from one to the other. "What are you talking about?"

"The guy in your dream," Ash said. "The eldest fate."

Bones shook his head. "No, what we're really talking about is you, Jenny. The visions you're experiencing and the people you're meeting in them are just something the spirits are doing to try to get your attention."

"I'm not sure I follow you," Jenny said.

"I don't know you," Bones said, "and you don't know me, so I don't know how much I should tell you. I don't know what you want to hear." He sounded regretful, but the crazy look in his eyes seemed to make a lie of that.

"What's that supposed to mean?" she asked.

"I don't want to piss you off. I mean, what's the percentage in it? What do either of us get out of me telling you something you don't want to hear?"

"I'm listening."

"But are you hearing? The spirits spoke to you and what did you do? You took their gift and instead of learning from it, you're trying to turn it to your own advantage." He shook his head. "Never works, you know."

Jenny could feel her face go stiff. "What the hell's that supposed to—"

"Anger's good," Bones told her, breaking in. "It's one of the ways the spirits tell you that you're alive."

"I'm not—" Jenny began, but she broke off.

Angry? No, she was furious at his cocky, know-it-all manner, but she heard an echo of what he'd said a few moments earlier—*I don't want to piss you off*—and that was enough to make her wonder just why she was so angry. She looked at Ash, but Ash didn't want to meet her gaze. She turned back to Bones. His face gave away nothing. Crazy eyes watched her back, solemn and laughing at the same time. She took a couple of steadying breaths and forced herself to calm down, to let the hostility go. It wasn't that she was suddenly into making nice. It was more that she realized that Bones seemed to understand the experiences she'd had—certainly better than she did—and he was right: he had nothing to gain in making her angry, or hurting her feelings. So maybe it was worth her while to hear him out.

"Okay," she said finally. "I am feeling angry. But I want to hear what you have to say."

"You sure?"

Ash elbowed him again before Jenny could reply.

"Okay," he said. "Let me put it this way. Does the sun rise and set just for you?"

Jenny shook her head.

"But it passes over you and makes you a part of its wheel, doesn't it?"

"I guess."

"Then perhaps you should learn to accept that you are a part of the world's wheel and not struggle so hard against what must be."

"So what are you telling me?" Jenny asked. "That I should just lie down and die?"

Bones grinned that crazy grin of his. "No, I'm saying you should get back on the wheel. Dream. Live. Don't look at the ground when you want to see the sky. What's the point of living forever if you don't experience life now?"

"Who says I'm not experiencing life?"

"You do. Your dreams-that-aren't dreams do. The spirits that have come across from the medicine lands to talk to you do."

The anger rose up in Jenny again, but this time she was quicker to deal with it. She looked away from them, bit at her lip. The dark place inside started to draw her down into its grasp and she couldn't seem to fight it.

"I'm sorry," Bones said, and she sensed that he meant it.

"You don't understand," she said finally. "That's the problem with living, nobody really understands. But we've got to carry on all the same. The trick isn't to save up our points for when we die so that maybe we can buy ourselves into a better life. The trick is to have that better life now. To make it for ourselves. To take it, if people are trying to keep it away from us."

Jenny still couldn't look at them. She picked at a loose thread on the seam near the knee of her jeans. The past was swallowing her again and this time she couldn't trick it into going away. It lay too thick inside her, that miasma of old hurts and griefs.

"Sometimes . . ." she began.

She had to stop and gather up her courage before could go on. This wasn't something she talked about. It was too hard to talk about. She took a steadying breath and tried again.

"Sometimes," she said in a small voice, "I don't feel I have anything to live for. Sometimes I feel like I don't deserve to live, but I'm more scared of dying." Finally she looked up. "I'm scared of dying and seeing them and of what they'll say to me, because I know it wasn't fair, that they had to die while I went on."

"Who died?" Ash asked softly.

"Everybody. My parents. My little sister. My older brother. My cousin did it. I was only . . . I was only twelve when it happened. He killed everybody except for me. I hid under my bed and waited for him to come . . . to come get me too, but he never did."

"Your own cousin?" Ash said. "Jesus. That's horrible."

"What happened to him?" Bones asked.

"He killed himself. That's why he never came after me. He . . . he killed everybody else and then he shot himself. I was under my bed for the rest of the night and most of the next day, just . . . just waiting for him."

Ash shook her head. "You poor thing. You were just a little kid."

"And then . . . then I went to live with my grandparents, but they died too."

"But your cousin . . . ?" Ash began.

"He . . . he didn't kill them. They just . . . died. . . ." It was getting harder and harder for Jenny to get it out. Starting had seemed tough, but going on was worse. Her chest was so tight she could barely breathe. She couldn't see because she was blinded with tears. Her throat felt thick, making her choke on the words before she could get the words out.

"None . . . none of them died easy. Not my own family. Not my grandfather from cancer, a few . . . a few years after I came to live with them. Not my grandmother . . . she had Alzheimer's. By the time she finally died she didn't even know who I was anymore. . . ."

She finally turned her face toward them. "Why did they all have to go like that? Why not me? I should have died with them. Instead, I've just got this emptiness inside where family's supposed to be. I feel so . . . so lonely . . . so guilty. . . ."

Ash came and sat beside her and put an arm around her, drawing Jenny's head down to her shoulder. Bones took her hand. She looked at him. Even through her tears she could see that crazy light in his eyes, but it didn't seem so strange anymore. It felt almost comforting.

"You've got to talk to those spirits one more time," he said. "This time you've got to tell them what you're feeling. That you don't want to die—not till it's your time—but you do want to live until it's your time. You want to be alive. You want to dream. You've got to ask them to help you let it all go."

"But she said the reason they came to me was *because* I don't dream. What's the point of me telling them what you're saying I should? Wouldn't they already know it?"

"The thing with spirits," Bones told her, "is they want you to work it out on your own. Then, when you ask them for the right gift, they might help you out."

"And . . . and if they won't?"

"Girl," Bones told her, "you've got a lot of strong medicine tucked away inside you. Everybody does. Those spirits don't want to help you, you come back and talk to me again and I'll see what I can do about waking it up for you."

"Why can't you just help her now?" Ash asked.

"Because these are spirits we're talking about," Bones said. "You don't mess with spirits unless you've got no choice, Ash—especially not spirits that are working their medicine mojo on someone else. There's no way I'm getting in between them until they get off this wheel and I can climb on it. That's the way it is."

8

So here I am, waiting for Death to show.

I'm trying to feel brave—or at least project a little courage even though I have none—but I don't think it's working. I don't know which I'm more afraid of: that I won't dream, that I know I'll never die and have to go on like this forever, or that maybe he'll take me away with him right now. Except in the end, it's not Death that joins me in my bedroom, but the middle fate, the spare-change girl.

"Where is he?" I ask her.

"You've decided to dream once more," she says, "so he's gone on to deal with other matters."

Harvesting other lives you mean—but I don't say that aloud. I don't know whether to feel relieved that it's not me this time, or angry that he even exists in the first place.

"Why can't he just leave us alone?"

She shakes her head. "Without his gift, what would you have?"

I'm sick of this idea that without death, that without knowing we're all going to die one day, rich and poor, whatever our creed or color, we can't appreciate life. Even if it is true.

"I wanted to talk to him," I say.

She gives me a long considering look. "Did you want to talk to him, or to the eldest of us?"

And then I understand. It hits me like a thunderclap booming under my skin. It's been her all along. *He's* the middle fate, Life; she's the one that cuts the thread and ferries us on. My heartbeat gets too fast, drumming in my chest. All my resolutions about facing the past and my fears drain away and I want to tell her that I've changed my mind again. I don't want to dream. I don't want to be more alive if it means I have to die.

"Is this it?" I ask her. "Have you come for me?"

"Would that be so bad?" she says.

She projects such a strange aura of comfort and happiness that I want to shake my head and agree with her.

"I'm scared," I tell her.

"Fear lets you know you're alive," she says, "but that doesn't mean you should embrace it."

"You're starting to sound like Bones."

"Ah, Bones."

"Do you know him?"

She smiles. "I know everybody."

I want to keep her talking. I want to put off the moment for as long as I can, so every time she finishes speaking, I try to fill the silence with another question.

"How do you decide when it's someone's time?" I ask.

"I told you," she says. "I don't choose when or how you die. I'm only there to meet you when you do."

"Do people get mad at you, or are they mostly just scared like me?"

The eldest fate shook her head. "Neither. Mostly they're too concerned with those they left behind to be angry or frightened. That old homily is true, you know: it's always harder for those left behind."

"So . . . so my family wasn't mad at me because I didn't die with them? And my grandparents . . ."

"How could they be? They loved you as much as you loved them."

"So I don't have to be scared of meeting them in . . . wherever it is I'll be going?"

"I don't know where you'll go or who you'll meet when you're there," the eldest fate says. "And I don't know what they'll say to you. But I don't think you have to be scared."

I take a deep breath. "Okay," I tell her, wondering as I'm saying it where I've found the courage. "I'm guess I'm ready."

I wonder how it'll happen. Maybe I'll be lucky. Maybe I'll be one of the ones who just drifts away in her sleep.

"I'm not here to take you," the eldest fate tells me.

I don't even have time to feel relief, I'm so confused. "But . . . then why are you here?"

"I came as a friend—to finish our earlier conversation."

"As a friend?"

"You know, returning a kindness," she says.

"But . . ."

"I'm everybody's friend," the eldest fate explains. "Most people just don't know it."

I think of what Bones told me. I think about what I can't let go of, how I'm always so afraid, how I'm too scared to get close to someone because I know they're just going to die on me, how most of the time I feel so lost and alone. I think about how sick I am of the way I've lived my life, how I want to change it, but I can't seem to do it. Not on my own. I think about all of this. I look in the eldest fate's eyes and I see she understands.

I'm not going to live forever. I know that. I don't expect that. I don't even really want it. All I've ever wanted is the chance to be normal, to have a piece of what everybody else seems to have: a respite from the hurt and pain. I don't have to die to find that.

"I could use a friend," I tell her.

If I Close My Eyes Forever

Beauty exists whether a person has the eye to
behold it or not. That principle also applies to
ugliness.

—*William Arthur Herring*
from A Horse of a Different Color

1

There are only a pair of old-fashioned cemeteries left in the Crowsea-
Foxville area. All Souls, over in Crowsea, hasn't been used in fifty years,
but it's under the protection of the Crowsea Heritage Society. Unfortunately, that protection only means that bodies haven't been moved, mausoleums, crypts, statuary, and other stonework haven't been torn down to
make room for condos. The place is seriously run-down and overgrown,
and the only people hanging there are drug dealers.

Foxville Cemetery is still a working graveyard, as witness the fresh
grave I've just laid flowers on. Neither's a fun place to be, but then being
here isn't about fun. It's about closure.

I think the same architect designed both places—someone with a serious jones for New Orleans-style graveyards. Has to be that, because
Newford's certainly not under sea level, so we don't need the crypts and
mausoleums. The closest we get to New Orleans is the seriously watered-
down Mardi Gras that's organized every year by the owners of the Good
Serpent Club. The parade they put together never gets to be much more

than a big block party, but you can't fault them for trying. It's not like we have a French Quarter here, primed and geared to be party central, or the tradition of Mardi Gras. The people who observe Lent in Newford aren't thinking along the lines of a carnival Fat Tuesday, and to everybody else, it's just another weekday.

I look down at the bouquet of six red roses lying on the freshly turned earth at my feet, then my gaze rises to the small stone and its incomplete inscription.

ELISE
Born, . . .–Died, July 23, 1994
R.I.P.

No one claimed the body and the police never did identify her beyond what little I had to tell them.

I was working late in my office the first time I met her. No, let's be honest. I was pushing papers around, killing time—trying to make myself so tired that by the time I did get home, I'd just fall into bed and sleep.

There was nothing left for me at home anymore. Peter took everything when he walked out on me.

What I missed the most was my confidence. My self-esteem.

2

Thursday night.

My business card says: FINDERS, LTD.—IF YOU NEED IT, WE CAN FIND IT. KIRA LEE, PROP., followed by my e-mail address, my phone and fax numbers, and finally my office address. The office is the least important part of the equation—at least insofar as dealing with clients. It's basically a tiny hole-in-the-wall of a room in the old Sovereign Building on Flood Street that barely manages to hold a desk, swivel chair, and file cabinet, with another chair parked across the desk for a visitor. A computer takes up most of the desktop—the tower sits on the floor beside the desk while my printer and fax machine are on a table over by the window. There's also a phone, stacks of papers and files, and, inevitably, a cup of coffee in some stage of depletion and usually cold.

I don't worry about clients coming by the office. With the kind of work I do, they don't have to. I get my contracts by phone or messenger; I get paid when I deliver the goods. It's a simple system and helps me keep my overhead low because usually by the time a client contacts me, all they're interested in is how fast can I get the job done, not how pretty my workspace is.

That night I'm sitting behind the desk, feet propped up on a corner while I flip through a fashion magazine. The window behind me's tuned to the usual dull channel: a nighttime view of an inner-city block, shops on the ground floor, apartments above them. The most predominant piece of color is a neon sign that just says BAR. Looking at all the models preening on the glossy pages propped up on my legs, I'm thinking that maybe what I need is a makeover. My idea of work clothing is comfort: jeans and hightops, a T-shirt with a lightweight shirt overtop, blonde hair tied back in a ponytail. About the only thing I have in common with these models is my height.

Of course a makeover means maintenance and I don't know if I have the patience for it. Shower, brush my hair, dab on some lipstick. Anything more and I'll be running even later than I usually am in the mornings. Then she comes walking in, drop-dead gorgeous like she stepped out of the magazine I'm holding, and I think, why even try?

Dark hair cut stylishly short, eyes darker still. The makeup's perfectly understated. The clothes, too. Custom fit, snug black dress and heels, clasp purse, and tailored silk jacket, also black. Her only jewelry is a short string of pearls.

"I need you to find someone for me," she says.

"That's not exactly my line of work, Ms . . . ?"

She lets my question hang there as she sits down across the desk from me, tugs her skirt down.

"It's extremely urgent," she says.

I have to smile. "It's always urgent, but I still can't help you. I don't do people—only things."

"I don't understand. Your card says . . ."

Well-manicured fingers take my business card from her purse and place it on the desk between us.

"I'm sorry if it's misled you," I tell her. "It just means that I find objects." She looks confused, so I go on to explain. "You know, like tickets to *Cats* for a visiting businessman. Props for a theater company or a film crew. Maybe some long out-of-print book. The kinds of things that people could find on their own if they had the time or the inclination. Instead they've got money and I do the legwork for them."

Now she takes a package of cigarettes from her purse.

"But it *is* an object I need you to find for me," she says.

It's my turn to look confused. "You started off saying you wanted me to find someone. . . ."

"I do. She stole my heart and I want it back."

The woman lights her cigarette and places the package and matches on the edge of the desk. I turn in my chair to look out the window. The same channel is still playing out there.

Well, this was a first. No one's ever contracted me to find a broken heart before. I want to send her right back out the door, except I start thinking about Peter, about how I felt when he walked out and took my heart away with him. So it was a woman who took hers instead of a man. Big deal. It had to hurt the same.

I turn back to look at her. "I have to level with you. I'm not really sure I can be of much help. What you really want is a private detective."

"I tried a few of them, but none of them would help me. The last one gave me your card."

I raise my eyebrows. "Can you remember his name?"

"A Peter Cross of the Vax Agency. He said it was just the odd sort of thing that would appeal to you."

Great. First he dumps me—"You're too intense, Kira,"—and now he's sending crumbs of work my way. Like I can't find work on my own. Though I'm not saying business has been good lately. . . .

I realize I'm frowning, but I can't seem to stop myself. Instead I reach for the woman's cigarette package.

"Do you mind?" I ask.

"Not at all."

"Thanks."

She gives me enough time to put a cigarette in my mouth.

"Will you help me?" she asks.

I pause with a lit match in my hand. "You know you can't ever get something like that back. When someone wants to walk out of your life, you can't force them to stay."

I'm thinking as I light the cigarette, trust me on this. I know. But I don't say it aloud.

She shakes her head. "Oh, no. You've misunderstood me. It's true we had a relationship, and it's true she left me, but I'm not looking to get her back. I just want my heart back. It's a pendant. She took it with her when she left."

"This is still a job for a private detective," I tell her. "Or maybe even the police, if you can prove ownership of the stolen property."

"It's not that simple."

It never is, is it?

I prop my elbow up on the desk, cup my chin with my hand. The cigarette smolders between the fingers of my free hand. It doesn't taste nearly as good as I was hoping it would.

"So tell me about it," I say.

"The heart was a gift to me from Faerie," she says.

This is getting kinkier by the minute. "So you're into gay, or I guess, bisexual guys, too?"

"Not at all."

"Hey, I don't have a problem with it," I tell her. "Live and let live, I say."

"When I say Faerie," she says, "I mean the Otherworld. I did a favor once for a prince of the realm and he gave me the pendant in gratitude. It allows one the gift of second sight. Of piercing the barriers between what we believe we see and what is actually there."

Scratch the kinky, I think. This woman belongs in a padded cell at the Zeb. Except she's so earnest. I can't help but lean forward as she talks, knowing it's all hogwash, but *wanting* it to be real. I mean, how many of us didn't go through a rainbow-and-unicorn phase when we were eleven or twelve?

So I let her ramble on about gifts from the faerie folk and how they don't work for everybody, but then what does? How her particular pendant not only gives its bearer this second sight, but also protects her from some of the, shall we say, less friendly denizens of the Otherworld. The friendlies pretty much ignore you, but the others . . .

See, the way she tells it, once you get their attention, once they know you can see them, you've got to have protection or your ass is grass. Sounds like life on the street to me, business as usual, except she's describing creatures with knives for fingers and worse.

I feel like I'm trapped in a video edition of *The Weekend Sun*, directed by Roger Corman—somewhere between "Nun Gives Birth to Pig Twins" and the Elvis Spotter page—so when I find myself agreeing to help her track down her friend and the pendant, I startle myself.

I mean, this really isn't my line of work. I'm strictly an over-the-phone girl. I do research, go electronic-tripping through the on-line services. Sometimes I have to leave the office to work the stacks at the Newford Library or something similar. I wouldn't know where to begin to find a missing person except from what I've seen in the movies.

My nameless client isn't stumped. She tells me to hit the girl bars on Gracie Street and gives me a photo of her friend. Tells me she'll be in touch with me tomorrow night. Leaves me sitting there in my office wondering, if she knows how to do it so well, why's she bothering to hire me? Leaves me wondering just how much Peter's leaving me has screwed me up that I'd agree to something like this.

I don't know my client's name. I don't know the name of the woman I'm looking for. My head's spinning with fairy tales. But at least she left her smokes. I give them up every couple of months. Right now I'm off them. Was.

So I stuff the pack in my pocket and hit the street. It's going on eleven, which means the action's just starting on Gracie Street. It's busy down here—not Times Square before Disney cleaned it up, but still big-city, inner-core, out-for-some-fun busy. The names of the bars range from the obvious to the less so: The North Star, Neon Sister, Girljock, Skirts. There's plenty of traffic on the pavement, cars cruising, cabs. Plenty of people on the sidewalk, too—street people, couples, single men and women. The couples I pass are all same sex: male and male, female and female. It's not too outrageous out on the street—you know, leather scenes and the like—but inside the clubs it's a whole different story.

Some of the women are femmes, some butch. Lots of sexy tops, short hair, body piercing, tattoos, dancing, smoking, drinking. I try not to do the tourist thing and gawk as I show around a photograph of two women standing on a street corner—one's my client. In the photo she's got her hair tied back. She's wearing a black T-shirt and jeans, black cowboy boots, and still looks like a million dollars. Around her neck, sparkling against the black shirt, is a small gold pendant in the shape of a heart. She has her arm around an attractive smaller woman who has short, spiky dark hair, angular features. The second woman is dressed in a short black dress and is barefoot. She's holding a pair of high heels by their straps with one hand and leaning against my client.

I show the photo around, but I seem to be generating more interest for who I am than the picture. I remember what I told my client earlier—live and let live—and I believe it. But I've never been hit on so many times in such a short period of time as I have in the past couple of hours. And not once by a guy.

It really isn't a problem for me. My best friend in high school, Sarah Jones, came out to me in our senior year and we're still good friends. But I'm being hit on so often right now that I find myself seriously wondering what it'd be like to go out with another woman.

I take a look at these cigarettes my client left behind and wonder what's in them, because first, she has me out here playing detective for her and now I'm actually considering . . .

There's an attractive woman with short red hair sitting at the other end of the bar, looking back at me, one eyebrow raised questioningly. She makes a victory sign with the first two fingers of her right hand and then flicks her tongue through them.

No, I don't think so.

I turn away quickly and bump into a tall black woman who's standing on the other side of my stool. She's wearing a white halter top, a short skirt and pumps, and has a ship captain's hat scrunching down her kinky black hair. There are three studs in her nose, half a dozen more in each ear, running up from the lobes.

"Easy now," she says, steadying me.

I jerk away from her. "Look, I'm not interested in—"

I break off when I realize the woman was just helping me keep my balance. She smiles at me, obviously non-aggressive, and I feel like a fool.

"I'm sorry," I tell her. "I'm just feeling a little . . ."

"Flustered?" she asks.

I nod.

"First time down here?"

"Yes, but it's not what you think."

When she cocks an eyebrow, I show her the photo and point to my client's companion.

"The other woman in the picture has got me looking for her," I say.

We're both leaning against the bar now, the photo lying on the bar between us. The music's still loud, making it hard to talk. All around us is the press of bodies, women dancing with each other, flirting with each other.

"I know them," the woman says. "Are you sure you're really into their scene?"

"What do you mean?"

"You know, the whole S&M thing. The girl you're looking for is your client's slave."

"Slave?"

The woman smiles. "You really are a virgin, aren't you? Your client's a top—you know, a leatherdyke."

I give her a blank look.

"The sexually dominant one of the pair. The other girl's a femme." She's still friendly, but maybe a little too friendly now. "Like you."

I shake my head. "No way."

And I mean it. Except even I can hear the trace of uncertainty in my voice.

My companion shrugs. "Then what're you doing with a recruiter?"

I'm getting more confused by the minute.

"I'm not sure I know what you mean," I tell her.

She gets a tired look on her face. "The leatherdykes are always looking for new blood, but the trouble is, you sweet young femmes don't always know you're looking for them, too."

She turns away, leaning against the bar with her elbows supporting her. She doesn't look at me anymore, her gaze on the crowd. I get the sense that this conversation is finished, thank you very much, but then she adds, "So people like your friend go out and recruit them."

"Oh."

What the hell have I gotten myself mixed up in?

The woman turns to look at me. "It's nothing heavy. Nobody's forced to do anything against her will. But sometimes people get talked into doing things that they regret later. The leather crowd can get a little rough."

"I'm really just trying to find this woman," I tell her. "After that, my job's over."

"Whatever."

She points to the photo then, finger resting on the chest of my client's ex-girlfriend.

"Somebody told me she's dancing at Chic Cheeks," she tells me. "That's a straight club over in the Combat Zone. I don't think her top knows about the gig. It's a big city. Easy to disappear in, especially if you go someplace where no one's going to look for you. At least no one in this crowd. We've got our own strip joints."

"Thanks," I say. "I really appreciate—"

"And considering the kind of clientele it caters to, you might want to go round the back like the girls who work there do."

"I will," I tell her.

"I'd say be careful, but you girls never listen, do you?"

I smile and leave with the photo in hand, pretending I didn't hear her.

Back out on Gracie Street, I find myself thinking about lesbian relationships again. Do women treat each other better than guys treat us, or is it the same-old same-old only with the gender changed? Call me naive, but I don't feel like that sailor girl would have treated me the way Peter did. But while I liked her, and I know she liked me, I still can't muster up a sexual interest in another woman.

I pause to light a cigarette.

I remember something another friend of mine said to me once. She told me she was attracted to lesbianism, but "It's not because I have the hots for another woman or anything," she confided. "What I'm attracted to is the kind of freedom the word implies. These women don't seem to worry so much about what everybody else is thinking; they just do what they think is right."

And that makes me think of what Sarah said about lesbian sex. "It's soft and slippery and it just never ends. There's no hard-on to worry about and one orgasm leads to the next. Who wants a guy, if that's what you get to do all day?"

As I light my cigarette, I see yet another woman watching me with interest from across the street. She looks as straight as I am, but I can tell she's getting ready to come over and chat. Before she crosses the street, I walk briskly on, trailing cigarette smoke.

No, I decide. I like guys. That's not going to change. I want my sexual partner to be tender, but I want him to have a hard-on, too. It's just the way Peter treated me that's got me all screwed up.

So . . . live and let live.

I catch a cab and have it drop me off in the Combat Zone. It's only a half block to Chic Cheeks from where the cab lets me out. When I get to the strip club, I stand in front of it for a long moment, frowning at the advertising posters and thinking about what I've been told.

What about my client? *Is* she a recruiter? I think of what the woman back at the club called her—a leatherdyke—and how she looked when she came into my office, and I don't know which is the mask. And how about all this talk about Faerie and magic and shit?

What was *that* all about?

I turn down the alleyway that runs alongside the club.

I'd pack it all in right now, except I've come this far and really, what else am I going to do? Go home and obsess about Peter? Or maybe go home and think too much about what I've seen tonight?

I don't have any trouble getting in through the side door—the bouncers are all out front. From the wings of the stage I watch a woman dressed like Alice in Wonderland go through her routine. She's got blonde hair— same cut as mine—but I recognize her, even with the blonde wig. She looks enough like me from a distance that I'd be amused, if I didn't feel a little sick. The Lovin' Spoonful's "Do You Believe in Magic?" is blasting from the sound system. She's playing the little girl, like she's twelve years old, and the freaks in the audience are lapping it up.

I find myself wishing I was back on Gracie Street. They're selling sex as blatantly there, but they're sure as hell not pandering to pedophiles.

I watch a little longer. The dancer's removed her blouse now. When she turns, I see the heartshaped pendant.

I go have a smoke while she finishes her act.

The dressing room's about what you'd expect in a dive like this. There's not even a door to allow the women some privacy. Anybody walking by backstage can stand in the doorway like I am and check things out. Some of the women are putting on costumes, or simply trying to relax. Some are smoking cigarettes, drinking. I can smell the joint that one of them's lit up.

My client's girlfriend has removed her blonde wig. She's dressed in street clothes now—jeans and a T-shirt—and is leaning close to a mirror adjusting her makeup.

I'd be wanting to take a shower after doing a "show" like that.

I wait until she's leaving the room. As she comes up to me, I step aside to let her go by, then touch her arm.

"Can I talk to you for a moment?" I ask.

"Sure. What's it about?"

I thought we could go for a coffee, but she's only got forty-five minutes until her next show so we sit on the steps of the alleyway entrance. We've both got cigarettes going. The alleyway's dark, but a slice of light from the door behind us cuts through the darkness, illuminating litter, the brick wall of the building on the other side of the alleyway, the photo that I've passed over to the dancer.

"You have to understand," she says. "I was never really into her scene. I mean, I swing both ways, but I'm not into pain. Or maybe I should say, my relationships are always painful, but it's not something I go looking for. It's not what I want. It just seems to happen. But with her . . ."

I nod encouragingly.

She shrugs. "The whips and the piercings and all that shit, it was just too much." She pauses for a beat, then adds, "Do you know anything about that kind of scene?"

"Not really."

"You really are their slave," she tells me. "You cook, you clean, you do the laundry—all for free. You don't get beaten as a punishment—that's how they reward you. You get to feeling that the worst thing that can happen is you'll be ignored. You start to crave the bondage and the fisting and the whips."

I watch her as she talks. Her expression is that of one both attracted and repulsed by what she's discussing.

"See," she goes on, "the thing is, pain brings on an endorphin high. You know it's just a biochemical thing, you're not *attracted* to being hurt, but after a while you can't stop craving it. You'll be a slave, if that's what it takes."

She jerks a thumb back toward the door of the club. "What did you think of the scene in there?"

"It made me feel a little sick," I tell her.

"Me, too. But at the same time it makes me feel strong. Because when I'm up there on the stage, I'm in control. I feel like they're my slaves and I could make them do anything I want."

I give her a sad look. "But it's not really true, is it?"

"No," she says with a humorless smile. "But it's what made me strong enough to get out of her grip. Don't get me wrong," she adds. "I'm not saying the women in the S&M scene shouldn't be doing what they want to do. It's just not for me."

I nod. "But you didn't know what you were getting into until it was too late. That's not right, either. Don't you think it should be consensual?"

Her expression when she replies is unreadable, distant. "The only thing I didn't know when I got into that scene was that I'd fall in love with her as hard as I did. But I should have known. I always do. I always fall in love with the ones that'll hurt me the most."

We sit there and smoke in silence for a few moments.

"So what does she want from me?" she asks finally. "Why did she send you out to look for me?"

"She just wants the pendant back."

The dancer reaches up and closes her hand around it.

"I figured as much," she says. "That's why I took it. It's like it was the only thing she really seemed to care about. If I couldn't get her to care for me, then at least I'd have something that she does care about."

She opens her hand and looks down at the pendant.

"If I give it back to her," she says, "I'll have nothing."

I nod. "Maybe it's better that way."

She closes her hand around the pendant again and gives it a sharp tug. The chain breaks. Standing up, she drops the pendant into my hand and goes back inside. She doesn't say anything. Not even goodbye.

I sit there for a while longer, looking down at the pendant with its broken chain where it lies in the palm of my hand.

I don't know what to say either.

3

Friday night.

I'm sitting in my office, looking out the window. It's raining, turning the streets slick with wet reflections. I'm waiting for my client, but she doesn't show. On my desk is the pack of cigarettes she left here last night. Beside it is the photo she gave me, the pendant lying on top of the photo with its broken chain.

I have no reason to worry about her, but I'm uneasy.

I keep going over what she told me about this business with the pendant. How it was given to her by this Faerie prince. How it doesn't work for everybody, but when it does it can give the person wearing it second sight. How it protects the person wearing it from the dark side of Faerie—the ghouls and the goblins and the things that go bump in the night.

Not that I believe any of it. Not for a moment.

My gaze leaves the pendant and goes back to the window. It's still raining.

But all day long, I haven't been able to shake the feeling that somebody's watching me. There's no one thing I can point to with certainty. It's just a prickling sensation that I feel on the nape of my neck. A sense of movement caught out of the corner of my eye. A kind of intuition . . .

I light one of the last two cigarettes.

Or second sight?

I stand up, picking up the pendant. I can't wait for her any longer. I'm getting the willies sitting in here on my own. There's no one in the building except me. And whatever might be watching me. . . .

I leave the office and cross the street to the bar, holding my trench coat closed with my hand. I've got to be around some people. I hate being alone. I think that's why my relationships always fall apart. I've got too much need. I *am* too intense—just like Peter said. But that's because when I'm alone, I think too much. My imagination gets carried away with itself. I imagine the worst. I start to believe there really is a burglar lurking about. Some crazed fanatic. A rapist. . . .

Nasty creatures from fairy tales is a new one for me.

It's pretty empty inside. A neighborhood bar with a few serious drinkers, a couple at a table near the back, oblivious to their surroundings, and me. I take a seat at a table by the window. The glass is fogged and streaked with rain, but I've cleared a portion of the pane with my hand so that I can look out. There are three beer bottles on my table, all empty. My glass is half full. The pack of cigarettes that I got from my client is beside it, also empty, plus a new fresh pack that has a couple of cigarettes missing. One of them's burning in the ashtray amidst the butts. My left hand is closed in a fist on the table.

I give the window another swipe to clear the fog again. I don't know what I'm looking for. My client? Or the things she's got me half-believing are out there, invisible to normal sight?

I open my hand to look at the pendant lying there in the middle of my palm.

Except maybe I don't have normal sight anymore. Maybe the pendant's working for me like it did for her.

I sigh and have another sip of beer.

I wish she'd just show up and take this stupid thing away with her.

All I see in the window is a reflection of my own face, raindrops streaking across the glass.

I wish I had someone to go home to.

4

A week later.

I'm sitting on the edge of my bed, reconsidering the idea of getting up and facing the day. I'm hung over and my bedroom feels claustrophobic. The room's small and the view's not exactly expansive. When I look past the fire escape, all I can see is the brick wall of the building next to mine—about the width of an alley away. My room's a mess. Clothes on the floor, the bedclothes rumpled, dresser covered with makeup, more clothes, magazines, and books. Ditto, my night table.

I'm a mess.

The cops found my business card in her purse, but no identification. That's why they had me come in to ID her. They didn't have anybody else and I didn't bother to mention my client's ex-girlfriend—not after viewing the body.

Ari—at least that's her stage name—took it hard when I went by the club to tell her the next night. I guess she was holding on to broken hopes, pretending that she and the woman she knew as Elise would get back together again—the same way I've been pretending Peter will come back.

I know that, for all our physical frailties, we humans are capable of inflicting incredible amounts of damage on each other, but there's no way Ari could have killed Elise, so why get her involved?

Nothing *human* killed her. The cops are saying she got torn apart by a dog, but I'm not so sure. I keep remembering the way she looked when she was telling me about how the pendant protected her from these creatures she described to me—the ones with knives for fingers and mouths full of barracuda teeth in the middle of their palms.

I finally get up, have a shower, get dressed. When I wander into my small kitchen it feels just as claustrophobic as my bedroom. I ignore the mess and put the kettle on, but coffee and a cigarette don't help my mouth taste any better. What I really want is another drink. I haven't been sober for a week now, because this way I can just put it all down to the booze. I use it as a crutch—the same way I've been using cigarettes since that night Elise first came into my office. The cigarettes for Peter, the booze for what happened to Elise.

I would've had nightmares all night, just thinking about what I saw there in the morgue, if I hadn't had so much to drink before I finally dragged myself home. If I'm drunk, I can pretend she didn't die the way I can so easily imagine she did, torn apart by some creatures from the dark side of the Brothers Grimm.

I can pretend they're not looking for me now.

I put my coffee mug down on the counter with all the other unwashed dishes and get my jacket from where I tossed it last night. I have to get out of here before my imagination runs too wild.

I mean, I know it's crazy. Nasty goblins didn't kill Elise. It *couldn't* have gone down that way. It's got to be like the cops said, she got attacked by some animal. A pack of feral dogs, ranging out of the Tombs, say.

When I step outside my apartment building, the sun hurts my eyes. But there's no one watching me except for the old guy down the street who stares at anybody who's got breasts, doesn't matter if they're no bigger than buttons, or old and sagging and hanging down to your waist.

But everything still feels different. There are undercurrents that I never sensed before the pendant came into my possession. I can't begin to explain it. I just know now that there *is* more to what's around us than what we can see. Things moving in our peripheral vision. Events. Possibilities. Omens and portents and the stuff of dreams. What I can't swear to is that they're necessarily malevolent.

I think what we call to ourselves is what we expect to see. We're still not seeing what's really *there*—only our perceptions of what we expect could be there. If you were haunted by inner demons and into S&M the way Elise was, then maybe you'd see a faerie world that was beautiful and dangerous. And you'd call the darkness to you, in the same way Elise's ex-girlfriend told me she was always attracted to those who would treat her the worst, allowing herself to keep falling into abusive relationships even when she knew better.

Which isn't to say that it's Ari's fault. If you're beat on all of your life, how can you be expected to gain a sudden change of attitude all by your-self? Confidence and strength accrue in direct proportion to the breaks you get—the help and support that only someone else can give you.

I guess I'm making it sound as though I've suddenly gained this huge boost of confidence myself, but in my own way, I'm just as bad as Ari. She's still shaking her ass on stage at Chic Cheeks, untouched by her con-tact with the pendant. She still thinks that stripping gives her some kind of power over the freaks. She's right on the edge of another bad relation-ship because she can't break the cycle.

And me? I still don't want to be alone. The focus of my life is still eddying around the fact that Peter left me, that there's something intrinsi-cally wrong with me, or why would my relationships always fall apart?

It can't just be that I get too intense. Love's *supposed* to be intense . . . isn't it?

And then there's this business with the pendant.

I still think something's watching me. Or some*things*. I don't know if they're stalking me, or simply curious.

I end up on the subway, not aware of what I'm doing until it takes me downtown. I get off and head up to street level and the first thing I see is a flower cart. I buy a half-dozen roses from the old man who runs the cart and catch a bus that takes me to the Foxville Cemetery. The gates loom up above me when I go inside and make my way to Elise's grave. When I get there, I kneel down and lay the roses on the dirt in front of her marker. It's just a small gravestone and cost a small fortune that I couldn't really afford. I had to dig deep into my rainy-day account to pay for it, but I felt she needed something and there was no one else to pitch in. Ari wanted nothing to do with it. I don't think she's willing to accept the idea that Elise is even dead.

My fingers rise to touch the pendant that I've taken to wearing. I don't think it affected Ari at all, but I can't say the same for myself.

It's funny how your whole life can change because of the smallest thing. Like someone walking in through the door of your office. . . . Everything still *looks* the same, but now I feel like the most common ob-ject has a secret history that most people can't see. The difference be-tween them and me is, they don't even think about it.

I'm certain this knowledge killed Elise, but somehow I can't believe it's dangerous, in and of itself. The real danger would be to ignore it. The real danger would be to see what your preconceptions have led you to expect, instead of striving to see what really is there.

I'm not going to make Elise's mistake.

I won't say I'm not nervous. The idea of all these . . . presences around me really creeps me out. But they don't have to be malevolent, do they? Are hopes always broken?

Maybe I'm being a Pollyanna. Maybe the world really is an ugly piece of work. But I don't want to believe that. I want to think I'm breaking a cycle. I think I can look into this unseen world of Faerie the way that friend of mine looked into the lesbian scene. She took from it the image of a strong ideal, someone in control of her own destiny, and it made her stronger. She took the idea of it—the knowledge that it can be done—and that was what let her do it for herself.

And that's what I want to do. I want to look into Faerie and know that everything can be different. I want to break the cycle of my old patterns. I want to throw away my crutches and addictions. I want to step into a world where anything is possible—where I can be anything or anybody.

I want to find strength in my solitude so that when I do interact with other people, I won't hold on so tightly when they're with me. So that I can let them go when we have to be apart.

I know the danger. All I have to do is remember what happened to Elise. If I close my eyes, I can see her ravaged body as clearly as though it were still lying stretched out in the morgue in front of me. . . .

By looking into Faerie, I might be calling the same savagery down upon myself. But there's no point in being afraid. The danger's all around anyway. I might have imagined all those psychotics and rapists that peopled my fears, but that doesn't mean they're not out there. All you have to do is pick up a paper or turn on the news.

The dangers of Faerie are out there, too.

I guess what I should be saying is that while I have to be careful, I can't let my fear overwhelm me the way I have in the past.

I reach into my pocket to take the package of cigarettes I'm currently working on and lay it down beside the roses.

Break the old patterns. The old cycles.

"It's funny how it works out, isn't it?" I say to my client's gravestone. "I failed you, but you—however inadvertently—you didn't fail me."

I stand up and brush the dirt from my knees.

"I can't pay you back, but maybe I can help other people the way you've helped me: trip them out of their old patterns and show them what they're doing to themselves. Jump-start their lives onto a new track and then try to be there for them when they begin to put their lives back together again."

I touch the stone, trace its smooth surface with my fingers.

"I don't know where you are," I tell Elise. "I don't know if you can hear me or if it'll make any difference if you can, but I promise I'll give it my best shot."

I turn away from the grave, continuing the one-sided conversation in my head.

I'm going to start with Ari and see if, together, we can't break the pattern of her pain. Her pain, and mine. That'd be a kind of magic, too, wouldn't it? Because we can't close our eyes to it. Not the magic, not the pain. If we do that, we might as well close them forever.

The gates of the graveyard loom over me again as I leave, but they don't feel as oppressive as they did when I first went in. In my mind's eye, I'm picturing little figures the size of mice, slipping out from behind Elise's gravestone. They look like they've been put together with twigs and leaves and other debris. Their heads are wide, eyes slightly oversized and slanted, noses small on some, prominent on others, mouths very wide. Their hair is matted like dreadlocks mixed up with leafy vines.

They climb over the roses. One of them pulls a cigarette from the pack I left there and is awkwardly holding it, nose quivering like a rabbit's as it sniffs the paper and tobacco. A few of them clamber up onto the lower base of the gravestone and are shading their eyes, looking in my direction.

I don't turn around and look back. So long as I don't turn around, they can really be there. The magic can be real. The pain can be put away.

*H*eartfires

Dance is the breath-of-life made visible.
—*seen on a T-shirt on 4th Avenue, Tucson, AZ*

1

Nobody tells you the really important stuff so in the end you have to imagine it for yourself. It's like how things connect. A thing is just a thing until you have the story that goes with it. Without the story, there's nothing to hold on to, nothing to relate this mysterious new thing to who you are—you know, to make it a part of your own history. So if you're like me, you make something up and the funny thing is, lots of times, once you tell the story, it comes true. Not *poof*, hocus-pocus, magic it comes true, but sure, why not, and after it gets repeated often enough, you and everybody else end up believing it.

It's like quarks. They're neither positive nor negative until the research scientists look at them. Right up until that moment of observation they hold the possibility of being one or the other. It's the *looking* that makes them what they are. Which is like making up a story for them, right?

The world's full of riddles like that.

The lady or the tiger.

Did she jump, or was she pushed?

The door standing by itself in the middle of the field—does it lead to somewhere, or from somewhere?

Or the locked room we found one night down in Old City, the part of it that runs under the Tombs. A ten-by-ten-foot room, stone walls, stone floor and ceiling, with a door in one wall that fits so snugly you wouldn't even know it was there except for the bolts—a set on either side of the door, big old iron fittings, rusted, but still solid. The air in that room is dry, touched with the taste of old spices and sagegrass. And the place is clean. No dust. No dirt. Only these scratches on that weird door, long gouges cut into the stone like something was clawing at it, both sides of the door, inside and out.

So what was it for? Before the quake dropped the building into the ground, that room was still below street level. Somebody from the long-ago built that room, hid it away in the cellar of what must have been a se-riously tall building in those days—seven stories high. Except for the top floor, it's all underground now. We didn't even know the building was there until Bear fell through a hole in the roof, landing on his ass in a pile of rubble which, luckily for him, was only a few feet down. Most of that top floor was filled with broken stone and crap, like someone had bull-dozed another tumbled-down building inside it and overtop of it, pretty much blocking any way in and turning that top floor into a small moun-tain covered with metal junk and weeds and every kind of trash you can imagine. It was a fluke we ever found our way in, it was that well hidden.

But why was it hidden? Because the building couldn't be salvaged, so cover it up, make it safe? Or because of that room?

That room. Was it to lock something in? Or keep something out?

Did our going into it make it be one or the other? Or was it the story we found in its stone confines?

We told that story to each other, taking turns like we usually do, and when we were done, we remembered what that room was. We'd never been in it before, not that room, in that place, but we remembered.

2

Devil's Night, October 30. It's not even nine o'clock and they've already got fires burning all over the Tombs: sparks flying, grass fires in the empty lots, trash fires in metal drums, the guts of derelict tenements and factory buildings going up like so much kindling. The sky overhead fills with an evil glow, like an aura gone bad, gone way bad. The smoke from the fires rises in streaming columns. It cuts through the orange glare hanging over that square mile or so of lost hopes and despair the way ink spreads in water.

The streets are choked with refuse and abandoned cars, but that doesn't stop the revelers from their fun, the flickering light of the fires playing across their features as they lift their heads and howl at the devil's glow. Does stop the fire department, though. This year they don't even bother to try to get their trucks in. You can almost hear the mayor telling the chiefs: "Let it burn."

Hell, it's only the Tombs. Nobody living here but squatters and hoboes, junkies and bikers. These are the inhabitants of the night side of the city—the side you only see out of the corner of your eye until the sun goes down and suddenly they're all over the streets, in your face, instead of back in the shadows where they belong. They're not citizens. They don't even vote.

And they're having some fun tonight. Not the kind of recreation you or I might look for, but a desperate fun, the kind that's born out of knowing you've got nowhere to go but down and you're already at the bottom. I'm not making excuses for them. I just understand them a little better than most citizens might.

See, I've run with them. I've slept in those abandoned buildings, scrabbled for food in Dumpsters over by Williamson Street, trying to get there before the rats and feral dogs. I've looked for oblivion in the bottom of a bottle or at the end of a needle.

No, don't go feeling sorry for me. I had me some hard times, sure, but everybody does. But I'll tell you, I never torched buildings. Even in the long-ago. When I'm looking to set a fire, I want it to burn in the heart.

3

I'm an old crow, but I still know a few tricks. I'm looking rough, maybe even used up, but I'm not yet so old I'm useless. You can't fool me, but I fool most everyone, wearing clothes, hiding my feathers, walking around on my hind legs like a man, upright, not hunched over, moving pretty fast, considering.

There were four of us in those days, ran together from time to time. Old spirits, wandering the world, stopped awhile in this place before we went on. We're always moving on, restless, looking for change so that things'll stay the same. There was me, Crazy Crow, looking sharp with my flat-brimmed hat and pointy-toed boots. Alberta the Dancer with those antlers poking up out of her red hair, you know how to look, you can see them. Bear, he was so big you felt like the sky had gone dark when he stood by you. And then there was Jolene.

She was just a kid that Devil's Night. She gets like that. One year she's about knee-high to a skinny moment and you can't stop her from tomfooling around, another year she's so fat even Bear feels small around her. We go way back, Jolene and me, knew each other pretty good, we met so often.

Me and Alberta were together that year. We took Jolene in like she was our daughter, Bear her uncle. Moving on the wheel like a family. We're dark-skinned—we're old spirits, got to be the way we are before the European look got so popular—but not so dark as fur and feathers. Crow, grizzly, deer. We lose some color when we wear clothes, walking on our hind legs all the time.

Sometimes we lose other things, too. Like who we really are and what we're doing here.

4

"Hey, 'bo."

I look up to see it's a brother calling to me. We're standing around an oil drum, warming our hands, and he comes walking out of the shadows like he's a piece of them, got free somehow, comes walking right up to me like he thinks I'm in charge. Alberta smiles. Bear lights a smoke, takes a couple of drags, then offers it to the brother.

"Bad night for fires," he says after he takes a drag. He gives the cigarette a funny look, tasting the sweetgrass mixed in with the tobacco. Not much, just enough.

"Devil's Night," Jolene says, grinning like it's a good thing. She's a little too fond of fires this year for my taste. Next thing you know she'll be wanting to tame metal, build herself a machine and wouldn't that be something?

"Nothing to smile about," the brother tells her. "Lot of people get hurt, Devil's Night. Gets out of hand. Gets to where people think its funny, maybe set a few of us 'boes on fire, you hear what I'm saying?"

"Times are always hard," I say.

He shrugs, takes another drag of the cigarette, then hands it back to Bear.

"Good night for a walk," he says finally. "A body might walk clear out of the Tombs on a night like this, come back when things are a little more settled down."

We all just look at him.

"Got my boy waiting on me," he says. "Going for that walk. You all take care of yourselves now."

We never saw the boy, standing there in the shadows, waiting on his pa, except maybe Jolene. There's not much she misses. I wait until the shadows almost swallow the brother before I call after him.

"Appreciate the caution," I tell him.

He looks back, tips a finger to his brow, then he's gone, part of the shadows again.

"Are we looking for trouble?" Bear asks.

"Uh-huh," Jolene pipes up, but I shake my head.

"Like he said," I tell them, jerking a thumb to where the brother walked away.

Bear leads the way out, heading east, taking a direct route and avoiding the fires we can see springing up all around us now. The dark doesn't bother us, we can see pretty much the same, doesn't matter if it's night or day. We follow Bear up a hillside of rubble. He gets to the top before us and starts dancing around, stamping his feet, singing, "Wa-hey, look at me. I'm the king of the mountain."

And then he disappears between one stamp and the next, and that's how we find the room.

5

I don't know why we slide down to where Bear's standing instead of him climbing back up. Curious, I guess. Smelling spirit mischief and we just have to see where it leads us, down, down, till we're standing on a dark street, way underground.

"Old City," Alberta says.

"Walked right out of the Tombs we did," Jolene says, then she shoots Bear a look and giggles. "Or maybe slid right out of it on our asses'd be a better way to put it."

Bear gives her a friendly whack on the back of the head but it doesn't budge a hair. Jolene's not looking like much this year, standing about halfway to nothing, but she's always solidly built, doesn't much matter what skin she's wearing.

"Let's take that walk," I say, but Bear catches hold of my arm.

"I smell something old," he tells me.

"It's an old place," I tell him. "Fell down here a long time ago and stood above ground even longer."

Bear shakes his head. "No. I'm smelling something older than that. And lower down."

We're on an underground street, I'm thinking. Way down. Can't get much lower than this. But Bear's looking back at the building we just came out of and I know what's on his mind. Basements. They're too much like caves for him to pass one by, especially when it's got an old smell. I look at the others. Jolene's game, but then she's always game when she's wearing this skin. Alberta shrugs.

"When I want to dance," she says, "you all dance with me, so I'm going to say no when Bear wants to try out a new step?"

I can't remember the last time we all danced, but I can't find any argument with what she's saying.

"What about you, Crazy Crow?" Bear asks.

"You know me," I tell him. "I'm like Jolene, I'm always game."

So we go back inside, following Bear who's following his nose, and he leads us right up to the door of that empty stone room down in the cellar. He grabs hold of the iron bolt, shoves it to one side, hauls the door open, rubs his hand on his jeans to brush off the specks of rust that got caught up on his palm.

"Something tried hard to get out," Alberta says.

I'm thinking of the other side of the door. "And in," I add.

Jolene's spinning around in the middle of the room, arms spread wide. "Old, old, old," she sings.

We can all smell it now. I get the feeling that the building grew out of this room, that it was built to hold it. Or hide it.

"No ghosts," Bear says. "No spirits here."

Jolene stops spinning. "Just us," she says.

"Just us," Bear agrees.

He sits down on the clean stone floor, cross-legged, rolls himself a smoke. We all join him, sitting in a circle, like we're dancing, except it's only our breathing that's making the steps. We each take a drag of the cigarette, then Bear sets the butt down in the middle of the circle. We watch the smoke curl up from it, tobacco with that pinch of sweetgrass. It makes a long curling journey up to the ceiling, thickens there like a small storm cloud, pregnant with grandfather thunders.

Somewhere up above us, where the moon can see it, there's smoke rising, too, Devil's Night fires filling the hollow of the sky with pillars of silent thunder.

Bear takes a shotgun cartridge out of his pocket, brass and red cardboard, twelve-gauge, and puts it down on the stone beside the smoldering butt, stands it on end, brass side down.

"Guess we need a story," he says. He looks at me. "So we can understand this place."

We all nod. We'll take turns, talking until one of us gets it right.

"Me first," Jolene says.

She picks up the cartridge and rolls it back and forth on that small dark palm of hers and we listen.

6

Jolene says:

It's like that pan-girl, always cooking something up, you know the one. You can smell the wild onion on her breath a mile away. She's got that box that she can't look in, tin box with a lock on it that rattles against the side of the box when she gives it a shake, trying to guess what's inside. There's all these scratches on the tin, inside and out, something trying to get out, something trying to get in.

That's this place, the pan-girl's box. You know she opened that box, let all that stuff out that makes the world more interesting. She can't get it back in, and I'm thinking why try?

Anyway, she throws that box away. It's a hollow now, a hollow place, can be any size you want it to be, any shape, any color, same box. Now we're sitting in it, stone version. Close that door and maybe we can't get out. Got to wait until another pan-girl comes along, takes a break from all that cooking, takes a peek at what's inside. That big eye of hers'll fill the door and ya-hey, here we'll be, looking right back at her, rushing past her, she's swatting her hands at us trying to keep us in, but we're already gone, gone running back out into the world to make everything a little more interesting again.

7

Bear says:

Stone. You can't get much older than stone. First house was stone. Not like this room, not perfectly square, not flat, but stone all the same. Found places, those caves, just like we found this place. Old smell in them. Sometimes bear. Sometimes lion. Sometimes snake. Sometimes the ones that went before.

All gone when we come. All that's left is their messages painted or scratched on the walls. Stories. Information. Things they know we have to figure out, things that they could have told us if they were still around. Only way to tell us now is to leave the messages.

This place is a hollow, like Jolene said, but not why she said it. It's hollow because there's no messages. This is the place we have to leave our messages so that when we go on we'll know that the ones to follow will be able to figure things out.

8

Alberta says:

Inside and out, same thing. The wheel doesn't change, only the way we see it. Door opens either way. Both sides in, both sides out. Trouble is, we're always on the wrong side, always want the thing we haven't got, makes no difference who we are. Restless spirits want life, living people look for something better to come. Nobody *here*. Nobody content with what they got. And the reason for that's to keep the wheel turning. That simple. Wheel stops turning, there's nothing left.

It's like the woman who feels the cage of her bones, those ribs they're a prison for her. She's clawing, clawing at those bone bars, making herself sick. Inside, where you can't see it, but outside, too.

So she goes to see the Lady of the White Deer—looks just like you, Jolene, the way you were last year. Big woman. Big as a tree. Got dark, dark eyes you could get lost in. But she's smiling, always smiling. Smiling as she listens, smiling when she speaks. Like a mother smiles, seen it all, heard it all, but still patient, still kind, still understanding.

"That's just living," she tells the caged woman. "Those aren't bars, they're the bones that hold you together. You keep clawing at them, you'll make yourself so sick you're going to die for sure."

"I can't breathe in here," the caged woman says.

"You're not paying attention," the Lady of the White Deer says. "All you're doing is breathing. Stop breathing and you'll be clawing at those same bones, trying to get back in."

"You don't understand," the caged woman tells her and she walks away.

So she goes to see the Old Man of the Mountains—looks just like you, Bear. Same face, same hair. A big old bear, sitting up there on the top of the mountain, looking out at everything below. Doesn't smile so much, but understands how everybody's got a secret dark place sits way deep down there inside, hidden but wanting to get out. Understands how you can be happy but not happy at the same time. Understands that sometimes you feel you got to go all the way out to get back in, but if you do, you can't. There's no way back in.

So not smiling so much, but maybe understanding a little more, he lets the woman talk and he listens.

"We all got a place inside us, feels like a prison," he tells her. "It's darker in some people than others, that's all. Thing is, you got to balance what's there with what's around you or you'll find yourself on a road that's got no end. Got no beginning and goes nowhere. It's just always this same thing, never grows, never changes, only gets darker and darker, like that candle blowing in the wind. Looks real nice till the wind blows it out—you hear what I'm saying?"

"I can't breathe in here," the woman tells him.

That Old Man of the Mountain he shakes his head. "You're breathing," he says. "You're just not paying attention to it. You're looking inside, looking inside, forgetting what's outside. You're making friends with that darkness inside you and that's not good. You better stop your scratching and clawing or you're going to let it out."

"You don't understand either," the caged woman says and she walks away.

So finally she goes to see the Old Man of the Desert—looks like you, Crazy Crow. Got the same sharp features, the same laughing eyes. Likes to collect things. Keeps a pocket full of shiny mementos that used to belong to other people, things they threw away. Holds onto them until they want them back and then makes a trade. He'd give them away, but he knows what everybody thinks: All you get for nothing is nothing. Got to put a price on a thing to give it any worth.

He doesn't smile at all when he sees her coming. He puts his hand in his pocket and plays with something while she talks. Doesn't say anything when she's done, just sits there, looking at her.

"Aren't you going to help me?" she asks.

"You don't want my help," the Old Man of the Desert says. "You just want me to agree with you. You just want me to say, aw, that's bad, really bad. You've got it bad. Everybody else in the world is doing fine, except for you, because you got it so hard and bad."

The caged woman looks at him. She's got tears starting in her eyes.

"Why are you being so mean to me?" she asks.

"The truth only sounds mean," he tells her. "You look at it from another side and maybe you see it as kindness. All depends where you're looking, what you want to see."

"But I can't breathe," she says.

"You're breathing just fine," he says right back at her. "The thing is, you're not thinking so good. Got clouds in your head. Makes it hard to see straight. Makes it hard to hear what you don't want to hear anyway. Makes it hard to accept that the rest of the world's not out of step on the wheel, only you are. Work on that and you'll start feeling a little better. Remember who you are instead of always crying after what you think you want to be."

"You don't understand either," she says.

But before she can walk away, the Old Man of the Desert takes that thing out of his pocket, that thing he's been playing with, and she sees it's her dancing. He's got it all rolled up in a ball of beads and cowrie shells and feathers and mud, wrapped around with a rope of braided sweet-grass. Her dancing. Been a long time since she's seen that dancing. She thought it was lost in the long-ago. Thought it disappeared with her breathing.

"Where'd you get that dancing?" she asks.

"Found it in the trash. You'd be amazed what people will throw out— every kind of piece of themselves."

She puts her hand out to take it, but the Old Man of the Desert shakes his head and holds it out of her reach.

"That's mine," she says. "I lost that in the long-ago."

"You never lost it," the Old Man of the Desert tells her. "You threw it away."

"But I want it back now."

"You got to trade for it," he says.

The caged woman lowers her head. "I got nothing to trade for it."

"Give me your prison," the Old Man of the Desert says.

She looks up at him. "Now you're making fun of me," she says. "I give you my prison, I'm going to die. Dancing's not much use to the dead."

"Depends," he says. "Dancing can honor the dead. Lets them breathe in the faraway. Puts a fire in their cold chests. Warms their bone prisons for a time."

"What are you saying?" the caged woman asks. "I give you my life and you'll dance for me?"

The Old Man of the Desert smiles and that smile scares her because it's not kind or understanding. It's sharp and cuts deep. It cuts like a knife, slips in through the skin, slips past the ribs of her bone prison.

"What you got caging you is the idea of a prison," he says. "That's what I want from you."

"You want some kind of . . . story?"

He shakes his head. "I'm not in a bartering mood—not about this kind of thing."

"I don't know how to give you my prison," she says. "I don't know if I can."

"All you got to do is say yes," he tells her.

She looks at that dancing in his hand and it's all she wants now. There's little sparks coming off it, the smell of smudge-sticks and licorice and gasoline. There's a warmth burning in it that she knows will drive the cold away. That cold. She's been holding that cold for so long she doesn't hardly remember what it feels like to be warm anymore.

She's looking, she's reaching. She says yes and the Old Man of the Desert gives her back her dancing. And it's warm and familiar, lying there in her hand, but she doesn't feel any different. She doesn't know what to do with it, now she's got it. She wants to ask him what to do, but he's not paying attention to her anymore.

What's he doing? He's picking up dirt and he's spitting on it, spitting and spitting and working the dirt until it's like clay. And he makes a box out of it and in one side of the box he puts a door. And he digs a hole in the dirt and he puts the box in it. And he covers it up again. And then he looks at her. "One day you're going to find yourself in that box again," he says, "but this time you'll remember and you won't get locked up again."

She doesn't understand what he's talking about, doesn't care. She's got other things on her mind. She holds up her dancing, holds it in the air between them.

"I don't know what to do with this," she says. "I don't know how to make it work."

The Old Man of the Desert stands up. He gives her a hand up. He takes the dancing from her and throws it on the ground, throws it hard, throws it so hard it breaks. He starts shuffling his feet, keeping time with a clicking sound in the back of his throat. The dust rises up from the ground and she breathes it in and then she remembers what it was like and who she was and why she danced.

It was to honor the bone prison that holds her breathing for this turn of the wheel. It was to honor the gift of the world underfoot. It was to celebrate what's always changing: the stories. The dance of our lives. The wheel of the world and the sky spinning above it and our place in it.

The bones of her prison weren't there to keep her from getting out. They were there to keep her together.

9

I'm holding the cartridge now, but there's no need for me to speak. The story's done. Somewhere up above us, the skies over the Tombs are still full of smoke, the Devil's Night fires are still burning. Here in the hollow of this stone room, we've got a fire of our own.

Alberta looks across the circle at me.

"I remember," she says.

"That was the first time we met," Jolene says. "I remember, too. Not the end, but the beginning. I was there at the beginning and then later, too. For the dancing."

Bear nods. He takes the cartridge from my fingers and puts it back into his pocket. Out of another pocket he takes packets of color, ground pigments. Red and yellow and blue. Black and white. He puts them on the floor, takes a pinch of color out of one of the packets and lays it in the palm of his hand. Spits into his palm. Dips a finger in. He gets up, that

Old Man of the Mountain, and he crosses over to one of the walls. Starts to painting. Starts to leave a message for the ones to follow.

Those colors, they're like dancing. Once someone starts, you can't help but twitch and turn and fidget until you're doing it, too. Next thing you know, we're all spitting into our palms, we're all dancing the color across the walls.

Remembering.

Because that's what the stories are for.

Even for old spirits like us.

We lock ourselves up in bone prisons same as everybody else. Forget who we are, why we are, where we're going. Till one day we come across a story we left for ourselves and remember why we're wearing these skins. Remember why we're dancing.

The Invisibles

What is unseen is not necessarily unknown.
                                        —*Wendelessen*

1

When I was twelve years old, it was a different world.

I suppose most people think that, turning their gazes inward to old times, the long trail of their memories leading them back into territory made unfamiliar with the dust of years. The dust lies so thick in places it changes the shape of what it covers, half-remembered people, places and events, all mixed together so that you get confused trying to sort them out, don't even recognize some, probably glad you can't make out others. But then there are places, the wind blows harder across their shapes, or maybe we visit them more often so the dust doesn't lie so thick, and the memories sit there waiting for us, no different now than the day they happened, good and bad, momentous occasions and those so trivial you can't figure out why you remember them.

But I know this is true: When I was twelve years old, kids my age didn't know as much as they do today. We believed things you couldn't get by most eight year olds now. We were ready to believe almost anything. All we required was that it be true—maybe not so much by the rules of the world around us, but at least by the rules of some intuitive inner logic. It wasn't ever anything that got talked out. We just believed. In

luck. In wishes. In how a thing will happen, if you stick to the right parade of circumstances.

We were willing to believe in magic.

Here's what you do, Jerry says. You get one of those little pipe tobacco
tins and you put stuff in it. Important stuff. A fingernail. Some hair. A
scab. Some dirt from a special place. You spit on it and mix it up like a
mud pie. Prick your finger and add a drop of blood. Then you wrap it all
up in a picture of the thing you like the best.

What if you don't have a picture of the thing you like the best? I ask.

Doesn't have to be a real picture, he says. You can just make a drawing
of it. Might be even better that way because then it really belongs
to you.

So what do you do with it? Rebecca asks.

I can see her so clearly, the red hairs coming loose from her braids,
picking at her knee where she scraped it falling off her bike.

You stick it in that tin, Jerry says, and close it up tight. Dig a hole under your porch and bury it deep.

He leans closer to us, eyes serious, has that look he always gets when
he's telling us something we might not believe is true, but he wants us to
know that it is.

This means something, he says. You do it right and you'll always have
that thing you like the best. Nothing will ever take it away.

I don't know where he heard about it. Read it in a book, or maybe his
grandmother told him. She always had the best stories. It doesn't matter.
We knew it was a true magic and that night each of us snuck out of our
house and did it. Buried those tins deep. Made a secret of it to make the
magic stronger is how Jerry put it.

I didn't need the magic to be any stronger. I just needed it to be true.
We were best friends, the three of us, and I didn't want that to ever
change. I really believed in magic, and the idea of the tin seemed to be
about the best magic kids like us could make.

Rebecca moved away when we were in ninth grade. Jerry died the last
year of high school, hit by a drunk driver.

Years later, this all came back to me. I'd returned to have a look at the
old neighborhood, but our houses were gone by then. Those acre lots we
grew up on had been subdivided, the roads all turned around on themselves and changed until there was nothing left of the neighborhood's old

patterns. They're identical, these new houses, poured out of the same mold, one after the other, row upon row, street after street.

I got out of the car that day and stood where I thought my house used to be, feeling lost, cut off, no longer connected to my own past. I thought of those tins then and wondered whatever had happened to them. I remembered the drawing I made to put in mine. It was so poorly drawn I'd had to write our names under our faces to make sure the magic knew who I meant.

The weird thing is I never felt betrayed by the magic when Rebecca moved away, or when Jerry died. I just . . . lost it. Forgot about it. It went away, or maybe I did. Even that day, standing there in a neighborhood now occupied by strangers, the memory of those tins was only bittersweet. I smiled, remembering what we'd done, sneaking out so late that night, how we'd believed. The tightness in my chest grew from good moments recalled, mixed up with the sadness of remembering friends I'd lost. Of course those tins couldn't have kept us together. Life goes on. People move, relationships alter, people die. That's how the world turns.

There isn't room for magic in it, though you'd never convince Ted of that.

2

Ted and I go back a long way. We met during my first year in college, almost twenty years ago, and we still see each other every second day or so. I don't know why we get along so well unless that old axiom's true and opposites do attract. Ted's about the most outgoing person you could meet; opinionated, I'll be the first to admit, but he also knows how to listen. He's the sort of person other people naturally gravitate to at a party, collecting odd facts and odder rumors the way a magpie does shiny baubles, then jump-starting conversations with them at a later date as though they were hors d'oeuvre.

I'm not nearly so social an animal. If you pressed me, I'd say I like to pick and choose my friends carefully; the truth is, I usually have no idea what to say to people—especially when I first meet them.

Tonight it's only the two of us, holding court in The Half Kaffe. I'm drinking espresso, Ted's got one of those decaf lattés made with skim milk that always has me wonder, what's the point? If you want to drink coffee that weak, you can find it down the street at Bruno's Diner for a quarter of the price. But Ted's gone health-conscious recently. It's all talk about decaf and jogging and macrobiotic this and holistic that, then he lights up a cigarette. Go figure.

"Who's that woman?" I ask when he runs out of things to say about this *T'ai Chi* course he's just started taking. "The one at the other end of the counter with the long straight hair and the sad eyes?"

I haven't been able to stop looking at her since we got here. I find her attractive, but not in a way I can easily explain. It's more the sum of the parts, because individually things are a little askew. She's tall and angular, eyes almost too wide-set, chin pointed like a cat's, a Picasso nose, very straight and angled down. She has the sort of features that look gorgeous one moment, then almost homely the next. Her posture's not great, but then, considering my own, I don't think I should be making that kind of judgment. Maybe she thinks like I do, that if you slouch a bit, people won't notice you. Doesn't usually work.

I suspect she's waiting for someone since all she's been doing is sitting there, looking out the window. Hasn't ordered anything yet. Or maybe it's because Jonathan's too caught up with the most recent issue of the *Utne Reader* to notice her.

I look away from her when I realize that Ted hasn't answered. I find him giving me a strange look.

"So what've you got in that cup besides coffee?" he asks.

"What's that supposed to mean?"

He laughs. "I'm not sure. All I know is I don't see anyone sitting at this counter, male or female. I see you and me and Jonathan."

I'm sure he's putting me on. "No, seriously. Who is she?"

And he, I realize, thinks I'm putting him on. He makes an exaggerated show of having a look, taking off non-existent glasses, cleaning them, putting them back on, looks some more, but his attention isn't even on the right stool.

"Okay," he says. "I see her now. I think . . . yes, she's a princess. Lost a shoe, or a half-dozen feet of hair, or a bag of beans or something. Or maybe turned the wrong key in the wrong lock and got turned out of her bearded husband's apartment and now she's here killing time between periods of sleep just like the rest of us."

"Enough," I tell him. "I get the picture."

He doesn't see her. And it's beginning to be obvious to me that Jonathan doesn't see her or he'd have taken her order by now. The group at the table behind us, all black jeans and intense conversation, they probably don't either.

"So what's this all about?" Ted asks.

He looks half amused, half intrigued, still unsure if it's a joke or something more intriguing, a piece of normal that's slid off to one side. He has a nose for that sort of thing, from Elvis sightings to nuns impregnated by aliens, and I can almost see it twitching. He doesn't read the tabloids in line at the supermarket, he buys them. Need I say more?

So when he asks me what it's all about, he seems the perfect candidate for me to tell because it's very confusing and way out of my line of experience. I've never been prone to hallucinations before and besides, I always thought they'd be more . . . well, surreal, I suppose. Dadaistic. Over the top. This is so ordinary. Just a woman, sitting in a coffee bar, that no one seems to be able to see. Except for me.

"Hello, Andrew," Ted says, holding the first syllable of my name and drawing it out. "You still with us?"

I nod and give him a smile.

"So are you going to fill me in or what?"

"It's nothing," I say. "I was just seeing if you were paying attention."

"Um-hmm."

He doesn't believe me for a moment. All I've managed to do is pique his curiosity more.

"No, really," I tell him.

The woman stands up from the counter, distracting me. I wonder why she came in here in the first place since she can't seem to place an order, but then I think maybe even invisible people need to get out, enjoy a little nightlife, if only vicariously.

Or maybe she's a ghost.

"Did anybody ever die in here?" I ask Ted.

Ted gives me yet another strange look. He leans across the table.

"You're getting seriously weird on me," he says. "What do you want to know that for?"

The woman's on her way to the door now. Portishead is playing on the café's sound system. "Sour Times." Lalo Schifrin and Smokey Brooks samples on a bed of scratchy vinyl sounds and a smoldering, low-key Eurobeat. Beth Gibbons singing about how nobody loves her. At one time we both worked at Gypsy Records and we're still serious music junkies.

It's one of the reasons we like The Half Kaffe so much; Jonathan has impeccable taste.

I pull a ten from my pocket and drop it on the table.

"I'll tell you later," I say as I get up from my stool.

"Andrew," Ted says. "You can't just leave me hanging like this."

"Later."

She's out the door, turning left. Through the café's window, I watch her do a little shuffle to one side as a couple almost walk right into her. They can't see her either. "Sour Times" dissolves into an instrumental, mostly keyboards and a lonesome electric guitar. Ted calls after me. He's starting to get up, too, but I wave him back. Then I'm out the door, jogging after the woman. "Excuse me!" I call after her. "Excuse me, miss!"

I can't believe I'm doing this. I have no idea what I'll say to her if she stops. But she doesn't turn. Gives no indication she's heard me. I catch up to her and touch her lightly on the elbow. I know a moment of surprise when I can feel the fabric of her sleeve instead of some cool mist. I half expected my fingers to go right through her.

"Excuse me," I say again.

She stops then and looks at me. Up close, her face, those sad eyes . . . they make my pulse quicken until my heartbeat sounds like a deep bass drum playing a march at double-time in my chest.

"Yes?"

"I . . ."

There's no surprise in her features. She doesn't ask how come I can see her and nobody else can. What I do see is a hint of fear in her eyes which shouldn't surprise me. A woman alone on the streets always has to be on her guard. I take a step back to ease the fear, feeling guilty and depressed for having put it there.

"I . . ."

There are a hundred things I want to ask her. About how she did what she did in The Half Kaffe. How come I can see her when other people can't. Why she's not surprised that I can see her. I'd even ask her out for a drink if I had the nerve. But nothing seems appropriate to the moment. Nothing makes sense.

I clear my throat and settle on: "Can you tell me how to get to Battersfield Road?"

The fear recedes in her eyes, but a wariness remains.

"Take a left at the next light," she tells me, "and just go straight. You can't miss it."

"Thanks."

I watch her continue on her way. Two women approach her from the other direction, moving aside to give her room when she comes abreast. So does what appears to be a businessman, suit and tie, briefcase in hand, working late, hurrying home. But the couple behind him don't see her at all; she has to dart to one side, press up against a store window so that they don't collide.

She's invisible again.

I follow her progress all the way to the end of the block as she weaves in and out of near collisions with the other pedestrians. Then she's at the crosswalk, a tall, slouching figure waiting for the light to change. She takes a right where she told me to take a left, and a storefront cuts her from my view.

I almost return to The Half Kaffe, but I don't feel up to being grilled by Ted. I almost go home, but what am I going to do at home on a Friday night? Instead, I run to the corner where she turned, cross against the light and almost get hit by a cab. The driver salutes me with one stiff finger and shouts something unintelligible at me, but I'm already past him, on the far curb now. I see her ahead of me, almost at the end of the block, and I do something I've never done before in my life. I follow a woman I don't know home.

3

The building she finally enters is one of those Crowsea brownstones that hasn't been renovated into condos yet—five stories, arches of tapered bricks over the windows, multi-gabled roof. There'd be at least twenty apartments in the place, crammed up against the other, shoulder to shoulder like commuters jostling in the subway. She could be living in any one of them. She could just be visiting a friend. She uses a key on the front door, but it could belong to anybody.

I know this. Just as I know she's not about to come walking out again. As I know she'd be able to see me if her window's facing this way and she looks out. But I can't help myself. I stand there on the street, looking at the face of the building as if it's the most interesting thing I've ever seen.

"She'll never tell you," a voice says from behind me, a kid's voice.

Here's what it's like, living in the city. The kid can't be more than twelve or thirteen. He's half my size, a scruffy little fellow in baggy jeans, hooded sweatshirt, air-pumped basketball shoes that have seen way better days. His hair is black, short and greasy, face looks as if it hasn't been washed in weeks, half-moons of dark shadow under darker eyes. I look at him and what do I do? Make sure he's alone. Try to figure out if he's carrying a gun or a knife. He's just a kid, and I'm checking out what possible threat he could pose.

I decide he's harmless, or at least means me no harm. He looks amused at the way I've been eyeing him, cocks his head. I look a little closer. There's something familiar about him, but I can't place it. Just the features, not the dirty hair, the grubby skin, the raggedy clothes.

"Who won't tell me what?" I finally ask.

"The invisible. She won't be able to tell you how it works. Half of them don't even know they go invisible. They just figure people treat them that way because that's all they're worth. Seriously low self-esteem."

I shake my head and can't stop the smile that comes. "So what are you? A psychiatrist?"

He looks back at me with a steadiness and maturity far belying his years and his appearance. There's a bead of liquid glistening under one nostril. He's a slight, almost frail figure, swamped in clothes that make him seem even smaller. But he carries himself with an assurance that makes me feel inadequate.

"No," he says. "Just someone who's learned to stay visible."

I'd laugh, but there's nothing to laugh about. I saw the woman in the café. I followed her home. If there's a conspiracy at work here, the number of people involved has to be immense and that doesn't make sense. No one would go through so much trouble over me—what would be the point? It's easier to believe she was invisible.

"So how come I could see her?" I ask.

The boy shrugs. "Maybe you're closer to her than you think."

I don't have to ask him what he means. Self-esteem's never been one of my strong suits.

"Or maybe it's because you believe," he adds.

"Believe in what?"

"Magic."

He says the word and I can see three small tobacco tins, the children burying them in the dirt under their porches. But I shake my head.

"Maybe I did once," I say. "But I grew out of it. There's nothing magic here. There's simply a . . . a phenomenon that hasn't been explained."

The boy grins and I lose all sense of his age. It's as if I've strayed into folklore, a fairy tale, tapped an innocent on the shoulder and come face to face with fanged nightmare. I feel I should turn my coat inside out or I'll never find my way back to familiar ground.

"Then explain this," the boy says around that feral grin.

He doesn't turn invisible. That'd be too easy, I guess. Instead it's like a sudden wind comes up, a dust devil, spinning the debris up from the street, candy wrappers, newspapers, things I can't identify. That vague sense of familiarity that's been nagging at me vanishes. There's nothing familiar about this. He's silhouetted against the swirling litter, then his shape loses definition. For one moment I see his dark eyes and that grin in the middle of a shape that vaguely resembles his, then the dust devil moves, comes part, and all that's left is a trail of debris leading up the sidewalk, away from me.

I stare down at the litter, my gaze slowly drifting toward the invisible woman's building. Explain this?

"I can't," I say aloud, but there's no one there to hear me.

4

I return to my studio, but I'm too restless to sleep, can't concentrate enough to work. I stand in front of the painting on my easel and try to make sense out of what I'm seeing. I can't make sense of the image it once depicted. The colors and values don't seem to relate to each other any more, the hard edges have all gone soft, there's no definition between the background and the foreground.

I work in watercolor, a highly detailed and realistic style that has me laboring on the same piece for weeks before I'm done. This painting started the same as they always do for me, with a buzz, a wild hum in my head that flares down my arms into my fingertips. My first washes go down fast, the bones of light and color building from abstract glazes until the forms appear and, as Sickert said, the painting begins to "talk back" to me. Everything slows down on me then because the orchestration of value and detail I demand of my medium takes time.

This one was almost completed, a cityscape, a south view of the Kick-aha River as seen from the Kelly Street Bridge, derelict warehouses running down to the water on one side, the lawns of Butler U. on the other. Tonight I can't differentiate between the river and the lawn, the edge of the bridge's railing and the warehouses beyond it. The image that's supposed to be on the paper is like the woman I followed earlier. It's taken on a kind of invisibility of its own. I stare at it for a long time, know that if I stay here in front of it, I'll try to fix it. Know as well that tonight that's the last thing I should be doing.

So I close the door on it, walk down the stairs from my studio to the street. It's only a few blocks to The Half Kaffe and still early for a Friday night, but when I get there, Ted's already gone home. Jonathan's behind the counter, but then Jonathan is always behind the counter. The servers he has working for him come and go, changing their shifts, changing their jobs, but Jonathan's always in his place, viewing the world by what he can see from his limited vantage point and through an endless supply of magazines.

He's flipping through the glossy pages of a British pop magazine when I come in. Miles Davis is on the sound system, a cut from his classic *Kind of Blue*, Evans's piano sounding almost Debussian, Davis's trumpet and Coltrane's tenor contrasting sharply with each other. I order an espresso from Jonathan and take it to the counter by the front window. The night goes about its business on the other side of the pane. I study the passers-by, wondering if any of them are invisibles, people only I can see, wonder if there are men and women walking by that I don't, that are invisible to me.

5

I find Ted at Bruno's Diner the next morning, having his usual breakfast of late. Granola with two-percent milk and freshly-squeezed orange juice. All around him are people digging into plates of eggs and bacon, eggs and sausages, western omelets, home fries on the side, toast slathered with butter. But he's happy. There's no esoteric music playing at Bruno's, just a golden oldies station issuing tinnily from a small portable radio behind the counter. The smell of toast and bacon makes my stomach rumble.

"So what happened to you last night?" Ted asks when I slide into his booth.

"Do you believe in magic?" I ask.

Ted pauses with a spoonful of granola halfway to his mouth. "What, like Houdini?" He puts down the spoon and smiles. "Man, I loved that stuff when I was a kid. I wanted to be a magician when I grew up more than just about anything."

He manages to distract me. Of all the things I can imagine Ted doing, stage magic isn't one of them.

"So what happened?" I ask.

"I found out how hard it is. And besides, you need dexterity and you know me, I'm the world's biggest klutz."

"But that stuff's all fake," I say. Time to get back on track. "I'm talking about real magic."

"Who says it's not real?"

"Come on. Everybody knows it's done with mirrors and smoke. They're illusions."

Ted's not ready to agree. "But that's a kind of magic on its own, wouldn't you say?"

I shake my head. "I'm talking about the real stuff."

"Give me a for instance."

I don't want to lose my momentum again—it's hard enough for me to talk about this in the first place. I just want an answer to the question.

"I know you read all those tabloids," I say, "and you always let on like you believe the things they print. I want to know if you really do. Believe in them."

"Maybe we should backtrack a bit here," he says.

So I explain. I don't know which is weirder—the story I tell him, or the fact that he takes me seriously when I tell it.

"Okay," he says. "To start with, all that stuff about Elvis and bigfoot and the like—it's not what I'd call magic. It's entertainment. It might be true and it might not. I don't know. It doesn't even matter. But magic . . ."

His voice trails off and he gets a kind of dreamy look on his face.

"There's a true sense of mystery with magic," he says. "Like you're having a meaningful dialogue with something bigger than you—bigger than anything you can imagine. The tabloids are more like gossip. Something like what's happened to you—that's the real thing. It reaches into what we've all agreed are the workings of the world and stirs them around a little, makes a person sit up and pay attention. Not simply to the experience itself, but to everything around them. That's why the great stage illusions—I don't care if it's a floating woman or someone walking through the Great Wall of China—when they're done properly, you come away questioning everything. Your eyes are opened to all sorts of possibilities."

He smiles then. "Of course, usually it doesn't last. Most people go right back to the reality we've all agreed on. Me, I think it's kind of sad. I *like* the idea that there's more to the world than I can see or understand and I don't want to ever forget it."

What he's saying reminds me of the feeling I got after I first started to do art. Up until then I'd been the perennial computer nerd, spending all my time in front of a screen because that way I didn't have to take part in any more than the minimum amount of social interaction to get by. Then one day, in my second year at Butler, I was short one course and for no reason that's made sense before or since, decided to take life drawing, realized I had an aptitude for it, realized I loved it more than anything I'd ever tried before.

After that, I never looked at anything the same again. I watched light, saw everything through an imaginary frame. Clouds didn't just mean a storm was coming; they were an ever-changing picture of the sky, a panorama of movement and light that affected everything around them—the landscape, the people in it. I learned to pay attention and realized that once you do, anything you look at is interesting. Everything has its own glow, its own place in the world that's related to everything else around it. I looked into the connectedness of it all and nothing was the same for me again. I got better at a lot of things. Meeting people. Art. General life skills. Not perfect, but better.

"Have you ever heard of these invisibles?" I ask Ted.

"That's what the practitioners of *voudoun* call their deities. *Les Invisibles.*"

I shake my head. "This kid wasn't speaking French. It wasn't like he was talking about that kind of thing at all. He was referring to ordinary people that go invisible because they just aren't *here* enough anymore." I stop and look across the table at Ted. "Christ, what am I saying? None of this is possible."

Ted nods. "It's easier to pretend it didn't happen."

"What's that supposed to mean?"

But I know exactly what he's talking about. You can either trust your senses and accept that there's more to the world than what you can see, or you can play ostrich. I don't know what to do.

"You had anything to eat yet?" Ted asks.

"Not since last night."

I let him order me breakfast, don't even complain when it's the same as his own.

"See, the thing is," he tells me while we're waiting for my cereal to arrive, "is that you're at the epicenter where two worlds are colliding."

"So now it's an earthquake."

He smiles. "But it's taking place on an interior landscape."

"I saw that woman last night—other people couldn't. That kid turned into a heap of litter right in front of my eyes. It happened here, Ted. In what's supposed to be the real world. Not in my head."

"I know. The quake hit you here, but the aftershocks are running through your soul."

I'd argue with him, except that's exactly how it feels.

"Why do you think that kid talked to me?" I ask.

I don't expect Ted to know, but it's part of what's been bothering me. Why'd he pick me to approach?

"I don't know," Ted says. "Next time you see him you should ask him."

"I don't think I want there to be a next time."

"You might not get a choice."

6

Maybe I could pretend to Ted that I didn't want any further involvement with invisible people and kids that turn into litter, but I couldn't lie to myself. I went looking for the boy, for the invisible woman, for things and people out of the ordinary.

There was still a pretense involved. I didn't wander aimlessly, one more lost soul out on the streets, but took a sketchbook and a small painting box, spent my time working on value drawings and color studies, gathering material for future paintings. It's hard for me to work *en plein*. I keep wanting to fuss and fiddle too much, getting lost in detail until the light changes and then I have to come back another day to get the values right.

A lot of those sketching sessions were spent outside the invisible woman's building, looking for her, expecting the boy to show up. I'd set up my stool, sit there flooding color onto the pages of my sketchbook, work in the detail, too much detail. I don't see the woman. Wind blows the litter around on the street but it doesn't rise up in the shape of a boy and talk to me.

I find myself thinking of fairy tales—not as stories, but as guideposts. Ted and I share a love of them, but for different reasons. He sees them as early versions of the tabloids, records kept of strange encounters, some real, some imagined, all of them entertaining. I think of them more metaphorically. All those dark forests and trials and trouble. They're the same things we go through in life. Maybe if more of us had the good heart of a Donkeyskin or the youngest son of three, the world would be a better place.

I'm thinking of this in front of the invisible woman's building on a blustery day. I've got the pages of my sketchbook clipped down, but the wind keeps flapping them anyway, making the paint puddle and run. Happy accidents, I've heard them called. Well, they're only happy when you can do something with them, when you don't work tight, every stroke counting. I'm just starting to clean up the latest of these so-called happy accidents when a ponytailed guy carrying a guitar walks right into me, knocking the sketchbook from my lap. I almost lose the paintbox as well.

"Jesus," he says. "I'm sorry. I didn't see you sitting there." He picks up my sketchbook and hands it over. "I hope I haven't totally ruined this."

"It's okay," I tell him. It's not, but what would be the point of being unpleasant?

"I'm really sorry."

I look down at the page I was working on. Now there's dirt smeared into the happy accident. Fixable it's not. My gaze lifts to meet his.

"Don't worry about it," I tell him. "It happens."

He nods, his relief plain. "I must've been dreaming," he says, "because I just didn't see you at all." He hesitates. "If you're sure it's okay . . ."

"I'm sure."

I watch him leave, think about what he said.

I just didn't see you.

So now what? I've become invisible, too? Then I remember the kid, something he said when I asked why I could see the invisible woman and others couldn't.

Maybe you're closer to her than you think.

Invisible. It comes to me, then. The world's full of invisible people and our not seeing them's got nothing to do with magic. The homeless.

Winos. Hookers. Junkies. And not only on the street. The housewife. The businessman's secretary. Visible only when they're needed for something. The man with AIDS. Famine victims. People displaced by wars or natural disasters. The list is endless, all these people we don't see because we don't want to see them. All these people we don't see because we're too busy paying attention to ourselves. I've felt it myself, my lack of self-confidence and how it translates into my behavior can have people look right through me. Standing in a store, waiting to be served. Sitting in the corner of a couch at a party and I might as well be a pillow.

The kid's face comes back to mind. I look down at my sketchbook, exchange the page smeared with happy accidents for a new one, draw the kid's features as I remember them. Now I know why he looked so familiar.

7

Ted opens his door on the first knock. He's just got off work and seems surprised to see me. I can smell herb tea steeping, cigarette smoke. Something classical is playing at low volume on the stereo. Piano. Chopin, I think. The preludes.

"Were we doing a movie or something tonight?" Ted asks.

I shake my head. "I was wondering if I could see that old photo album of yours again."

He studies me for a moment, then steps aside so that I can come in. His apartment's as cluttered as ever. You can't turn for fear of knocking over a stack of books, magazines, CDs, cassettes. Right by the door there's a box of newspapers and tabloids ready to go out for recycling. The one on top has a headline that shouts in bold caps: TEENAGER GIVES BIRTH TO FISH BOY!!

"You don't have to look at the album," he tells me. "I'll 'fess up."

Something changes in me when he says those words. I thought I knew him, like I thought I knew the world, but now they've both become alien territory. I stand in the center of the room, the furniture crouched around me like junkyard dogs. I have a disorienting static in my ears. I feel as though I'm standing on dangerous ground, stepped into the fairy tale, but Stephen King wrote it.

"How did you do it?" I ask.

Ted gives me a sheepish look. "How first? Not even why?"

I give the sofa a nervous look, but it's just a sofa. The vertigo is receding. My ears pop, as though I've dropped altitude, and I can hear the piano music coming from the speakers on either side of the room. I'm grounded again, but nothing seems the same. I sit down on the sofa, set my stool and sketching equipment on the floor between my feet.

"I don't know if I can handle why just yet," I tell him. "I have to know how you did it, how you made a picture of yourself come to life."

"Magic."

"Magic," I repeat. "That's it?"

"It's not enough?" He takes a seat in the well-worn armchair across from me, leans forward, hands on his knees. "Remember this morning, when I told you about wanting to be an illusionist?"

I nod.

"I lied. Well, it was partly a lie. I didn't give up stage magic, I just never got the nerve to go up on a stage and do it."

"So the kid . . . he was an illusion?"

Ted smiles. "Let's say you saw what I wanted you to see."

"Smoke and mirrors."

"Something like that."

"But . . ." I shake my head. He was right earlier. There's no point in asking for details. Right now, how's not as important as . . . "So why?" I ask.

He leans back in the chair. "The invisibles need a spokesperson—someone to remind the rest of the world that they exist. People like that woman you saw in The Half Kaffe last night. If enough people don't see her, she's simply going to fade away. She can't speak up for herself. If she could, she wouldn't be an invisible. And she's at the high end of the scale. There are people living on the streets that—"

"I know," I say, breaking in. "I was just thinking about them this afternoon. But their invisibility is a matter of perception, of people ignoring them. They're not literally invisible like the woman last night. There's nothing *magic* about them."

"You're still missing the point," Ted says "Magic's all about perception. Things are the way they are because we've agreed that's the way they are. An act of magic is when we're convinced we're experiencing something that doesn't fit into the conceptual reality we've all agreed on."

"So you're saying that magic is being tricked into thinking an illusion is real."

"Or seeing through the illusion, seeing something the way it really is for the first time."

I shake my head, not quite willing to concede the argument for all that it's making uncomfortable sense.

"Where does your being a spokesperson fit in?" I ask.

"Not me. You."

"Oh, come on."

But I can tell he's completely serious.

"People have to be reminded about the invisibles," he says, "or they'll vanish."

"Okay," I say. "For argument's sake, let's accept that as a given. I still don't see where I come into it."

"Who's going to listen to me?" Ted asks. "I try to talk about it, but I'm a booking agent. People'd rather just think I'm a little weird."

"And they're not going to think the same of me?"

"No," he says. "And I'll tell you why. It's the difference between art and argument. They're both used to get a point across but the artist sets up a situation and, if he's good enough, his audience understands his point on their own, through how they assimilate the information he's given them and the decisions they can then make based on that information. The argument is just someone telling you what you're supposed to think or feel."

"Show, don't tell," I say, repeating an old axiom appropriate to all the arts.

"Exactly. You've got the artistic chops and sensibility to show people, to let them see the invisibles through your art, which will make them see them out there." He waves a hand towards the window. "On the street. In their lives."

He's persuasive, I'll give him that.

"Last night in The Half Kaffe," I begin.

"I didn't see the woman you saw," Ted says. "I didn't see her until you stopped her down the street."

"And after? When she went invisible again?"

"I could still see her. You made me see her."

"That's something anybody could do," I tell him.

"But only if they can see the invisibles in the first place," he says. "And you can't be everywhere. Your paintings can. Reproductions of them can."

I give him a look that manages to be both tired and hold all my skepticism with what he's saying. "You want me to paint portraits of invisible people so that other people can see them."

"You're being deliberately obtuse now, aren't you? You know what I mean."

I nod. I do know exactly what he means.

"Why bring this all up now?" I ask him. "We've known each other for years."

"Because until you saw the invisible woman, you never would have believed me."

"How do I know she's not another illusion—like the boy made of litter that was wearing your twelve-year-old face?"

"You don't."

8

He's wrong about that. I do know. I know in that part of me that he was talking about this morning over breakfast, the part that had a meaningful dialogue with something bigger than me, the part that's willing to accept a momentary glimpse behind the curtain of reality as a valid experience. And I know why he sent the illusion of the boy after me, too. It's the same reason he didn't admit to any of this sooner, played the innocent when I came to him with my story of invisible people. It was to give me my own words to describe the experience. To make me think about the invisibles, to let me form my own opinions about what can be readily seen and what's hidden behind a veil of expectations. Showing, not telling. He's better than he thinks he is.

I stand in my studio, thinking about that. There's a board on my easel with a stretched full-sized piece of three-hundred-pound Arches hot-pressed paper on it. I squeeze pigments into the butcher's tray I use as a palette, pick up a brush. There's a light pencil sketch on the paper. It's a cityscape, a street scene. In one corner, there's a man, sleeping in a doorway, blanketed with newspapers. The buildings and street overwhelm him. He's a small figure, almost lost. But he's not invisible.

I hope to keep him that way.

I dip my brush into my water jar, build up a puddle in the middle of the tray. Yellow ochre and alizarin crimson. I'm starting with the features that can be seen between the knit woolen cap he's wearing and the edge of his newspaper blanket, the gnarled hand that grips the papers, holding them in place. I want him to glow before I add in the buildings, the street, the night that shrouds them.

As I work, I think of the tobacco tins that Rebecca, Jerry, and I buried under our porches all those years ago. Maybe magic doesn't always work. Maybe it's like life, things don't always come through for you. But being disappointed in something doesn't mean you should give up on it. It doesn't mean you should stop trying.

I think of the last thing Ted said to me before I left his apartment.

"It goes back to stage magicians," he told me. "What's so amazing about them isn't so much that they can make things disappear, as that they can bring them back."

I touch the first color to the paper and reach for a taste of that amazement.

Seven for a Secret

It's a mistake to have only one life.
—*Dennis Miller Bunker, 1890*

1

Later, he can't remember which came first, the music or the birds in the trees. He seems to become aware of them at the same time. They call up a piece of something he thinks he's forgotten; they dredge through his past, the tangle of memories growing as thick and riddling as a hedgerow, to remind him of an old story he heard once that began, "What follows is imagined, but it happened just so. . . ."

2

The trees are new growth, old before their time. Scrub, leaves more brown than green, half the limbs dead, the other half dying. They struggle for existence in what was once a parking lot, a straggling clot of vegetation fed for years by some runoff, now baking in the sun. Something diverted the water—another building fell down, supports torched by Devil's Night fires, or perhaps the city bulldozed a field of rubble, two or three blocks over, inadvertently creating a levee. It doesn't matter. The trees are dying now, the weeds and grass surrounding them already baked dry.

And they're full of birds. Crows, ravens . . . Jake can't tell the difference. Heavy-billed, black birds with wedge-shaped tails and shaggy ruffs at their throats. Their calls are hoarse, croaking *kraaacks*, interspersed with hollow, knocking sounds and a sweeter *klu-kluck*.

The fiddle plays a counterpoint to the uneven rhythm of their calls, an odd, not quite reasonable music that seems to lie somewhere between a slow dance tune and an air that manages to be at once mournful and jaunty. The fiddle, he sees later, is blue, not painted that color, rather the varnish lends the wood that hue so its grain appears to be viewed as though through water.

Black birds, blue fiddle.

He might consider them portents if he were given to looking for omens, but he lives in a world that is always exactly what it should be, no more and no less, and he has come here to forget, not foretell. He is a man who stands apart, always one step aside from the crowd, an island distanced from the archipelago, spirit individual as much as the flesh. But though we are all islands, separated from one another by indifferent seas that range as wide as we allow them to be, we still congregate. We are still social animals. And Jake is no different. He comes to where the fires burn in the oil drums, where the scent of cedar smudge sticks mingles with cigarette smoke and dust, the same as the rest of us.

The difference is, he watches. He watches, but rarely speaks. He rarely speaks, but he listens well.

"They say," the woman tells him, "that where ravens gather, a door to the Otherworld stands ajar."

He never heard her approach. He doesn't turn.

"You don't much like me, do you?" she says.

"I don't know you well enough to dislike you, but I don't like what you do."

"And what is it that you think I do?"

"Make-believe," he says. "Pretend."

"Is that what you call it?"

But he won't be drawn into an argument.

"Everybody sees things differently," she says. "That's the gift and curse of free will."

"So what do you hear?" he asks. His voice is a sarcastic drawl. "Fairy music?"

The city died here, in the Tombs. Not all at once, through some natural disaster, but piece by piece, block by block, falling into disrepair, buildings abandoned by citizens and then claimed by the squatters who've got no reason to take care of them. Some of them fall down, some burn.

It's the last place in the world to look for wonder.

"I hear a calling-on music," she says, "though whether it's calling us to cross over, or calling something to us, I can't tell."

He turns to look at her finally, with his hair the glossy black of the ravens, his eyes the blue of that fiddle neither of them has seen yet. He notes the horn that rises from the center of her brow, the equine features that make her face seem so long, the chestnut dreadlocks, the dark, wide-set eyes and the something in those eyes he can't read.

"Does it matter?" he asks.

"Everything matters on some level or other."

He smiles. "I think that depends on what story we happen to be in."

"Yours or mine," she says, her voice soft.

"I don't have a story," he tells her.

Now she smiles. "And mine has no end."

"Listen," he says.

Silence hangs in the air, a thick gauze dropped from the sky like a blanket, deep enough to cut. The black birds are silent. They sit motionless in the dying trees. The fiddler has taken the bow from the strings. The blue fiddle holds its breath.

"I don't hear anything," she says.

He nods. "This is what my story sounds like."

"Are you sure?"

He watches as she lifts her arm and makes a motion with it, a graceful wave of her hand, as though conducting an orchestra. The black birds lift from the trees like a dark cloud, the sound of their wings cutting through the gauze of silence. The fiddle begins to play again, the blue wood vibrating with a thin distant music, a sound that is almost transparent. He looks away from the departing birds to find her watching him with the same lack of curiosity he had for the birds.

"Maybe you're not listening hard enough," she says.

"I think I'd know if—"

"Remember what I said about the ravens," she tells him.

He returns his attention to the trees, the birds all gone. When he looks for her again, she's already halfway down the block, horn glinting, too far away for him to read the expression in her features even if she was looking at him. If he even cared.

"I'd know," he says, repeating the words for himself.

He puts her out of his mind, forgets the birds and the city lying just beyond these blocks of wasteland, and goes to find the fiddler.

3

I probably know her better than anyone else around here, but even I forget about the horn sometimes. You want to ask her, why are you hiding out in the Tombs, there's nothing for you here. It's not like she's an alkie or a squatter, got the need for speed or any other kind of jones. But then maybe the sunlight catches that short length of ivory rising up out of her brow, or you see something equally impossible stirring in her dark eyes, and you see that horn like it's the first time all over again, and you understand that it's her difference that puts her here, her strangeness.

Malicorne, is what Frenchy calls her, says it means unicorn. I go to the Crowsea Public Library one day and try to look the word up in a dictionary, but I can only find it in pieces. Now Frenchy got the *corne* right because she's sure enough got a horn. But the word can also mean hoof, while *mal* or *mali* . . . you get your pick of what it can mean. Cunning or sly, which aren't exactly compliments, but mostly it's things worse than that: wickedness, evil, hurt, harm. Maybe Frenchy knows more than he's saying, and maybe she does, too, because she never answers to that name. But she doesn't give us anything better to use instead so the name kind of sticks—at least when we're talking about her among ourselves.

I remember the first time I see her, I'm looking through the trash after the Spring Festival, see if maybe I can sift a little gold from the chaff, which is a nice way of saying I'm a bum and I'm trying to make do. I see her sitting on a bench, looking at me, and at first I don't notice the horn, I'm just wondering, who's this horsy-faced woman and why's she looking at me like she wants to know something about me. Not what I'm doing here, going through the trash, but what put me here.

We've all got stories, a history that sews one piece of who we were to another until you get the reason we're who we are now. But it's not something we offer each other, never mind a stranger. We're not proud of who we are, of what we've become. We don't talk much about it, we never ask each other about it. There's too much pain in where we've been to go back, even if it's just with words. We don't even want to think about it— why do you think we're looking for oblivion in the bottom of a bottle?

I want to turn my back on her, but even then, right from the start, Malicorne's got this pull in her eyes, draws you in, draws you to her, starts you talking. I've seen rheumy-eyed old alkies who can't even put together "Have you got some spare change?" with their heads leaning close to hers, talking, the slur gone from their voices, some kind of sense working its way back into what they're saying. And I'm not immune. I turn my back, but it's on that trash can, and I find myself shuffling, hands stuck deep into my pockets, over to the bench where she's sitting.

"You're so innocent," she says.

I have to laugh. I'm forty-five and I look sixty, and the last thing I am is innocent.

"I'm no virgin," I tell her.

"I didn't say you were. Innocence and virginity aren't necessarily synonymous."

Her voice wakes something in me that I don't want to think about.

"I suppose," I say.

I want to go and get on with my business. I want to stay.

She's got a way of stringing together words so that they all seem to mean more than what you think they're saying, like there's a riddle lying in between the lines, and the funny thing is, I can feel something in me re-sponding. Curiosity. Not standing around and looking at something strange, but an intellectual curiosity—the kind that makes you think.

I study her, sitting there beside me on the bench, raggedy clothes and thick chestnut hair so matted it hangs like fat snakes from her head, like a Rasta's dreadlocks. Horsy features. Deep, dark eyes, like they're all pu-pil, wide-set. And then I see the horn. She smiles when she sees my eyes go wide.

"Jesus," I say. "You've got a—"

"Long road to travel and the company is scarce. Good company, I mean."

I don't much care for weird shit, but I don't tell her that. I tell her things I don't tell anybody, not even myself, how it all went wrong for me, how I miss my family, how I miss having something in my life that means anything. And she listens. She's good at the listening, everybody says so, except for Jake. Jake won't talk to her, says she's feeding on us, feeding on our stories.

"It's give and take," I try to tell him. "You feel better after you've talked to her."

"You feel better because there's nothing left inside to make you feel bad," he says. "Nothing good, nothing bad. She's taking all the stories that make you who you are and putting nothing back."

"Maybe we don't want to remember those things anyway," I say.

He shakes his head. "What you've done is who you are. Without it, you're really nothing." He taps his chest. "What's left inside that belongs to you now?"

"It's not like that," I try to explain. "I still remember what put me here. It doesn't hurt as much anymore, that's all."

"Think about that for a moment."

"She tells you stuff, if you're willing to listen."

"Everything she says is mumbo-jumbo," Jake says. "Nothing that makes sense. Nothing that's worth what she's taken from you. Don't you *see?*"

I don't see it and he won't be part of it. Doesn't want to know about spirits, things that never were, things that can't be, made-up stories that are supposed to take the place of history. Wants to hold on to his pain, I guess.

But then he meets Staley.

4

The fiddler's a woman, but she has no sense of age about her; she could be thirty, she could be seventeen. Where Malicorne's tall and angular, horse-lanky, Staley's like a pony, everything in miniature. There's nothing dark about her, nothing gloomy except the music she sometimes wakes from that blue fiddle of hers. Hair the color of straw and cut like a boy's, a slip of a figure, eyes the green of spring growth, face shaped like a heart. She's barefoot, wears an old pair of overalls a couple of sizes too big, some kind of white jersey, sleeves pushed up on her forearms. There's a knapsack on the ground beside her, an open fiddle case. She's sitting on a chunk of stone—piece of a wall, maybe, piece of a roof—playing that blue fiddle of hers, her whole body playing it, leaning into the music, swaying, head crooked to one side holding the instrument to her shoulder, a smile like the day's just begun stretching across her lips.

Jake stands there, watching her, listening. When the tune comes to an end, he sits down beside her.

"You're good," he tells her.

She gives him a shy smile in return.

"So did you come over from the other side?" he asks.

"The other side of what?"

Jake's thinking of Malicorne, about black birds and doors to other places. He shrugs.

"Guess that answers my question," he says.

She hears the disappointment in his voice, but doesn't understand it.

"People call me Jake," he tells her.

"Staley Cross," she says as they shake hands.

"And are you?"

The look of a Michelle who's been called *ma belle* too often moves across her features, but she doesn't lose her humor.

"Not often," she says.

"Where'd you learn to play like that?"

"I don't know. Here and there. I just picked it up. I'm a good listener, I guess. Once I hear a tune, I don't forget it." The fiddle's lying on her lap. She plays with her bow, loosening and tightening the frog. "Do you play?" she asks.

He shakes his head. "Never saw a blue fiddle before—not blue like that."

"I know. It's not painted on—the color's in the varnish. My grandma gave it to me a couple of years ago. She says it's a spirit fiddle, been in the family forever."

"Play something else," he asks. "Unless you're too tired."

"I'm never too tired to play."

She sets the bow to the strings, wakes a note, wakes another, and then they're in the middle of a tune, a slow reel. Jake leans back, puts his hands behind his head, looks up into the bare branches of the trees. Just before he closes his eyes, he sees those birds return, one after the other, leafing the branches with their black wings. He doesn't hear a door open, all he hears is Staley's fiddle. He finishes closing his eyes and lets the music take him to a place where he doesn't have to think about the story of his life.

5

I'm lounging on a bench with Malicorne near a subway station in that no-man's-land between the city and the Tombs, where the buildings are falling down but there's people still living in them, paying rent. Frenchy's sitting on the curb with a piece of cardboard cut into the shape of a guitar, dark hair tied back with a piece of string, holes in his jeans, hole in his heart where his dreams all escaped. He strums the six drawn strings on that cardboard guitar, mouthing "Plonkety, plonkety" and people are actually tossing him quarters and dimes. On the other side of him Casey's telling fortunes. He looks like the burned-out surfer he is, too many miles from any ocean, still tanned, dirty blond hair falling into his face. He gives everybody the same piece of advice: "Do stuff."

Nobody's paying much attention to us when Jake comes walking down the street, long and lanky, hands deep in the pockets of his black jeans. He sits down beside me, says, "Hey, William," nods to Malicorne. Doesn't even look at her horn.

"Hey, Jake," I tell him.

He leans forward on the bench, talks across me. "You ever hear of a spirit fiddle?" he asks Malicorne.

She smiles. "Are you finally starting a story?"

"I'm not starting anything. I'm just wondering. Met that girl who was making the music and she's got herself a blue fiddle—says it's a spirit fiddle. Been in her family a long time."

"I heard her playing," I say. "She's good."

"Her name's Staley Cross."

"Don't know the name," Malicorne says. There's a hint of surprise in her voice, as though she thinks she should. I'm not the only one who hears it.

"Any reason you should?" Jake asks.

Malicorne smiles and looks away, not just across the street, it seems, but further than that, like she can see through the buildings, see something we can't. Jake's looking at that horn now but I can't tell what he's thinking.

"Where'd she go?" I ask him.

He gets a puzzled look, like he thinks I'm talking about Malicorne for a second, then he shrugs.

"Downtown," he says. "She wanted to busk for a couple of hours, see if she can't get herself a stake."

"Must be nice, having a talent," I say.

"Everybody's got a talent," Malicorne says. "Just like everybody's got a story."

"Unless they give it to you," Jake breaks in.

Malicorne acts like he hasn't interrupted. "Trouble is," she goes on, "some people don't pay much attention to either and they end up living with us here."

"You're living here," Jake says.

Malicorne shakes her head. "I'm just passing through."

I know what Jake's thinking. Everybody starts out thinking, this is only temporary. It doesn't take them long to learn different. But then none of them have a horn pushing out of the middle of their forehead. None of them have mystery sticking to them like they've wrapped themselves up in double-sided tape and whatever they touch sticks to them.

"Yeah, well, we'll all really miss you when you're gone," Jake tells her.

It's quiet then. Except for Frenchy's cardboard guitar. "Plonkety-plonk." None of us are talking. Casey takes a dime from some kid who wants to know the future. His pale blue eyes stand out against his surfer's tan as he gives the kid a serious look.

"Do stuff," he says.

The kid laughs, shakes his head and walks away. But I think about what Malicorne was saying, how everybody's got a story, everybody's got a talent, and I wonder if maybe Casey's got it right.

6

"Blue's the rarest color in nature," Staley says.

Jake smiles. "You ever look up at the sky?"

They're sharing sandwiches her music bought, coffee in cardboard cups, so hot you can't hold the container. If Jake's still worrying about magic and spirit fiddles, it doesn't show.

Staley returns his smile. "I don't mean it's hard to find. But it's funny you should mention the sky. Of all the hundreds of references to the sky and the heavens in a book like the bible, the color blue is never mentioned."

"You read the bible a lot?"

"Up in the hills where I come from, that's pretty much the only thing there is to read. That, and the tabloids. But when I was saying blue's the rarest color—"

"You meant it's the most beautiful."

She nods. "It fills the heart. Like the blue of twilight when anything's possible. Blue makes me feel safe, warm. People think of it as a cool color, but you know, the hottest fire has a blue-white flame. Like stars. The comparatively cooler stars have the reddish glow." She takes a sip of her coffee, looks at him over the brim. "I make up for all the reading I missed by spending a lot of time in libraries."

"Good place to visit," Jake says. "Safe, when you're in a strange town."

"I thought you'd understand. You can put aside all the unhappiness you've accumulated by opening a book. Listening to music."

"You think forgetting is a good thing?"

She shrugs. "For me, it's a necessary thing. It's what keeps me sane."

She looks at him and Jake sees himself through her eyes: a tall, gangly hobo of a man, seen better times, but seen worse ones, too. The worse ones are why he's where he is.

"You know what I mean," she says.

"I suppose. Don't know if I agree, though." She lifts her eyebrows, but he doesn't want to take that any further. "So tell me about the spirit in that fiddle of yours," he says instead.

"It hasn't got a spirit—not like you mean, anyway. It comes from a spirit place. That's why it's blue. It's the color of twilight and my grandma says it's always twilight there."

"In the Otherworld."

"If that's what you want to call it."

"And the black of a raven's wing," Jake says, "that's really a kind of blue, too, isn't it?"

She gives him a confused look.

"Don't mind me," he tells her. "I'm just thinking about what someone once told me."

"Where I come from," she says, "the raven's an unlucky bird."

"Depends on how many you see," Jake says. He starts to repeat the old rhyme for her then. "One for sorrow, two for mirth . . ."

She nods, remembering. "Three for a wedding, four for a birth."

"That's it. Five for silver, six for gold . . ."

". . . seven for a secret never to be told . . ."

". . . eight for heaven, nine for hell . . ."

". . . and ten for the devil's own sel'." She smiles. "But I thought that was for crows."

He shrugs. "I've heard it used for magpies, too. Guess it's for any kind of black bird." He looks up at the trees, empty now. "That music of yours," he goes on. "It called up an unkindness of ravens this afternoon."

"An unkindness of ravens," she repeats, smiling. "A murder of crows. Where do they come up with that kind of thing?"

He shrugs. "Who knows? Same place they found once in a blue moon, I guess."

"There was a blue moon the night my great-great-grandma got my fiddle," Staley tells him. "Least that's how the story goes."

"That's what I meant about forgetting," he says. "Maybe you forget some bad things, but work at it hard enough and you forget a story like that, too."

They're finished eating now, the last inch of coffee cooling in their cups.

"You up to playing a little more music?" Jake asks. "See what it calls up?"

"Sure."

She takes the instrument from its case, tightens the bow, runs her finger across the strings to check the tuning, adjusts a couple of them. Jake likes to watch her fingers move, even doing this, without the music having started yet, tells her that.

"You're a funny guy," she says as she brings the fiddle up under her chin.

Jake smiles. "Everybody says that," he tells her.

But he's thinking of something else, he's thinking of how the little pieces of her history that she's given him add to his own without taking anything away from her. He's thinking about Malicorne and the stories she takes, how she pulls the hurt out of them by listening. He's thinking—

But then Staley starts to play and the music takes him away again.

"I was working on a tune this afternoon," she says as the music moves into three-four time. "Maybe I'll call it 'Jake's Waltz.' "

Jake closes his eyes, listening, not just to her music, but for the sound of wings.

7

It's past sundown. The fires are burning in the oil drums and bottles are being passed around. Cider and apple juice in some, stronger drink in others. Malicorne's not drinking, never does, least not that I can ever remember seeing. She's sitting off by herself, leaning against a red brick wall, face a smudge of pale in the shadows, horn invisible. The wall was once the side of a factory, now it's standing by itself. There's an owl on top of the wall, three stories up, perched on the bricks, silhouetted by the moon. I saw it land and wonder what owls mean around her. Jake told me about the ravens.

After a while, I walk over to where she's sitting, offer her some apple juice. She shakes her head. I can see the horn now.

"What's it with you and Jake?" I ask.

"Old arguments never die," she says.

"You go back a long time?"

She shakes her head. "But the kind of man he is and I do. Live long enough, William, and you'll meet every kind of person, hear every kind of story, not once, but a hundred times."

"I don't get what you mean," I say.

"No. But Jake does."

We hear the music then, Staley's fiddle, one-two-three, one-two-three, waltz time, and I see them sitting together on the other side of the fires, shadow shapes, long tall Jake with his raven hair and the firefly glow of Staley's head bent over her instrument. I hear the sound of wings and think of the owl on the wall above us, but when I check, it's gone. These are black birds, ravens, a flock of them, an unkindness, and I feel something in the air, a prickling across my skin and at the nape of my neck, like a storm's coming, but the skies are clear. The stars seem so close we could be up in the mountains instead of here, in the middle of the city.

"What are you thinking about?" Malicorne asks.

I turn to her, see the horn catch the firelight. "Endings," I find myself saying. "Where things go when they don't fit where they are."

She smiles. "Are you reading my mind?"

"Never was much inclined for that sort of thing."

"Me, either."

That catches me by surprise. "But you . . ." You're magic, I was going to say, but my voice trails off.

"I've been here too long," she says. "Stopped to rest a day or so, and look at me now. Been here all spring and most of the summer."

"It's been a good summer."

She nods. "But Jake's right, you know. Your stories do nourish me. Not like he thinks, it's not me feeding on them and you losing something, it's that they connect me to a place." She taps a finger against the dirt we're sitting on. "They connect me to something real. But I also get you to talk because I know talking heals. I like to think I'm doing some good."

"Everybody likes you," I tell her. I don't add, except for Jake.

"But it's like Scheherazade," she says. "One day the stories are all told and it's time to move on."

I'm shaking my head. "You don't have to go. When you're standing at the bottom of the ladder like we are, nobody can tell you what to do anymore. It's not much, but at least we've got that."

"There's that innocence of yours again," she says.

"What the hell's that supposed to mean?"

She smiles. "Don't be angry."

"Then don't treat me like a kid."

"But isn't this like Neverneverland?" she asks. "You said it yourself. Nobody can tell you what to do anymore. Nothing has to ever change. You can be like this forever."

"You think any of us want to be here? You think we chose to live like this?"

"She's not talking about you, William," Jake says. "She's talking about me."

I never heard the music stop, never heard them approach, Jake and the fiddler, standing near us now. I don't know how long they've been there, how much they've heard. Staley lifts her hand to me, says hi. Jake, he's just looking at Malicorne. I can't tell what he's thinking.

"So I guess what you need is my story," he says, "and then you can go."

Malicorne shakes her head. "My coming or going has nothing to do with you."

Jake doesn't believe her. He sits down on the dirt in front of us, got that look in his eye I've seen before, not angry, just he won't be backing down. Staley sits down, too, takes out her fiddle, but doesn't play it. She holds the instrument on her lap, runs the pad of her thumb along the strings, toys with the wooden curlicues on the head, starts to finger a tune, pressing the strings against the fingerboard, soundlessly. I wish I had something to do with my hands.

"See," Jake's saying, "it's circumstances that put most of these people here, living on the street. They're not bad people, they're just weak, maybe, or had some bad luck, some hard times, that's all. Some of them'll die here, some of them'll make a second chance for themselves and your guess is as good as mine, which of them'll pull through."

"But you chose to live like this," Malicorne says.

"You know, don't you? You already know all about me."

She shakes her head. "All I know is you're hiding from something and nobody had to tell me that. I just had to look at you."

"I killed a man," Jake says.

"Did he deserve it?"

"I don't even know anymore. He was stealing from me, sent my business belly-up and just laughed at me when I confronted him with it. Asked me what I was going to do, the money was all spent and what the hell could I prove anyway? He'd fixed the books so it looked like it was all my fault."

"That's hard," I say.

I'm where I am because I drank too much, drank all the time and damned if I can tell you why. Got nobody to blame but myself. Don't drink anymore, but it's too late to go back. My old life went on without me. Wife remarried. Kids think I'm dead.

"It was the laughing I couldn't take," Jake says. "He was just standing there, looking so smug and laughing at me. So I hit him. Grabbed the little turd by the throat and started whacking the back of his head against the wall and when I stopped, he was dead. First time I ever saw a dead person. First time I ever hit anybody, except for goofing around with the guys in high school." He looks at me. "You know, the old push and shove, but it's nothing serious."

I give him a nod.

"But this was serious. The thing is, when I think about it now, what he did to me, the money he stole, none of it seems so important anymore."

"Are you sorry?" Malicorne asks.

"I'm not sorry he's dead, but I'm sorry I was the one that killed him."

"So you've been on the run ever since."

Jake nods. "Twelve years now and counting." He gives her a long, steady look. "So that's my story."

"Do you feel any better having told us about it?"

"No."

"I didn't think you would," she says.

"What's that supposed to mean?"

"You've got to want to heal before you can get out of this prison you've made for yourself."

I'm expecting this to set him off, but he looks at the ground instead, shoulders sagging. I've seen a lot of broken men on the skids—hell, all I've had to do for years is look in a mirror—but I've never imagined Jake as one of them. Never knew why he was down here with the rest of us, but always thought he was stronger than the rest of us.

"I don't know how," he says.

"Was he your brother?" Staley asks. "This man you killed."

I've been wondering how she was taking this, sitting there so still, listening, not even her fingers moving anymore. It's hard to see much of anything, here in the shadows. Our faces and hands are pale blurs. The light from the fires in the oil drums catches Malicorne's horn, Staley's hair, awakes a shine on her lap where the blue fiddle's lying.

Jake shakes his head. "He was my best friend. I would've given him anything, all he had to do was ask."

"I'm sorry for you," Malicorne says, standing up. "I'm sorry for you both, the one dead and the other a long time dying."

She's going then, nothing to pack, nothing to carry, leaving us the way she came with her hands empty and her heart full. Over by the oil drums, nobody notices. Frenchy is rolling himself a cigarette from the butts he collected during the day. Casey's sleeping, an empty bottle of wine lying in the dirt beside his hand. I can't see the black birds, but I can hear them, feathers rustling in the dark all around us. I guess if you want to believe in that kind of thing, there's a door standing open nearby.

"Let me come with you," Jake says.

Malicorne looks at him. "The road I'm traveling goes on forever," she says.

"I kind of guessed that, what with the horn and all."

"It's about remembering, not forgetting."

He nods. "I know that, too. Maybe I can learn to be good company."

"Nobody ever said you weren't," she tells him. "What you have to ask yourself is, are you trying to escape again or are you really ready to move on?"

"Talking about it—that's a start, isn't it?"

Malicorne smiles. "It's a very good start."

8

Staley and I, we're the only ones to see them go. I don't know if they just walked off into the night, swallowed by the shadows, or if they stepped through a door, but I never see either of them again. We sit there for a while, looking up at the stars. They still seem so big, so near, like they want to be close to whatever enchantment happened here tonight. After a while Staley starts to play her fiddle, that same tune she played earlier, the one in three-four time. I hear wings, in behind the music, but it's the black birds leaving, not gathering. Far off, I hear hoofbeats and I don't know what to make of that.

Frenchy gets himself a job a few weeks later, sweeping out a bar over on Grasso Street, near the Men's Mission. Casey goes back to the coast, says he's thinking of going back to school. Lots of the others, things start to look up a little for them, too. Not everybody, not all of us, but more than tried to take a chance before Malicorne came into our lives.

Me, I find myself a job as a custodian in a Kelly Street tenement. The job gives me a little room in the basement, but there's no money in it. I get by with tips from the tenants when I do some work for them, paint a room, fix a leaky faucet, that kind of thing. I'm looking for something better, but times are still hard.

Staley, she hangs around for a few days, then moves on.

I remember thinking there's a magic about her, too, but now I know it's in the music she calls up from that blue fiddle of hers, the same kind of magic any good musician can wake from an instrument. It takes you away. Calls something to you maybe, but it's not necessarily ravens or enchantment.

Before she goes, I ask her about that night, about what brought her down to the Tombs.

"I wanted to see the unicorn," she says. "I was playing in a pick-up band in a roadhouse up on Highway 14 and overheard somebody talking about her in the parking lot at the end of the night—a couple of 'boes, on their way out of the city. I just kind of got distracted with Jake. He seemed like a nice guy, you know, but he was so lonely."

"The unicorn . . . ?"

For a minute there I don't know what she's talking about, but then Malicorne's horsy features come to mind, the chestnut dreadlocks, the wide-set eyes. And finally I remember the horn and when I do, I can't figure out how I forgot.

"You know," Staley's saying. "White horse, big spiraling horn coming out of her forehead."

"But she was a woman," I begin.

Staley smiles. "And Jake was a man. But when they left I saw a white horse and a black one."

"I didn't. But I heard hoofbeats. . . ." I give her a puzzled look. "What happened that night?"

Staley shoulders her knapsack, picks up her fiddlecase. She stands on tip-toes and kisses me lightly on the cheek.

"Magic," she says. "And wasn't it something—just that little piece of it?"

I'm nodding when she gives me a little wave of her hand.

"See you, William," she says. "You take care now."

I wave back, stand there, watching her go. I hear a croaking cry from the top of the derelict building beside me, but it's a crow I see, beating its black wings, lifting high above the ragged roofline, not a raven.

Sometimes I find myself humming that waltz she wrote for Jake.

Sometimes I dream about two horses, one black and one white with a horn, the two of them running, running along the crest of these long hills that rise and fall like the waves of the sea, and I wake up smiling.

Crow Girls

I remember what somebody said about nostalgia, he said it's okay to look back, as long as you don't stare.

—*Tom Paxton,*
  from an interview with Ken Rockburn

People have a funny way of remembering where they've been, who they were. Facts fall by the wayside. Depending on their temperament they either remember a golden time when all was better than well, better than it can be again, better than it ever really was: a first love, the endless expanse of a summer vacation, youthful vigor, the sheer novelty of being alive that gets lost when the world starts wearing you down. Or they focus in on the bad, blow little incidents all out of proportion, hold grudges for years, or maybe they really did have some unlucky times, but now they're reliving them forever in their heads instead of moving on.

But the brain plays tricks on us all, doesn't it? We go by what it tells us, have to I suppose, because what else do we have to use as touchstones? Trouble is we don't ask for confirmation on what the brain tells us. Things don't have to be real, we just have to believe they're real, which pretty much explains politics and religion as much as it does what goes on inside our heads.

Don't get me wrong; I'm not pointing any fingers here. My people aren't guiltless either. The only difference is our memories go back a lot further than yours do.

*   *   *

"I don't get computers," Heather said.

Jilly laughed. "What's not to get?"

They were having cappuccinos in the Cyberbean Café, sitting at the long counter with computer terminals spaced along its length the way those little individual jukeboxes used to be in highway diners. Jilly looked as though she'd been using the tips of her dark ringlets as paintbrushes, then cleaned them on the thighs of her jeans—in other words, she'd come straight from the studio without changing first. But however haphazardly messy she might allow herself or her studio to get, Heather knew she'd either cleaned her brushes, or left them soaking in turps before coming down to the café. Jilly might seem terminally easygoing, but some things she didn't blow off. No matter how the work was going—good, bad or indifferent—she treated her tools with respect.

As usual, Jilly's casual scruffiness made Heather feel overdressed, for all that she was only wearing cotton pants and a blouse, nothing fancy. But she always felt a little like that around Jilly, ever since she'd first taken a class from her at the Newford School of Art a couple of winters ago. No matter how hard she tried, she hadn't been able to shake the feeling that she looked so typical: the suburban working mother, the happy wife. The differences since she and Jilly had first met weren't great. Her blonde hair had been long then while now it was cropped short. She was wearing glasses now instead of her contacts.

And two years ago she hadn't been carrying an empty wasteland around inside her chest.

"Besides," Jilly added. "You use a computer at work, don't you?"

"Sure, but that's work," Heather said. "Not games and computer-screen romances and stumbling around the Internet, looking for information you're never going to find a use for outside of Trivial Pursuit."

"I think it's bringing back a sense of community," Jilly said.

"Oh, right."

"No, think about it. All these people who might have been just vegging out in front of a TV are chatting with each other in cyberspace instead—hanging out, so to speak, with kindred spirits that they might never have otherwise met."

Heather sighed. "But it's not real human contact."

"No. But at least it's contact."

"I suppose."

Jilly regarded her over the brim of her glass coffee mug. It was a mild gaze, not in the least probing, but Heather couldn't help but feel as though Jilly was seeing right inside her head, all the way down to where desert winds blew through the empty space where her heart had been.

"So what's the real issue?" Jilly asked.

Heather shrugged. "There's no issue." She took a sip of her own coffee, then tried on a smile. "I'm thinking of moving downtown."

"Really?"

"Well, you know. I already work here. There's a good school for the kids. It just seems to make sense."

"How does Peter feel about it?"

Heather hesitated for a long moment, then sighed again. "Peter's not really got anything to say about it."

"Oh, no. You guys always seemed so . . ." Jilly's voice trailed off. "Well, I guess you weren't really happy, were you?"

"I don't know what we were anymore. I just know we're not together. There wasn't a big blow up or anything. He wasn't cheating on me and I certainly wasn't cheating on him. We're just . . . not together."

"It must be so weird."

Heather nodded. "Very weird. It's a real shock, suddenly discovering after all these years, that we really don't have much in common at all."

Jilly's eyes were warm with sympathy. "How are you holding up?"

"Okay, I suppose. But it's so confusing. I don't know what to think, who I am, what I thought I was doing with the last fifteen years of my life. I mean, I don't regret the girls—I'd have had more children if we could have had them—but everything else . . ."

She didn't know how to begin to explain.

"I married Peter when I was eighteen and I'm forty-one now. I've been a part of a couple for longer than I've been anything else, but except for the girls, I don't know what any of it meant anymore. I don't know who I am. I thought we'd be together forever, that we'd grow old together, you know? But now it's just me. Casey's fifteen and Janice is twelve. I've got another few years of being a mother, but after that, who am I? What am I going to do with myself?"

"You're still young," Jilly said. "And you look gorgeous."

"Right."

"Okay. A little pale today, but still."

Heather shook her head. "I don't know why I'm telling you this. I haven't told anybody."

"Not even your mom or your sister?"

"Nobody. It's . . ."

She could feel tears welling up, the vision blurring, but she made herself take a deep breath. It seemed to help. Not a lot, but some. Enough to carry on. How to explain why she wanted to keep it a secret? It wasn't as though it was something she could keep hidden forever.

"I think I feel like a failure," she said.

Her voice was so soft she almost couldn't hear herself, but Jilly reached over and took her hand.

"You're not a failure. Things didn't work out, but that doesn't mean it was your fault. It takes two people to make or break a relationship."

"I suppose. But to have put in all those years . . ."

Jilly smiled. "If nothing else, you've got two beautiful daughters to show for them."

Heather nodded. The girls did a lot to keep the emptiness at bay, but once they were in bed, asleep, and she was by herself, alone in the dark, sitting on the couch by the picture window, staring down the street at all those other houses just like her own, that desolate place inside her seemed to go on forever.

She took another sip of her coffee and looked past Jilly to where two young women were sitting at a corner table, heads bent together, whispering. It was hard to place their ages—anywhere from late teens to early twenties, sisters, perhaps, with their small builds and similar dark looks, their black clothing and short blue-black hair. For no reason she could explain, simply seeing them made her feel a little better.

"Remember what it was like to be so young?" she said.

Jilly turned, following her gaze, then looked back at Heather.

"You never think about stuff like this at that age," Heather went on.

"I don't know," Jilly said. "Maybe not. But you have a thousand other anxieties that probably feel way more catastrophic."

"You think?"

Jilly nodded. "I know. We all like to remember it as a perfect time, but most of us were such bundles of messed-up hormones and nerves I'm surprised we ever managed to reach twenty."

"I suppose. But still, looking at those girls . . ."

Jilly turned again, leaning her head on her arm. "I know what you mean. They're like a piece of summer on a cold winter's morning."

It was a perfect analogy, Heather thought, especially considering the winter they'd been having. Not even the middle of December and the snowbanks were already higher than her chest, the temperature a seriously cold minus-fifteen.

"I have to remember their faces," Jilly went on. "For when I get back to the studio. The way they're leaning so close to each other—like confidantes, sisters in their hearts, if not by blood. And look at the fine bones in their features . . . how dark their eyes are."

Heather nodded. "It'd make a great picture."

It would, but the thought of it depressed her. She found herself yearning desperately in that one moment to have had an entirely different life, it almost didn't matter what. Perhaps one that had no responsibility but to draw great art from the world around her the way Jilly did. If she hadn't had to support Peter while he was going through law school, maybe she would have stuck with her art. . . .

Jilly swiveled in her chair, the sparkle in her eyes deepening into concern once more.

"Anything you need, anytime," she said. "Don't be afraid to call me."

Heather tried another smile. "We could chat on the Internet."

"I think I agree with what you said earlier: I like this better."

"Me, too," Heather said. Looking out the window, she added, "It's snowing again."

Maida and Zia are forever friends. Crow girls with spiky blue-black hair and eyes so dark it's easy to lose your way in them. A little raggedy and never quiet, you can't miss this pair: small and wild and easy in their skins, living on Zen time. Sometimes they forget they're crows, left their feathers behind in the long-ago, and sometimes they forget they're girls. But they never forget that they're friends.

People stop and stare at them wherever they go, borrowing a taste of them, drawn by they don't know what, they just have to look, try to get close, but keeping their distance, too, because there's something scary/craving about seeing animal spirits so pure walking around on a city street. It's a shock, like plunging into cold water at dawn, waking up from the comfortable familiarity of warm dreams to find, if only for a moment, that everything's changed. And then, just before the way you know the world to be comes rolling back in on you, maybe you hear giddy laughter, or the slow flap of crows' wings. Maybe you see a couple of dark-haired girls sitting together in the corner of a café, heads bent together, pretending you can't see them, or could be they're perched on a tree branch, looking down at you looking up, working hard at putting on serious faces but they can't stop smiling.

It's like that rhyme, "two for mirth." They can't stop smiling and neither can you. But you've got to watch out for crow girls. Sometimes they wake a yearning you'll be hard pressed to put back to sleep. Sometimes only a glimpse of them can start up a familiar ache deep in your chest, an ache you can't name, but you've felt it before, early mornings, lying alone in your bed, trying to hold onto the fading tatters of a perfect dream. Sometimes they blow bright the coals of a longing that can't ever be eased.

Heather couldn't stop thinking of the two girls she'd seen in the café earlier in the evening. It was as though they'd lodged pieces of themselves inside her, feathery slivers winging dreamily across the wasteland. Long after she'd played a board game with Janice, then watched the end of a Barbara Walters special with Casey, she found herself sitting up by the big picture window in the living room when she should have been in bed herself. She regarded the street through a veil of falling snow, but this time she wasn't looking at the houses—so alike that, except for the varying heights of their snowbanks, they might as well all be the same one. Instead, she was looking for two small women with spiky black hair, dark shapes against the white snow.

There was no question but that they knew exactly who they were, she thought when she realized what she was doing. Maybe they could tell her who she was. Maybe they could come up with an exotic past for her so that she could reinvent herself, be someone like them, free, sure of herself. Maybe they could at least tell her where she was going.

But there were no thin, dark-haired girls out on the snowy street, and why should there be? It was too cold. Snow was falling thick with another severe winter storm warning in effect tonight. Those girls were safe at home. She knew that. But she kept looking for them all the same because in her chest she could feel the beat of dark wings—not the sudden panic that came out of nowhere when once again the truth of her situation reared without warning in her mind, but a strange, alien feeling. A sense that some otherness was calling to her.

The voice of that otherness scared her almost more than the grey landscape lodged in her chest.

She felt she needed a safety net, to be able to let herself go and not have to worry about where she fell. Somewhere where she didn't have to think, be responsible, to do anything. Not forever. Just for a time.

She knew Jilly was right about nostalgia. The memories she carried forward weren't necessarily the way things had really happened. But she yearned, if only for a moment, to be able to relive some of those simpler times, those years in high school before she'd met Peter, before they were married, before her emotions got so complicated.

And then what?

You couldn't live in the past. At some point you had to come up for air and then the present would be waiting for you, unchanged. The wasteland in her chest would still stretch on forever. She'd still be trying to understand what had happened. Had Peter changed? Had she changed? Had they both changed? And when did it happen? How much of their life together had been a lie?

It was enough to drive her mad.

It was enough to make her want to step into the otherness calling to her from out there in the storm and snow, step out and simply let it swallow her whole.

Jilly couldn't put the girls from the café out of her mind either, but for a different reason. As soon as she'd gotten back to the studio, she'd taken her current work-in-progress down from the easel and replaced it with a fresh canvas. For a long moment she stared at the texture of the pale ground, a mix of gesso and a light burnt-ochre acrylic wash, then she took up a stick of charcoal and began to sketch the faces of the two dark-haired girls before the memory of them left her mind.

She was working on their bodies, trying to capture the loose splay of their limbs and the curve of their backs as they'd slouched in toward each other over the café table, when there came a knock at her door.

"It's open," she called over her shoulder, too intent on what she was doing to look away.

"I could've been some mad, psychotic killer," Geordie said as he came in.

He stamped his feet on the mat, brushed the snow from his shoulders and hat. Setting his fiddlecase down by the door, he went over to the kitchen counter to see if Jilly had any coffee on.

"But instead," Jilly said, "it's only a mad, psychotic fiddler, so I'm entirely safe."

"There's no coffee."

"Sure there is. It's just waiting for you to make it."

Geordie put on the kettle, then rummaged around in the fridge, trying to find which tin Jilly was keeping her coffee beans in this week. He found them in one that claimed to hold Scottish shortbreads.

"You want some?" he asked.

Jilly shook her head. "How's Tanya?"

"Heading back to L.A. I just saw her off at the airport. The driving's horrendous. There were cars in the ditch every couple of hundred feet and I thought the bus would never make it back."

"And yet, it did," Jilly said.

Geordie smiled.

"And then," she went on, "because you were feeling bored and lonely, you decided to come visit me at two o'clock in the morning."

"Actually, I was out of coffee and I saw your light was on." He crossed the loft and came around behind the easel so that he could see what she was working on. "Hey, you're doing the crow girls."

"You know them?"

Geordie nodded. "Maida and Zia. You've caught a good likeness of them—especially Zia. I love that crinkly smile of hers."

"You can tell them apart?"

"You can't?"

"I never saw them before tonight. Heather and I were in the Cyberbean and there they were, just asking to be drawn." She added a bit of shading to the underside of a jaw, then turned to look at Geordie. "Why do you call them the crow girls?"

Geordie shrugged. "I don't. Or at least I didn't until I was talking to Jack Daw and that's what he called them when they came sauntering by. The next time I saw them I was busking in front of St. Paul's, so I started to play 'The Blackbird,' just to see what would happen, and sure enough, they came over to talk to me."

"Crow girls," Jilly repeated. The name certainly fit.

"They're some kind of relation to Jack," Geordie explained, "but I didn't quite get it. Cousins, maybe."

Jilly was suddenly struck with the memory of a long conversation she'd had with Jack one afternoon. She was working up sketches of the Crowsea Public Library for a commission when he came and sat beside her on the grass. With his long legs folded under him, black brimmed hat set at a jaunty angle, he'd regaled her with a long, rambling discourse on what he called the continent's real first nations.

"Animal people," she said softly.

Geordie smiled. "I see he fed you that line, too."

But Jilly wasn't really listening—not to Geordie. She was remembering another part of that old conversation, something else Jack had told her.

"The thing we really don't get," he'd said, leaning back in the grass, "is these contracted families you have. The mother, the father, the children, all living alone in some big house. Our families extend as far as our bloodlines and friendship can reach."

"I don't know much about bloodlines," Jilly said. "But I know about friends."

He'd nodded. "That's why I'm talking to you."

Jilly blinked and looked at Geordie. "It made sense what he said."

Geordie smiled. "Of course it did. Immortal animal people."

"That, too. But I was talking about the weird way we think about families and children. Most people don't even like kids—don't want to see, hear, or hear about them. But when you look at other cultures, even close to home . . . up on the rez, in Chinatown, Little Italy . . . it's these big rambling extended families, everybody taking care of everybody else."

Geordie cleared his throat. Jilly waited for him to speak but he went instead to unplug the kettle and finish making the coffee. He ground up some beans and the noise of the hand-cranked machine seemed to reach out and fill every corner of the loft. When he stopped, the sudden silence was profound, as though the city outside was holding its breath along with the inheld breath of the room. Jilly was still watching him when he looked over at her.

"We don't come from that kind of family," he said finally.

"I know. That's why we had to make our own."

* * *

It's late at night, snow whirling in dervishing gusts, and the crow girls are perched on the top of the wooden fence that's been erected around a work site on Williamson Street. Used to be a parking lot there, now it's a big hole in the ground on its way to being one more office complex that nobody except the contractors want. The top of the fence is barely an inch wide at the top and slippery with snow, but they have no trouble balancing there.

Zia has a ring with a small spinning disc on it. Painted on the disc is a psychedelic coil that goes spiraling down into infinity. She keeps spinning it and the two of them stare down into the faraway place at the center of the spiral until the disc slows down, almost stops. Then Zia gives it another flick with her fingernail, and the coil goes spiraling down again.

"Where'd you get this anyway?" Maida asks.

Zia shrugs. "Can't remember. Found it somewhere."

"In someone's pocket."

"And you never did?"

Maida grins. "Just wish I'd seen it first, that's all."

They watch the disc some more, content.

"What do you think it's like down there?" Zia says after awhile. "On the other side of the spiral."

Maida has to think about that for a moment. "Same as here," she finally announces, then winks. "Only dizzier."

They giggle, leaning into each other, tottering back and forth on their perch, crow girls, can't be touched, can't hardly be seen, except someone's standing down there on the sidewalk, looking up through the falling snow, his worried expression so comical it sets them off on a new round of giggles.

"Careful now!" he calls up to them. He thinks they're on drugs—they can tell. "You don't want to—"

Before he can finish, they hold hands and let themselves fall backward, off the fence.

"Oh, Christ!"

He jumps, gets a handhold on the top of the fence and hauls himself up. But when he looks over, over and down, way down, there's nothing to be seen. No girls lying at the bottom of that big hole in the ground, nothing at all. Only the falling snow. It's like they were never there.

His arms start to ache and he lowers himself back down the fence, lets go, bending his knees slightly to absorb the impact of the last couple of feet. He slips, catches his balance. It seems very still for a moment, so still he can hear an odd rhythmical whispering sound. Like wings. He looks up, but there's too much snow coming down to see anything. A cab comes by, skidding on the slick street, and he blinks. The street's full of city sounds again, muffled, but present. He hears the murmuring conversation of a couple approaching him, their shoulders and hair white with snow. A snowplow a few streets over. A distant siren.

He continues along his way, but he's walking slowly now, trudging through the drifts, not thinking so much of two girls sitting on top of a fence as remembering how, when he was a boy, he used to dream that he could fly.

After fiddling a little more with her sketch, Jilly finally put her charcoal down. She made herself a cup of herbal tea with the leftover hot water in the kettle and joined Geordie where he was sitting on the sofa, watching the snow come down. It was warm in the loft, almost cozy compared to the storm on the other side of the windowpanes, or maybe because of the storm. Jilly leaned back on the sofa, enjoying the companionable silence for a while before she finally spoke.

"How do you feel after seeing the crow girls?" she asked.

Geordie turned to look at her. "What do you mean, how do I feel?"

"You know, good, bad . . . different . . ."

Geordie smiled. "Don't you mean 'indifferent?' "

"Maybe." She picked up her tea from the crate where she'd set it and took a sip. "Well?" she asked when he didn't continue.

"Okay. How do I feel? Good, I suppose. They're fun, they make me smile. In fact, just thinking of them now makes me feel good."

Jilly nodded thoughtfully as he spoke. "Me, too. And something else as well."

"The different," Geordie began. He didn't quite sigh. "You believe those stories of Jack's, don't you?"

"Of course. And you don't?"

"I'm not sure," he replied, surprising her.

"Well, I think these crow girls were in the Cyberbean for a purpose," Jilly said. "Like in that rhyme about crows."

Geordie got it right away. "Two for mirth."

Jilly nodded. "Heather needed some serious cheering up. Maybe even something more. You know how when you start feeling low, you can get on this descending spiral of depression . . . everything goes wrong, things get worse, because you expect them to?"

"Fight it with the power of positive thinking, I always say."

"Easier said than done when you're feeling that low. What you really need at a time like that is something completely unexpected to kick you out of it and remind you that there's more to life than the hopeless, grey expanse you think is stretching in every direction. What Colin Wilson calls absurd good news."

"You've been talking to my brother."

"It doesn't matter where I got it from—it's still true."

Geordie shook his head. "I don't buy the idea that Maida and Zia showed up just to put your friend in a better mood. Even bird people can get a craving for a cup of coffee, can't they?"

"Well, yes," Jilly said. "But that doesn't preclude their being there for Heather as well. Sometimes when a person needs something badly enough, it just comes to them. A personal kind of steam-engine time. You might not be able to articulate what it is you need, you might not even know you need something—at least, not at a conscious level—but the need's still there, calling out to whatever's willing to listen."

Geordie smiled. "Like animal spirits."

"Crow girls."

Geordie shook his head. "Drink your tea and go to bed," he told her. "I think you need a good night's sleep."

"But—"

"It was only a coincidence. Things don't always have a meaning. Sometimes they just happen. And besides, how do you even know they had any effect on Heather?"

"I could just tell. And don't change the subject."

"I'm not."

"Okay," Jilly said. "But don't you see? It doesn't matter if it was a co-incidence or not. They still showed up when Heather needed them. It's more of that 'small world, spooky world' stuff Professor Dapple goes on about. Everything's connected. It doesn't matter if we can't see how, it's still all connected. You know, chaos theory and all that."

Geordie shook his head, but he was smiling. "Does it ever strike you as weird when something Bramley's talked up for years suddenly becomes an acceptable element of scientific study?"

"Nothing strikes me as truly weird," Jilly told him. "There's only stuff I haven't figured out yet."

Heather barely slept that night. For the longest time she simply couldn't sleep, and then when she finally did, she was awake by dawn. Wide awake, but heavy with an exhaustion that came more from heartache than lack of sleep.

Sitting up against the headboard, she tried to resist the sudden tightness in her chest, but that sad, cold wasteland swelled inside her. The bed seemed depressingly huge. She didn't so much miss Peter's presence as feel adrift in the bed's expanse of blankets and sheets. Adrift in her life. Why was it he seemed to have no trouble carrying on when the simple act of getting up in the morning felt as though it would require far more energy than she could ever hope to muster?

She stared at the snow swirling against her window, not at all relishing the drive into town on a morning like this. If anything, it was coming down harder than it had been last night. All it took was the suggestion of snow and everybody in the city seemed to forget how to drive, never mind common courtesy or traffic laws. A blizzard like this would snarl traffic and back it up as far as the mountains.

She sighed, supposing it was just as well she'd woken so early since it would take her at least an extra hour to get downtown today.

Up, she told herself, and forced herself to swing her feet to the floor and rise. A shower helped. It didn't really ease the heartache, but the hiss of the water made it easier to ignore her thoughts. Coffee, when she was dressed and had brewed a pot, helped more, though she still winced when Janice came bounding into the kitchen.

"It's a snow day!" she cried. "No school. They just announced it on the radio. The school's closed, closed, closed!"

She danced about in her flannel nightie, pirouetting in the small space between the counter and the table.

"Just yours," Heather asked, "or Casey's, too?"

"Mine, too," Casey replied, following her sister into the room.

Unlike Janice, she was maintaining her cool, but Heather could tell she was just as excited. Too old to allow herself to take part in Janice's spontaneous celebration, but young enough to be feeling giddy with the unexpected holiday.

"Good," Heather said. "You can look after your sister."

"*Mom!*" Janice protested. "I'm not a baby."

"I know. It's just good to have someone older in the house when—"

"You can't be thinking of going in to work today," Casey said.

"We could do all kinds of stuff," Janice added. "Finish decorating the house. Baking."

"Yeah," Casey said, "all the things we don't seem to have time for anymore."

Heather sighed. "The trouble is," she explained, "the real world doesn't work like school. We don't get snow days."

Casey shook her head. "That is *so* unfair."

The phone rang before Heather could agree.

"I'll bet it's your boss," Janice said as Heather picked up the phone. "Calling to tell you it's a snow day for you, too."

Don't I wish, Heather thought. But then what would she do at home all day? It was so hard being here, even with the girls and much as she loved them. Everywhere she turned, something reminded her of how the promises of a good life had turned into so much ash. At least work kept her from brooding.

She brought the receiver up to her ear and spoke into the mouthpiece. "Hello?"

"I've been thinking," the voice on the other end of the line said. "About last night."

Heather had to smile. Wasn't that so Jilly, calling up first thing in the morning as though they were still in the middle of last night's conversation.

"What about last night?" she said.

"Well, all sorts of stuff. Like remembering a perfect moment in the past and letting it carry you through a hard time now."

If only, Heather thought. "I don't have a moment that perfect," she said.

"I sort of got that feeling," Jilly told her. "That's why I think they were a message—a kind of perfect moment now that you can use the same way."

"What *are* you talking about?"

"The crow girls. In the café last night."

"The crow . . ." It took her a moment to realize what Jilly meant. Their complexions had been dark enough so she supposed they could have been Indians. "How do you know what tribe they belonged to?"

"Not Crow, Native American," Jilly said, "but crow, bird people."

Heather shook her head as she listened to what Jilly went on to say, for all that only her daughters were here to see the movement. Glum looks had replaced their earlier excitement when they realized the call wasn't from her boss.

"Do you have any idea how improbable all of this sounds?" she asked when Jilly finished. "Life's not like your paintings."

"Says who?"

"How about common sense?"

"Tell me," Jilly said. "Where did common sense ever get you?"

Heather sighed. "Things don't happen just because we want them to," she said.

"Sometimes that's *exactly* why they happen," Jilly replied. "They happen because we need them to."

"I don't live in that kind of a world."

"But you could."

Heather looked across the kitchen at her daughters once more. The girls were watching her, trying to make sense out of the one-sided conversation they were hearing. Heather wished them luck. She was hearing both sides and that didn't seem to help at all. You couldn't simply reinvent your world because you wanted to. Things just were how they were.

"Just think about it," Jilly added. "Will you do that much?"

"I . . ."

That bleak landscape inside Heather seemed to expand, growing so large there was no way she could contain it. She focused on the faces of her daughters. She remembered the crow girls in the café. There was so much innocence in them all, daughters and crow girls. She'd been just like them once and she knew it wasn't simply nostalgia coloring her memory. She knew there'd been a time when she lived inside each particular day, on its own and by itself, instead of trying to deal with all the days of her life at once, futilely attempting to reconcile the discrepancies and mistakes.

"I'll try," she said into the phone.

They said their goodbyes and Heather slowly cradled the receiver.

"Who was that, Mom?" Casey asked.

Heather looked out the window. The snow was still falling, muffling the world. Covering its complexities with a blanket as innocent as the hope she saw in her daughters' eyes.

"Jilly," she said. She took a deep breath, then smiled at them. "She was calling to tell me that today really is a snow day."

The happiness that flowered on their faces helped ease the tightness in her chest. The grey landscape waiting for her there didn't go away, but for some reason, it felt less profound. She wasn't even worried about what her boss would say when she called in to tell him she wouldn't be in today.

Crow girls can move like ghosts. They'll slip into your house when you're not home, sometimes when you're only sleeping, go walking spirit-soft through your rooms and hallways, sit in your favorite chair, help themselves to cookies and beer, borrow a trinket or two which they'll mean to return and usually do. It's not breaking and entering so much as simple curiosity. They're worse than cats.

Privacy isn't in their nature. They don't seek it and barely understand the concept. Personal property is even more alien. The idea of ownership— that one can lay proprietary claim to a piece of land, an object, another person or creature—doesn't even register.

"Whatcha looking at?" Zia asks.

They don't know whose house they're in. Walking along on the street, trying to catch snowflakes on their tongues, one or the other of them suddenly got the urge to come inside. Upstairs, the family sleeps.

Maida shows her the photo album. "Look," she says. "It's the same people, but they keep changing. See, here's she's a baby, then she's a little girl, then a teenager."

"Everything changes," Zia says. "Even we get old. Look at Crazy Crow."

"But it happens so fast with them."

Zia sits down beside her and they pore over the pictures, munching on apples they found earlier in a cold cellar in the basement.

Upstairs, a father wakes in his bed. He stares at the ceiling, wondering what woke him. Nervous energy crackles inside him like static electricity, a sudden spill of adrenaline, but he doesn't know why. He gets up and checks the children's rooms. They're both asleep. He listens for intruders, but the house is silent.

Stepping back into the hall, he walks to the head of the stairs and looks down. He thinks he sees something in the gloom, two dark-haired girls sitting on the sofa, looking through a photo album. Their gazes lift to meet his and hold it. The next thing he knows, he's on the sofa himself, holding the photo album in his hand. There are no strange girls sitting there with him. The house seems quieter than it's ever been, as though the fridge, the furnace, and every clock the family owns are holding their breath along with him.

He sets the album down on the coffee table, walks slowly back up the stairs and returns to his bed. He feels like a stranger, misplaced. He doesn't know this room, doesn't know the woman beside him. All he can think about is the first girl he ever loved and his heart swells with a bittersweet sorrow. An ache pushes against his ribs, makes it almost impossible to breathe.

What if, what if . . .

He turns on his side and looks at his wife. For one moment her face blurs, becomes a morphing image that encompasses both her features and those of his first true love. For one moment it seems as though anything is possible, that for all these years he could have been married to another woman, to that girl who first held, then unwittingly, broke his heart.

"No," he says.

His wife stirs, her features her own again. She blinks sleepily at him.

"What . . . ?" she mumbles.

He holds her close, heartbeat drumming, more in love with her for being who she is than he has ever been before.

Outside, the crow girls are lying on their backs, making snow angels on his lawn, scissoring their arms and legs, shaping skirts and wings. They break their apple cores in two and give their angels eyes, then run off down the street, holding hands. The snow drifts are undisturbed by their weight. It's as though they, too, like the angels they've just made, also have wings.

"This is so cool," Casey tells her mother. "It really feels like Christmas. I mean, not like Christmases we've had, but, you know, like really being part of Christmas."

Heather nods. She's glad she brought the girls down to the soup kitchen to help Jilly and her friends serve a Christmas dinner to those less fortunate than themselves. She's been worried about how her daughters would take the break from tradition, but then realized, with Peter gone, tradition was already broken. Better to begin all over again.

The girls had been dubious when she first broached the subject with them—"I don't want to spend Christmas with *losers*," had been Casey's first comment. Heather hadn't argued with her. All she'd said was, "I want you to think about what you just said."

Casey's response had been a sullen look—there were more and more of these lately—but Heather knew her own daughter well enough. Casey had stomped off to her room, but then come back half an hour later and helped her explain to Janice why it might not be the worst idea in the world.

She watches them now, Casey having rejoined her sister where they are playing with the homeless children, and knows a swell of pride. They're such good kids, she thinks as she takes another sip of her cider. After a couple of hours serving coffee, tea and hot cider, she'd really needed to get off her feet for a moment.

"Got something for you," Jilly says, sitting down on the bench beside her.

Heather accepts the small, brightly-wrapped parcel with reluctance. "I thought we said we weren't doing Christmas presents."

"It's not really a Christmas present. It's more an everyday sort of a present that I just happen to be giving you today."

"Right."

"So aren't you going to open it?"

Heather peels back the paper and opens the small box. Inside, nestled in a piece of folded Kleenex, are two small silver earrings cast in the shapes of crows. Heather lifts her gaze.

"They're beautiful."

"Got them at the craft show from a local jeweler. Rory Crowther. See, his name's on the card in the bottom of the box. They're to remind you—"

Heather smiles. "Of crow girls?"

"Partly. But more to remember that this—" Jilly waves a hand that could be taking in the basement of St. Vincent's, could be taking in the whole world. "It's not all we get. There's more. We can't always see it, but it's there."

For a moment, Heather thinks she sees two dark-haired slim figures standing on the far side of the basement, but when she looks more closely they're only a baglady and Geordie's friend Tanya, talking.

For a moment, she thinks she hears the sound of wings, but it's only the murmur of conversation. Probably.

What she knows for sure is that the grey landscape inside her chest is shrinking a little more, every day.

"Thank you," she says.

She isn't sure if she's speaking to Jilly or to crow girls she's only ever seen once, but whose presence keeps echoing through her life. Her new life. It isn't necessarily a better one. Not yet. But at least it's on the way up from wherever she'd been going, not down into a darker despair.

"Here," Jilly says. "Let me help you put them on."

Wild Horses

Chance is always powerful. Let your hook be
always cast; in the pool where you least expect
it, there will be a fish.

—Ovid

1

The horses run the empty length of the lake shore, strung out like a
long ragged necklace, perfect in their beauty. They run wild. They run
like whitecaps in choppy water, their unshod hooves kicking up sand
and spray. The muffled sound of their galloping is a rough music, pure
rhythm. Palominos. Six, seven . . . maybe a dozen of them. Their white
manes and tails flash, golden coats catch the sunlight and hold it under
the skin the way mine holds a drug.

The city is gone. Except for me, transfixed by the sight of them, gaze
snared by the powerful motion of their muscles propelling them forward,
the city is gone, skyline and dirty streets and dealers and the horse that
comes in a needle instead of running free along a beach. All gone.

And for a moment, I'm free, too.

I run after them, but they're too fast for me, these wild horses, can't be
tamed, can't be caught. I run until I'm out of breath and stumble and fall
and when I come to, I'm lying under the overpass where the freeway cuts
through Squatland, my works lying on my coat beside me, empty now. I

look out across a landscape of sad tenements and long-abandoned factories and the only thing I can think is, I need another hit to take me back.
Another hit, and this time I'll catch up to them.

I know I will. I have to.

There's nothing for me here.

But the drugs don't take me anywhere.

2

Cassie watched the young woman approach. She was something, sleek
and pretty, newly shed of her baby fat. Nineteen, maybe; twenty-one,
twenty-two, tops. Wearing an old sweater, raggedy jeans and sneakers—
nothing fancy, but she looked like a million dollars. Bottle that up, Cassie
thought, along with the long spill of her dark curly hair, the fresh-faced,
perfect complexion, and you'd be on easy street. Only the eyes hinted
at what must have brought her here, the lost, hopeful look in their
dark depths. Something haunted her. You didn't need the cards to tell
you that.

She was out of place—not a tourist, not part of the bohemian coterie
of fortune-tellers, buskers, and craftspeople who were set up along this
section of the Pier either. Cassie tracked her gaze as it went from one card
table to the next, past the palmist, the other card readers, the Gypsy, the
lovely Scottish boy with his Weirdin discs, watched until that gaze met
her own and the woman started to walk across the boards, aimed straight
for her.

Somebody was playing a harp, over by one of the weavers' tables. A
sweet melody, like a lullaby, rose above the conversation around the tables and the sound of the water lapping against the wooden footings below. It made no obvious impression on the approaching woman, but
Cassie took the music in, letting it swell inside her, a piece of beauty
stolen from the heart of commerce. The open-air market and sideshow
that sprawled along this section of the Pier might look alternative, but it
was still about money. The harper was out to make a buck, and so was
Cassie.

She had her small collapsible table set up with a stool for her on one
side, its twin directly across the table for a customer. A tablecloth was
spread over the table, hand-embroidered with ornate hermetic designs.

On top of the cloth, a small brass change bowl and her cards, wrapped in silk and boxed in teak.

The woman stood behind the vacant stool, hesitating before she finally sat down. She pulled her knapsack from her back and held it on her lap, arms hugging it close to her chest. The smile she gave Cassie was uncertain.

Cassie gave her a friendly smile back. "No reason to be nervous, girl. We're all friends here. What's your name?"

"Laura."

"And I'm Cassandra. Now what sort of a reading were you looking for?"

Laura reached out her hand, not quite touching the box with its cards. "Are they real?" she asked.

"How do you mean, real?"

"Magic. Can you work magic with them?"

"Well, now . . ."

Cassie didn't like to lie, but there was magic and there was magic. One lay in the heart of the world and was as much a natural part of how things were as it was deep mystery. The other was the thing people were looking for to solve their problems with and it never quite worked the way they felt it should.

"Magic's all about perception," she said. "Do you know what I mean?"

Laura shook her head. She'd drawn her hand back from the cards and was hugging her knapsack again. Cassie picked up the wooden box and put it to one side. From the inside pocket of her matador's jacket, she pulled out another set of cards. These ones were tattered around the edges, held together by an elastic band. When she placed them on the tablecloth, the woman's gaze went to the top card and was immediately caught by the curious image on it. The card showed the same open-air market they were sitting in, the crowds of tourists and vendors, the Pier, the lake behind.

"Those . . . are those regular cards?" Laura asked.

"Do I look like a regular reader?"

The question was academic. Cassie didn't look like a regular anything, not even on the Pier. She was in her early thirties, a dark-eyed woman with coffee-colored skin and hair that hung in a hundred tiny beaded braids. Today she wore tight purple jeans and yellow combat boots; under her black matador's jacket was a white T-shirt with the words DON'T! BUY! THAI! emblazoned on it. Her ears were festooned with studs, dangling earrings, and simple hoops. On each wrist she had a dozen or so plastic bracelets in a rainbow palette of Day-Glo colors.

"I guess not," the woman said. She leaned a little closer. "What does your T-shirt mean? I've seen that slogan all over town, on T-shirts, spray-painted on walls, but I don't know what it means."

"It's a boycott to try to stop the child-sex industry in Thailand."

"Are you collecting signatures for a petition or something?"

Cassie shook her head. "You just do like the words say. Check out what you're buying and if it's made in Thailand, don't buy it and explain why."

"Do you really think it'll help?"

"Well, it's like magic," Cassie said, bringing the conversation back to what she knew Laura really wanted to talk about. "And like I said, magic's about perception, that's all. It means anything is possible. It means taking the way we usually look at a thing and making people see it differently. Or, depending on your viewpoint, making them see it properly for the first time."

"But—"

"For instance, I could be a crow, sitting on this stool talking to you, but I've convinced everybody here that I'm Cassandra Washington, card reader, so that's what you all see."

Laura gave her an uneasy look that Cassie had no trouble reading: Pretty sure she was being put on, but not entirely sure.

Cassie smiled. "The operative word here is *could*. But that's how magic works. It's all about how we perceive things to be. A good magician can make anything seem possible and pretty soon you've got seven-league boots and people turning invisible or changing into wolves or flying—all sorts of fun stuff."

"You're serious, aren't you?"

"Oh, yeah. Now fortune-telling—that's all about perception, too, except it's looking inside yourself. It works best with a ritual because that allows you to concentrate better—same reason religion and church works so well for some people. Makes them all pay attention and focus and the next thing you know they're either looking inside themselves and working out their problems, or making a piece of magic."

She picked up the cards and removed the elastic band. Shuffled them. "Think of these as a mirror. Pay enough attention to them and they'll lay out a pattern that'll take you deep inside yourself."

Laura appeared disappointed. But they always did, when it was put out in front of them like this. They thought you'd pulled back the curtain and shown the Wizard of Oz, working all the levers of his machine, not realizing that you'd let them into a deeper piece of magic than something they might buy for a few dollars in a place like the Pier.

"I . . . I thought it might be different," Laura said.

"You wanted it all laid out for you, simple, right? Do this, and this'll happen. Do this, and it'll go like this. Like reading the sun signs in the newspaper, except personal."

Laura shook her head. "It wasn't about me. It was about my brother."

"Your brother?"

"I was hoping you could, you know, use your cards to tell me where he is."

Cassie stopped shuffling her pack and laid it face down on the table.

"Your brother's missing?" she said.

Laura nodded. "It's been two years now."

Cassie was willing to give people a show, willing to give them more than what they were asking for, sometimes, or rather what they were really asking for but weren't articulating, but she wasn't in the business of selling false hopes or pretenses. Some people could do it, but not her. Not and sleep at night.

"Laura," she said. "Girl. You've come to the wrong place. You want to talk to the police. They're the ones who deal with missing persons."

And you'll have wanted to talk to them a lot sooner than now, she thought, but she left that unsaid.

"I did," Laura told her.

Cassie waited. "And what?" she asked finally. "They told you to come here?"

"No. Of course not. They—a Sergeant Riley. He's been really nice, but I guess there's not much they can do. They say it's been so long and the city's so big and Dan could have moved away months ago. . . ."

Her eyes filled with tears and voice trailed off. She swallowed, tried again.

"I brought everything I could think of," she said, holding up her knapsack for a moment before clutching it tightly to her chest again. "Pictures.

His dental records. The last couple of postcards I got from him. I . . ."
She had to swallow again. "They have all these pictures of . . . of uniden-
tified bodies and I . . . I had to look at them all. And they sent off copies
of the stuff I brought—sent it off all over the country, but it's been over a
month and I know Dan's not dead. . . ."

She looked up, her eyes still shiny with unshed tears. Cassie nodded
sympathetically.

"Can I see one of the pictures?" she said.

A college-aged boy looked back at her from the small snapshot Laura
took out of her knapsack. Not handsome, but there was a lot of character
in his features. Short brown hair, high cheek bones, strong jawline. Something in his eyes reflected the same mix of loss and hopefulness that was
now in his sister's. What had *he* been looking for?

"You say he's been missing for two years?" Cassie asked.

Laura nodded. Showing the picture seemed to have helped steady her.

"Your parents didn't try to find him?"

"They never really got along. It's—I don't know why. They were always fighting, arguing. He left the house when he was sixteen—as soon as
he could get out. We live—we *lived* just outside of Boston. He moved
into Cambridge, then maybe four years ago, he moved out here. When I
was in college he'd call me sometimes and always send me postcards."

Cassie waited. "And then he stopped?" she said finally.

"Two years ago. That's when I got the last card. I saw him a couple of
months before that."

"Do you get along with your parents?"

"They've always treated me just the opposite from how they treated
him. Dan couldn't do anything right and I can't do anything wrong."

"Why did you wait so long?"

"I . . ." Her features fell. "I just kept expecting to hear from him. I was
finishing up my master's and working part-time at a restaurant and . . . I
don't know. I was just so busy and I didn't realize how long it had really
been until all of a sudden two years have gone by since he wrote."

She kept looking at the table as she spoke, glancing up as though to
make sure Cassie was still listening, then back down again. When she
looked up now, she straightened her back.

"I guess it was pretty crazy of me to think you could help," she said.

No, Cassie thought. More like a little sad. But she understood need and how it could make you consider avenues you'd never normally take a walk down.

"Didn't say I wouldn't try," she told Laura. "What do you know about what he was doing here?"

"The last time I saw him, all he could talk about were these horses, wild horses running along the shore of the lake."

Cassie nodded encouragingly when Laura's voice trailed off once more.

"But there aren't any, are there?" Laura said. "It's all . . ." She waved her hand, encompassing the Pier, the big hotels, the Williamson Street Mall further up the beach. "It's all like this."

"Pretty much. A little further west there's the Beaches, but that's all private waterfront and pretty upscale. And even if someone would let him onto their land, I've never heard of any wild horses out there."

Laura nodded. "I showed his picture around at the racetrack and every riding stable I could find listed in the Yellow Pages, but no one recognized him."

"Anything else?" Cassie asked.

She hesitated for a long moment before replying. "I think he was getting into drugs again." Her gaze lifted from the card table to meet Cassie's. "He was pretty bad off for a few years, right after he got out of the house, but he'd cleaned up his act before he moved out here."

"What makes you think he got back into them?"

"I don't know. Just a feeling—the last time I saw him. The way he was all fidgety again, something in his eyes. . . ."

Maybe that was what she'd seen in his picture, Cassie thought. That need in his eyes.

"What kind of drugs?" she asked.

"Heroin."

"A different kind of horse."

Laura sighed. "That's what Sergeant Riley said."

Cassie tapped a fingernail, painted the same purple as her jeans, on the pack of cards that lay between them.

"Where are you staying?" she asked.

"The Y. It's all I can afford. I'm getting kind of low on money and I haven't had much luck getting a job."

Cassie nodded. "Leave me that picture," she said. "I'll ask around for you, see what I can find out."

"But . . ."

She was looking at the cards. Cassie laid her hand over them and shook her head.

"Let me do this my way," Cassie said. "You know the pay phone by the front desk? I'll give you a call there tomorrow, around three, say, and then we can talk some more."

She put out her hand and Laura looked confused.

"Um," she began. "How much do you want?"

Cassie smiled. "The picture, girl. I'll do the looking as a favor."

"But I'm putting you to so much trouble—"

"I've been where you are," Cassie said. "If you want to pay me back, do a good turn for someone else."

"Oh."

She didn't seem either confident or happy with the arrangement, but she left the picture and stood up. Cassie watched her make her way back through the other vendors, then slowly turned over three cards from the top of the deck. The first showed a set of works lying on worn blue denim. A jacket, Cassie decided. The second had a picture of an overpass in the Tombs. The last showed a long length of beach, empty except for a small herd of palominos cantering down the wet sand. In the background, out in the water, was the familiar shape of Wolf Island, outlined against the horizon.

Cassie lifted her head and turned to look at the lake. Beyond the end of the Pier she could see Wolf Island, the ferry on a return trip, halfway between the island and the mainland. The image on her card didn't show the city, didn't show docking facilities on the island, the museum and gift shop that used to be somebody's summer place. The image on her card was of another time, before the city got here. Or of another place that you could only reach with your imagination.

Or with magic.

3

Cassie and Joe had made arrangements to meet at The Rusty Lion that night. He'd been sitting outside on the patio waiting for her when she arrived, a handsome Native man in jeans and a plain white T-shirt, long black braid hanging down his back, a look in his dark eyes that was usually half solemn, half tomfool Trickster. Right now it was concerned.

"You don't look so good," he said as she sat down.

She tried to make a joke of it. "People ask me why I stay with you," she said, "and I always tell them, you just know how to make a girl feel special."

But Joe would have none of it.

"You've got trouble," he told her, "and that means we have trouble. Tell me about it."

So she did.

Joe knew why she was helping this woman she'd never seen before. That was one of the reasons it was so good between them: Lots of things didn't need to be explained, they were simply understood.

" 'Course you found Angie too late," he said.

He reached across the table and took her hand, wanting to ease the sting of his words. She nodded and took what comfort she could from the touch of his rough palm and fingers. There was never any comfort in thinking about Angie.

"It might be too late for Laura's brother, too," she said.

Joe shrugged. "Depends. The cops could be right. He could be long gone from here, headed off to some junkie heaven like Seattle. I hear they've got one of the best needle-exchange programs in the country and you know the dope's cheap. Twenty bucks'll buy you a 30 piece."

Cassie nodded. "Except the cards . . ."

"Oh, yeah. The cards."

The three cards lay on the table between them, still holding the images she'd found in them after Laura walked away. Joe had recognized the place where the horses were running the same as she had.

"Except I never heard of dope taking someone into the spiritworld before," he said.

"So what does it mean?" Cassie asked.

He put into words what she'd only been thinking. "Either he's clean, or he's dead."

She nodded. "And if he's clean, then why hasn't he called her, or sent another postcard? They were close."

"She says."

"You don't think so?"

Joe shrugged. "I wasn't the one who met her. But she waited two years."

"I waited longer to go looking for Angie."

There was nothing Joe could say to that.

4

It was a long time ago now.

Cassie shows them all, the white kids who wouldn't give her the time of day and the kids from the projects that she grew up with. She makes top of her graduating class, valedictorian, stands there at the commencement exercises, out in front of everybody, speech in hand. But when she looks out across the sea of mostly white faces, she realizes they still don't respect her and there's nobody she cares about sitting out there. The one person who ever meant something to her is noticeably absent.

Angie dropped out in grade nine and they really haven't seen each other since. Somewhere between Angie dropping out and Cassie resolving to prove herself, she and her childhood best friend have become more than strangers. They might as well never have known each other, they're so different.

So Cassie's looking out at the crowd. She wants to blow them off, but that's like giving in, so she follows through, reads her speech, pretends she's a part of the celebration, but she skips the bullshit parties that follow, doesn't listen to the phony praise for her speech, won't talk to her teachers who want to know what she plans to do next. She goes home and takes off that pretty new dress that cost her two months' working after school and weekends at McDonald's. Puts on sweats and hightops. Washes the makeup from her face and looks in the mirror. The face that looks back at her is soft, that of a little girl. The only steel is in the eyes.

Then she goes out looking for Angie, but Angie's not around any more. Word on the street is she went the junkie route, mixing crack and horse, selling herself to pay for her jones, long gone now or dead, and why would Cassie care anyway? It's like school, only in reverse. She's got no street smarts, no one takes her seriously, no one respects her.

She finds herself walking out of the projects, still looking for Angie, but keeping to herself now, walking all over the city, looking into faces but finding only strangers. Her need to find Angie is maybe as strong as Angie's was for the drugs, everything's focused on it, looking not only for Angie but for herself—the girl she was before she let other people's opinions become more important than her best friend. She's not ready to say that her turning her back on Angie pushed her toward the street life, but it couldn't have helped either. But she does know that Angie had a need that Cassie filled and the drugs took its place. Now Cassie has a need and she doesn't know what's going to fill it, but something has to or she feels like she's just going to dry up and blow away.

She keeps walking further and further until one day that jones of hers takes her to an old white clapboard house just north of the city, front yard's got a bottle tree growing in the weeds and dirt, an old juju woman sitting on the porch looking at her with dark eyes, skin so black Cassie feels white. Cassie doesn't know which is scarier, the old woman or her saying, " 'Bout time you showed up, girl. I'd just about given up on you."

All Cassie can do is stand there, can't walk away, snared by the old woman's gaze. A breeze comes up and those bottles hanging in the tree clink against each other. The old woman beckons to her with a crooked finger and the next thing Cassie knows she's walking up to the porch, climbing the rickety stairs, standing right in front of the woman.

"I've been keeping these for someone like you," she says and pulls a pack of tattered cards out of the pocket of her black dress.

Cassie doesn't want to take them, but she reaches for them all the same. They're held together with an elastic band. When the old woman puts them in her hand, something like a static charge jumps between them. She gets a dizzy feeling that makes her sway, almost lose her balance. She closes her hand, fingers tight around the cards and the feeling goes away.

The old woman's grinning. "You felt that, didn't you, girl?"

"I . . . I felt something."

"Aren't you a caution."

None of this feels real, none of it makes sense. The old woman, the house, the bottle tree. Cassie tries to remember how she got here, when the strip malls and fast-food outlets suddenly gave way to a dirt road and this place. Is this how it happened to Angie? All of a sudden she looks at herself one day and she's a junkie?

Cassie's gaze goes down to the cards the old woman gave her. She removes the elastic and fans a few of them out. They have a design on one side; the other side is blank. She lifts her head to find the old woman still grinning at her.

"What are these?" she asks.

"What do they look like, girl? They're cards. Older than Egypt, older than China, older than when the first mama woke up in Africa and got to making babies so that we could all be here."

"But . . ." It's hard to think straight. "What are they for?"

"Fortunes, girl. Help you find yourself. Let you help other people find themselves."

"But . . ."

She was valedictorian, she thinks. She has more of a vocabulary than her whole family put together and all she can say is "but."

"But there's nothing on them."

She doesn't know much about white people's magic, but she's heard of telling fortunes with cards—playing cards, Tarot cards. She doesn't know much about her own people's magic either.

The old juju woman laughs. "Oh, girl. 'Course there isn't. There won't be nothing on them until you need something to be there."

None of this is making sense. It's only making her dizzy again. There's a stool beside the woman's chair and she sits on it, closes her eyes, still holding the cards. She takes a few deep breaths, steadies herself. But when she opens her eyes again she's sitting on a concrete block in the middle of a traffic median. There's no house, no bottle tree. No old woman. Only the traffic going by on either side of her. A discount clothing store across the street. A factory outlet selling stereos and computers on the other side.

There's only the cards in her hands and at her feet, lying on the pavement of the median, an elastic band.

She's scared. But she bends down, picks up the elastic. She turns over the top card, looks at it. There's a picture now, where before it was blank. It shows an abandoned tenement in the Tombs, one of the places where the homeless people squat. She's never been in it, but she recognizes the building. She's passed it a hundred times on the bus, going from school to the McDonald's where she worked. She turns another card and now she's looking at a picture of the inside of a building—probably the same one. The windows are broken, there's garbage all over, a heap of rags in one corner. A third card takes her closer to the rags. Now she can see there's somebody lying under those rags, somebody so thin and wasted there's only bone covered with skin.

She doesn't turn a fourth card.

She returns the cards to the pack, puts the elastic around them, sticks the pack in her pocket. Her mouth feels baked and dry. She waits for a break in the traffic and goes across to the discount clothing store to ask for a drink of water, but they tell her the restroom is only for staff. She has to walk four blocks before a man at a service station gives a sympathetic look when she repeats her request, hands her the key to the woman's room.

She drinks long and deep, then feels sick and has to throw up. When she returns to the sink, she rinses her mouth, washes her face. The man's busy with a customer, so she hangs the key on the appropriate hook by the door in the office and thanks him as she goes by, walking back toward downtown.

Normal people don't walk through the Tombs, not even along well-trafficked streets like Williamson or Flood. It's too dangerous, a no-man's-land of deserted tenements and abandoned factories. But she doesn't see she has a choice. She walks until she sees the tenement that was on the card, swallows hard, then crosses an empty lot overgrown with weeds and refuse until she's standing in front of it. It takes her a while to work up her nerve, but finally she steps into its foyer.

It smells of urine and garbage. Something stirs in a corner, sits up. Her pulse jumps into overtime, even when she sees it's only a raggedy boy, skinny, hollow-eyed.

"Gimme something," he says. "I don't need to get high, man. I just need to feel well again."

"I . . . I don't have anything."

She's surprised she can find her voice. She's surprised that he only nods and lies back down in his nest of newspapers and rags.

It doesn't take her long to find the room she saw on the second card. Something pulls her down a long hall. The doors are all broken down. Things stir in some of the rooms. People. Rats. Roaches. She doesn't know and doesn't investigate. She just keeps walking until she's in the room, steps around the garbage littering the floor to the heap of rags in the corner.

A half hour later she's at a pay phone on Gracie Street, phoning the police, telling them about the dead body she found in the tenement.

"Her name's Angie," she says. "Angie Moore."

She hangs up and starts to walk again, not looking for anything now, hardly able to see because of the tears that swell in her eyes.

She doesn't go home again. She can't exactly explain why. Meeting the old woman, the cards she carries, finding Angie, it all gets mixed up in her head with how hard she tried to do well and still nobody really cared about her except for the friend she turned her back on. Her parents were happy to brag about her marks, but there was no warmth there. She is eighteen and can't remember ever being embraced. Her brothers and sisters were like the other kids in the projects, ragging on her for trying to do well. The white kids didn't care about anything except for the color of her skin.

It all came down to no one respecting her except for Angie, and she'd turned her back on Angie because Angie couldn't keep up.

But the cards mean something. She knows that.

She's still working at the McDonald's, only now she saves her money and lives in a squat in the Tombs. Nobody comes to find out why she hasn't returned home. Not her family, not her teachers. Some of the kids from school stop by, filling up on Big Macs and fries and soft drinks, and she can hear them snickering at their tables, studiously not looking at her.

She takes to going to the library and reading about cards and fortune telling, gets to be a bit of an expert. She buys a set of Tarot cards in The Occult Shop and sometimes talks to the people who work there, some of the customers. She never reads or hears anything about the kind of cards the old woman gave her.

Then one day she meets Joseph Crazy Dog in the Tombs, just down from the Kickaha rez, wild and reckless and a little scary, but kind, too, if you took the time to get to know him. Some people say he's not all there, supposed to be on medication, but won't take it. Others say he's got his feet in two worlds, this one and another place where people have animal faces and only spirits can stay for more than a few days, the kind of place you come back from either a poet or mad. First thing he tells her is he can't rhyme worth a damn.

Everybody calls him Bones because of how he tells fortunes with a handful of small-animal and bird bones, reads auguries in the way they fall upon the buckskin when he throws them. But she calls him Joe and something good happens between them because he respects her, right away he respects her. He's the first person she tells about the old juju woman and she knows she was right to wait because straightaway he can tell her where she went that day and what it means.

5

It was almost dark by the time Cassie and Joe reached the overpass in the Tombs that was pictured on the card. At one time it had been a hobo camp, but now it was one more junkie landmark, a place where you could score and shoot without being hassled. The cops didn't bother coming by much. They had bigger fish to fry.

"A lot of hard times bundled up in a place like this," Joe said.

Cassie nodded.

Some of the kids they walked by were so young. Most of them were already high. Those that weren't, were looking to score. It wasn't the sort of place you could ask questions, but neither Cassie nor Joe were strangers to the Tombs. They still squatted themselves and most people knew of them, if they'd never actually met. They could get away with showing around a picture, asking questions.

"When did heroin get so popular again?" Cassie said.

Joe shrugged. "Never got unpopular—not when it's so easy to score. You know the drill. The only reason solvents and alcohol are so popular up on the rez is no one's bringing in this kind of shit. That's the way it works everywhere—supply and demand. Here the supply's good."

And nobody believed it could hurt them, Cassie thought. Because it wouldn't happen to them and sure people got addicted, but everybody knew somebody who'd used and hadn't got strung out on it. Nobody set out to become an addict. Like most bad things, it just snuck up on you when you weren't paying attention. But the biggest problem was that kids got lied to about so much, it was hard for them to accept this warning as a truth.

They made a slow pass of the three or four blocks where most of the users congregated, showing the photo of Laura's brother when it seemed appropriate, but without much luck. From there they headed back downtown, following Williamson Street down Gracie. It was on the gay bar strip on Gracie Street that they finally found someone who could help.

"I like the hair, Tommy," Cassie said.

It was like a close-cut Afro, the corkscrew curls so purple they had to come from a bottle. Tommy grinned, but his good humor vanished when Joe showed him the picture.

"Yeah, I know him," Tommy said. "Danny Packer, right? Though he sure doesn't look like that now. How come you're looking for him?"

"We're not. His sister is and we're just helping her out. Any idea where we could find him?"

"Ask at the clinic."

Cassie and Joe exchanged glances.

"He's working there?" Cassie asked.

Tommy shook his head.

6

"What is this place?" Laura asked.

They were standing in front of an old yellow brick house on McKennitt Street in Lower Crowsea. Cassie had picked her up outside the Y a little after four and Joe drove them across town in a cab he'd borrowed from a friend.

"It's a hospice," Cassie said. "It was founded by a writer who died of AIDS a few years ago—Ennis Thompson."

"I've read him. He was a wonderful writer."

Cassie nodded. "His royalties are what keeps it running."

The house was on a quiet stretch of McKennitt, shaded by a pair of the tall, stately oaks that flourished in Crowsea. There wasn't much lawn. Geraniums grew in terra cotta planters going up the steps to the front door, adding a splash of color and filling the air with their distinctive scent. They didn't seem to make much of an impression on Laura. She was too busy studying the three-storied building, a small frown furrowing the skin between her eyebrows.

"Why did Dan want me to meet him here?" she asked.

Cassie hesitated. When they'd come to see him last night, Laura's brother had asked them to let him break the news to her. She understood, but it left her in the awkward position of having to be far too enigmatic in response to Laura's delight that her brother had been found. She'd been fending off Laura's questions ever since they'd spoken on the phone earlier and arranged to drive out here.

"Why don't we let him tell you himself," Cassie said.

Joe held the door for them. He nodded a greeting to the young woman stationed at a reception desk in what would once have been a front parlor.

"Go ahead," she told them. "He's expecting you."

"Thanks," Joe said.

He led the way down the hall to Dan's room. Rapping softly on the door, he opened it when a weak voice called out, "It's open."

Laura stopped and wouldn't go on.

"Come on," Cassie said, her voice gentle.

But Laura could only shake her head. "Oh god, how could I have been so stupid? He's a patient here, isn't he?"

Cassie put a hand on her arm and found it trembling. "He's still your brother."

"I know. It's not that. It's just—"

"Laura?"

The voice pulled her to the door and through it, into the room. Cassie had been planning to allow them some privacy for this meeting, but now she followed in after Laura to lend her moral support in case it was needed.

Dan was in bad shape. She only knew him from the picture that Laura had lent her yesterday, but he bore no resemblance to the young man in that photograph. Not anymore. No doubt he had already changed somewhat in the years since the picture had been taken, but now he was skeletal, the skin hanging from his bones, features hollow and sunken. Sores discolored his skin in great blotches and his hair was wispy and thin.

But Laura knew him.

Whatever had stopped her outside the room was gone. She crossed the room quickly now, sat down on the edge of the bed, carefully took his scrawny hands in her own, leaned forward and kissed his brow.

"Oh, Danny. What have you done to yourself?"

He gave her a weak smile. "Screwed things up as usual."

"But this . . ."

"I want you to know—it wasn't from a needle."

Laura threw a glance over her shoulder at Cassie, then returned her attention to her brother.

"I always knew," she said.

"You never said anything."

"I was waiting for you to tell me."

He shook his head slowly. "I could never put one past you."

"When were you going to tell me?" Laura asked.

"That's why I came back the last time. But I lost my nerve. And then when I got back to the city, I wasn't just HIV-positive anymore, but had full-blown AIDS and . . ."

His voice, already weak, trailed off.

"Oh, Danny, why? What did you think—that I wouldn't love you anymore?"

"I didn't know what to think. I just didn't want to be a bother."

"That's the last thing you are," Laura assured him. "I know . . ." She had to swallow and start again. "I know you won't be getting better, but you've got to at least have your family with you. Come home with me."

"No."

"Why not? Mom and Dad will want to—"

Dan cut her off, anger giving his voice some strength. "They won't want anything to do with me."

"But—"

"You never understood, did you? We lived in the same house, but it was two different worlds. I lived in one and the rest of you lived in the other. I don't know why things worked out that way, but you've got to accept that it's never going to change. That not even something like this could change it."

Laura didn't say anything for a long moment. She simply sat there, holding his hands, looking at him.

"It was so awful for you," she said finally. "Wasn't it?"

He nodded. "Everything, except for you."

That seemed to be too much for her, knowing that on top of his dying, how hard his life had been, right from when he was a child. She bowed down over him, holding him, shoulders shaking as she wept.

Cassie backed out of the room to join Joe where he was waiting in the hall.

"It's got to be tough," he said.

Cassie nodded, not trusting her voice. Her own gaze was blurry with tears.

7

"You never told her how you found me," Dan said later.

When Laura had gone to get tea, Cassie and Joe came back into the room, sitting on hardbacked chairs beside the bed. It was still hours until dusk but an overcast sky cast a gloomy light into the room.

"And you won't, will you?" he added.

Cassie shook her head.

"Why not?"

"It's hard to explain," she said. "I guess I just don't want her to get the wrong idea about the cards. You don't use them or any oracular device to find answers; you use them to ask questions. Some people don't get that."

He nodded slowly. "Laura wouldn't. She was always looking for miracles to solve everything. Like the way it was for me back home."

"Her heart was in the right place," Joe said.

Dan glanced at him. "Still is." He returned his attention to Cassie. "But those cards aren't normal Tarot cards."

Cassie had shown him the cards the night before, the three images that had taken her and Joe up into the Tombs and eventually to Dan's room here in the hospice.

"No," she said. "They're real magic."

"Where did you get them? I mean, can I ask you that?"

Cassie smiled. "Of course you can. They come from the same place where your wild horses are running."

"They . . . they're real?"

"Depends on how you translate real," Joe said.

Cassie gave him a light tap on his shoulder with a closed fist. "Don't start with that."

"What place are you talking about?" Dan asked.

For once, Joe was more forthcoming than he usually was with a stranger.

"The spiritworld," he said. "It's a lot closer than most people think. Open yourself up to it and it comes in close, so close it's like it's right at hand, no further away than what's out there on the other side of that window." He paused a moment, then added, "Dangerous place to visit, outside of a dream."

"It wasn't a dream that took me there," Dan said.

"Wasn't the drugs either," Joe told him.

"But—"

"Listen to me, what took you there is the same thing that called Cassie to the old juju woman who gave her those cards. You had a need. Doesn't happen often, but sometimes that's enough to take you across."

"I still have that need."

Joe nodded. "But first the drugs you kept taking got in the way. And now you're dying and your body knows better than to let your spirit go visiting. It wants to hang on and the only thing that's keeping you going is spirit."

"What about Laura's need when she was looking for me?" Dan asked. "Why didn't the spiritworld touch her?"

"It brought her to me, didn't it?" Cassie said.

"That's true."

Dan looked away, out the window. The view he had through it was filled with the boughs of one of those big oak trees. Cassie didn't think he was seeing them.

"You know," he said after a moment, not looking away from the window. "Before all of this, I wouldn't have believed you for a moment. Wouldn't have even listened to you. But you start thinking about spiritual things at a time like this. When you *know* you're going to die, it's hard not to." His gaze returned to them, moving slowly from one to the other. "I'd like to see them again . . . those horses."

Cassie glanced at Joe and he nodded.

"When you're ready to leave," he said, "give me a call."

"You mean that? You can do that?"

"Sure."

Dan started to reach for the pen and paper that was on the table beside his bed. "What's your number?"

"We don't have a phone," Joe said. "You just think about me and those horses hard enough and I'll come take you to them."

"But—"

"He can do it," Cassie said. "Even at the best of times, he's walking with one foot in either world. He'll know when you're ready and he'll take you there."

Dan studied Joe for a moment and Cassie knew what he was seeing, the dark Coyote eyes, the crow's head sitting just under his human skin. There was something solemn and laughing wild about him, all at once, as though he knew a joke no one else did that wrapped him in a feral kind of wisdom that could scare you silly. But Dan was past fear.

"That's something else you discover when you're this close to the edge," he said. "You get this ability to cut away the bullshit and look right into a person, see them for exactly as they are."

"So what are you seeing?" Joe asked.

Dan smiled. "Damned if I know. But I know I can trust you."

Cassie knew exactly what he meant.

8

Summer gave way to fall. On a cold October night, Cassie woke near dawn to find Joe sitting on the edge of the bed, pulling on his boots. He came over to the bed and kissed her cheek.

"Go back to sleep," he said. "I might be awhile."

They'd been up late that night and she fell back asleep before she could think to ask where he was going.

9

Dan's funeral was two days later. It was a small service with few in attendance. Laura. Cassie. A few of the caregivers from the hospice. After the service, Cassie took Laura down to the lakefront. They sat on a bench at the end of the Pier where they'd first met, looking out at Wolf Island. A cold wind blew in off the lake and they sat close to each other for warmth.

"Where's Joe?" Laura asked.

"He had to go out of town."

Laura looked different to Cassie, more sure of herself, less haunted for all her sadness. She'd been working as a bartender for the past few months—"See, I knew that M.A. would be useful for something," she'd joked—spending her afternoons with Dan.

"It's been really hard," she said. "Especially the last couple of weeks."

Cassie put her arm around Laura's shoulders. "Probably the hardest thing you'll ever do."

"But I wouldn't give up any of it. What Dan had to go through, yes, but not my being with him."

"He was lucky you found him in time."

"It wasn't luck," Laura said.

Cassie raised her eyebrows.

"He told me about the cards." She shook her head before Cassie could say anything. "No, it's okay. I understand. I know it would be so tempting to use something like that to make all your decisions for you. I'm not asking for that." She hesitated a moment, then added, "But I was wondering . . . can they show me Dan one last time? Just so I can know if he finally caught up with those horses? Just so I can know he's okay?"

"I don't know," Cassie said. "I think the only way we ever find out where we go in the end, is when we make the journey ourselves."

Laura gave a slow nod, unable to hide her disappointment. "I . . . I guess I understand."

"But that doesn't mean we can't look."

She took her arm away from Laura's shoulders and brought out the set of cards the old juju woman had given her, sitting there on her porch with the bottle tree clinking on the lawn. Removing the elastic, she gave the cards a shuffle, then offered the pack to Laura.

"Pick one," she said.

"Don't you have to lay them out in some kind of pattern?"

"Ordinary Tarot cards, yes. But you're looking to see into someplace they can't take you now."

Laura placed her fingers on the top of the deck. She held off for a long moment, then finally took the card and turned it over. There were horses running along the lakeshore on it, golden horses with white manes and tails. The image was too small to make out details, but they could see a figure on the back of one of them, head thrown back. Laughing, perhaps. Finally free.

Smiling, Laura returned the card to the pack.

"Where he goes," she said, "I hope he'll always be that happy."

Cassie wound the elastic back around the cards and returned them to her pocket.

"Maybe if we believe it strongly enough it'll be true," she said.

Laura turned to look at her. Her eyes where shiny with tears but that lost, haunted look Cassie had seen in them that first time they met was gone.

"Then I'll believe it," Laura said.

They leaned back against the bench, looking out across the water. The sound of the ferry's horn echoed faintly across the water, signaling its return from the island.

In the Land of the Unforgiven

> No people sing with such pure voices as those
> who live in deepest hell; what we take for the
> song of angels is their song.
>
> —*Franz Kafka*

The little dead boy shows up in his dreams, the night after Cray hears how he died. Stands there in a place that's only half-light and shadows. Stands there singing, part of a chorus of children's voices, the other singers hidden in the darkness.

The pure, sweet sound of their voices wakes Cray and puts tears in his eyes. The springs creak as he turns to lie on his back. He stares up at the cracks in the ceiling and can't get the sound out of his head.

Cray waits in the shadows pooling at the mouth of the alley, his gaze on the lit window. Third floor of a brownstone, middle apartment. A swollen moon is just setting, so big and close it feels like it's going down only a few blocks over. He watches the last fat sliver slip away, then returns his gaze to the apartment.

A silhouette moves across the window. Cray starts to take a step back, stops himself when he realizes what he's doing. Like Erwin could see him.

The guys he came up with in the old neighborhood wouldn't have let it go so long. Something like this, you moved in, hard, fast. You didn't take time to think. You just popped him, end of story.

But Cray's a long way from the old neighborhood. Not so much where he is, but who he is.

Earlier that afternoon, Danny Salmorin comes into the gym for a work-out. He's stand-up for a cop. Detective, Crowsea Precinct. There's nothing soft about him. He's in here regular as clockwork, three days a week. Free weights, jogs on the machines.

"Hey, Joe," Danny says. "How's it hanging?"

Cray doesn't have time for small talk. This thing's been on his mind for a couple of days now.

"Sonny Erwin," he says. "You know him?"

"He's scum. What's to know?"

"He's selling babies, Danny. Selling them for sex, body parts—whatever people are buying."

Something flickers darkly in Danny's eyes. "You've got something solid on this?"

Cray tells him about Juanita's little boy.

"Let me talk to her," Danny says. "I'll set up a meeting with the D.A.'s office and—"

He breaks off when Cray shakes his head.

"She's illegal," Cray says. "No way she'll talk to the D.A."

"You're tying my hands."

"This guy's a freak—you know what I'm saying?"

Danny nods. "I don't need an excuse to look for some way to take him down, Joe. We've been on him for two years now and we can't touch him. He plays it too clean."

"These kids . . ."

Cray lets his voice trail off. He sees it in Danny's eyes. No forgiveness. Shame for how the system keeps a freak like Erwin on the street. The law's reactive these days—it can't protect anymore, it can barely avenge, and even then you need hard facts to grease the wheels of justice and get them moving. Danny's carrying the weight of all those lives taken, all those lives that will be taken, and he can't do a damn thing to stop it.

"Something was to happen to Erwin," Danny says, measuring the words out, careful, "and there was any kind of a problem, I'd be the one to call."

Cray doesn't get it, not then, but he nods to let Danny know he's listening.

Later he's sitting up in his office, can't concentrate on the paperwork. All he can think of is what Mona told him about Juanita and her little boy. He looks out through the window, down to where Danny's jogging on one of the machines. The darkness has settled deep in Danny's eyes. Sweat's dripping from his brow, soaking his T-shirt. He's been on the machine for forty minutes now and he hasn't begun to burn off his frustration and anger.

Cray remembers the last stretch he pulled. He's been clean a long time, but you never forget what it's like inside. He swore he'd never go back, and he's held good to that promise, but he's thinking now that maybe there are some things worth giving up your freedom for.

All he has to do is ask himself, what kind of freedom did Juanita's kid have?

Cray squares his shoulders and crosses the street. As he walks up to the entrance of the brownstone, he hears the sound of a steel door closing. The sound's in his head, only he can hear it. A piece of memory he's going to be reliving soon.

It takes him maybe six seconds to jimmy the door—the lock's crap. It's been ten years since he's creeped a joint, but he could've done this one in his sleep.

He cracks the door, steps inside. Starts up the stairs. Takes them two at a time. He's not even winded when he reaches the third floor landing.

The sound in his head now is that of a children's chorus.

"Let it go," Mona says before he leaves for the day.

She's standing in the door to his office, tall and rangy in purple and pink Spandex shorts, black halter top. Red hair pulled back into a tight ponytail. She's got an aerobics class in ten minutes. Anywhere from eight to fifteen out-of-shape, well-heeled yuppies who never come up against the kind of thing he can't get out of his head.

Guys like Erwin know the drill. They're hitting the poor and the illegals. The ones who can't complain, can't defend themselves.

The closest Mona's class is going to come to it is maybe a couple of lines in the morning papers—if one of the kids gets even that much coverage. Most of them simply disappear and nobody hears about it, nobody cares except for their families.

"Juanita's got to come forward," he says. "Without her, they can't do a thing."

"She's got three other kids. What's going to happen to them if she gets deported?"

"That's what I told Danny."

She waits a beat, then says, "We did what we could."

He can see it cost her to say that, but she's got to know he can't let it go now.

"And the next kid he snatches?" he asks.

She looks at him, knows where this is taking him.

"I should never have told you," she says.

He shrugs.

"You'll never get away with it."

"I don't plan to," he tells her. "If there's one thing I've learned, you've got to take responsibility for your actions."

"But Erwin—"

Cray knows how cold his voice is. "That's something Erwin still has to learn."

It goes easy. Three A.M. and Erwin doesn't even ask who's at the door. He just opens it up, smiles. He probably gets deliveries all the time—whenever opportunity presents itself to those who're snatching the kids and babies for him.

The thing that gets to Cray is, Sonny Erwin looks so normal. Just an average joe. The monster's hiding there in his eyes, but you have to know it's there to see it.

"You know why I'm here?" Cray asks.

Erwin's brows rise in a question. He's still smiling. Cocksure.

Cray straight-arms him and sends Erwin backpedaling for balance. He follows him into the apartment, kicks the door closed behind him with the heel of his boot. Erwin's finally lost the smile. The switchblade drops from Cray's sleeve, into his palm. The blade slides into place with a *snik* that seems loud in the confined space of the apartment.

"Somebody's got to stand up for those kids," he says.

He never gives Erwin time to reply.

*   *   *

Danny Salmorin shows up with his partner in tow. Cray doesn't know why he's here. All Cray did was call 911; he never mentioned Danny to the dispatcher. Never even mentioned his own name. Just said, "There's a dead man here," gave the address, then hung up. Sat down and waited for them to come.

Roland Johns is a tall black man, almost as broad-shouldered as Cray. He's from the neighborhood—like Danny, he's one of the few of them that made good. He looks at the body sprawled in the middle of the living room floor, takes in the cut throat, the blood that's soaking Erwin's thick plush.

"What are you doing here?" Cray asks. "Where's the uniforms?"

"I like him in red," Roland says around the toothpick he's chewing on. "It's really his color, don't you think? Someone should've done a makeover on him years ago."

Danny ignores his partner. "We were in the area and caught the call," he tells Cray.

Cray gets the sense that maybe they were waiting for the call. But that's okay. Dealing with people he knows'll make it easier to get through this.

"Was he carrying?" Danny asks.

Cray shakes his head. He watches Danny reach behind his back and pull a .38 from the waistband of his pants. Danny wipes the piece clean with a cloth he takes from the pocket of his jacket, then kneels down. He puts the .38 in Erwin's hand, presses the fingers around the grip, then lays the gun on the carpet, like it fell there.

For a moment Cray doesn't understand what Danny's doing. Then he gets it. The .38's Danny's throwdown, serial numbers eaten away with acid. A clean weapon he's been hanging on to for an occasion like this. No history. Can't be traced. Lots of cops carry them.

"This is the way it went down," Danny says. "Sonny sets up a meet. When he tells you he wants access to the youth programs in the gym, you argue. He pulls his piece. You struggle, next thing you know he's dead. You call us like a good citizen and here we are."

Cray shakes his head. "I can't do it. That's playing the game his way."

"You already played it his way," Danny says. "He's dead, isn't he?"

"That's right. And I'll take the fall for it."

"Bullshit. You want to do time for getting rid of a piece of crap like that, makes his living selling kids to short-eyes and worse?"

"Maybe we should start arresting people for killing rats and roaches, too?" Roland adds.

"It's not right," Cray says. "I did what I had to do, but now I've got to stand up for it."

"Let me tell you what's not right," Danny says. "You going back inside, the gym closing up—that's not right. You think we don't know what you do in there? The women's self-defense courses. The youth programs. The sliding scale on memberships so nobody gets turned away. You're bringing some sense of community back into the neighborhood, Joe. You think losing that's worth this dipshit's life? Play this my way and you're not even going to court."

"I crossed a line—"

"Yeah, and now you're crossing right back over it again. Sonny Erwin *lived* on the other side of the line, Joe, and we couldn't touch him. You did us all a favor."

Beside him, Roland nods. "You broke a big link in the chain," he says. "This is going to put a serious cramp in a lot of freaks' lifestyles."

"I still broke the law," Cray says. "Where are we going to be if everybody settles their problems this way?"

"You making a career of this?" Danny asks. "You gonna be some kind of superhero vigilante now?"

"You know it wasn't like that," Cray says.

Danny nods. He looks tired.

"Yeah, I know," he says. "Thing I need to know is, do you?"

The next day Danny catches up with Cray outside the cemetery, after the service. He offers his condolences to Juanita, treats her respectfully. Holds the door of the cab for her so that she and her kids can get in. Mona's sitting in the front with the driver. She nods to Danny.

Cray and Danny watch as the cab pulls away from the curb, drives away under skies as dirty grey as the pavement under its tires.

"You clear on last night?" Danny asks.

Cray shakes his head. "Not really."

"You think Roland and me, we're on the pad or something? Running our own businesses on the side?"

"I've got no reason to think that."

Danny nods. "We're living in a war zone now, Joe. The old neighborhood's turned into a no-man's-land where a freak like Sonny Erwin can market kids and we can't touch him. When we were growing up we could leave our doors unlocked—remember that? Sure, we had to deal with the wiseguys and their crap, but things still made sense. Now nothing seems to anymore. Now there's no justice, no forgiveness—it's like we're not even human anymore. Nobody's looking out for anybody but themselves. Christ, half the department's on the pad."

"What're you trying to say?" Cray asks.

"I'm saying it's not right. We've lost something and I don't know that we can ever get it back. All of us who live down here, who don't have the money or the moneymen in our pocket, we get tarnished with the same brand, like there's no right, no wrong. Just us. The unforgiven."

"What I did last night wasn't right," Cray says. "I'm pretty clear on this."

Danny shakes his head. "It was against the law, but it was right, Joe. It was something that had to be done only nobody else had the balls to do it. Who wanted to do the time?"

"I could've done it."

"You're already doing time," Danny says. "That's what I'm trying to tell you. The way we're living now . . . we're all doing time. That's what it's come to." He shakes his head. "You tell me. Where's the difference?"

"You ever been inside?" Cray asks.

"No, but you have. Why do you think I'm asking you?"

Cray nods slowly. He looks down the street, but he's not seeing it. He's thinking about being kept four to a cell that was built to hold two. How you couldn't scratch your ass without a screw watching you. How you had to walk the line between the sides, the blacks and the Aryans, and if you couldn't fit in, you did your time in the hole. How you fought back with whatever it took so you didn't end up somebody's girlfriend.

"We have choices out here," he says. "We can make a difference."

"You make a difference," Danny says. "With the gym and with what you did last night."

"Last night I deliberately set out to kill a man. I never knew I had that in me. Never knew that I could plan it and do it, like I was ordering a new piece of equipment for the gym."

Cray frowns as he's speaking. The words seem inadequate to express the bleakness that has lodged inside him.

"There's a big difference," he adds, "between what I did and killing someone who's in my face, somebody jumps me in an alley, tries to hurt my family. I got through this by knowing I'd have to pay for it. You understand? But now . . ."

"Now you have to live with it."

Cray nods.

"You see what I'm trying to tell you?" Danny says. "You *are* paying for it. You're doing your time, only you're doing it on the outside where you can still make a difference. Same as me."

"Same as you?"

"Accessory after the fact." Danny gives him a long, serious look. "You think I don't respect this badge I'm carrying . . . what it stands for? You think what went down with Erwin didn't keep me up all night? I'm asking myself the same questions you are and I figure we handed ourselves life sentences. We're doing time like everybody else, except we know it. And we know why."

Cray nods again.

There's a long moment of silence.

"So if you could roll back time," Danny finally asks. "Would you do it the same?"

Cray wonders if Danny hears the children's voices, the sweet angel chorus that echoes faintly in the back of his head and makes his heart break to hear. He wonders if it ever goes away.

"I don't know," he says. "I'd have to stop him." Their gazes meet. "I'd have to do whatever it took."

"Yeah," Danny tells him. "Me, too."

There's nothing more either of them has to say.

My Life as a Bird

From the August, 1996 issue of the Spar Distributions catalogue:

The Girl Zone, No. 10. Written & illustrated by Mona Morgan. Latest issue features new chapters of The True Life Adventures of Rockit Grrl, Jupiter Jewel & My Life As A Bird. Includes a one-page jam with Charles Vess. My Own Comix Co., $2.75 Back issues available.

"MY LIFE AS A BIRD"
MONA'S MONOLOGUE FROM CHAPTER THREE:

The thing is, we spend too much time looking outside ourselves for what we should really be trying to find inside. But we can't seem to trust what we find in ourselves—maybe because that's where we find it. I suppose it's all a part of how we ignore who we really are. We're so quick to cut away pieces of ourselves to suit a particular relationship, a job, a circle of friends, incessantly editing who we are until we fit in. Or we do it to someone else. We try to edit the people around us.

I don't know which is worse.

Most people would say it's when we do it to someone else, but I don't think either one's a very healthy option.

Why do we love ourselves so little? Why are we suspect for trying to love ourselves, for being true to who and what we are rather than what someone else thinks we should be? We're so ready to betray ourselves, but we never call it that. We have all these other terms to describe it: Fitting in. Doing the right thing. Getting along.

I'm not proposing a world solely ruled by rank self-interest; I know that there have to be some limits of politeness and compromise or all we'll have left is anarchy. And anyone who expects the entire world to adjust to them is obviously a little too full of their own self-importance.

But how can we expect others to respect or care for us, if we don't respect and care for ourselves? And how come no one asks, "If you're so ready to betray yourself, why should I believe that you won't betray me as well?"

"And then he dumped you—just like that?"

Mona nodded. "I suppose I should've seen it coming. All it seems we've been doing lately is arguing. But I've been so busy trying to get the new issue out and dealing with the people at Spar who are still being such pricks. . . ."

She let her voice trail off. Tonight the plan had been to get away from her problems, not focus on them. She often thought that too many people used Jilly as a combination den mother/emotional junkyard, and she'd promised herself a long time ago that she wouldn't be one of them. But here she was anyway, dumping her problems all over the table between them.

The trouble was, Jilly drew confidences from you as easily as she did a smile. You couldn't not open up to her.

"I guess what it boils down to," she said, "is I wish I was more like Rockit Grrl than Mona."

Jilly smiled. "Which Mona?"

"Good point."

The real-life Mona wrote and drew three ongoing strips for her own bi-monthly comic book, *The Girl Zone*. Rockit Grrl was featured in "The True Life Adventures of Rockit Grrl," the pen-and-ink-Mona in a semi-autobiographical strip called "My Life as a Bird." Rounding out each issue was "Jupiter Jewel."

Rockit Grrl, aka "The Menace from Venice"—Venice Avenue, Crowsea, that is, not the Italian city or the California beach—was an in-your-face punkette with an athletic body and excellent fashion sense, strong and unafraid; a little too opinionated for her own good, perhaps, but that only allowed the plots to pretty much write themselves. She spent her time righting wrongs and combating heinous villains like Didn't-Phone-When-He-Said-He-Would Man and Honest-My-Wife-and-I-Are-as-Good-as-Separated Man.

The Mona in "My Life as a Bird" had spiky blonde hair and jean overalls just as her creator did, though the real life Mona wore a T-shirt under her overalls and she usually had an inch or so of dark roots showing. They both had a quirky sense of humor and tended to expound at length on what they considered the mainstays of interesting conversation—love and death, sex and art—though the strip's monologues were far more coherent. The stories invariably took place in the character's apartment or the local English-styled pub down the street from it, which was based on the same pub where she and Jilly were currently sharing a pitcher of draught.

Jupiter Jewel had yet to make an appearance in her own strip, but the readers all felt as though they already knew her since her friends—who did appear—were always talking about her.

"The Mona in the strip, I guess," Mona said. "Maybe life's not a smooth ride for her either, but at least she's usually got some snappy come-back line."

"That's only because you have the time to think them out for her."

"This is true."

"But then," Jilly added, "that must be half the fun. Everybody thinks of what they should have said after the fact, but you actually get to use those lines."

"Even more true."

Jilly refilled their glasses. When she set the pitcher back down on the table there was only froth left in the bottom.

"So did you come back with a good line?" she asked.

Mona shook her head. "What could I say? I was so stunned to find out that he'd never taken what I do seriously that all I could do was look at him and try to figure out how I ever thought we really knew each other."

She'd tried to put it out of her mind, but the phrase "that pathetic little comic book of yours" still stung in her memory.

"He used to like the fact that I was so different from the people where he works," she said, "but I guess he just got tired of parading his cute little Bohemian girlfriend around to office parties and the like."

Jilly gave a vigorous nod which made her curls fall down into her eyes. She pushed them back from her face with a hand that still had the inevitable paint lodged under the nails. Ultramarine blue. A vibrant coral.

"See," she said. "That's what infuriates me about the corporate world. The whole idea that if you're doing something creative that doesn't earn big bucks, you should consider it a hobby and put your real time and effort into something serious. Like your art isn't serious enough."

Mona took a swallow of beer. "Don't get me started on that."

Spar Distributions had recently decided to cut back on the non-superhero titles they carried and *The Girl Zone* had been one of the casualties. That was bad enough, but then they also wouldn't cough up her back issues or the money they owed her from what they had sold.

"You got a lousy break," Jilly told her. "They've got no right to let things drag on the way they have."

Mona shrugged. "You'd think I'd have had some clue before this," she said, more willing to talk about Pete. At least she could deal with him. "But he always seemed to like the strips. He'd laugh in all the right places and he even cried when Jamaica almost died."

"Well, who didn't?"

"I guess. There sure was enough mail on that story."

Jamaica was the pet cat in "My Life as a Bird"—Mona's one concession to fantasy in the strip since Pete was allergic to cats. She'd thought that she was only in between cats when Crumb ran away and she first met Pete, but once their relationship began to get serious she gave up on the idea of getting another one.

"Maybe he didn't like being in the strip," she said.

"What wasn't to like?" Jilly asked. "I loved the time you put me in it, even though you made me look like I was having the bad hair day from hell."

Mona smiled. "See, that's what happens when you drop out of art school."

"You have bad hair days?"

"No, I mean—"

"Besides, I didn't drop out. You did."

"My point exactly," Mona said. "I can't draw hair for the life of me. It always looks all raggedy."

"Or like a helmet, when you were drawing Pete."

Mona couldn't suppress a giggle. "It wasn't very flattering, was it?"

"But you made up for it by giving him a much better butt," Jilly said.

That seemed uproariously funny to Mona. The beer, she decided, was making her giddy. At least she hoped it was the beer. She wondered if Jilly could hear the same hysterical edge in her laugh that she did. That made the momentary good humor she'd been feeling scurry off as quickly as Pete had left their apartment earlier in the day.

"I wonder when I stopped loving him," Mona said. "Because I did, you know, before we finally had it out today. Stop loving him, I mean."

Jilly leaned forward. "Are you going to be okay? You can stay with me tonight if you like. You know, just so you don't have to be alone your first night."

Mona shook her head. "Thanks, but I'll be fine. I'm actually a little relieved, if you want to know the truth. The past few months I've been wandering through a bit of a fog, but I couldn't quite figure out what it was. Now I know."

Jilly raised her eyebrows.

"Knowing's better," Mona said.

"Well, if you change your mind . . ."

"I'll be scratching at your window the way those stray cats you keep feeding do."

When they called it a night, an hour and another half pitcher of draught later, Mona took a longer route home than she normally would. She wanted to clear her head of the decided buzz that was making her stride less than steady, though considering the empty apartment she was going home to, maybe that wasn't the best idea, never mind her brave words to Jilly. Maybe, instead, she should go back to the pub and down a couple of whiskey's so that she'd really be too tipsy to mope.

"Oh, damn him anyway," she muttered and kicked at a tangle of crumpled newspapers that were spilling out of the mouth of an alleyway she was passing.

"Hey, watch it!"

Mona stopped at the sound of the odd gruff voice, then backed away as the smallest man she'd ever seen crawled out of the nest of papers to glare at her. He couldn't have stood more than two feet high, a disagreeable and ugly little troll of a man with a face that seemed roughly carved and then left unfinished. His clothes were ragged and shabby, his face bristly with stubble. What hair she could see coming out from under his cloth cap was tangled and greasy.

Oh my, she thought. She was drunker than she'd realized.

She stood there swaying for a long moment, staring down at him and half expecting him to simply drift apart like smoke, or vanish. But he did neither and she finally managed to find her voice.

"I'm sorry," she said. "I just didn't see you down . . . there." This was coming out all wrong. "I mean . . ."

His glare deepened. "I suppose you think I'm too small to be noticed?"

"No. It's not that. I . . ."

She knew that his size was only some quirk of genetics, an unusual enough trait to find in someone out and about on a Crowsea street at midnight, but at the same time her imagination or, more likely, all the beer she'd had, was telling her that the little man scowling up at her had a more exotic origin.

"Are you a leprechaun?" she found herself asking.

"If I had a pot of gold, do you think I'd be sleeping on the street?"

She shrugged. "No, of course not. It's just . . ."

He put a finger to the side of his nose and blew a stream of snot onto the pavement. Mona's stomach did a flip and a sour taste rose up in her throat. Trust her that, when she finally did have some curious encounter like the kind Jilly had so often, it had to be with a grotty little dwarf such as this.

The little man wiped his nose on the sleeve of his jacket and grinned at her.

"What's the matter, princess?" he asked. "If I can't afford a bed for the night, what makes you think I'd go out and buy a handkerchief just to avoid offending your sensibilities?"

It took her a moment to digest that. Then digging in the bib pocket of her overalls, she found a couple of crumpled dollar bills and offered them to him. He regarded the money with suspicion and made no move to take it from her.

"What's this?" he said.

"I just . . . I thought maybe you could use a couple of dollars."

"Freely given?" he asked. "No strings, no ties?"

"Well, it's not a loan," she told him. Like she was ever going to see him again.

He took the money with obvious reluctance and a muttered "Damn."
Mona couldn't help herself. "Most people would say thank you,"
she said.

"Most people wouldn't be beholden to you because of it," he replied.

"I'm sorry?"

"What for?"

Mona blinked. "I meant, I don't understand why you're indebted to
me now. It was just a couple of dollars."

"Then why apologize?"

"I didn't. Or I suppose I did, but—" This was getting far too confusing. "What I'm trying to say is that I don't want anything in return."

"Too late for that." He stuffed the money in his pocket. "Because your
gift was freely given, it means I owe you now." He offered her his hand.
"Nacky Wilde, at your service."

Seeing it was the same one he'd used to blow his nose, Mona decided
to forgo the social amenities. She stuck her own hands in the side pockets
of her overalls.

"Mona Morgan," she told him.

"Alliterative parents?"

"What?"

"You really should see a doctor about your hearing problem."

"I don't have a hearing problem," she said.

"It's nothing to be ashamed of. Well, lead on. Where are we going?"

"*We're* not going anywhere. I'm going home and you can go back to
doing whatever it was you were doing before we started this conversation."

He shook his head. "Doesn't work that way. I have to stick with you
until I can repay my debt."

"I don't think so."

"Oh, it's very much so. What's the matter? Ashamed to be seen in my
company? I'm too short for you? Too grubby? I can be invisible, if you
like, but I get the feeling that'd only upset you more."

She had to be way more drunk than she thought she was. This wasn't
even remotely a normal conversation.

"Invisible," she repeated.

He gave her an irritated look. "As in, not perceivable by the human
eye. You do understand the concept, don't you?"

"You can't be serious."

"No, of course not. I'm making it up just to appear more interesting to you. Great big, semi-deaf women like you feature prominently in my day-dreams, so naturally I'll say anything to try to win you over."

Working all day at her drawing desk didn't give Mona as much chance to exercise as she'd like, so she was a bit touchy about the few extra pounds she was carrying.

"I'm not big."

He craned his neck. "Depends on the perspective, sweetheart."

"And I'm not deaf."

"I was being polite. I thought it was kinder than saying you were mentally disadvantaged."

"And you're *certainly* not coming home with me."

"Whatever you say," he said.

And then he vanished.

One moment he was there, two feet of unsavory rudeness, and the next she was alone on the street. The abruptness of his disappearance, the very weirdness of it, made her legs go all watery and she had to put a hand against the wall until the weak feeling went away.

I am *way* too drunk, she thought as she pushed off from the wall.

She peered into the alleyway, then looked up and down the street. Nothing. Gave the nest of newspapers a poke with her foot. Still nothing. Finally she started walking again, but nervously now, listening for footsteps, unable to shake the feeling that someone was watching her. She was almost back at her apartment when she remembered what he'd said about how he could be invisible.

Impossible.

But what if . . . ?

In the end she found a phonebooth and gave Jilly a call.

"Is it too late to change my mind?" she asked.

"Not at all. Come on over."

Mona leaned against the glass of the booth and watched the street all around her. Occasional cabs went by. She saw a couple at the far end of the block and followed them with her gaze until they turned a corner. So far as she could tell, there was no little man, grotty or otherwise, anywhere in view.

"Is it okay if I bring my invisible friend?" she said.

Jilly laughed. "Sure. I'll put the kettle on. Does your invisible friend drink coffee?"

"I haven't asked him."

"Well," Jilly said, "if either of you is feeling as woozy as I am, I'm sure you could use a mug."

"I could use something." Mona said after she'd hung up.

"MY LIFE AS A BIRD"
MONA'S MONOLOGUE FROM CHAPTER EIGHT:

Sometimes I think of God as this little man sitting on a café patio somewhere, bewildered at how it's all gotten so out of his control. He had such good intentions, but everything he made had a mind of its own and, right from the first, he found himself unable to contain their conflicting impulses. He tried to create paradise, but he soon discovered that free will and paradise were incompatible because everybody has a different idea as to what paradise should be like.

But usually when I think of him, I think of a cat: a little mysterious, a little aloof, never coming when he's called. And in my mind, God's always a he. The bible makes it pretty clear that men are the doers; women can only be virgins or whores. In God's eyes, we can only exist somewhere in between the two Marys, the mother of Jesus and the Magdalene.

What kind of a religion is that? What kind of religion ignores the rights of half the world's population just because they're supposed to have envy instead of a penis? One run by men. The strong, the brave, the true. The old boys' club that wrote the book and made the laws.

I'd like to find him and ask him, 'Is that it, God? Did we really get cloned from a rib and because we're hand-me-downs, you don't think we've got what it takes to be strong and brave and true?"

But that's only part of what's wrong with the world. You also have to ask, what's the rationale behind wars and sickness and suffering?

Or is there no point? Is God just as bewildered as the rest of us? Has he finally given up, spending his days now on that café patio, sipping strong espresso, and watching the world go by, none of it his concern anymore? Has he washed his hands of it all?

I've got a thousand questions for God, but he never answers any of them. Maybe he's still trying to figure out where

I fit on the scale between the two Marys and he can't reply
until he does. Maybe he doesn't hear me, doesn't see me,
doesn't think of me at all. Maybe in his version of what the
world is, I don't even exist.

Or if he's a cat, then I'm a bird, and he's just waiting to
pounce.

"You actually believe me, don't you?" Mona said.

The two of them were sitting in the windowseat of Jilly's studio loft,
sipping coffee from fat china mugs, piano music playing softly in the
background, courtesy of a recording by Mitsuko Uchida. The studio was
tidier than Mona had ever seen it. All the canvases that weren't hanging
up had been neatly stacked against one wall. Books were in their shelves,
paintbrushes cleaned and lying out in rows on the worktable, tubes of
paint organized by color in wooden and cardboard boxes. The drop cloth
under the easel even looked as though it had recently gone through
a wash.

"Spring clean-up and tidying," Jilly had said by way of explanation.

"Hello? It's September."

"So I'm late."

The coffee had been waiting for Mona when she arrived, as had been a
willing ear as she related her curious encounter after leaving the pub. Jilly,
of course, was enchanted with the story. Mona didn't know why she was
surprised.

"Let's say I don't disbelieve you," Jilly said.

"I don't know if I believe me. It's easier to put it down to those two
pitchers of beer we had."

Jilly touched a hand to her head. "Don't remind me."

"Besides," Mona went on. "Why doesn't he show himself now?" She
looked around Jilly's disconcertingly tidy studio. "Well?" she said, aiming
her question at the room in general. "What's the big secret, Mr. Nacky
Wilde?"

"Well, it stands to reason," Jilly said. "He knows that I could just give
him something as well, and then he'd indebted to me, too."

"I don't *want* him indebted to me."

"It's kind of late for that."

"That's what he said."

"He'd probably know."

"Okay. I'll just get him to do my dishes for me or something."

Jilly shook her head. "I doubt it works that way. It probably has to be something that no one else can do for you except him."

"This is ridiculous. All I did was give him a couple of dollars. I didn't mean anything by it."

"Money doesn't mean anything to you?"

"Jilly. It was only two dollars."

"It doesn't matter. It's still money and no matter how much we'd like things to be different, the world revolves around our being able to pay the rent and buy art supplies and the like, so money's important in our lives. You freely gave him something that means something to you and now he has to return that in kind."

"But anybody could have given him the money."

Jilly nodded. "Anybody could have, but they didn't. You did."

"How do I get myself into these things?"

"More to the point, how do you get yourself out?"

"You're the expert. You tell me."

"Let me think about it."

Nacky Wilde didn't show himself again until Mona got back to her own apartment the next morning. She had just enough time to realize that Pete had been back to collect his things—there were gaps in the bookshelves and the stack of CDs on top of the stereo was only half the size it had been the previous night—when the little man reappeared. He was slouched on her sofa, even more disreputable looking in the daylight, his glower softened by what could only be the pleasure he took from her gasp at his sudden appearance.

She sat down on the stuffed chair across the table from him. There used to be two, but Pete had obviously taken one.

"So," she said. "I'm sober and you're here, so I guess you must be real."

"Does it always take you this long to accept the obvious?"

"Grubby little men who can appear out of thin air and then disappear back into it again aren't exactly a part of my everyday life."

"Ever been to Japan?" he asked.

"No. What's that got to—"

"But you believe it exists, don't you?"

"Oh, please. It's not at all the same thing. Next thing you'll be wanting me to believe in alien abductions and little green men from Mars."

He gave her a wicked grin. "They're not green and they don't come from—"

"I don't want to hear it," she told him, blocking her ears. When she saw he wasn't going to continue, she went on, "So was Jilly right? I'm stuck with you?"

"It doesn't make me any happier than it does you."

"Okay. Then we have to have some ground rules."

"You're taking this rather well," he said.

"I'm a practical person. Now listen up. No bothering me when I'm working. No sneaking around being invisible when I'm in the bathroom or having a shower. No watching me sleep—*or* getting into bed with me."

He looked disgusted at the idea. Yeah, me too, Mona thought.

"And you clean up after yourself," she finished. "Come to think of it, you could clean up yourself, too."

He glared at her. "Fine. Now for my rules. First—"

Mona shook her head. "Uh-uh. This is my place. The only rules that get made here are by me."

"That hardly seems fair."

"None of this is fair," she shot back. "Remember, nobody asked you to tag along after me."

"Nobody asked you to give me that money," he said and promptly disappeared.

"I *hate* it when you do that."

"Good," a disembodied voice replied.

Mona stared thoughtfully at the now-empty sofa cushions and found herself wondering what it would be like to be invisible, which got her thinking about all the ways one could be nonintrusive and still observe the world. After a while, she got up and took down one of her old sketchbooks, flipping through it until she came to the notes she'd made when she'd first started planning her semi-autobiographical strip for *The Girl Zone.*

"My Life as a Bird"
Notes for Chapter One:

(Mona and Hazel are sitting at the kitchen table in Mona's apartment having tea and muffins. Mona is watching Jamaica, asleep on the windowsill, only the tip of her tail twitching.)

MONA: Being invisible would be the coolest, but the next best thing would be, like, if you could be a bird or a cat— something that no one pays any attention to.

HAZEL: What kind of bird?

MONA: I don't know. A crow, all blue-black wings and shadowy. Or, no. Maybe something even less noticeable, like a pigeon or a sparrow.

(She gets a happy look on her face.)

MONA: Because you can tell. They pay attention to everything, but no one pays attention to them.

HAZEL: And the cat would be black, too, I suppose?

MONA: Mmm. Lean and slinky like Jamaica. Very Egyptian. But a bird would be better—more mobility—though I guess it wouldn't matter, really. The important thing is how you'd just be there, another piece of the landscape, but you'd be watching everything. You wouldn't miss a thing.

HAZEL: Bit of a voyeur, are we?

MONA: No, nothing like that. I'm not even interested in high drama, just the things that go on every day in our lives— the stuff most people don't pay attention to. That's the real magic.

HAZEL: Sounds boring.

MONA: No, it would be very Zen. Almost like meditating.

HAZEL: You've been drawing that comic of yours for too long.

The phone rang that evening while Mona was inking a new page for "Jupiter Jewel." The sudden sound startled her and a blob of ink fell from the end of her nib pen, right beside Cecil's head. At least it hadn't landed on his face.

I'll make that a shadow, she decided as she answered the phone.

"So do you still have an invisible friend?" Jilly asked.

Mona looked down the hall from the kitchen table where she was working. What she could see of the apartment appeared empty, but she didn't trust her eyesight when it came to her uninvited houseguest.

"I can't see him," she said, "but I have to assume he hasn't left."

"Well, I don't have any useful news. I've checked with all the usual sources and no one quite knows what to make of him."

"The usual sources being?"

"Christy. The professor. An old copy of *The Newford Examiner* with a special section on the fairy folk of Newford."

"You're kidding."

"I am," Jilly admitted. "But I did go to the library and had a wonderful time looking through all sorts of interesting books, from K. M. Briggs to *When the Desert Dreams* by Anne Bourke, neither of whom writes about Newford, but I've always loved those fairy lore books Briggs compiled and Anne Bourke lived here, as I'm sure you knew, and I really liked the picture on the cover of her book. I know," she added, before Mona could break in. "Get to the point already."

"I'm serenely patient and would never have said such a thing," Mona told her.

"Humble, too. Anyway, apparently there are all sorts of tricksy fairy folk, from hobs to brownies. Some relatively nice, some decidedly nasty, but none of them quite fit the Nacky Wilde profile."

"You mean sarcastic, grubby and bad mannered, but potentially helpful?"

"In a nutshell."

Mona sighed. "So I'm stuck with him."

She realized that she'd been absently doodling on her art and set her pen aside before she completely ruined the page.

"It doesn't seem fair, does it?" she added. "I finally get the apartment to myself, but then some elfin squatter moves in."

"How *are* you doing?" Jilly asked. "I mean, aside from your invisible squatter?"

"I don't feel closure," Mona said. "I know how weird that sounds, considering what I told you yesterday. After all, Pete stomped out and then snuck back while I was with you last night to get his stuff—so I *know* it's over. And the more I think of it, I realize this had to work out the way it did. But I'm still stuck with this emotional baggage, like trying to figure out why things ended up the way they did, and how come I never noticed."

"Would you take him back?"

"No."

"But you miss him?"

"I do," Mona said. "Weird, isn't it?"

"Perfectly normal, I'd say. Do you want someone to commiserate with?"

"No, I need to get some work done. But thanks."

After she hung up, Mona stared down at the mess she'd made of the page she'd been working on. She supposed she could try to incorporate all the squiggles into the background, but it didn't seem worth the bother. Instead she picked up a bottle of white acrylic ink, gave it a shake and opened it. With a clean brush she began to paint over the doodles and the blob of ink she'd dropped by Cecil's head. It was obvious now that it wouldn't work as shadow, seeing how the light source was on the same side.

Waiting for the ink to dry, she wandered into the living room and looked around.

"Trouble with your love life?" a familiar, but still disembodied voice asked.

"If you're going to talk to me," she said, "at least show your face."

"Is this a new rule?"

Mona shook her head. "It's just disorienting to be talking into thin air—especially when the air answers back."

"Well, since you asked so politely . . ."

Nacky Wilde reappeared, slouching in the stuffed chair this time, a copy of one of Mona's comic books open on his lap.

"You're not actually reading that?" Mona said.

He looked down at the comic. "No, of course not. Dwarves can't read—their brains are much too small to learn such an obviously complex task."

"I didn't mean it that way."

"I know you didn't, but I can't help myself. I have a reputation to maintain."

"As a dwarf?" Mona asked. "Is that what you are?"

He shrugged and changed the subject. "I'm not surprised you and your boyfriend broke up."

"What's that supposed to mean?"

He stabbed the comic book with a short stubby finger. "The tension's so apparent—if this bird story holds any truth. One never gets the sense that any of the characters really likes Pete."

Mona sat down on the sofa and swung her feet up onto the cushions. This was just what she needed—an uninvited, usually invisible squatter of a houseguest who was also a self-appointed analyst. Except, when she thought about it, he was right. "My Life as a Bird" was emotionally true, if not always a faithful account of actual events, and the Pete character in it had never been one of her favorites. Like the real Pete, there was an underlying tightness in his character; it was more noticeable in the strip because the rest of the cast was so Bohemian.

"He wasn't a bad person," she found herself saying.

"Of course not. Why would you let yourself be attracted to a bad person?"

Mona couldn't decide if he was being nice or sarcastic.

"They just wore him down," she said. "In the office. Won him over to their way of thinking, and there was no room for me in his life anymore."

"Or for him in yours," Nacky said.

Mona nodded. "It's weird, isn't it? Generosity of spirit seems to be so old-fashioned nowadays. We'd rather watch somebody trip on the sidewalk than help them climb the stairs to whatever it is they're reaching for."

"What is it you're reaching for?" Nacky asked.

"Oh, god." Mona laughed. "Who knows? Happiness, contentment. Some days all I want is for the lines to come together on the page and look like whatever it is that I'm trying to draw." She leaned back on the arm of the sofa and regarded the ceiling. "You know, that trick you do with invisibility is pretty cool." She turned her head to look at him. "Is it something that can be taught or do you have to be born magic?"

"Born to it, I'm afraid."

"I figured as much. But it's always been a fantasy of mine. That, or being able to change into something else."

"So I've gathered from reading this,' Nacky said, giving the comic another tap with his finger. "Maybe you should try to be happy just being yourself. Look inside yourself for what you need—the way your character recommends in one of the earlier issues."

"You really have been reading it."

"That is why you write it, isn't it—to be read?"

She gave him a suspicious look. "Why are you being so nice all of a sudden?"

"Just setting you up for the big fall."

"Uh-huh."

"Thought of what I can do for you yet?" he asked.

She shook her head. "But I'm working on it."

"MY LIFE AS A BIRD"
NOTES FOR CHAPTER SEVEN:

(So after Mona meets Gregory, they go walking in Fitzhenry Park and sit on a bench from which they can see Wendy's Tree of Tales growing. Do I need to explain this, or can it just be something people who know will understand?)

GREGORY: Did you ever notice how we don't tell family stories anymore?

MONA: What do you mean?

GREGORY: Families used to be made up of stories—their history—and those stories were told down through the generations. It's where a family got its identity, the same way a neighborhood or even a country did. Now the stories we share we get from television and the only thing we talk about is ourselves.

(Mona realizes this is true—maybe not for everybody, but it's true for her. Argh. How do I draw this???)

MONA: Maybe the family stories don't work anymore. Maybe they've lost their relevance.

GREGORY: They've lost nothing.

(He looks away from her, out across the park.)

GREGORY: But we have.

In the days that followed, Nacky Wilde alternated between the sarcastic grump Mona had first met and the surprisingly good company he could prove to be when he didn't, as she told him one night, "have a bee up his butt." Unfortunately, the good of the one didn't outweigh the frustration of having to put up with the other and there was no getting rid of him. When he was in one of his moods, she didn't know which was worse: having to look at his scowl and listen to his bad-tempered remarks, or telling him to vanish but knowing that he was still sulking around the apartment, invisible and watching her.

A week after Pete had moved out, Mona met up with Jilly at the Cyberbean Café. They were planning to attend the opening of Sophie's latest show at The Green Man Gallery and Mona had once again promised herself not to dump her problems on Jilly, but there was no one else she could talk to.

"It's so typical," she found herself saying. "Out of all the hundreds of magical beings that populate folk tales and legends, I had to get stuck with the one that has a multiple personality disorder. He's driving me crazy."

"Is he with us now?" Jilly asked.

"Who knows? Who cares?" Then Mona had to laugh. "God, listen to me. It's like I'm complaining about a bad relationship."

"Well, it is a bad relationship."

"I know. And isn't it pathetic?" Mona shook her head. "If this is what I rebounded to from Pete, I don't want to know what I'll end up with when I finally get this nasty little man out of my life. At least the sex was good with Pete."

Jilly's eyes went wide. "You're not . . . ?"

"Oh, please. That'd be like sleeping with the eighth dwarf, Snotty— the one Disney kept out of his movie and with good reason."

Jilly had to laugh. "I'm sorry, but it's just so—"

Mona wagged a finger at her. "Don't say it. You wouldn't be laughing if it was happening to you." She looked at her watch. "We should get going."

Jilly took a last sip of her coffee. Wrapping what she hadn't finished of her cookie in a napkin, she stuck it in her pocket.

"What are you going to do?" she asked as they left the café.

"Well, I looked in the Yellow Pages, but none of the exterminators have cranky dwarves listed among the household pests they'll get rid of, so I guess I'm stuck with him for now. Though I haven't looked under exorcists yet."

"Is he Catholic?" Jilly asked.

"I didn't think it mattered. They just get rid of evil spirits, don't they?"

"Why not just ask him to leave? That's something no one else but he can do for you."

"I already thought of that," Mona told her.

"And?"

"Apparently it doesn't work that way."

"Maybe you should ask him what he can do for you."

Mona nodded thoughtfully. "You know, I never thought of that. I just assumed this whole business was one of those Rumpelstiltskin kind of things—that I had to come up with it on my own.

"What?" Nacky said later that night when Mona returned from the gallery and asked him to show himself. "You want me to list my services like on a menu? I'm not a restaurant."

"Or computer software," Mona agreed, "though it might be easier if you were either, because then at least I'd know what you can do without having to go through a song and dance to get the information out of you."

"No one's ever asked this kind of thing before."

"So what?" she asked. "Is against the rules?"

Nacky scowled. "What makes you think there are rules?"

"There are always rules. So come on. Give."

"Fine," Nacky said. "We'll start with the most popular items." He began to count the items off on his fingers. "Potions, charms, spells, incantations—"

Mona held up a hand. "Hold on there. Let's back up a bit. What are these potions and charms and stuff?"

"Well, take your ex-boyfriend," Nacky said.

Please do, Mona thought.

"I could put a spell on him so that every time he looked at a woman that he was attracted to, he'd break out in hives."

"You could do that?"

Nacky nodded. "Or it could just be a minor irritation—an itch that will never go away."

"How long would it last?"

"Your choice. For the rest of his life, if you want."

Wouldn't that serve Pete right, Mona thought. Talk about a serious payback for all those mean things he'd said about her and *The Girl Zone*.

"This is so tempting," she said.

"So what will it be?" Nacky asked, briskly rubbing his hands together. "Hives? An itch? Perhaps a nervous tic under his eye so that people will always think he's winking at them. Seems harmless, but it's good for any number of face slaps and more serious altercations."

"Hang on," Mona told him. "What's the big hurry?"

"I'm in no hurry. I thought you were. I thought the sooner you got rid of Snotty, the eighth dwarf, the happier you'd be."

So he had been in the café.

"Okay," Mona said. "But first I have to ask you. These charms and things of yours—do they only do negative stuff?"

Nacky shook his head. "No. They can teach you the language of birds, choose your dreams before you go to sleep, make you appear to not be somewhere when you really are—"

"Wait a sec. You told me I had to be born magic to do that."

"No. You asked about, and I quote, 'the trick *you* do with invisibility,' the emphasis being mine. How I do it, you have to be born magic. An invisibility charm is something else."

"But it does the same thing?"

"For all intents and purposes."

God, but he could be infuriating.

"So why didn't you tell me that?"

Nacky smirked. "You didn't ask."

I will not get angry, she told herself. I am calmness incarnate.

"Okay," she said. "What else?"

He went back to counting the items on his fingers, starting again with a tap of his right index finger onto his left. "Potions to fall in love, to fall out of love. To make hair longer, or thicker. To make one taller, or shorter, or—" he gave her a wicked grin "—slimmer. To speak with the recent dead, to heal a person who's sick—"

"Heal them of what?" Mona wanted to know.

"Whatever ails them," he said, then went on in a bored voice. "To turn kettles into foxes, and vice versa. To—"

Mona was beginning to suffer overload.

"Enough already," she said. "I get the point."

"But you—"

"Shh. Let me think."

She laid her head back in her chair and closed her eyes. Basically, what it boiled down to was that she could have whatever she wanted. She could have revenge on Pete—not for leaving her, but for being so mean-spirited about it. She could be invisible, or understand the language of bird and animals. And though he'd claimed not to have a pot of gold when they first met, she could probably have fame and fortune, too.

But she didn't really want revenge on Pete. And being invisible probably wasn't such a good idea since she already spent far too much time on her own as it was. What she should really do is get out more, meet more people, make more friends of her own, instead of all the people she knew through Pete. As for fame and fortune . . . corny as it might sound, she really did believe that the process was what was important, the journey her art and stories took her on, not the place where they all ended up.

She opened her eyes and looked at Nacky.

"Well?" he said.

She stood up and picked up her coat from where she'd dropped it on the end of the sofa.

"Come on," she said as she put it on.

"Where are we going?"

"To hail a cab."

She had a taxi take them to the children's hospital. After paying the fare, she got out and stood on the lawn. Nacky, invisible in the vehicle, popped back into view. Leaves crackled underfoot as he joined her.

"There," Mona said, pointing at the long square block of a building. "I want you to heal all the kids in there."

There was a long moment of silence. When Mona turned to look at her companion, it was to find him regarding her with a thoughtful expression.

"I can't do that," he said.

Mona shook her head. "Like you couldn't make me invisible?"

"No, semantics this time," he said. "I can't heal them all."

"But that's what I want."

Nacky sighed. "It's like asking for world peace. It's too big a task. But I could heal one of them."

"Just one?"

Nacky nodded.

Mona turned to look at the building again. "Then heal the sickest one."

She watched him cross the lawn. When he reached the front doors, his figure shimmered and he seemed to flow through the glass rather than step through the actual doors.

He was gone a long time. When he finally returned, his pace was much slower and there was a haunted look in his eyes.

"There was a little girl with cancer," he said. "She would have died later tonight. Her name—"

"I don't want to know her name," Mona told him. "I just want to know, will she be all right?"

He nodded.

I could have had anything, she found herself thinking.

"Do you regret giving the gift away," Nacky asked her.

She shook her head. "No. I only wish I had more of them." She eyed him for a long moment. "I don't suppose I could freely give you another couple of dollars . . . ?"

"No. It doesn't—"

"Work that way," she finished. "I kind of figured as much." She knelt down so that she wasn't towering over him. "So now what? Where will you go?"

"I have a question for you," he said.

"Shoot."

"If I asked, would you let me stay on with you?"

Mona laughed.

"I'm serious," he told her.

"And what? Things would be different now, or would you still be snarly more often than not?"

He shook his head. "No different."

"You know I can't afford to keep that apartment," she said. "I'm probably going to have to get a bachelor somewhere."

"I wouldn't mind."

Mona knew she'd be insane to agree. All she'd been doing for the past week was trying to get him out of her life. But then she thought of the look in his eyes when he'd come back from the hospital and knew that he wasn't all bad. Maybe he was a little magic man, but he was still stuck living on the street and how happy could that make a person? Could be, all he needed was what everybody needed—a fair break. Could be, if he was treated fairly, he wouldn't glower so much, or be so bad-tempered.

But could she put up with it?

"I can't believe I'm saying this," she told him, "but, yeah. You can come back with me."

She'd never seen him smile before, she realized. It transformed his features.

"You've broken the curse," he said.

"Say what?"

"You don't know how long I've had to wait to find someone both selfless and willing to take me in as I was."

"I don't know about the selfless—"

He leaned forward and kissed her.

"Thank you," he said.

And then he went whirling off across the lawn, spinning like a dervishing top. His squatness melted from him and he grew tall and lean, fluid as a willow sapling, dancing in the wind. From the far side of the lawn he waved at her. For a long moment, all she could do was stare, openmouthed. When she finally lifted her hand to wave back, he winked out of existence, like a spark leaping from a fire, glowing brightly before it vanished into the darkness.

This time she knew he was gone for good.

"MY LIFE AS A BIRD"
MONA'S CLOSING MONOLOGUE FROM CHAPTER ELEVEN:

The weird thing is I actually miss him. Oh, not his crankiness, or his serious lack of personal hygiene. What I miss is the kindness that occasionally slipped through—the piece of him that survived the curse.

Jilly says that was why he was so bad-tempered and gross. He had to make himself unlikeable, or it wouldn't have been so hard to find someone who would accept him for who he seemed to be. She says I stumbled into a fairy tale, which is pretty cool when you think about it, because how many people can say that?

Though I suppose if this really were a fairy tale, there'd be some kind of "happily ever after" wrap up, or I'd at least have come away with a fairy gift of one sort or another. That invisibility charm, say, or the ability to change into a bird or a cat.

But I don't really need anything like that.

I've got *The Girl Zone*. I can be anything I want in its

pages. Rockit Grrl, saving the day. Jupiter, who can't seem to physically show up in her own life. Or just me.

I've got my dreams. I had a fun one last night. I was walking downtown and I was a birdwoman, spindly legs, beak where my nose should be, long wings hanging down from my shoulders like a ragged cloak. Or maybe I was just wearing a bird costume. Nobody recognized me, but they knew me all the same and thought it was way cool.

And I've touched a piece of real magic. Now, no matter how grey and bland and pointless the world might seem sometimes, I just have to remember that there really is more to everything than what we can see. Everything has a spirit that's so much bigger and brighter than you think it could hold.

Everything has one.

Me, too.

China Doll

> In theory there is free will, in practice every-
> thing is predetermined.
>
> *—Ramakrishna,*
> *nineteenth-century Bengali saint*

The crows won't shut up. It's late, close on midnight. The junkyard's more shadow than substance and the city's asleep. The crows should be sleeping, too—roosting somewhere, doing whatever it is that crows do at night. Because you don't normally see them like this, cawing at each other, hoarse voices tearing raggedly across the yard, the birds shifting, restless on their perches, flecks of rust falling in small red clouds every time they move.

They can't sleep and they won't shut up.

Coe can't sleep either, but at least he's got an excuse.

The dead don't sleep.

He's sitting there on the hood of a junked car, three nights dead. Watching the flames lick up above the rim of an old steel barrel where he's got a trash fire burning. Waiting for China to show up. China with her weird tribal tags: the white mud dried on her face, eyes darkened with rings of soot, lips blackened with charcoal, cheeks marked with black hi-eroglyphic lines. He looks about the same. The two of them are like matched bookends in a chiaroscuro still life. Like they just stepped out of some old black and white movie, except for that red dress of hers.

He's not exactly looking forward to seeing her. First thing you know, she'll start in again on who they're supposed to kill and why, and he's no more interested in listening to her tonight than he was the day he came back.

He thinks of standing by the barrel, holding his hands up to the flames for warmth, but that's a comfort he's never going to know again. The cold's lodged too deep inside him and it's never going away, doesn't matter what China says.

Killing's not the answer. But neither's this.

"Just shut up," he tells the birds.

They don't listen to him any more than they ever do, but China comes walking out of the shadows like his voice summoned her.

"Hey, Leon," she says.

She jumps lightly up onto the hood of the car, stretches out her legs, leans back against the windshield. Her dress rides up her legs, but the sight of it doesn't do anything for him. She's too young. Hell, she could be his daughter.

Coe gives her a nod, waits for her to start in on him. She surprises him. She just sits there, quiet for a change, checking out the birds.

"What do you think they're talking about?" she asks after awhile.

"You don't know?"

Ever since they came back, it's like she knows everything. Maybe she was like that before they died. He doesn't know. First time he saw her she was in that tight red dress, running down a narrow alleyway, black combat boots clumping on the pavement. Came bursting out of the alley and ran right into him where he was just walking along, minding his own business. They fall in a tumble, and before they can get themselves untangled, there's a couple of Oriental guys there, standing over them. One's got a shotgun, the other a Uzi. For a moment, Coe thinks he's back in the jungle.

He doesn't get a chance to say a word.

The last thing he sees are the muzzles of their guns, flashing white. Last thing he hears is the sound of the shots. Last thing he feels are the bullets tearing into him. When he comes back, he's lying in a junkyard—this junkyard—and China's bending over him, wiping wet clay on his face. He starts to push her away, but she shakes her head.

"This is the way it's got to be," she says.

He doesn't know what she's talking about then. Now that he does, he wishes he didn't. He looks at her, lounging on the car, and wonders, was she always so bloodthirsty, or did dying bring it out in her? Dying didn't bring it out in him and it wouldn't have had to dig far to find the capacity for violence in his soul.

She sits up, pulls her knees to her chin, gazes over them to where he's sitting on the hood.

"Look," she tells him, her voice almost apologetic. "I didn't choose for things to work out the way they did."

He doesn't reply. There's nothing to say.

"You never asked why those guys were chasing me," she says.

Coe shrugs.

"Don't you want to know why you died?"

"I know why I died," he says. "I was in the wrong place at the wrong time, end of story."

China shakes her head. "It's way more complicated than that."

It usually is, Coe thinks.

"You know anything about how the Tongs run their prostitution rings?" she goes on.

Coe nods. It's an old story. The recruiters find their victims in Southeast Asia, "loaning" the girls the money they need to buy passage to North America, then make them work off the debt in brothels over here. The fact that none of their victims ever pays off that debt doesn't seem to stop the new girls from buying into it. There's always fresh blood. Some of those girls are so young they've barely hit puberty. The older ones— late teens, early twenties—make out like they're preteens, because that's where the big money is.

He gives China a considering look. Her name accentuates the Chinese cast to her features. Dark eyes the shape of almonds, black hair worn in a classic pageboy, bangs in front, the rest a sleek shoulder-length curve. He'd thought she was sixteen, seventeen. Now he's not so sure anymore.

"That what happened to you?" he asks.

She shakes her head. "I never knew a thing about it until I ran into one of their girls. According to a card she was carrying, she was the property of the Blue Circle Boys Triad—at least the card had their chop on it. She was on the run and I took her in."

"And the Tong found out."

She shakes her head again. "She could barely speak a word of English, but a woman in the Thai grocery under my apartment was able to translate for us. That's how I heard about what they're doing to these girls."

There's a look in her eyes that Coe hasn't seen there before, but he recognizes it. It's like an old pain that won't go away. He knows all about old pain.

"So what put the Tong onto you?" he asks, curious in spite of himself.

"I turned them in."

Coe thinks he didn't hear her right. "You what?"

"I turned them in. The cops raided their brothel and busted a couple of dozen of them. Don't you read the papers?"

Coe shook his head. "I don't—didn't—need more bad news in my life."

"Yeah, well. I've been there."

Coe's still working his head around what she did. Blowing the whistle on the Blue Circle Boys. She had to have known there'd be cops in their pocket, happy to let them know who was responsible. It was probably only dumb luck that the cop she'd taken her story to was a family man, walking the straight and narrow.

"And you didn't think the Tong'd find out?' he asks.

"I didn't care," she says. She's quiet for a long moment, then adds, "I didn't think I cared. Dying kind of changes your perspective on this kind of thing."

Coe nods. "Yeah. Dying brings all kinds of changes."

"So I was out clubbing—the night they were chasing me. Feeling righteous about what I'd done. Celebrating, I guess. I was heading for home, trying to flag down a cab, when they showed up. I didn't know what to do, so I just took off and ran."

"And we know how well that turned out," Coe says.

"It wasn't like I was trying to get you killed. I liked being alive myself."

Coe shrugs. "I'm not blaming you. It's like I said. I was just in the wrong place."

"But our dying still means something. Doesn't matter if there's crooked cops, or that they rolled me over to the Tong. The brothel still got shut down and the Blue Circle Boys are hurting bad. And now those girls have a chance at a better life."

"Sure. They're going to do really well once they're deported back to Thailand or Singapore or wherever they originally came from."

Anger flares in her eyes. "What are you saying?"

"That nothing's changed. The Tong's had a bit of a setback, but give it a month or two and everything'll be back to business as usual. That's the way it works."

"No," she says. "This means something. Just like what we've got to do now means something."

Coe shakes his head again. "Some things you can't change. It's like the government. The most you can do is vote in another set of monkeys, but it doesn't change anything. It's always business as usual."

"Have you always been such a chickenshit?"

"I'm a pacifist. I don't believe violence solves anything."

"Same difference."

Coe looks at her. He's guessing now that she's maybe twenty, twenty-two. At least half his age. When he was younger than she is now, the government gave him a gun and taught him how to kill. He was good at it, too. Did two tours, in country, came back all in one piece and with no other skills. So they hired him on. Same work, different jungle. There was always work for a guy like him who was good at what he did, good at doing what he was told. Good at keeping his mouth shut.

Until the day an op went bad and a little girl got caught in the crossfire. After that he couldn't do it anymore. He looked at that dead kid and all he could do was put the gun down and disappear. Stopped living like a king, the best hotels, the best restaurants, limos when he wanted them, working only nine, ten times a year. He retired from it all, just like that. Vanished into the underground world of the homeless where he was just one more skell, nobody a citizen'd give a second look.

It had to be that way. The people he worked for didn't exactly have a retirement plan for their employees. At least, not one that included your staying alive.

"You don't know what I am," he tells her.

He slides down from the hood of the car and starts walking.

"Leon!" she calls after him.

The crows lift up around the junkyard, filling the air with their raucous cries. It's like they think he's going to follow them, that he's going to let them lead him back to where an eye for an eye makes sense again. But it isn't going to happen. Dying hasn't changed that. They want to take down the shooters who killed China and him, they can do it themselves.

"Leon!" China calls again.

He doesn't turn, and she doesn't follow.

* * *

He walks until he finds himself standing in front of a familiar building. Looks like any of the hundreds of other office buildings downtown, nothing special, except the people he'd worked for had a branch in it. There are lights up on the twelfth floor where they have their offices.

His gaze is drawn to the glass doors of the foyer, to the reflection he casts on their dark surfaces. He looks like he's got himself made up for Halloween, like he's wearing warpaint. Back when he was a grunt, there'd been an Indian in his platoon. Joey Keams, a Black Hills Lakota. Keams used to talk about his grandfather, how the same government they were fighting for had outlawed the Ghostdance and the Sun Dances, butchered his people by the thousands, but here he was anyway, fighting for them all the same.

Keams was a marvel. It was like he had a sixth sense, the way he could spot a sniper, a mine, an ambush. Handy guy to have around. Eight months into his tour, they were out on patrol and he stepped on a mine that his sixth sense hadn't bothered to warn him about. There wasn't enough left of him to ship home.

Coe glances around, but the birds are all gone. All that's left is one dark shape sitting on a lamppost, watching him.

Funny the things you forget, he thinks. Because now he remembers that Keams talked about crows, too. How some people believed they carried the souls of the dead on to wherever we go when we die. How sometimes they carried them back when they had unfinished business. He'd have got along real well with China.

"I don't have any unfinished business," he tells the bird.

It cocks its head, stares right back at him like it's listening.

Coe hasn't had anything for a long time. Once he stopped killing, he went passive. Eating at soup kitchens, sleeping under overpasses, cadging spare change that he gave away to those who needed it more than he did. He didn't drink, didn't smoke, didn't do drugs. Didn't need anything that you couldn't get as a handout.

He gives the building a last look, gaze locked on his reflection in the glass door. He looks like what he is: a bum, pushing fifty. Wearing raggedy clothes. No use to anyone. No danger to anyone. Not anymore.

The only thing that doesn't fit is the face-painting job that China did on him. Pulling out his shirttails, he tries to wipe off the war paint, but all he does is smear the clay, make it worse. Screw it, he thinks. He turns away, heading up the street.

It's close to dawn and except for the odd cab that wouldn't stop for him anyway, he's pretty much got the streets to himself. Even the whores are finally asleep.

The crow leaves its perch, flies overhead, lands on the next lamppost.

"So what are you?" he asks it. "My personal guide?"

The bird caws once. Coe pauses under the lamppost, puts his head back to look at it.

"Okay," he says. "Show me what you've got."

The crow flies off again and this time he follows. He's still not bought into any of it, but he can't help being curious, now that he's heard China's story. And sure enough the bird leads him into Chinatown, up where it meets the no-man's-land of the Tombs. As far as Coe can see, there's nothing but abandoned tenements and broken-down factories and warehouses. He follows the crow across an empty lot, gravel and dirt crunching underfoot.

Used to be he could walk without a sound, like a ghost. Now that he is one, you can hear him a mile away.

He stops in the shadows of one of the factories. There are no streetlights down here. But dawn's pinking the horizon and in its vague light he can make out the graffiti chops on the walls of the building across the street that mark it as Blue Circle Boys' turf.

He hears footsteps coming up behind him, but he doesn't look. His crow is perched on the roof of an abandoned car. A moment later, it's joined by a second bird. Finally he turns around.

"You were in the trade, right?" he says to China.

She nods. "I guess you could say that. I was an exotic dancer."

"China . . . ?"

"Was my stage name. China Doll. Cute, huh? My real name's Susie Wong, but I can't remember the last time I answered to it."

"Why'd the cops listen to a stripper?"

"Dumb luck. Got a real family man, hungry for a righteous bust."

"And now?" Coe asks.

"We have to take them out. The ones the cops didn't pick up."

Coe doesn't say anything.

"The ones that killed us."

"The crows tell you all that?" he asks. He lifted a hand to his cheek. "Like they told you about this warpaint?"

She nods.

He shakes his head. "They don't say anything to me. All I hear is their damned cawing."

"But you'll help me?" China asks. "We died together, so we have to take them out together."

More crow mumbo-jumbo, Coe supposes.

"I told you," he says. "I won't buy into this Old Testament crap."

"I don't want to argue with you."

"No, you just want me to kill a few people so that we can have a happy ending and float off to our just reward."

She cocks her head and looks at him, reminding him of one the crows.

"Is that what you're scared of?" she asks. "Of what might be waiting for you when we cross over to the other side?"

Coe hasn't even been thinking of himself, of other vengeful spirits that might be waiting for him somewhere. But now that China's brought it up, he has to wonder. Why haven't the crows brought back any of the people he's killed? And then there was the part he'd played in the death of at least one little girl who really hadn't deserved to die. . . .

"It's not fear," he tells her. "It's principle."

She gives him a blank look.

Coe sighs. "We play out this eye-for-an-eye business, then we're no better than them."

"So what are you doing here?" she asks. She points at the Tong's building with her chin.

He doesn't have an answer for her.

"We'd be saving lives," she says.

"By taking lives."

It's an old argument. It's how he got started in the business he fell into after his two tours in 'Nam.

China nods. "If that's what it takes. If we stop them, they won't kill anybody else."

Except it never stops. There's always one more that needs killing, just to keep things tidy. And the next thing you know, the body count keeps rising. One justification feeding the next like endless dominos knocking against each other. It never stops anything, and it never changes anything, because evil's like kudzu. It can grow anywhere, so thick and fast that you're choking on it before you know it. The only way to eradicate it is to refuse to play its game. Play the game and you're letting it grow inside of you.

But there's no way to explain that so that she'll really understand. She'd have to see through his eyes. See how that dead little girl haunts him. How she reminds him, every day, of how she'd still be alive if he hadn't been playing the game.

The thing to aim for is to clear the playing board. If there's nothing left for evil to feed on, it'll feed on itself.

It makes sense. Believing it is what's kept him sane since that little girl died in the firefight.

"So why are you here?" China asks again.

"I'm just checking them out. That's all."

He leaves her again, crosses the street. Along the side of the building he spots a fire escape. He follows its metal rungs with his gaze, sees they'll take him right to the roof, four stories up. The two crows are already on their way.

Just checking things out, he thinks as he starts up the fire escape.

He hears China climbing up after him, but he doesn't look down. When he gets to the end of the ladder he hauls himself up and swings onto the roof. Gravel crunches underfoot. He thinks he's alone until the crows give a warning caw. He sees the shadow of a man pull away from a brick, box-like structure with a door in it. The roof access, he figures. The man's dark-haired, wearing a long, black raincoat, motorcycle boots that come up to his knees. He's carrying a Uzi, the muzzle rising to center on Coe as he approaches.

He and Coe recognize each other at the same time.

Coe's had three days to get used to this, this business of coming back from the dead. The shooter's had no time at all, but he doesn't waste time asking questions. His eyes go wide. You can see he's shaken. So he does what men always do when they're scared of something—he takes the offense.

The first bullet hits Coe square in the chest. He feels the impact. He staggers. But he doesn't go down. Coe doesn't know which of them's more surprised—him or the shooter.

"You don't want to do this," Coe tells him.

He starts to walk forward and the shooter starts backing away. His finger takes up the slack on the Uzi's trigger and he opens it up. Round after round tears through Coe's shirt, into his chest. He feels each hit, but he's over his surprise, got his balance now, and just keeps walking forward.

And the shooter keeps backing up, keeps firing.

Coe wants to take the gun away. The sound of it, the fact that it even exists, offends him. He wants to talk to the shooter. He doesn't know what he's going to say, but he knows the man needs to get past this business of trying to kill what you don't understand.

The trouble is, the shooter sees Coe's approach through his own eyes, takes Coe's steady closing of the distance between them for a threat. He turns suddenly, misjudges where he is. Coe cries out a warning, but it's too late. The shooter hits his knees against the low wall at the edge of the roof and goes over.

Coe runs to the wall, but the shooter's already gone.

There's an awful, wet sound when the man hits the pavement four stories down. Coe's heard it before; it's not a sound you forget. The shooter's gun goes off, clatters across the asphalt. The crows are out there, riding air currents down toward the body, gliding, not even moving their wings.

"That's one down," China says.

She steps up to the wall beside him to have a look. Coe hadn't even heard her footsteps on the gravel behind him. He frowns at her, but before he can speak, they hear the roof access door bang open behind them. They turn to see a half-dozen men coming out onto the gravel. They fan out into a half circle, weapons centered on the two of them. Shotguns with pistol grips, automatics. A couple more Uzis.

Coe makes the second shooter from the alleyway. The man's eyes go as wide as his partner's had, whites showing. He says something, but Coe doesn't understand the language. Chinese, maybe. Or Thai.

"Party time," China says.

"Can it," Coe tells her.

But all she does is laugh and give the men the finger.

"Hey, assholes," she yells. *"Ni deh!"*

Coe doesn't understand her either, but the meaning's clear. He figures the men are going to open fire, but then they give way to a new figure coming out from the doorway behind them. From the deference the men give him, he's obviously their leader. The newcomer's a tall, Chinese man. Coe's age, late forties. Handsome, black hair cut short, eyes dark.

Now it's Coe's turn to register shock. He doesn't see a ghost of the dead, like the shooters from the alleyway did, but it's a ghost all the same.

A ghost from Coe's past.

"Jimmy," Coe says softly. "Jimmy Chen."

Jimmy doesn't even seem surprised. "I knew I'd be seeing you again," he says. "Sooner or later, I knew you'd surface."

"This an agency op?" Coe asks.

"What do you think?"

"I think you're flying solo."

"Wait a minute," China breaks in. "You guys *know* each other?"

Coe nods. "We have history."

Sometimes the office sent in a team, which was how Coe ended up on a rooftop with this psychopath Jimmy Chen. The target was part of a RICO investigation, star witness kept in a safehouse that was crawling with feds. In a week's time he'd be up on the witness stand, rolling over on a half-dozen crime bosses. Trouble was, he'd also be taking down a few congressmen and industry CEOs. The office wanted to keep the status quo so far as the politicos and moneymen were concerned.

That was where he and Jimmy Chen came in. If the witness couldn't make it into court, the attorney general'd lose his one solid connection between the various defendants and his RICO case would fall apart. The office didn't want to take any chances on this hit, so they sent in a team to make sure the job got done.

Coe wasn't one to argue, but he knew Jimmy by reputation and nothing he'd heard was good. He set up a meet with the woman who'd handed out the assignment.

"Look," he said. "I can do this on my own. Jimmy Chen's a psycho freak. You turn him loose in a downtown core like this and we're going to have a bloodbath on our hands."

"We don't have a problem with messy," the woman told him. "Not in this case. It'll make it look like a mob hit."

He should have backed out then, but he was too used to taking orders. To doing what he was told. So he found himself staking out the safehouse with Jimmy. He forced himself to concentrate on the hit, and a safe route out once the target was down, to ignore the freak as best he could.

The feds played their witness close to the vest. They never took him out. No one went in unless they were part of the op. In the end, Coe and Jimmy realized they'd have to do it on the day of the trial.

They took up their positions as the feds' sedan pulled up in front of the safehouse to pick up the witness. The feds had two more vehicles on the street—one parked two cars back, one halfway up the block. Coe counted six men, all told. And then there were the men inside the house with the witness. But when they brought him out, he was accompanied by a woman and a child. The witness held the child as they came down the steps—a little girl, no more than six with blonde curly hair. It was impossible to get a clear shot at him.

Now what? Coe thought.

But Jimmy didn't have any problem with the situation.

"How d'you like that?" he said. "They're using the kid as a shield. Like that's going to make a difference."

Before Coe could stop him, Jimmy fired. His first bullet tore through the girl and the man holding her. His second took the woman—probably the man's wife. All Coe could do was stare at the little girl as she hit the pavement. He was barely aware of Jimmy dropping the feds as they scattered for cover. Jimmy picked off four of them before Coe's paralysis broke.

He hit Jimmy on the side of his head with stock of his rifle. For a moment he stood over the fallen man, ready to shoot the damned freak. Then he simply dropped the weapon onto Jimmy's chest and made his retreat.

"Oh, yeah," Jimmy says. "We have history."

He laughs and Coe decides he liked the sound of the crows better. Jimmy's men give way as he moves forward.

"That's one way to put it, Leon," Jimmy goes on. "Hell, if it wasn't for you, I wouldn't even be here."

"What's that supposed to mean?" Coe asks.

But he already knows. He and Jimmy worked for the same people—men so paranoid they put conspiracy buffs to shame. When it came to that, they'd probably been on that grassy knoll in '63. Or if not them, then one of their proxies.

When Coe went underground, Jimmy must have taken the heat for it, sent him running till he ended up with the Blue Circle Boys. The fact that he's still alive says more for Jimmy's ability to survive than it does for the competence of the feds or any kindness in the hearts of their former employers. Unless Jimmy's new business *is* part of an op run by their old employers. Coe wouldn't put it past them. The Blue Circle Boys' war chest had to look good in these days of diminishing budgets, especially for an agency that didn't officially exist.

"How do you know this guy?" China asks.

"That's Leon," Jimmy says, smiling. "He always was a close-mouthed bastard. Best damn wet-boy assassin to come out of 'Nam and he doesn't even confide in his girlfriend."

"She's not my girlfriend," Coe tells him. "She's got nothing to do with this."

Because now he knows why he's here. Why the crows brought him back from the dead and to this place.

Jimmy's giving China a contemplative look.

"Oh, I don't know," he says. "Can you say 'stoolie,' Leon?"

"I'm telling you—"

"But it's a funny thing," Jimmy goes on, like he was never interrupted. "She's supposed to be dead, and here she shows up with you. You did kill her, didn't you, Gary?"

He doesn't turn around, but the surviving shooter from the alleyway is starting to sweat.

"We shot them both, Mr. Chen," he says. "I swear we did. When we dumped them in the junkyard, they were both dead."

"But here they are anyway," Jimmy says softly. "Walking tall." He looks thoughtful, his gaze never leaves Coe's face. "Why now, Leon?" he asks. "After all these years, why're you sticking your nose in my business now?"

Coe shrugs. "Just bad luck, I guess."

"And it's all yours," Jimmy says, smiling again.

"Screw this," China tells them.

As she lunges forward, Coe grabs her around the waist and hauls her back.

"Not like this," he says.

She struggles in his grip, but she can't break free.

"Kill them," Jimmy tells his men. "And this time do it right." He pauses for a heartbeat, then adds, "And aim for their heads. That Indian war paint's not going to be Kevlar like the flak vests they've got to be wearing."

That what you want to believe? Coe has time to think. China couldn't fit a dime under that dress of hers.

But then the men open up. The dawn fills with the rattle of gunfire. Coe's braced for it, but the impact of the bullets knocks China hard against him and like the shooter did earlier, he loses his balance. The backs of his legs hit the wall and the two of them go tumbling off the roof.

For a long moment, Jimmy watches the crows that are wheeling in the dawn air, right alongside the edge of the building where Coe and his little china doll took their fall. There have to be a couple of dozen of them, though they're making enough noise for twice that number.

Jimmy's never liked crows. It's the Japanese that think they're such good luck. Crows, any kind of black bird. They just give him the creeps.

"Somebody go clean up down there," he tells his men. "The last thing we need is for a patrol car to come by and find them."

But when his men get down to the street, there's only the body of the dead shooter lying on the pavement.

Coe and China watch them from the window of an abandoned factory nearby. The men. The crows. China runs her finger along the edge of a shard of broken glass that's still stuck in the windowframe. It doesn't even break the skin. She turns from the window.

"Why'd you drag us in here?" she asks. "We could've taken them."

Coe shakes his head. "That wasn't the way."

"What are you so scared of? You saw for yourself—we can't die. Not from their guns, not from the fall."

"Maybe we only have so many lives we can use up," Coe tells her.

"But—"

"And I've got some other business to take care of first."

China gives him a long considering look.

"Was it true?" she asks. "What the guy you called Jimmy said, about you being an assassin?"

"It was a long time ago. A different life."

"No wonder the crows wanted you for this gig."

Coe sighs. "If our being here's about retribution," he says, "it's got nothing to do with us. What does the universe care about some old bum and a stripper?"

"According to your friend, you're not just some—"

"That freak's not anybody's friend," Coe tells her, his voice hard.

"Okay. But—"

"This is about something else."

He tells her about the hit that went sour, the little girl that died. Tells her how Jimmy Chen shot right through her to get the job done.

China shivers. "But . . . *you* didn't kill her."

"No," Coe says. "But I might as well have. It's because of who I was, because of people like me, that she died."

China doesn't say anything for a long moment. Finally she asks, "You said something about some kind of business?"

"We're going to a bank," he tells her.

"A bank."

She lets the words sit there.

Coe nods. "So let's wash this crap off our faces or we'll give my financial advisor the willies. It'll be bad enough as it is."

"Why's that?"

"You'll see."

Coe can see the questions build up in China's eyes as he takes her into an office building that's set up snug against Cray's Gym over in Crowsea, but she keeps them to herself. The "bank" is up on the second floor, in back. A single-room office with a glass door. Inside there's a desk with a laptop computer on it, a secretary's chair, a file cabinet, and a couple of straightbacks for visitors. The man sitting at the desk is overweight and balding. He's wearing a cheap suit, white shirt, tie. He's got a take-out coffee sitting on his desk. Nothing about him or the office reflects the penthouse he goes home to with the security in the lobby and a view of the lake that upped the price of the place by another hundred grand.

The man looks up as they come in, his already pale skin going white with shock.

"Jesus," he says.

The hint of a smile touches Coe's lips. "Yeah, it's been a while. China, this is Henry, my bank manager. Henry, China."

Henry gives her a nod, then returns his gaze to Coe.

"I heard you were dead," he says.

"I am."

Henry laughs, like it's a joke. Whatever works, Coe thinks.

"So how're my investments doing?" he asks.

Henry calls up the figures on the laptop that always travels with him between the office and home. After a while he starts to talk. When the figures start to add up into the seven digits, Coe knows that Henry's been playing fair. In Coe's business, people disappear, sometimes for years, then they show up again out of the blue. It's the kind of situation that a regular financial institution can't cope with all that well. Which keeps men like Henry in business.

"I want to set up a trust fund," he tells Henry. "Something to help kids."

"Help them how?"

Coe shrugs. "Get them off the streets, or give them scholarships. Maybe set it up like one of those wish foundations for dying kids or something. Whatever works. Can you do it?"

"Sure."

"You'll get your usual cut," Coe tells him.

Henry doesn't bother to answer. That'd go without saying.

"And I want it named in memory of Angelica Ciccone."

Henry's eyebrows go up. "You mean Bruno's kid? The one that died with him the day he was going to testify?"

"You've got a long memory," Coe tells him.

Henry shrugs. "It's the kind of thing that sticks in your mind."

Tell me about it, Coe thinks.

"So you can do this?" he says.

"No problem."

"And we're square?"

Henry smiles. "We're square. I like this idea, Leon. Hell, I might even throw in a few thou' myself to help sweeten the pot."

"Where'd you get that kind of money?" China asks when they're back out on the street again.

Coe just looks at her. "Where do you think?"

"Oh. Right." But then she shakes her head. "You had all that money and you lived like a bum. . . ."

"Blood money."

"But still . . ."

"Maybe now it can do some good. I should've thought of this sooner."

"To make up for all the people you killed?" China asks.

Coe looks down the street to where a pair of crows are playing tag around a lamppost.

"You don't make up for that kind of thing," he says. "The foundation's just to give a little hope to some kids who might not get to see it otherwise. So that they don't grow up all screwed up like me."

China's quiet for a long moment.

"Or like me," she says after a while.

Coe doesn't say anything. There's nothing he can say.

"So now what?" China asks after they've been walking for a few blocks.

Coe spies a phone booth across the street and leads her to it.

"Now we make a call," he says. "You got a watch?"

She lifts her wrist to show him the slim, knock-off Rolex she's wearing.

"Time me," he says as he drops a quarter into the slot, punches in a number. "And tell me when three minutes are up. Exactly three minutes. Starting . . ." He waits until the connection's made. "Now."

While China dutifully times the call, Coe starts talking about Jimmy Chen, the hit on Bruno Ciccone, what Jimmy's up to these days, where he can be found, how many men he's got.

"Two-fifty-eight," China says. "Two-fifty-nine."

At the three-minute mark, Coe drops the phone receiver, lets it bang against the glass wall of the booth. He grabs China's hand and runs with her, back across the street, down the block and onto the next, ducks into an alley.

"Okay," he says. "Watch."

He barely gets the words out before the first cruiser comes squealing around a corner, blocks the intersection the pair of them just crossed, cherry lights flashing. Moments later, another one pulls across the intersection at the other end of the block. They're joined by two more cruisers, an unmarked car, and then a couple of dark sedans. The feds step out of those, four of them in their dark suits, looking up and down the street.

China turns to Coe. "Jesus. That was seriously fast."

Coe's smiling. "A guy who kills as many feds as Jimmy did is going to give them a hard-on that won't go away. C'mon," he adds as the police start to fan out, heading up and down the sidewalks, checking doorways, alleys. "We're done here."

China keeps her questions in check again. She lets Coe take the lead and he slips them out of the net the police are setting up like he doesn't even have to think about it. Some skills you just don't lose.

He takes her back to the junkyard. They ease in through the gates when the old man running the place isn't looking and make their way back to the rear. The dogs the old man keeps won't even come near them. But the crows follow, a thickening flock of them that settle on the junked cars and trash around them.

"That business with the phone call and the cops," China wants to know. "What was all that about?"

"We just dealt with Jimmy."

She shakes her head. "His lawyers'll have him back on the streets before the end of the day."

"Unless he resists," Coe says. "What do you think, China? Think Jimmy's the kind of guy who'll go quietly and stand trial on murder one charges for killing a half-dozen cops?"

"No. I guess not. But if he gets away . . ."

"What do the crows tell you?" Coe asks.

She sits quietly for a moment, looking at them, head cocked, like she's listening. Coe doesn't hear anything except for their damned cawing. Finally she turns back to look at him.

"It's over," she says. "We're done."

Coe raps a knuckle against the fender he's sitting on. It's solid. So's he.

"How come we're still here?" he asks.

"I guess we'll cross over tonight."

Coe nods. There's a kind of symmetry to that.

"I like you better without the war paint," he says.

"Yeah? I think on you it was an improvement."

She smiles, but then she gets a serious look.

"I'm glad we did it your way, Leon," she says. "I feel better for it. Cleaner."

Coe doesn't say anything. His own soul's stained with too much killing for him to ever feel clean again. He didn't do this for himself, or because of the pacifism he's embraced since Angelica Ciccone was killed. He did it for China. He did it so she wouldn't have to carry what he does when the crows take them over to wherever it is they're going next. Into some kind of afterworld, he guesses, if there really is such a place.

He's been thinking. Maybe there is, considering the crows and how they brought the two of them back. And the thing is, if there *is* someplace else to go, he figures she deserves a shot at it with a clean slate.

Him, he'll settle for simple oblivion.

*   *   *

It's late at night now, close on to the anniversary hour of their dying. The crows are leading them back to where Jimmy Chen's boys shot them down. When they reach the mouth of the alley, Coe hesitates. The skin at the nape of his neck goes tight and a prickle of something walks down his spine.

"It's okay," China tells him.

The air above them's thick with crows, wheeling and cawing. Coe still can't make any kind of sense out of them.

China takes his hand.

"If you can't trust them," she says, "then trust me."

Coe nods. He doesn't know where they're going, but he knows for sure that there's nothing left for him here. So he lets her lead him out of the world, the crows flying on ahead of them, into a tunnel of light.

In the Quiet After Midnight

It's a winter's night, the stars are bright
And the world keeps spinning around. . . .
—*Kiya Heartwood, from "Robert's Waltz"*

1

I'm fifteen when I realize that I don't remember my mother anymore. I mean, I still recognize her in pictures and everything, but I can't call her face up just before I fall asleep the way I once did. I used to tell her about my day, the little things that happened to me, all the things I was thinking about, and it made the loneliness seem less profound—having her listening, I mean. Now I can't remember her. It's like she isn't inside me anymore and I don't even know when she went away.

I still remember I had a mother. I'm not stupid. But the immediacy of the connection is gone. Now it's like something I read in a history book in school, not something that was ever part of my life and it scares me because it was never supposed to go away. She was always supposed to be with me.

It's a seriously hot day in the middle of June and I'm walking home from school when it hits me, when it stops me dead in my tracks right there in the middle of the sidewalk, near the corner of Williamson and Kelly. I can't tell you what makes it come to me the way it does, so true and hard, bang, right out of nowhere. But all of a sudden it's like I can't breathe, like the hot air's pressing way too close around me.

I look around—I don't know what I'm looking for, I just know I have to get off the street, away from all the people and their ordinary lives— and that's when I see this little Catholic church tucked away on a side street. Kelly Street was a main thoroughfare years ago, back when the church was really impressive, too, I guess. Now they're both looking long neglected.

I don't know why I go in. I'm not even Catholic. But it's cool inside, dark after the sunlight I just left behind, and quiet. I sit down in a pew near the back and look up toward the front. I've heard of the Stations of the Cross, but I don't know what they are, if they're even something you can see. But I see Jesus hanging there, front and center, a statue of his mother off to one side, pictures of the saints. I wonder which one is the patron of memory.

I bring my gaze back to the front of the church. This time I look at the candles. There must thirty, forty of them, encased in short red glasses. Only five or six are lit. They're prayers, I'm guessing, or votive offerings. Whoever lit them doesn't seem to be around.

I slouch in the pew and stare up at the vaulted ceiling. It's easier to breathe in here, the world doesn't seem to press down on me the way it did outside, but the sick, lost feeling doesn't go away.

I don't know how long I've been sitting there when there's a rustle of cloth behind me. I turn to see a hooded man kneeling, two pews back, head bent in prayer. He's all in black, cloak and hood, shadows swallowing his features. A priest, I think, except they don't dress like that, do they? At least none of the ones I've ever seen—on the street or in the movies.

Maybe he's not even a man, I find myself thinking. Maybe he's a she, a nun, except they don't dress like that either. I guess I'm thinking about him so hard that my thoughts pull his head up. I still can't see anything but the hint of features in the spill of shadows under the hood, but the voice is definitely male.

"A curious sanctuary, is it not?" he says, sitting back on the pew behind him.

I have no idea what he means, but I nod my head.

"Here we sit, neither of us parishioners, yet we have the place to ourselves."

"The priest must be around here someplace," I say, hoping it's true.

It's suddenly occurred to me that this guy could easily be some kind of pervert, following young girls into an out-of-the-way place like this and hitting on them. I'm very aware of how quiet it is in here, how secluded.

He shakes his head. "They are all long gone," he says. "Priest and parishioners all."

Now I'm really getting the creeps. I don't want to turn my back on him so I gesture with my chin toward the front of the church. I clear my throat.

"Somebody lit those candles," I say.

"At one time," he agrees. "But now we see only the memory of their light, the way starlight is but a memory of what burns in the heavens, crossing an unthinkable distance from where they flared to where we stand when we regard them."

"My, um, dad's expecting me," I tell him. "He knows where I am."

As if, but it seems like a good thing to say. I might be alone in here, but I don't want him thinking I'm an easy mark. I sit up a little straighter and try to look bigger than I am. Tougher. If worse comes to worst, I'll go down kicking and screaming. I may be small, but I can be fierce, only ferocity doesn't seem to be the issue since all he's doing is sitting there looking at me from under the shadows of his hood. A footnoted script would be good, though, since nothing he's saying really makes much sense.

"What is it you have lost?" he asks.

The confused look I give him isn't put on like my bravado. "What do you mean, lost?"

"We've all lost something precious," he says. "Why else would we find ourselves in this place?"

Maybe I'm not a Catholic, but I know this conversation has nothing to do with their doctrines. I should get up and see if I can make it back out the door. Instead I ask, "What have you lost?"

"My life."

Okay. Way too creepy. But I can't seem to get up. It's like it's really late at night and I know I have to get up for school the next day, but I still have to finish the book first. I can't go to sleep, not knowing how it ends.

"You don't look dead," I say.

"I don't believe in death," he tells me.

There's a glint of white in the shadows under his hood. Teeth, I realize. He just smiled. I don't feel at all comforted.

I clear my throat again. "But . . ."

I can't see his eyes, but I can feel the weight of his gaze.

"I have lost my life," he says, "but I cannot die."

He shrugs and I realize there's something wrong under that hood of his, the way the folds of the cloth fall. He's bumpy, but in the wrong places.

"And you?" he asks.

"My mother," I find myself saying. I remember what he said about the candles and starlight. "The memory of my mother."

I don't even know why I'm telling him this. It's not the kind of thing I'd tell my dad, or my best friend Ellie, but here I am, sharing this horrible lost feeling with a perfect stranger who doesn't exactly make me feel like he's got my best interests at heart.

"Some would embrace the loss of memory," he says, "rather than lament its absence."

I shake my head. "I don't understand."

"Remembering can keep the pain too fresh," he explains. "It is so much easier to forget—or at least it is more comfortable. But you and I, we are not seeking comfort, are we? We know that to forget is to give in to the darkness, so we walk in the light, that we hold fast to our joys and our pains."

At first I thought he had a real formal way of speaking, but now I'm starting to get the idea that maybe English isn't his first language, that he's translating in his head as he talks and that's what makes everything sound so stiff and proper.

"There was a glade in my homeland," he says. He settles further back against his pew and I catch a glimpse of a russet beard, a pointed chin, high cheekbones before the hood shadows them again. "It had about it a similar air as does this church. It was a place for remembering, a sanctuary hidden in a grove where the lost could gather the fraying tatters of their memories and weave them strong once more."

"The lost . . ."

Again that flash of a smile. There's no humor in it.

"Such as we."

"I just came in here to get out of the heat," I tell him.

"Mmm."

"I was feeling a little dizzy."

"And why here, do you suppose?" he asks. "I will tell you," he goes on before I can answer. "Because like us, this place also seeks to hold on to what it has lost. We help each other. You. I. The church."

"I'm not . . ."

Remembering anything, I'm about to say, but my voice trails off because suddenly it's not true. I am remembering. If I close my eyes, I know I can call my mother's face up again—not stiff, like in a photo, but the way it was when she was still alive, mobile and fluid. And not only her face. I can smell the faint rose blush of her perfume. I can almost feel her hand on my head, tousling the curls that are pulled back in a French braid right now.

I look at him. "How . . . ?"

He smiles again and stands. He's not as tall as I was expecting from his broad shoulders.

"You see?" he says. "And I, too, am remembering. Reeds by a river and a woman hidden in them. I should never have cut a pipe from those reeds. Her voice was far sweeter."

He's lost me again.

"I can pretend it was preordained," he says. "That the story needed to play out the way it did. But you and I, we know better, don't we? The story can't be told until the deed is done. Only the Fates can look into the future and I have known them to be wrong."

"I'm not sure I know what you're talking about," I say.

He nods. "Of course. Why should you? They are my memories and it is an old story, forgotten now. But remember this: There is always a choice. Perhaps destiny will quicken the plot, but what we do with the threads we are given is our choice."

I've taken this in school.

"You mean free will."

He has to think about that.

"Perhaps I do," he says finally. "But it comes without instruction and the price of it can be dear."

"What do you mean?"

He shrugs. "I can only speak of what is pertinent to my own experience, but if there were any advice I would wish I had been given, it would be to believe in death."

"How can you not believe in it?" I say. "It's all around us."

There's a tightness in my chest again, but this time it's because I can remember. It's because my memories are immediate and clear, the good and the bad, the joy of my mother's love and the way she was taken away from me.

"It was not always so," he says.

"Then it was a better time."

"You think so?" he asks. "Consider the alternative. Imagine being alive when all consider you dead. You walk through the changing world as a ghost. You can touch no one. No one can see you."

I could really use those footnotes now.

"But—"

"Be careful with your choices," he says and turns away.

I hear the rustling of cloth as he moves, the faint click of his heels on the stone floor, except they don't sound like leather-soled shoes. There's a hollow ring to them, like a horse's hoof on pavement. He turns to face me again when he reaches the door, pushes back his hood. He has strong, handsome features, with a foreign cast. Dark, olive skin, but his hair is as red as his beard, and standing up among the curls are two small horns, curled like a goat's.

"You . . . you're the devil," I say.

I can't believe he's here in a church. I want to look up above the altar, to see if the statue of Jesus is turning away in horror at this unholy invasion, but I can't move, can't pull my gaze from the horned man. I feel sick to my stomach.

"Where one might see a devil," he says, "another might see a friend."

I'm shaking my head. I may not be much of a churchgoer, but even I've heard about what happens to people who make deals with the devil.

"Remember what I said about choices," he tells me.

And then he's gone.

It's forever before I can get up the nerve to walk back out through that door myself and go home.

2

They'd all gotten together at The Harp to share a pitcher of beer after finishing the evening classes they taught at the Newford School of Art. After the quiet of the school, the noisy pub with its Irish session in full swing in one corner was exactly what they needed to wind down. They commandeered a table far enough away from the music so that they could talk and hold forth, but close enough so that they could still hear the music.

They made a motley group. Jilly and Sophie, alike enough in the pub's low light that they could be sisters, except Jilly was thinner, with the scruffier clothes and the longer, curlier hair; Sophie was tidier, more buxom. Hannah, all in black as usual, blonde hair cropped short, blue eyes sparkling with the buzz her second glass of beer was giving her. Desmond, dreadlocked and smiling, dressed as though he was still living on the Islands, wearing only a thin cotton jacket, despite the below-zero temperatures outside. Angela, the intensity of her dark eyes softened by her pixy features and a fall of silky Pre-Raphaelite hair.

It was Hannah who'd come up with the question—"What's the strangest thing that ever happened to you?"—and then looked around the table. She'd expected something from Jilly because Jilly could always be counted on for some outlandish story or other. Hannah was never quite sure if they were true or not, but that didn't really matter. The stories were always entertaining, everything from affirmation that Bigfoot had indeed been seen wandering around the Tombs to a description of the strange goblin kingdom that Jilly would insist existed in Old Town, that part of the city that had dropped underground during the Big Quake and then been built over during the reconstruction.

And, of course, she told them so well.

But the first story had come from Angela and instead of giving them a fit of the giggles, it made them all fall quiet. Her calm recitation created a pool of stillness in the middle of the general hubbub of the tavern as they regarded her with varying degrees of belief and wonder: Jilly completely accepting the story at face value, Desmond firmly in the rational camp, Sophie somewhere in between the two. Hannah supposed she was closest to Sophie—she'd like to believe, but she wasn't sure she could.

Angela smiled. "Not exactly what you were expecting, was it?"

"Well, no," Hannah said.

"I think it's lovely," Jilly put in. "And it feels so absolutely true."

"Well, you would," Sophie told her. She looked around the table. "Maybe we should order another pitcher so that we can all work at seeing the world the way Jilly does."

"We'll be needing a lot more than beer for that," Desmond put in.

Jilly stuck out her tongue at him.

"So?" Angela asked. "Was he the devil?"

Desmond shook his head. "As if."

"What do you think?" Hannah asked.

"I have no idea," Angela replied. "I was young and impressionable and certainly upset at the time. Maybe I saw what I thought I saw, or maybe I imagined it. Or maybe he was suffering from one of those de-forming diseases like elephantiasis and those weren't horns I saw coming up out of his hair, but some sort of unfortunate growth."

"I'll side with Desmond on this one," Jilly said.

Everyone looked at her in surprise. Jilly and Desmond never agreed on anything except that their students needed a firm grounding in the basics of classical art—figure studies, anatomy, color theory, and the like—before they could properly go on to create more experimental works.

Jilly rolled her eyes at the way they were all looking at her. "I mean that Angela didn't meet the devil," she said. "Or at least not the devil according to Christian doctrine. What she met was something far older— what the Christians used as a template for their fallen angel."

"I definitely need that beer," Desmond said and got up to order an-other pitcher.

"But in a church?" Hannah found herself saying.

Jilly turned to her. "Why not?"

"Who exactly are we talking about here?" Sophie asked.

"Well, think about it," Jilly replied. "You've got him talking about chasing a nymph into the reeds and making music that can't compare to her singing. He had goat's horns and probably goat's feet—Angela says his footsteps sounded like hooves on the floor."

Angela nodded in agreement.

"And then," Jilly went on, "there's this business of being dead but liv-ing forever."

She sat back, obviously pleased with herself.

Hannah shook her head. "I still don't see what you're getting at."

"Old gods," Jilly said. "She met Pan. Like it says in the stories, 'Great Pan is dead. Long live Pan!'"

"Not to be picayune," Sophie put in with a smile, "but I think you're quoting the Waterboys."

Jilly shrugged. "Whatever. It doesn't change anything."

"I thought about that, too," Angela said, "but it makes no sense. What would Pan be doing here, thousands of miles from Arcadia, even if he ever did exist and was still alive?"

"I think he travels the world," Jilly told her. "Like the Wandering Jew. And besides, Newford's a cool city. We all live here, don't we? Why *shouldn't* Pan show up here as well?"

"Because," Desmond said, having returned with a brimming pitcher in time to hear the last part of the conversation, "Roman gods aren't real. Aren't now, never were, end of story."

"He was Greek, actually," Sophie said.

"Whose side are you on?" Desmond asked.

He poured them all fresh glasses, then set the empty pitcher down in the middle of the table.

Sophie clinked her glass against his. "The side of truth, justice, and equality for all—including obstinate, if talented, sculptors."

"Flatterer," he said.

"Hussy."

"Men can't be hussies."

"Can too!" all four women cried at once.

3

The talk went on for hours along with another couple of pitchers of The Harp's draught lager. By the time Sophie said they should probably call it a night—"It's a night!" Jilly pronounced to a round of giggles—Hannah was feeling dizzy from both.

She and Angela had the same bus stop, so after a chorus of goodbyes, they left together, slightly unsteady on their feet, breath clouding in the cold air. Happily the bus stop wasn't far and there was a bench where they could sit while they waited. Hannah settled back in her seat, not really feeling the cold yet. She looked up at the sky, wishing she was out in the country somewhere so that she could fully appreciate the stars that were cloaked by the city's light pollution. That was one of the things she missed the most about having moved to the city—deep night skies and country quiet.

"Did that really happen?" she asked after a moment.

Angela didn't need to ask what.

"I don't know," she said. "I can joke about it, but the truth is, that was a pivotal moment for me—one of those crossroads they talk about where your life could have gone one way or the other. It doesn't matter to me whether it was real or not—or rather, if I had some extraordinary experience or not. I still came away from it with the realization that I always have to think my choices through carefully, and then, when I make a decision, take full responsibility for it."

Like moving to the city, Hannah thought. It was no use bemoaning the things she missed, though of course that didn't stop her from worrying a half-dozen times a week over whether she'd made the right decision. She wanted to be a painter, and the community and contacts she'd come here to find were what she needed to be able to do it—not to mention the fact that back home she could never make her living with the odd sorts of jobs she held here: art instructor, sometime artist's model, waitress, messenger, the occasional commission for an ad or a poster. Maybe when she was somewhat better established she could afford to move back to the country, but not now. Not and feel that her career was actually moving forward.

But that didn't stop her from missing everything she'd left behind.

"Think it through first," Hannah said, "but then don't look back."

Angela nodded. "Exactly. If you embrace the decision you've made, everything seems that much clearer because you're not fighting self-doubt."

"You got all that when you were fifteen?"

"Not the way you're thinking. It wasn't this amazing epiphany and my whole life changed. But I couldn't get him—whoever or whatever he was—out of mind. Nor what he'd told me. And whatever else happened, I had my mom back." Angela touched a mittened hand to her chest. "In here." She got a far-away look in her eyes. "Jilly's always saying that magic's never what you expect it to be, but it's often what you need. I think she's right. And it doesn't really matter if the experience comes from outside or inside. *Where* it comes from isn't important at all. What's important is that it *does* come—and that we're receptive enough to recognize and accept it."

"I could use a piece of magic to change my life," Hannah said. "I seem to be in this serious rut—always scrambling to make ends meet, which also means that I never have the time to do enough of my own work to do more than participate in group shows."

"Well, you know what they say: Visualize it. If you see yourself as having more time, being more successful, whatever, you can make it happen."

"I think if I'm going to visualize magic, I'd rather it was dancing on a hilltop with your horned man."

Angela's eyebrows rose.

Hannah smiled. "Well, that's what I think magic should be. Not this." She waved a hand to take in the city around them. "Not being successful or whatever, but just having a piece of something impossible to hold on to, if only for a moment."

"So visualize that."

"As if."

They fell silent for a time, watching the occasional car go by.

"Did you ever see him again?" Hannah asked.

Angela smiled and shook her head. "I think it was pretty much a once-in-a-lifetime sort of experience. That piece of something impossible you were talking about that I only got to hold on to for a moment."

Her bus arrived then.

"Can you get home okay?" she asked.

"I'm not *that* tipsy," Hannah told her.

"But almost."

"Oh, yes."

Her own bus took another five minutes to arrive.

4

Later that night, Hannah lay in bed, studying the splotchy plaster on her ceiling, and let her mind drift. Visualize, she thought. How would she visualize Angela's mysterious visitor? Like that painting in *The Wandering Wood*, she decided. The watercolor by Ellen Wentworth that depicted the spirit of the forest as some kind of hybrid Greek/Native American being—goat legs and horns, but with beads and feathers and cowrie shells braided into the red hair and beard, even into the goaty leg hair.

She smiled, remembering how she'd copied the painting from out of the book when she was twelve or thirteen and had kept it hanging up in her room for ages—right up until her last year of high school when the sheer naiveté of its rendering finally made her put it away. She was doing such better work by that time. Her grasp of anatomy alone made it difficult to look at the piece anymore. What had become of it? she wondered.

She got up out of bed, but not to go searching through stacks of old art—most of that early juvenile stuff was still stored in boxes on the farm anyway. No, she'd had a cup of herbal tea when she got home and now she had to pay the price with a trip to the bathroom. She got as far as putting a thick flannel housecoat on top of the oversized T-shirt she slept in before being distracted by the scene that lay outside her bedroom window.

There was nothing particularly untoward to catch her eye. Back yards and fences, half of the latter in desperate need of repair that they'd probably never get. Narrow lanes made more narrow by garbage cans, Dumpsters and snowbanks. Above them, fire escapes and brick walls, windows—mostly dark, but a few lit from within by the blue flicker of television screens—rooflines, telephone poles and drooping wires criss-crossing back and forth across the alleys and lanes.

The snow covering softened some of the usual harshness of the scene, and yes, it could be almost magical during a snowfall, the kind when big sleepy flakes came drifting down, but it was still hard to imagine the city holding anything even remotely as enchanting as Jilly's stories of gemmin, which were a kind of earth spirit that lived in abandoned cars, or Angela's mysterious goatman—even if such things were possible in the first place. If she were a magical being, she wouldn't live here, not when there were deep forests and mountains an hour or so's drive north of the city, or the lake right smack at the southern end of the urban sprawl. She'd run through the woods like one of Ellen Wentworth's elfish tree people, or sail off across the lake in a wooden shoe.

She smiled. Leaving the window, she went and had her pee, but in-stead of getting back into bed, she pulled on a pair of jeans under her housecoat, stuck her feet into her boots and left her apartment. She took the stairs up to the roof. The door was stuck so she had to give it a good shove before she could get it open and step outside into the chilly air.

She wasn't sure what time it was. After four, at any rate. Late enough that you could almost tune out the occasional siren and the vague bits of traffic that drifted from the busier streets a few blocks over. The wide ex-panse of the rooftop was covered with a thin layer of snow, granulated and hard, clinging to the surface of the roof like carbuncles. Her flower-boxes were up here, a half-dozen of them in which she grew all sorts of vegetables and flowers—a piece of the farm transplanted here so that she didn't feel quite so cut off from the land. The dirt in the boxes was all frozen now and snow covered them. She'd pulled most of the dead growth out in the autumn, but there were still a few browned stalks push-ing hardily out of the snow that she hadn't gotten to. Cosmos and purple coneflowers. Some kale, which was better after a frost anyway, only it was finished now.

She shivered, but didn't go back inside right away. She looked out across the rooftops, a checkerboard of white squares and black streets and yards. There was a sort of magic, she supposed, about the city this late at night. The stillness, the dark, the sensation that time seemed to have stopped. The knowing that she was one of a select few who were awake and outside at this hour. If you were going to discover a secret, if you were going to get the chance to peer under the skin of the world, if only for a moment, this was the time for it.

Are you out there? she wondered, addressing the mysterious man Angela had met in a church long before Hannah had even thought of moving to the city herself. *Will you show yourself to me? Because I could use a piece of magic right about now, a piece of something impossible that shouldn't exist, but does, if only for this moment.*

Her straits weren't as desperate as Angela's had been. And compared to how so many people had to live—out of work, on the streets, cadging spare change just to get a bowl of soup or a cup of coffee—what she had was luxury. But she still had a deficit, a kind of hollow in her heart from which bits and pieces of her spirit trickled away, like coins will from a hole in your pocket. Nothing she couldn't live without, but she missed them all the same.

She wasn't sure that magic could change that. She wasn't sure anything could, because what she really needed to find was a sense of peace. Within herself. With the choices she'd made that had brought her here. Magic would probably confuse the issue. She imagined it would be like an instant addiction—having tasted it once, you'd never be satisfied not tasting it again. She didn't know how Angela did it.

Except, not having tasted it created just as much yearning. This wanting to believe it was real. This asking for the smallest, slightest tangible proof.

She remembered what Angela had said. Visualize it.

Okay. She'd pretend she was thinking up a painting—a made-up landscape. She closed her eyes and tried to ignore the cold air. It wasn't winter, but a summer's night, somewhere near the Mediterranean. This wasn't a tenement rooftop, but a hilltop with olive trees and grape vines and . . . the details got a little vague after that.

Oh, just try, she told herself.

Some white buildings with terra-cotta roofs in the distance, like stairs going down to the sea. Maybe some goats, or sheep. A stone wall. It's night. The sky's like velvet and the stars feel as though they're no more than an elbow-length away.

Where would he be?

Under one of the olive trees, she decided. Right at the top of the hill. Starlight caught on the curve of his goat horns. And he'd be playing those reed pipes of his. A low breathy sound like . . . like . . . She had to use her father's old Zamfir records for a reference, stripping away the sappy accompaniment and imagining the melody to be more mysterious. Older. No, timeless.

For a moment there, she could almost believe it. Could almost smell the sea, could feel the day's heat still trapped in the dirt under her feet. But then a cold gust of wind made her shiver and took it away. The warm night, olive trees and all.

Except . . . except . . .

She blinked in confusion. She *was* on a hilltop, only it was in the middle of the city. The familiar roofs of the tenements surrounding her apartment were all still there, but her own building was gone, replaced by a snowy hilltop, cleared near the top where she stood, skirted with pine and cedar as it fell away to the street.

She shook her head slowly. This couldn't . . .

The sound she heard was nothing like the one she'd been trying to imagine. It still originated from a wind instrument, was still breathy and low, but it held an undefinable quality that she couldn't have begun to imagine. It was like a heartbeat, the hoot of an owl, the taste of red wine and olives, all braided together and drawn out into long, resonating notes. In counterpoint she heard footsteps, the crunch of snow and the soft sound of shells clacking together.

"Dance with me," a voice said from behind her.

When she turned, he was there. Ellen Wentworth's forest spirit, horns and goat legs, the hair entwined with feathers, beads and shells. She seemed to fall into his eyes, tumbling down into the deep mystery of them and unable to look away. He was a northern spirit, as much a part of the winter and the hills north of the city as a wolf or a jack pine, but the Mediterranean goatman was there, too, the sense of him growing sharper and clearer, the further she was drawn into his gaze.

"You . . . I . . ."

Her throat couldn't shape the words. Truth was, she had no idea what she was trying to say. Perhaps his name—the name Jilly had given him.

She let him take her in his warm arms and felt ridiculous in her tatty housecoat, cowboy boots, and jeans. He smelled of pine sap and cedar boughs, and then of something else, a compelling musky scent she couldn't place, old and dark and secret. His biceps were corded and hard under her hands, but his touch was light, gentle as she remembered the brush of wildflowers to be against her legs when she crossed a summer meadow.

The music had acquired a rhythm, a slow waltz time. His music. He was dancing with her, but somehow he was still making that music.

"How . . . ?" she began.

His smile made her voice falter. The question grew tattered in her head and came apart, drifted away. Magic, she decided. Pure and simple. Visualized. Made real. A piece of impossible, a couldn't-be, but here it was all the same and what did it matter where it came from, or how it worked?

He led beautifully, and she was content to let everything else fall away and simply dance with him.

5

She woke to find that she'd spent the night sleeping on the landing outside the door that led out onto the roof of her building. She was stiff from having slept on the hard floor, cold from the draft coming in from under the door. But none of that seemed to matter. Deep in her chest she could still feel the rhythm of that mysterious music she'd heard last night, heard while she danced on a hilltop that didn't exist, danced with a creature that couldn't possibly exist.

She remembered one of the things that Angela had said last night.

Jilly's always saying that magic's never what you expect it to be, but it's often what you need.

Lord knows she had needed this.

"Hey, *chica*. You drink a little too much last night?"

Mercedes Muñoz, her upstairs neighbor, was standing on the stairs leading up to where Hannah lay. Hand on her hip, Mercedes wore her usual smile, but worry had taken up residence in her dark eyes.

"You okay?" she added when Hannah didn't respond.

Hannah slowly sat up and drew her housecoat close around her throat.

"I've never felt better in my life," she assured Mercedes. It was true. She didn't even have a hangover. "For the first time since I've moved to this city, I finally feel like I belong."

It made no sense. How could it make her feel this way? A dream of dancing with some North American version of a small Greek god, on a hilltop that resembled the hills that rose up behind the farm where she'd grown up. But it had all the same. Maybe it was simply the idea of the experience—wonderful, impossible, exhilarating.

But she preferred to believe it hadn't been a dream. That like Angela, she'd met a piece of old-world magic, however improbable it might seem. That the music she was still carrying around inside her had been his. That the experience had been real. Because if something like that could happen, then other dreams could come true as well. She could make it here, on her own, away from the farm. It hadn't been a mistake to come.

Mercedes offered her a hand up.

"And now what?" Mercedes asked. "You going to try sleeping in a cardboard house in some alley next?"

Hannah smiled. "If that's what it takes, maybe I will."

The Pennymen

. . . and then there are the pennymen, linked to
the trembling aspens, or penny trees, so called
because their leaves, when moving in a breeze,
seem like so many twinkling coins.

—*Christy Riddell,*
from Fairy Myths of North America

1

It's a Sunday morning in January and there's a tree outside my window,
full of birds. I'm not exactly sure what kind. They look like starlings with
their winter-dark feathers and speckled breasts and heads, but I could be
wrong. I've never been much good at identifying birds. Pigeon, crow,
robin, seagull, sparrow . . . after that, I'm pretty much guessing. But the
tree's a rowan, a mountain ash. I know that because Jilly named it for me
when she helped the boy and me first move into this apartment.

Jilly says they're also called wicken, or quicken trees, an old name that
seems both quaint and evocative to me. She claims they're a magic tree—
real magic, she insists, like faeries dancing on hilltops, Rhine maidens rising up from the river bottom, little hobgoblins scurrying down the street
that you might glimpse from the corner of your eye. As if. All I can do
when she starts in on that sort of thing is smile and nod and try not to roll
my eyes. Jilly's sweet, but she does take some things way too seriously. I
mean, you can have all the romantic notions in the world, but just be-

cause you think you feel a tickle of enchantment, like you're peeking through a loose board in the fence that divides what we know from what could be, doesn't mean it's real.

Magic belongs in stories, it's that simple. Real life and that kind of story don't mix.

Except lying here in bed this morning, pillows propped up on the headboard and looking out the window, for some reason I feel as though I'm in a story. Nothing overly dramatic, mind you. It's not like I expect spies to come crashing in through the front door, or to find a body in the bathtub when I get up to have a pee. It's more like an establishing shot in a movie, something glimpsed in passing, a scene to set the mood of what's to come.

So if this is a movie, here's what the audience would see: It's a blustery day, the sky thick with fat snow that blurs the world outside the glass panes. Against a backdrop of a Crowsea street, there are the birds and the tree, or more properly the stand of trees, since the rowans are growing in a bunch, trunks no thicker than my forearms. The berries are orange, not the bright orange of autumn. They're a deeper color this time of year, but they still stand out against the white snow, the dark lines of the branches, and those birds. Tiny splashes of color. The ground under the tree is littered with them, though the snow's covering them up now.

I can't hear the starlings through the glass. They're probably not making any noise. Too busy chowing down on the berries and keeping their perches as the wind makes the branches sway wildly in sudden snowy gusts. I should get up, but I don't want to lose this moment. I want to lie here and let it stretch out as far as it can go.

I wish the boy were home. I'd ask her to bring me some tea, only she's off working at the gallery this morning. Commerce stops for no one, not even on Sunday anymore.

Have I confused you? Sorry. I started calling Eliza "the boy" after she got her hair cut. The longest she lets it grow anymore is about the length of my pinky finger. It used to fall to the middle of her back like mine still does and then we really looked like the sisters some people think we are.

The boy and I aren't really a couple, like we don't sleep together or anything, but we're closer than friends and don't date, which tends to confuse people when they first meet us and try to fit us into an appropriate mental pigeonhole. Sorry, I don't have one that really works any better myself. You could call us soul mates, I guess, though that's not much clearer, is it?

We met when we were both going through a particularly rough time. Neither of us had friends or family or any kind of support system to fall back on. We were solitary sadnesses until we literally bumped into each other at a La-La-La Human Steps performance and acquired each other. I can't explain it, but things just clicked between us, right there in the foyer of the Standish, and we've been pretty much inseparable ever since.

The boy's the creative one. Long before we met, she was always drawing and painting and making something out of nothing—an amazing ability if you ask me. Forget fairy-tale stuff; that's the only real magic we're going to find in this world. The creative impulse, and the way that people can connect—you know, we might be separate islands of muscle, bone, and flesh, but something in our souls is still able to bridge that impossible gap.

Okay, that's two magics. So sue me.

It's through the boy that we got involved with the Crowsea arts crowd and met Jilly, Sophie, and the others. Me? Well, when I was younger, the only thing I was any good at was being a troublemaker. These days my claim to fame is that I've cleaned up my act and don't cause problems for people anymore.

The boy and I opened the gallery about a year and a half ago, now. The Bone Circus Gallery—don't ask where we got the name. It was just there waiting for us when we decided this was what we wanted to do. We have a different artist showcased every month as well as a general selection of miscellaneous artists' work, postcards, posters, and prints. We carry art supplies, too, and the boy has a studio in back. The art supplies really pay the rent some months, plus it's a way for the boy to get a deep discount on the stuff she needs for her own work.

So life's been treating us well. Maybe we're not rich, and the boy's not famous—yet—but we pay the bills. Better still, she gets to work at what she loves and I've discovered that not only do I like running this little shop and gallery of ours, but I'm good at it, too. It's the first time I've ever been good at anything.

Of course the way the world works is, you don't ever get too comfortable with what you've got, because if you do, something'll come along to pull the rug out from under you. In our case, it's how the boy got co-opted into this fairyland of Jilly's.

It starts while I'm lying in bed, watching the starlings gorge on rowan berries.

2

Eliza Casey loved a winter's day such as this. Clouds of fat, lazy snow drifting down, the sounds of the city muffled by the ever-deepening white blanket—footsteps, traffic, sirens, all. She didn't mind being bundled up like a roly-poly teddy bear as she trundled down the snowy streets, nor that it was her turn to open the gallery this Sunday morning. Not when it entailed her getting up early and out into this weather.

Too much of winter in the city involved dirty slush and bitter cold, frayed tempers and complaints about the wind chill, the icy pavement, the perceived interminable length of the season. A snowfall like this, early in the morning when she pretty much had the streets to herself, was like a gift, a whisper of quiet magic. A piece of enchanted time stolen from the regular whirl and spin of the world in which it felt as though anything could happen.

She was humming happily to herself by the time she reached the gallery. A gust of wind rocked the store sign as she went up the steps, dropping a clump of snow on her head and making her laugh even as some of it went sliding down the back of her neck. She swept the porch and steps, then went inside and stomped the snow from her boots in the hall. By the time she'd put the cash float in the register and made a cup of tea, another inch or so of snow had already accumulated on the porch. Since she wasn't opening for another twenty minutes, she decided to wait until then before sweeping again. First she'd have her tea.

Her studio at the back of the store tempted her, but she resolutely ignored its lure. Carrying her tea mug around the gallery with her, she busied herself with dusting, straightening the prints and postcards in their racks, tidying and restocking the art supplies that provided the gallery with its main bread and butter. By the time she was done, it was a few minutes before opening.

She put her parka back on and went out into the hall. It was as she was reaching for the broom where it was leaning up in the corner by the door that she noticed the coppery glint of a penny lying on the floor. The old rhyme went through her mind:

Find a penny, pick it up, and all the day you'll have good luck.

She bent down, fingers stretched out to pluck it up from the hardwood floor, then jumped back as the penny made a turtle-like transformation from coin into a tiny man. Legs, arms, and a head popped out from a suddenly plump little body and he scurried off, quick as a cockroach. Hardly able to believe what her own two eyes were showing her, she watched as he sped toward a crack between the baseboard and the floor, squeezed in through the narrow opening, and was gone.

Slowly she sat down on the floor, gaze locked on where he'd disappeared.

"Oh my," she said, unaware that she was speaking aloud.

She looked up and down the length of the hall, wishing there was someone with her to confirm what she'd just seen. It was like something out of Mary Norton's *The Borrowers*, or one of William Dunthorn's *Smalls* come to life. But she was alone with the impossibility of the experience and already the rational part of her mind was reshuffling the memory of what she'd seen, explaining it away.

It hadn't been a penny in the first place, so of course it hadn't turned into a little man. It was only a bug that she'd startled. A beetle, though it wasn't summer. A cockroach, though they'd never had them in the building before.

Except . . . except . . .

She could so clearly call up the round swell of the little man's tummy and his spindly limbs. The tiny startled gaze that had met her own before he had scooted away.

"Oh, my," she said again.

3

It's not that I don't want to believe; it's that I can't.

I'm as romantically inclined as the next person and can fully appreciate the notion of faeries dancing in some moonlit glade, or dwarves laboring over their silver and gold jewelry in some hidden kingdom, deep underground. Really, I can. But I also believe it's important to differentiate between fact and fiction—to keep one's daydreams separate from the realities of day-to-day life. It's when you mix the two that the trouble starts. Trust me. Living the first seventeen years of my life with a seriously schizophrenic mother, I know all about this.

So I subscribe to the scientific contention that nothing is proven until it can be shown to be repeatable. It makes perfect sense to me that anything that only happens once should be considered anecdotal, and therefore worthless from a scientific point of view. If faeries live at the bottom of the garden, they should always be observable. Even if you have to stand on one foot during the second night of the full moon, with a pomegranate in your pocket and your head cocked a certain way. Every time you complete the specifications, you should see them.

"The problem with that," Jilly said when we were talking about it a while ago, "is that *everything* happens only once."

"You're being too literal," I told her.

"Maybe you're not being literal enough."

I shook my head. "No. I just think it's important to be grounded, that's all. To know that if I drop something, gravity will do its thing. That if I open the door to my room, I won't find some forgotten ruin of Atlantis there instead of my bed and dresser. I couldn't live in a world where anything can happen."

"That's not what it's about. It's about staying open to the possibility that there's more to the world than what most of us have agreed is there to be seen. Just because something can't be measured and weighed in a laboratory doesn't mean it doesn't exist."

"I don't know," I said. "Sounds like a pretty good guideline to me."

But Jilly shook her head. "If you're going to be like that, what makes it any less of a leap in faith to believe in something that you need a microscope or other special equipment to see? Who's to say how much your observations are being manipulated by electronics and doodads?"

"Now you're just being silly."

Jilly smiled. "Depends on your point of view. Lots of people would say I was only being practical."

"Right. The same people who didn't believe in elephants at the turn of the century because they'd never seen one themselves."

"It's the same difference with an otherworldly being," Jilly said. "Just because you've never seen one, doesn't mean they don't exist."

I refuse to accept that. Accepting that would only lead to craziness and I've had enough of that to last me a lifetime. My mother spent more time with her imaginary companions, arguing and fighting and crying, than she did with us kids. There's no way I'm even cracking the door on the possibility of that happening to me.

4

It was a long moment before Eliza finally stood up again. Mechanically, she took the broom, went outside and swept the porch and steps once more, then returned to the gallery. She hung her parka in the closet and sat down behind the cash counter, started to reach for the phone, then thought better of it. What would she say? Sarah would think she'd gone mad. But she felt she had to tell someone.

Picking up a pencil, she turned over one of the flyers advertising a Zeffy Lacerda concert at the YoMan next weekend and made a sketch of what she'd seen. Thought she'd seen. The tiny man with his round moon of a body and twig-thin arms and the little startled eyes. She drew him changing from penny to little man. Another of him looking up at her. Another of him squeezing in through the crack between the baseboard and floor, fat little rear end sticking out and legs wiggling furiously.

No, she thought, looking at her drawings. Sarah definitely wouldn't believe that she'd seen this little man. No one would. She hardly believed it herself. Truth was, the whole experience had left her feeling vaguely nervous and unsettled. It was as though the floor had suddenly gone spongy underfoot, as though the whole world had become malleable, capable of stretching in ways it shouldn't be able to. It was hard to trust that anything was the way it seemed to be. She found herself looking around the shop, constantly imagining movement in the corner of her eye. She grew increasingly more tense with the pressure of feeling that at any moment the unknown and previously unseen was about to manifest again.

But at the same time she was filled with a giddy exhilaration, a kind of heady, senseless good humor that stretched a grin on her lips and made her feel that everything she looked at she was seeing for the first time. The art hanging from the walls was vibrant, the colors almost pulsing. The spiraling grain in the room's wooden trim, window frames, and wainscotting pulled at her gaze, drawing it down into its twists and turns. The smell of the turps and solvents from her studio behind her had never had such a presence and bite before. It wasn't so much unpleasant as so very immediate.

This, she realized suddenly, was what Jilly meant when she talked about the epiphany of experiencing magic, howsoever small a piece of the mystery you stumbled upon. It redefined everything. It wasn't a scary thing, in and of itself; it only felt scary at first because it was so surprising.

She smiled. That's who she could call, she thought. She laid her pencil down and reached for the phone, but before she could dial, she heard the front door open and someone stamping their feet in the hall. When she looked up, it was to find Jilly standing in the doorway. Jilly gave her a wave, then shook the snow from her tangled hair, brushed it from her parka.

"Oh, good," she said, removing her mittens. "You are open. I wasn't sure when I saw the closed sign in the window, but I could see that the steps had been swept so I thought I'd give it a try anyway."

Eliza blinked in surprise. "I can't believe you're here."

"Oh, come on. The weather's not that bad. In fact, I rather like this kind of a snowfall. Pooh on the winter grinches, I say."

"No, I mean I was just about to call you."

"With the most tremendous good news, I hope."

"Well, I . . ."

But by that point Jilly was standing by the counter and looking down at Eliza's sketches. Her eyes, already a startling blue, sparkled even brighter with merriment.

"Pennymen!" she said. "Oh, aren't they just the best?"

"You know what he is?"

Jilly gave her a puzzled look. "You don't? But they're your drawings."

"No. I mean, they are, but I've never heard of a pennyman before. I just thought . . . I just saw one a few moments ago . . . out in the hall . . . and . . ."

Her voice trailed off.

Jilly smiled. "And now you don't know what to make of it at all."

You didn't have to spend much time with Jilly for the conversation to turn to things not quite of this world. She claimed an intimate knowledge with the curious magical beings that populated many of her paintings, a point of view that frustrated die-hard realists such as Sarah at the same time as it enchanted those like Eliza who would love to believe, couldn't quite, but definitely leaned in that direction under the spell of Jilly's stories and firm belief. Or at least Eliza did so for the duration of the story.

"I guess that's pretty much it," Eliza admitted.

Jilly took off her parka and dropped it on the floor, then settled down in the extra chair that they kept behind the counter for visitors.

"Well," she said, "pennymen are very lucky. Christy wrote about them in one of his books."

She cocked an eyebrow, but Eliza had to shake her head. Christy Riddell was a friend of Jilly's, a local author considered to be quite the expert on urban folklore and myths. Eliza had lost count of how many books he'd written.

"I guess I haven't read that one," she said.

Jilly nodded. "Who can keep up with the man?" She scrunched her brow for a moment, thinking, then went on. "Anyway, the pennymen are all tied up with penny folklore. They start their lives in the branches of the penny trees."

Eliza gave her a blank look.

"Which is another name for trembling aspens," Jilly told her.

"Their leaves *do* look like coins," Eliza said. "The way they move in a breeze."

"Exactly. Except the pennymen are a coppery color—skin, hair, clothes, and all—and sort of turtlelike, since they can draw in their limbs and head and lie flat on the ground, looking exactly like a coin. Seeing one is like picking up the penny for luck. When they live in your house, they project a . . . I suppose you could call it an aura that promotes thriftiness and honesty."

Eliza smiled. "As in pennywise?"

"You've got it. And then there's that business with 'a penny for your thoughts.' Supposedly, every time that's offered, the pennymen acquire those thoughts and add them to what Christy calls 'the long memory'— the history of a people, or a family, or a city, or a social circle; a kind of connective stream of thoughts and memories that define the collective. A non-monetary wealth of song and poetry, stories and gossip, that we can access through dreams."

"Really?"

Jilly shrugged. "That's what Christy says—though they have to take a liking to you first. The problem is, they can also be mischievous little buggers if they decide you need to be taken down a notch or two. Not malicious, but definitely . . ." She looked for the word she wanted. "Vexing."

"But they're so small—what could they do?"

"Being small doesn't necessarily mean they can't be a bother. They can be very good at hiding your keys, or the pen you were sure you put down, right there, just a moment ago. Maybe they'll switch all the auto-dial numbers on your phone. Or wet your postage stamps so they're all stuck together when you go to use them. Little things."

Jilly looked down at Eliza's sketches again.

"I've never seen one myself," she said, "but you've drawn them exactly the way I imagined they'd look from Christy's descriptions."

"So what does it mean—my seeing one the way I did?"

Jilly laughed. "Mostly, it doesn't mean anything. It just is. It's like seeing a murder of crows, or a particularly wonderful sunset—you just appreciate the experience for what it is. The beauty of it. And the wonder. And how it can make you smile."

"But everything feels so different now," Eliza said. "It's like . . . I don't know. It's like I feel as though anything can happen now."

"And somewhere, it probably does."

"You know what I mean."

Jilly nodded. "Let me see if I can remember how Christy first explained it to me. What's happened is that you've now cracked open a door in the wall set up by the rational part of your brain—the part that makes it easier for us to function in what everybody perceives as the regular, logical world—and your own logic is struggling to shut it while the part of you that leans toward whimsy and wonder wants to push it as wide open as it can go. You have to learn to balance the two, though most people end up simply shutting the door again and not even remembering that it's there. They're not even aware that they're doing it; it's simple self-preservation because living with the door open, or simply ajar, can be very confusing."

"I'll say."

"But not necessarily a bad thing."

Eliza sighed. "Unless you're Sarah."

"There's that," Jilly agreed sympathetically.

5

There's something different about the boy when she comes home that night, but I can't quite put my finger on it. She's wearing a glow, but that could just be the weather. She loves the kind of snowfall we've had today. Some people get grumpy during a Newford winter; the boy only gets more cheerful. It's in the summer that she wilts.

I've finally gotten out of bed and made up for my earlier laziness by tidying the apartment and putting together dinner—a chicken curry, with nan and a yogurt-cucumber salad on the side. We have dinner and later we watch a video, a remake of *Sabrina* that I decide was much better in the original with Hepburn and Bogey, but the boy likes it.

Later, when I stop by the door of her bedroom to say goodnight, I find her looking at sketches of little round cartoon men that it turns out she did at the gallery earlier today. I'm surprised to see them because she usually works in a much more realistic mode, like the project she's been working on for the past few months, a series of landscapes, the connective thread being that each has a ladder in it. You don't always spot it right away, but it's there. The nice thing about the paintings is that the inclusion of the ladder is never forced. Odd, sometimes. Even a little startling. But never forced.

These drawings . . . they're more along the lines of what Jilly does. Fat-bellied miniature men—I know they're tiny because of the size references she's included in a couple of the drawings. A running shoe in one. Tubes of oil paint in another. They're fun—whimsical—and I find myself wondering if she's taken on a commission for a poster or something. Or maybe she's decided to develop a comic strip. There're worse things than having your work syndicated in hundreds of morning papers.

"What are these?" I ask.

"Pennymen," she tells me. "Coins that turn into little people when they think we're not looking."

I see the connection now. Lose the little heads and skinny limbs and they'd look just like pennies. In fact, there are coins in a couple of the sketches, which must be the pennymen at rest.

"Cute," I say.

She shrugs and bundles the sketches together, tosses them onto her desk. I wonder again why she's drawing them, but she doesn't say, and I don't ask. I get that funny feeling again—like I did when she first came home—that there's something different, something changed, only then she smiles and says goodnight, and I stop worrying about it.

But in the days that follow, I find myself thinking about it again because the boy seems to have developed a few odd mannerisms. Sometimes I see her sitting with her head cocked, listening, when there's nothing to hear. Or she'll turn quickly, as though she caught movement from the corner of her eye, but there're only the two of us in the room.

There's something familiar about all of this, but I don't place the familiarity immediately. Then one day it hits me.

She reminds me of my mother—my mother and her invisible companions—and my heart sinks.

6

It was two weeks before Eliza caught another glimpse of a pennyman. She was sitting in her studio, working on a canvas, when from the corner of her eye, she saw the slow, careful movement along the baseboard. As soon as she turned toward him, the little man dropped to the ground and there was only what appeared to be a penny lying there on the floor.

Eliza put her brush down and stepped around her easel. The pennyman remained motionless as she approached it. She knelt down for a closer look and cleared her throat. Feeling a little self-conscious, she addressed the coin.

"You don't have to be afraid," she said. "I would never hurt you. Honestly."

Not surprisingly, the copper penny made no reply. She didn't even get a small head poking its way turtlelike out of the body to look back at her. What response she did get came from the doorway to the gallery where Sarah was now standing, a puzzled look on her face.

"Eliza," she said. "*Who* are you talking to?"

"The pennyman," Eliza said, without thinking.

She'd looked over at Sarah, then back at where the pennyman had turned into a coin, but neither penny nor little man were there now.

"The pennyman," Sarah repeated.

Slowly Eliza returned her attention to her roommate.

"It's not like what you think," she told Sarah.

"How's that?"

You don't have to be afraid, Eliza wanted to say. I'm not going crazy like your mother did.

But of course she couldn't.

"They're real," Eliza said instead. "I didn't make them up."

Sarah nodded and Eliza watched her roommate's features close up, could feel the distance grow between them.

"Of course you didn't," Sarah said.

She turned away and went back into the gallery. Eliza gave the empty stretch of wooden floor a last scrutinizing look, then rose from where she'd been kneeling.

"Sarah!" she called.

Sarah reappeared in the doorway.

"Don't," she said, before Eliza could speak. "Don't make it worse."

"But there really are pennymen. I've seen them. It's true."

Sarah shook her head. "No, it's only true for you."

7

I know I'm being a lousy friend. I should be more sympathetic, but the boy should know that this is the last thing in the world I can deal with. I can't *ever* go through this again. It's not like she doesn't know. It's not like we haven't talked it out a hundred times before—the separate sorrows that we each had to carry and deal with on our own until that day we met. My mother and the boy's fiancé.

She got left at the altar, which is weird enough, except he was the one who wanted to get married so badly, he wanted the huge wedding, he's the one who blew it all up way out of proportion so that when he abandoned her in the church, the embarrassment and lack of self-worth she felt was exaggerated all out of proportion as well. And somehow the whole sorry mess became her fault. Her family blamed her. His family blamed her. She became the pariah in their circle of friends, none of whom would stand by her when she needed them, not even those who'd been her friends before she'd met him.

We helped each other. We made each other. Being an artist was something she'd only ever dreamed of before; I'm the one who stood by her and convinced her to make it a reality. I don't say this to make it seem like I should be getting some kind of a medal for perseverance and support above and beyond the call of duty, because she went through just as much for me. She's the one who finally made me believe I could be a normal functioning human being myself, that my mother's genes weren't going to tune me into broadcasts from loopyville and everything that would subsequently entail.

Except now she's the one who's gone all *X Files* on me. The truth isn't out there; it's on TV and it's not truth at all, it's just tabloid stories brought to life by writers trying to make a buck. The truth is we can't buy into the paranormal because it undermines everything that grounds us, that lets us function in the real world. And never forget, whatever little fairy-tale encounters we think we've had, whatever mysterious voices we hear whispering in our ears, or lights we see in the sky that can't be explained, at some point, we all have to return to the real world.

I guess the worst thing is that now there's a part of the boy that I don't recognize anymore. Now there's a whole side to her that's stopped making sense and that scares me. Because if part of her can become a stranger, what's to stop the rest of her from doing the same?

She could become anyone. She could have been anyone all along and I was just kidding myself that we knew each other. I find myself needing to ask, is this how we spend our lives—imagining each other? Because you can never really *know* what another person's thinking or feeling, can you? And just because they're thinking or feeling one thing at one time, what's to stop them from changing their minds about it?

Someone once told me never to fall in love with a place or a person because they're only on loan. What kind of a way is that to live? I thought when I first heard that. But now I understand a little better. It's because what you fall in love with doesn't last. Everything changes. Sometimes you can grow with it, but sometimes you just grow apart instead.

Earlier I said that magic belongs in stories and that the real world isn't a story. Not that kind, anyway.

I still believe that. Only now I wish I didn't.

8

Jilly found Eliza sitting in the window booth of The Dear Mouse Diner on Lee Street, nursing a cup of coffee that had long since gone cold. Outside, the snow had turned to freezing rain, making the footing more than a little slippery. Jilly was on her way home from an evening course she was teaching at the Newford School of Art and had almost taken a fall more than once before spying Eliza in the window and deciding to come in to join her.

"Hey, you," she said, sliding into the booth across from Eliza.

Eliza looked up and nodded hello. "Hey, yourself."

Jilly leaned over the table and peered into Eliza's cup. Her cold coffee looked about as appealing as old bathwater, complete with a dark ring at surface level crusted on the white china.

"You want a refill?" she asked.

Eliza shrugged, which Jilly took to mean yes. She brought the cup over to the counter and returned with a fresh one for each of them. They were busy for a moment, opening creamers and sugar packets, stirring the contents into their cups. Then Eliza sighed and looked out the window again.

"I feel this is all my fault," Jilly said.

Eliza looked back at her. "Don't. I'm the one who saw what Sarah can't handle as being real."

"But if I hadn't talked them up to you . . ."

Eliza shook her head. "It still wouldn't change my having seen the pennymen. I didn't mean to ever say that I believed they were real. Not to her. I mean, of all people, I *know* how she feels about that kind of thing. But she caught me off guard and it kind of slipped out and then, well, I wasn't about to start lying to her. That's just not something we'd do to each other."

"Of course not."

"Lying by omission was bad enough."

Jilly nodded. "So what's she doing now?"

"I'm not sure. I know she's staying at the Y, but she hasn't been back to the gallery in a week and she won't talk to me at all."

"I don't understand. Was it that bad with her mother?"

"Probably worse. I think she's scared of two things, actually. The first is that the pennymen aren't real, and that means I'm going to go the same route her mother did."

"And the second?"

"That the pennymen are real and so maybe her mother wasn't crazy."

"But she was diagnosed—"

"By the same terms of reference that say pennymen can't exist."

Jilly gave a slow nod. "I get it."

"The guilt would kill Sarah. You know, what if the voices and the invisible people were real?"

"Except there's a big difference between mental illness and an encounter with magic," Jilly said.

"But you can see how some people wouldn't see it that way. For them it has to be one or the other with no grey areas in between."

"Too true," Jilly said. "Unfortunately."

"And it was so hard for Sarah," Eliza went on. "I mean, by all accounts, her mother was way out there. Violent, if she stopped taking her medication. Imagine growing up in an environment like that. Screaming and flailing at things no one else could see. And maybe the worst thing was that her father wouldn't accept that it was an actual illness they were dealing with, so he wouldn't let her be hospitalized during the worst of it. He'd go off to work during the day, hang out with his buds in the evening, and there'd be Sarah and her little brother, left at home, trying to deal with all of this."

Eliza looked away, out the window again. The freezing rain was still coming down.

"Anyway," she said without looking away. "You can see why she wouldn't want to go through it again."

"So what are you going to do?"

"I don't know," Eliza said. "All I know is I miss her terribly."

"Would it help if I tried to talk to her?"

That woke the first smile Jilly had gotten from her so far this evening.

"What do *you* think?" Eliza said.

"This is true," Jilly admitted. "I'm not exactly renowned for my objective point of view when it comes to this sort of thing."

"But thanks awfully for offering."

Jilly nodded. "I guess we'll just have to hope that when she really thinks about it, when she weighs your friendship against how she has to deal with what you've experienced, the friendship will win out. That she'll realize that you're not her mother."

"I suppose," Eliza said. "But I'm not holding my breath waiting for it to happen."

"But you can hope."

"Of course," Eliza said. "There's always hope."

She didn't sound convinced. Jilly reached across the table and took her hand.

"The one thing I refuse to do," she said, "is give up on anyone. We're all carrying around devils inside us, but the thing to remember is, we're carrying angels, too. Sometimes we just have to wait a little longer for the angels to show up, that's all."

"Thanks," Eliza said. "I needed to hear something like that."

9

I've taken to riding the subways this past week—like I used to before I met the boy. Somehow I don't feel quite so lost and all alone sitting in one of these rattling cars, watching the dark tunnels go by. I don't know what I'm trying to find—or maybe hide from. I'm not really thinking at all. Except that's a lie, because at the same time as my head feels like a numbed bruise that can't hold one clear thought, I'm thinking about everything, all at once. The boy and my mother and coins that can turn into little men. Or is it vice versa?

I went to the Crowsea Public Library, to the Newford Room, and took down the faerie-myth book of Christy's. There's a whole section on the boy's pennymen in it and I read it through a few times. Doesn't make it any more real. I mean, where's the proof? Where's some straightforward empirical evidence? Surely if they actually existed we'd be reading about them in the real newspapers. They'd have pennymen in labs somewhere, running experiments on them, scientists would be publishing their findings. But there's nada. Just a few inches of type in an admittedly entertaining, but hardly textbook-factual collection of folk tales and myths.

The train pulls into the Williamson Street Station. The three people sharing my car get off. Nobody gets on. I stare down at my feet as the train pulls away again, heading for the next station. My clunky shoes don't hold a lot of interest, so I keep going, looking at the floor in the middle of the aisle, attention traveling across the car, under the opposite seat. Then I stop, gaze locked on the shiny copper penny lying there beside a candy wrapper.

I smile mirthlessly.

Penny? Or pennyman?

If I reach over to pick it up, will it scurry away? Or will it hold to its shape? Would I pick up a coin, or something soft and fleshy, squirming in between my fingers as it tries to escape?

We hit a rough patch of track and I grab for the nearest pole to keep my balance. When I look back under the opposite seat, the coin is gone. Did it simply roll away, or did it sprout limbs and walk away?

I realize it doesn't matter. Somewhere between seeing the coin and its disappearance, I remember how much the boy means to me. Her friendship is more important than the question of whether or not pennymen exist. Where does it say that we both have to agree on everything to be friends? Where does it say that just because she's convinced her pennymen are real, she's going to slide away from me the way my mother did?

I get off at the next station and find a pay phone. I'm calling home, but the boy doesn't answer. That's okay. I'd rather talk to her in person, anyway.

I decide to walk back to the apartment. Maybe she'll be back by the time I get there. If not, I can wait.

I don't know what I'll say to her when I see her. I won't say I believe— I can't do that because it wouldn't be true. I guess I'll just start with I'm sorry and see where that takes us.

Twa Corbies

As I was walkin' all alane
I heard twa corbies makin' mane . . .
—*from "Twa Corbies," Scots traditional*

1

Gerda couldn't sleep again. She stood by the upright piano, wedding picture in hand, marveling at how impossibly young she and Jan had been. Why, they were little more than children. Imagine making so serious a commitment at such an age, raising a family and all.

Her insomnia had become a regular visitor over the past few years—often her only one. The older she got, the less sleep she seemed to need. She went to bed late, got up early, and the only weariness she carried through her waking hours was in her heart. A loneliness that was stronger some nights than others. But on those nights, the old four-poster double bed felt too big for her. All that extra room spread over the map of the quilt like unknown territories, encroaching on her ability to relax, even with the cats lolling across the hills and vales of the bed's expanse.

It hadn't always been that way. When Jan was still alive—before the children were born, and after they'd moved out to accept the responsibility of their own lives—she and Jan could spend the whole day in bed, passing the time with long conversations and silly little jokes, sharing tea and biscuits while they read the paper, making slow and sweet love. . . .

She sighed. But Jan was long gone and she was an old woman with only her cats and piano to keep her company now. This late at night, the piano could offer her no comfort—it wouldn't be fair to her neighbors. The building was like her, old and worn. The sound of the piano would carry no matter how softly she played. But the cats . . .

One of them was twining in and out against her legs now—Swarte Meg, the youngest of the three. She was just a year old, black as the night sky, as gangly and unruly as a pumpkin vine. Unlike the other two, she still craved regular attention and loved to be carried around in Gerda's arms. It made even the simplest of tasks difficult to attend to, but there was nothing in Gerda's life that required haste anymore.

Replacing the wedding picture on the top of the piano, she picked Swarte Meg up and moved over to the window that provided her with a view of the small, cobblestoned square outside.

By day there was always someone to watch. Mothers and nannies with their children, sitting on the bench and chatting with each other while their charges slept in prams. Old men smoking cigarettes, pouring coffee for each other out of a thermos, playing checkers and dominoes. Neighborhood gossips standing by the river wall, exaggerating their news to give it the desired impact. Tourists wandering into the square and looking confused, having wandered too far from the more commercial streets.

By this time of night, all that changed. Now the small square was left to fend for itself. It seemed diminished, shadows pooling deep against the buildings, held back only by the solitary street lamp that rose up behind the wrought-iron bench at its base.

Except . . .

Gerda leaned closer to the windowpane.

What was this . . . ?

2

Sophie's always telling me to pace myself. The trouble is, when I get absorbed in a piece, I can spend whole days in front of the canvas, barely stopping to eat or rest until the day's work is done. My best times, though, are early in the morning and late at night—morning for the light, the late hours for the silence. The phone doesn't ring, no one knocks on your door. I usually seem to finish a piece at night. I know I have to see it again in the morning light, so to stop myself from fiddling with it, I go out walking—anywhere, really.

When the work's gone well, I can feel a deep thrumming build up inside me and I wouldn't be able to sleep if I wanted to, doesn't matter how tired I might be. What I need then is for the quiet streets of the city and the swell of the dark night above them to pull me out of myself and my painting. To render calm to my quickened pulse. Walking puts a peace in my soul that I desperately need after having had my nose up close to a canvas for far too long.

Any part of the city will do, but Old Market's the best. I love it here, especially at this time of night. There's a stillness in the air and even the houses and shops seem to be holding their breath. All I can hear is the sound of my boots on the cobblestones. One day I'm going to move into one of the old brick buildings that line these streets—it doesn't matter which one, I love them all. As much for where they are, I suppose, as for what they are.

Because Old Market's a funny place. It's right downtown, but when you step into its narrow, cobblestoned streets, it's like you've stepped back in time, to an older, other place. The rhythms are different here. The sound of traffic seems to disappear far more quickly than should be physically possible. The air tastes cleaner and it still carries hints of baking bread, Indonesian spices, cabbage soups, fish, and sausages long after midnight.

On a night like this I don't even bother to change. I just go out in my paint-stained clothes, the scent of my turps and linseed trailing along behind me. I don't worry about how I look because there's no one to see me. By now, all the cafés are closed up and except for the odd cat, everybody's in bed, or checking out the nightlife downtown. Or almost everybody.

I hear the sound of their wings first—loud in the stillness. Then I see them, a pair of large crows that swoop down out of the sky to dart down a street no wider than an alleyway, just ahead of me.

I didn't think crows were nocturnal, but then they're a confusing sort of animal at the best of times. Just consider all the superstitions associated with them. Good luck, bad luck—it's hard to work them all out.

Some say that seeing a crow heralds a death.

Some say a death brings crows so that they can ferry us on from this world to the next.

Some say it just means there's a change coming.

And then there's that old rhyme. One for sorrow, two for mirth . . .

It gets so you don't know what to think when you see one. But I do know it's definitely oh so odd to see them at this time of night. I can't help but follow in their wake. I don't even have to consider it, I just go, the quickened scuff of my boots not quite loud enough to envelop the sound of their wings.

The crows lead me through the winding streets, past the closed shops and cafés, past the houses with their hidden gardens and occasional walkways overhead that join separate buildings, one to the other, until we're deep in Old Market, following a steadily narrowing lane that finally opens out onto a small town square.

I know this place. Christy used to come here and write sometimes, though I don't think he's done it for a while. And he's certainly not here tonight.

The square is surrounded on three sides by tall brick buildings leaning against each other, cobblestones underfoot. There's an old-fashioned streetlight in the center of the square with a wrought-iron bench underneath, facing the river. On the far side of the river I can barely see Butler Common, the wooded hills beyond its lawns, and on the tops of the hills, a constellation of twinkling house lights.

By the bench is an overturned shopping cart with all sorts of junk spilling out of it. I can make out bundles of clothes, bottles and cans, plastic shopping bags filled with who knows what, but what holds my gaze is the man lying beside the cart. I've seen him before, cadging spare change, pushing that cart of his. He looks bigger than he probably is because of the layers of baggy clothes, though I remember him as being portly anyway. He's got a touque on his head and he's wearing fingerless gloves and mismatched shoes. His hairline is receding, but he still has plenty of long, dirty blonde hair. His stubble is just this side of an actual beard, greyer than his hair. He's lying face-up, staring at the sky.

At first I think he's sleeping, then I think he's collapsed there. It's when I see the ghost that I realize he's dead.

The ghost is sitting on the edge of the cart—an insubstantial version of the prone figure, but this one is wearing a rough sort of armor instead of those layers of raggedy clothes. A boiled leather breastplate over a rough sort of tunic, leggings and leather boots. From his belt hangs an empty scabbard. Not big enough for a broadsword, but not small either.

I start forward, only I've forgotten the crows. The flap of their descending wings draws my gaze up and then I can't hold onto the idea of the dead man and his ghost anymore, because somewhere between the moment of their final descent and landing, the pair change from crows into girls.

They're not quite children, but they don't have adult physiques either. I'm just over five feet, but they're shorter and even slighter of build. Their skin is the color of coffee with a dash of milk, their hair an unruly lawn of blue-black spikes, their faces triangular in shape with large green eyes and sharp features. I can't tell them apart and decide they must be twins, even dressing the same in black combat boots, black leggings, and black oversized raggedy sweaters that seem to be made of feathers. They look, for all the world, like a pair of . . .

"Crow girls," I hear myself say in a voice that's barely a whisper.

I lower myself down onto the cobblestones and sit with my back against the brick wall of the house behind me. This is a piece of magic, one of those moments when the lines between what is and what might be blur like smudged charcoal. Pentimento. You can still see the shapes of the preliminary sketch, but now there are all sorts of other things hovering and crowding at the edges of what you initially drew.

I remember how I started thinking about superstitions when I first saw these two girls as crows. How there are so many odd tales and folk beliefs surrounding crows and other black birds, what seeing one, or two, or three might mean. I can't think of one that says anything about seeing them flying at night. Or what to do when you stumble upon a pair of them that can take human form and hold a conversation with a dead man. . . .

One of the girls perches by the head of the corpse and begins to play with its hair, braiding it. The other sits cross-legged on the ground beside her twin and gives her attention to the ghost.

"I was a knight once," the ghost says.

"We remember," one of the girls tells him.

"I'm going to be a knight again."

The girl braiding the corpse's hair looks up at the ghost. "They might not have knights where you're going."

"Do you know that?"

"We don't know anything," the first girl says. She makes a steeple with her hands and looks at him above it. "We just are."

"Tell us about the King's Court again," her twin says.

The ghost gives a slow nod of his head. "It was the greatest court in all the land. . . ."

I close my eyes and lean my head back against the wall of the building I'm sitting against, the bricks pulling at the tangles of my hair. The ghost's voice holds me spellbound and takes me back, in my mind's eye, to an older time.

"It was such a tall building, the tallest in all the land, and the King's chambers were at the very top. When you looked out the window, all creation lay before you."

I start out visualizing one of the office buildings downtown, but the more I listen, the less my mind's eye can hold the image. What starts out as a tall, modern office skyscraper slowly drifts apart into mist, re-forms into a classic castle on top of a steep hill with a town spread out along the slopes at its base. At first I see it only from the outside, but then I begin to imagine a large room inside and I fill it with details. I see a hooded hawk on a perch by one window. Tapestries hang from the walls. A king sits on his throne at the head of a long table around which are numerous knights, dressed the same as the ghost. The ghost is there, too. He's younger, taller, his back is straighter. Hounds lounge on the floor.

In Old Market, the dead man talks of tourneys and fairs, of border skirmishes and hunting for boar and pheasant in woods so old and deep we can't imagine their like anymore. And as he speaks, I can see those tourneys and country fairs, the knights and their ladies, small groups of armed men skirmishing in a moorland, the ghost saying farewell to his lady and riding into a forest with his hawk on his arm and his hound trotting beside his horse.

Still, I can't help but hear under the one story he tells, another story. One of cocktail parties and high-rise offices, stocks and mergers, of drops in the market and job losses, alcohol and divorce. He's managed to recast the tragedy of his life into a story from an old picture book. King Arthur. Prince Valiant. The man who lost his job, his wife, and his family, who ended up dying, homeless and alone on the streets where he lived, is an errant knight in the story he tells.

I know this, but I can't see it. Like the crow girls, I'm swallowed by the fairy tale.

The dead man tells now of that day's hunting in the forests near the castle. How his horse is startled by an owl and rears back, throwing him into a steep crevice where he cracks his head on a stone outcrop. The hawk flies from his wrist as he falls, the laces of its hood catching on a branch and tugging off its hood. The hound comes down to investigate, licks his face, then lies down beside him.

When night falls, the horse and hound emerge from the forest. Alone. They approach the King's castle, the hawk flying overhead. And there, the ghost tells us, while his own corpse lies at the bottom of the crevice, his lady stands with another man's arm around her shoulders.

"And then," the ghost says, "the corbies came for their dinner and what baubles they could find."

I open my eyes and blink, startled for a moment to find myself still in Old Market. The scene before me hasn't changed. One of the crow girls has cut off the corpse's braid and now she's rummaging through the items spilled from the shopping cart.

"That's us," the other girl says. "We were the corbies. Did we eat you?"

"What sort of baubles?" her companion wants to know. She holds up a Crackerjack ring that she's found among the litter of the ghost's belongings. "You mean like this?"

The ghost doesn't reply. He stands up and the crow girls scramble to their feet as well.

"It's time for me to go," he says.

"Can I have this?" the crow girl holding the Crackerjack ring asks.

The other girl looks at the ring that's now on her twin's finger. "Can I have one, too?"

The first girl hands her twin the braid of hair that she's cut from the corpse.

After his first decisive statement, the ghost now stands there looking lost.

"But I don't know where to go," he says.

The crow girls return their attention to him.

"We can show you," the one holding the braid tells him.

Her twin nods. "We've been there before."

I watch them as they each take one of his hands and walk with him toward the river. When they reach the low wall, the girls become crows again, flying on either side of the dead man's ghostly figure as he steps through the wall and continues to walk, up into the sky. For one long moment the impossible image holds, then they all disappear. Ghost, crow girls, all.

I sit there for a while longer before I finally manage to stand up and walk over to the shopping cart. I bend down and touch the corpse's throat, two fingers against the carotid artery, searching for a pulse. There isn't any.

I look around and see a face peering down at me from a second-floor window. It's an old woman and I realize I saw her earlier, that she's been there all along. I walk toward her house and knock on the door.

It seems to take forever for anyone to answer, but finally a light comes on in the hall and the door opens. The old woman I saw upstairs is standing there, looking at me.

"Do you have a phone?" I ask. "I need to call 911."

3

What a night it had been, Gerda thought.

She stood on her front steps with the rather self-contained young woman who'd introduced herself as Jilly, not quite certain what to do, what was expected at a time such as this. At least the police had finally gone away, taking that poor homeless man's body with them, though they had left behind his shopping cart and the scatter of his belongings that had been strewn about it.

"I saw you watching from the window," Jilly said. "You saw it all, but you didn't say anything about the crow girls."

Gerda smiled. "Crow girls. I like that. It suits them."

"Why didn't you say anything?"

"I didn't think they'd believe me." She paused for a moment, then added, "Why don't you come in and have a cup of tea?"

"I'd like that."

Gerda knew that her kitchen was clean, but terribly old-fashioned. She didn't know what her guest would think of it. The wooden kitchen table and chairs were the same ones she and Jan had bought when they'd first moved in, more years past than she cared to remember. A drip had put a rusty stain on the porcelain of her sink that simply couldn't be cleaned. The stove and fridge were both circa 1950—bulky, with rounded corners. There was a long wooden counter along one wall with lots of cupboards and shelves above and below it, all loaded with various kitchen accoutrements and knickknacks. The window over the sink was hung with lacy curtains, the sill a jungle of potted plants.

But Jilly seemed delighted by her surroundings. While Gerda started the makings for tea, putting the kettle on the stove, teacups on the table, she got milk from the fridge and brought the sugar bowl to the table.

"Did you know him?" Gerda asked.

She took her Brown Betty teapot down from the shelf. It was rarely used anymore. With so few visitors, she usually made her tea in the cup now.

"The man who died," she added.

"Not personally. But I've seen him around—on the streets. I think his name was Hamish. Or at least that's what people called him."

"The poor man."

Jilly nodded. "It's funny. You forget that everyone's got their own movie running through their heads. He'd pretty much hit rock bottom here, in the world we all share, but the whole time, in his own mind, he was living the life of a questing knight. Who's to say which was more real?"

When the water began to boil, Gerda poured some into the pot to warm it up. Emptying the pot into the sink, she dropped in a pair of teabags and filled the pot, bringing it to the table to steep. She sat down across from her guest, smoothing down her skirt. The cats finally came in to have a look at the company, Swarte Meg first, slipping under the table and up onto Gerda's lap. The other two watched from the doorway.

"Did . . . we really see what I think we saw?" Gerda asked after a moment's hesitation.

Jilly smiled. "Crow girls and a ghost?"

"Yes. Were they real, or did we imagine them?"

"I'm not sure it's important to ask if they were real or not."

"Whyever not?" Gerda said. "It would be such a comfort to know for certain that some part of us goes on."

To know there was a chance one could be joined once more with those who had gone on before. But she left that unsaid.

Jilly leaned her elbow on the table, chin on her hand, and looked toward the window, but was obviously seeing beyond the plants and the view on the far side of the glass panes, her gaze drawn to something that lay in an unseen distance.

"I think we already know that," she finally said.

"I suppose."

Jilly returned her attention to Gerda.

"You know," she said. "I've seen those crow girls before, too—just as girls, not as crows—but I keep forgetting about them, the way the world forgets about people like Hamish." She sat up straighter. "Think how dull we'd believe the world to be without them to remind us. . . ."

Gerda waited a moment, watching her guest's gaze take on that dreamy distant look once more.

"Remind us of what?" she asked after a moment.

Jilly smiled again. "That anything is possible."

Gerda thought about that. Her own gaze went to the window. Outside she caught a glimpse of two crows, flying across the city skyline. She stroked Swarte Meg's soft black fur and gave a slow nod. After what she had seen tonight she could believe it, that anything was possible.

She remembered her husband Jan—not as he'd been in those last years before the illness had taken him, but before that. When they were still young. When they had just married and all the world and life lay ahead of them. That was how she wanted it to be when she finally joined him again.

If anything was possible, then that was how she would have it be.

The Fields Beyond the Fields

I just see my life better in ink.

—*Jewel Kilcher, from an interview on*
MuchMusic, 1997

Saskia is sleeping, but I can't. I sit up at my rolltop desk, writing. It's late, closer to dawn than midnight, but I'm not tired. Writing can be good for keeping sleep at bay. It also helps me make sense of things where simply thinking about them can't. It's too easy to get distracted by a wayward digression when the ink's not holding the thoughts to paper. By focusing on the page, I can step outside myself and look at the puzzle with a clearer eye.

Earlier this evening Saskia and I were talking about magic and wonder, about how it can come and go in your life, or more particularly, how it comes and goes in my life. That's the side of me that people don't get to see when all they can access is the published page. I'm as often a skeptic as a believer. I'm not the one who experiences those oddities that appear in the stories; I'm the one who chronicles the mystery of them, trying to make sense out of what they can impart about us, our world, our preconceptions of how things should be.

The trouble is, mostly life seems to be exactly what it is. I can't find the hidden card waiting to be played because it seems too apparent that the whole hand is already laid out on the table. What you see is what you get, thanks, and do come again.

I want there to be more.

Even my friends assume I'm the knowledgeable expert who writes the books. None of them knows how much of a hypocrite I really am. I listen well and I know exactly what to say to keep the narrative flowing. I can accept everything that's happened to them—the oddest and most absurd stories they tell me don't make me blink an eye—but all the while there's a small voice chanting in the back of my head.

As if, as if, as if. . . .

I wasn't always like this, but I'm good at hiding how I've changed, from those around me, as well as from myself.

But Saskia knows me too well.

"You used to live with a simple acceptance of the hidden world," she said when the conversation finally turned into a circle and there was nothing new to add. "You used to live with magic and mystery, but now you only write about it."

I didn't know how to reply.

I wanted to tell her that it's easy to believe in magic when you're young. Anything you couldn't explain was magic then. It didn't matter if it was science or a fairy tale. Electricity and elves were both infinitely mysterious and equally possible—elves probably more so. It didn't seem particularly odd to believe that actors lived inside your TV set. That there was a repertory company inside the radio, producing its chorus of voices and music. That a fat, bearded man lived at the North Pole and kept tabs on your behavior.

I wanted to tell her that I used to believe she was born in a forest that only exists inside the nexus of a connection of computers, entangled with one another where they meet on the World Wide Web. A Wordwood that appears in pixels on the screen, but has another, deeper existence somewhere out there in the mystery that exists concurrent to the Internet, the way religion exists in the gathering of like minds.

But not believing in any of it now, I wasn't sure that I ever had.

The problem is that even when you have firsthand experience with a piece of magic, it immediately begins to slip away. Whether it's a part of the enchantment, or some inexplicable defense mechanism that's been wired into us either by society or genetics, it doesn't make any difference. The magic still slips away, sliding like a melted icicle along the slick surface of our memories.

That's why some people need to talk about it—the ones who want to hold on to the marvel of what they've seen or heard or felt. And that's why I'm willing to listen, to validate their experience and help them keep it alive. But there's no one around to validate mine. They think my surname Riddell is a happy coincidence, that it means I've solved the riddles of the world instead of being as puzzled by them as they are. Everybody assumes that I'm already in that state of grace where enchantment lies thick in every waking moment, and one's dreams—by way of recompense, perhaps?—are mundane.

As if, as if, as if. . . .

The sigh that escapes me seems self-indulgent in the quiet that holds the apartment. I pick up my pen, put it down when I hear a rustle of fabric, the creak of a spring as the sofa takes someone's weight. The voice of my shadow speaks then, a disembodied voice coming to me from the darkness beyond the spill of the desk's lamplight, but tonight I don't listen to her. Instead I take down volumes of my old journals from where they're lined up on top of my desk. I page through the entries, trying to see if I've really changed. And if so, when.

I don't know what makes sense anymore; I just seem to know what doesn't.

When I was young, I liked to walk in the hills behind our house, looking at animals. Whether they were big or small, it made no difference to me. Everything they did was absorbing. The crow's lazy flight. A red squirrel scolding me from the safety of a hemlock branch, high overhead. The motionless spider in a corner of its patient web. A quick russet glimpse of a fox before it vanished in the high weeds. The water rat making its daily journeys across Jackson's Pond and back. A tree full of cedar waxwings, gorging on berries. The constantly shifting pattern of a gnat ballet.

I've never been able to learn what I want about animals from books or nature specials on television. I have to walk in their territories, see the world as they might see it. Walk along the edges of the stories they know.

The stories are the key, because for them, for the animals, everything that clutters our lives, they keep in their heads. History, names, culture, gossip, art. Even their winter and summer coats are only ideas, genetic imprints memorized by their DNA, coming into existence only when the seasons change.

I think their stories are what got me writing. First in journals, accounts as truthful as I could make them, then as stories where actuality is stretched and manipulated, because the lies in fiction are such an effective way to tell emotional truths. I took great comfort in how the lines of words marched from left to right and down the page, building up into a meaningful structure like rows of knitting. Sweater stories. Mitten poems. Long, rambling journal entries like the scarves we used to have when we were kids, scarves that seemed to go on forever.

I never could hold the stories in my head, though in those days I could absorb them for hours, stretched out in a field, my gaze lost in the expanse of forever sky above. I existed in a timeless place then, probably as close to Zen as I'll ever get again. Every sense alert, all existence focused on the present moment. The closest I can come to recapturing that feeling now is when I set pen to paper. For those brief moments when the words flow unimpeded, everything I am is simultaneously focused into one perfect detail and expanded to encompass everything that is. I own the stories in those moments, I am the stories, though, of course, none of them really belongs to me. I only get to borrow them. I hold them for a while, set them down on paper, and then let them go.

I can own them again, when I reread them, but then so can anyone.

According to Jung, at around the age of six or seven we separate and then hide away the parts of ourselves that don't seem acceptable, that don't fit in the world around us. Those unacceptable parts that we secret away become our shadow.

I remember reading somewhere that it can be a useful exercise to visualize the person our shadow would be if it could step out into the light. So I tried it. It didn't work immediately. For a long time, I was simply talking to myself. Then, when I did get a response, it was only a spirit voice I heard in my head. It could just as easily have been my own. But over time, my shadow took on more physical attributes, in the way that a story grows clearer and more pertinent as you add and take away words, molding its final shape.

Not surprisingly, my shadow proved to be the opposite of who I am in so many ways. Bolder, wiser, with a better memory and a penchant for dressing up with costumes, masks, or simply formal wear. A cocktail dress in a raspberry patch. A green man mask in a winter field. She's short, where I'm tall. Dark-skinned, where I'm light. Red-haired, where mine's dark. A girl to my boy, and now a woman as I'm a man.

If she has a name, she's never told me it. If she has an existence outside the times we're together, she has yet to divulge it either. Naturally I'm curious about where she goes, but she doesn't like being asked questions and I've learned not to press her because when I do, she simply goes away.

Sometimes I worry about her existence. I get anxieties about schizophrenia and carefully study myself for other symptoms. But if she's a delusion, it's singular, and otherwise I seem to be as normal as anyone else, which is to say, confused by the barrage of input and stimuli with which the modern world besets us, and trying to make do. Who was it that said she's always trying to understand the big picture, but the trouble is, the picture just keeps getting bigger? Ani DiFranco, I think.

Mostly I don't get too analytical about it—something I picked up from her, I suppose, since left to my own devices, I can worry the smallest detail to death.

We have long conversations, usually late at night, when the badgering clouds swallow the stars and the darkness is most profound. Most of the time I can't see her, but I can hear her voice. I like to think we're friends; even if we don't agree about details, we can usually find common ground on how we'd like things to be.

There are animals in the city, but I can't read their stories the same as I did the ones that lived in the wild. In the forested hills of my childhood.

I don't know when exactly it was that I got so interested in the supernatural, you know, fairy tales and all. I mean, I was always interested in them, the way kids are, but I didn't let them go. I collected unusual and odd facts, read the Brothers Grimm, Lady Gregory, Katharine Briggs, but *Famous Monsters* and ghost stories, too. They gave me something the animals couldn't—or didn't—but I needed it all the same.

Animal stories connected me to the landscape we inhabited—to their world, to my world, to all the wonder that can exist around us. They grounded me, but were no relief from unhappiness and strife. But fairy tales let me escape. Not away from something, but *to* something. To hope. To a world beyond this world where other ways of seeing were possible. Where other ways of treating each other were possible.

An Irish writer, Lord Dunsany, coined the phrase "Beyond the Fields We Know" to describe fairyland, and that's always appealed to me. First there's the comfort of the fields we do know, the idea that it's familiar and friendly. Home. Then there's the otherness of what lies beyond them that so aptly describes what I imagine the alien topography of fairyland to be. The grass is always greener in the next field over, the old saying goes. More appealing, more vibrant. But perhaps it's more dangerous as well. No reason not to explore it, but it's worthwhile to keep in mind that one should perhaps take care.

If I'd thought that I had any aptitude as an artist, I don't think I'd ever have become a writer. All I ever wanted to capture was moments. The trouble is, most people want narrative, so I tuck those moments away in the pages of a story. If I could draw or paint the way I see those moments in my head, I wouldn't have to write about them.

It's scarcely an original thought, but a good painting really can hold all the narrative and emotional impact of a novel—the viewer simply has to work a little harder than a reader does with a book. There are fewer clues. Less taking the viewer by the hand and leading him or her through all the possible events that had to occur to create this visualized moment before them.

I remember something Jilly once said about how everyone should learn to draw competently at an early age, because drawing, she maintains, is one of the first intuitive gestures we make to satisfy our appetites for beauty and communication. If we could acknowledge those hungers, and do so from an early age, our culture would be very different from the way it is today. We would understand how images are used to compel us, in the same way that most of us understand the subtleties of language.

Because, think of it. As children, we come into the world with a natural desire to both speak and draw. Society makes sure that we learn language properly, right from the beginning, but art is treated as a gift of innate genius, something we either have or don't. Most children are given far too much praise for their early drawings, so much so that they rarely learn the ability to refine their first crude efforts the way their early attempts at language are corrected.

How hard would it be to ask children what they see in their heads? How big should the house be in comparison to the family standing in front of it? What is it about the anatomy of the people that doesn't look right? Then let them try it again. Teach them to learn how to see and ask questions. You don't have to be Michelangelo to teach basic art, just as you don't have to be Shakespeare to be able to teach the correct use of language.

Not to be dogmatic about it, because you wouldn't want any creative process to lose its sense of fun and adventure. But that doesn't mean you can't take it seriously as well.

Because children know when they're being patronized. I remember, so clearly I can remember, having the picture in my head and it didn't look at all like what I managed to scribble down on paper. When I was given no direction, in the same way that my grammar and sentence struc- ture and the like were corrected, I lost interest and gave up. Now it seems too late.

I had a desk I made as a teenager—a wide board laid across a couple of wooden fruit crates. I'd set out my pens and ink, my paper, sit cross- legged on a pillow in front of it and write for hours. I carried that board around with me for years, from rooming house to apartments. I still have it, only now it serves as a shelf that holds plants underneath a window in the dining room. Saskia finds it odd, that I remain so attached to it, but I can't let it go. It's too big a piece of my past—one of the tools that helped free me from a reality that had no room for the magic I needed the world to hold, but could only make real with words.

I didn't just like to look at animals. I'd pretend to be them, too. I'd scrab- ble around all day on my hands and knees through the bush to get an understanding of that alternative viewpoint. Or I'd run for miles, the horse in me effortlessly carrying me through fields, over fences, across streams. Remember when you'd never walk, when you could run? It never made any *sense* to go so slow.

And even at home, or at school, or when we'd go into town, the ani- mals would stay with me. I'd carry them secreted in my chest. That horse, a mole, an owl, a wolf. Nobody knew they were there, but I did. Their se- cret presence both comforted and thrilled me.

I write differently depending on the pen I use. Ballpoints are only good for business scribbles, or for making shopping lists, and even then, I'll often use a fountain pen. When I first wrote, I did so with a dip pen and ink. Colored inks, sometimes—sepia, gold, and a forest green were the most popular choices—but usually India ink. I used a mapping nib, writing on cream-colored paper with deckled edges and more tooth than might be recommended for that sort of nib. The dip pen made me take my time, think about every word before I committed to it.

But fountain pens grew to be my writing implement of choice. A fat, thick-nibbed, deep green Cross from which the ink flowed as though sliding across ice, or a black Waterman with a fine point that made tiny, bird-track-like marks across the page.

When I began marketing my work, I typed it up—now I use a computer—but the life of my first drafts depends on the smooth flow of a fountain pen. I can, and did, and do, write anywhere with them. All I need is the pen and my notebook. I've written standing up, leaning my notebook on the cast-iron balustrade of the Kelly Street Bridge, watching the dark water flow beneath me, my page lit by the light cast from a streetlamp. I've written in moonlight and in cafés. In the corner of a pub and sitting at a bus stop.

I can use other implements, but those pens are best. Pencil smears, pen and ink gets too complicated to carry about, Rapidographs and rollerballs don't have enough character, and ballpoints have no soul. My fountain pens have plenty of both. Their nibs are worn down to the style of my hand, the shafts fit into my fingers with the comfort of the voice of a long-time friend, met unexpectedly on a street corner, but no less happily for the surprise of the meeting.

Time passes oddly. Though I know the actual contrast is vast, I don't feel much different now from when I was fifteen. I still feel as clumsy and awkward and insecure about interacting with others, about how the world sees me, though intellectually, I understand that others don't perceive me in the same way at all. I'm middle-aged, not a boy. I'm at that age when the boy I was thought that life would pretty much be over, yet now I insist it's only begun. I have to. To think otherwise is to give up, to actually *be* old.

That's disconcerting enough. But when a year seems to pass in what was only a season for the boy, a dreamy summer that would never end, the long cold days of winter when simply stepping outside made you feel completely alive, you begin to fear the ever-increasing momentum of time's passage. Does it simply accelerate forever, or is there a point when it begins to slow down once again? Is that the real meaning of "over the hill"? You start up slow, then speed up to make the incline. Reach the top and gravity has you speeding once more. But eventually your momentum decreases, as even a rolling stone eventually runs out of steam.

I don't know. What I do know is that the antidote for me is to immerse myself in something like my writing, though simply puttering around the apartment can be as effective. There's something about familiar tasks that keeps at bay the unsettling sense of everything being out of my control. Engaging in the mundane, whether it be watching the light change in the sky at dusk, playing with my neighbor's cat, or enjoying the smell of freshly brewed coffee, serves to alter time. It doesn't so much stop the express, as allow you to forget it for a while. To recoup, catch your breath.

But writing is best, especially the kind that pulls you out of yourself, off the page, and takes you into a moment of clarity, an instant of happy wonder, so perfect that words, stumbling through the human mind, are inadequate to express.

The writer's impossible task is to illuminate such moments, yes, but also the routines, the things we do or feel or simply appreciate, that happen so regularly that they fade away into the background the way street noise and traffic become inaudible when you've lived in the city long enough. It's the writer's job to illuminate such moments as well, to bring them back into awareness, to acknowledge the gift of their existence and share that acknowledgment with others.

By doing this, we are showing deference to the small joys of our lives, giving them meaning. Not simply for ourselves, but for others as well, to remind them of the significance to be found in their lives. And what we all discover, is that nothing is really ordinary or familiar after all. Our small worlds are more surprising and interesting than we perceive them to be.

But we still need enchantment in our lives. We still need mystery. Something to connect us to what lies beyond the obvious, to what, perhaps, *is* the obvious, only seen from another, or better-informed, perspective.

Mystery.

I love that word. I love how, phonetically, it seems to hold both "myth" and "history." The Kickaha use it to refer to God, the Great Mystery. But they also ascribe to animism, paying respect to small, mischievous spirits that didn't create the world, but rather, are *of* the world. They call them mysteries, too. *Manitou.* The little mysteries.

We call them faerie.
We don't believe in them.
Our loss.

Saskia is still sleeping. I look in on her, then slowly close the bedroom door. I put on my boots and jacket and go downstairs, out onto the pre-dawn streets. It's my favorite time of day. It's so quiet, but everything seems filled with potential. The whole world appears to hold its breath, waiting for the first streak of light to lift out of the waking eastern skies.

After a few blocks, I hear footsteps and my shadow falls in beside me.

"Still soul searching?" she asks.

I nod, expecting a lecture on how worrying about "what if" only makes you miss out on "what is," but she doesn't say anything. We walk up Lee Street to Kelly, past the pub and up onto the bridge. Halfway across, I lean my forearms on the balustrade and look out across the water. She puts her back to the rail. I can feel her gaze on me. There's no traffic. Give it another few hours and the bridge will be choked with commuters.

"Why can't I believe in magic?" I finally say.

When there's no immediate response, I look over to find her smiling.

"What do you think I am?" she asks.

"I don't know," I tell her honestly. "A piece of me. Pieces of me. But you must be more than that now, because you've had experiences I haven't shared since you . . . left."

"As have you."

"I suppose." I turn my attention back to the water flowing under us. "Unless I'm delusional."

She laughs. "Yes, there's always the risk of that, isn't there?"

"So which is it?"

She shrugs.

"At least tell me your name," I say.

Her only response is another one of those enigmatic smiles of hers that would have done Leonardo proud. I sigh, and try one more time.

"Then tell me this," I say. "Where do you go when you're not with me?"

She surprises me with an answer.

"To the fields beyond the fields," she says.

"Can you take me with you some time?" I ask, keeping my voice casual. I feel like Wendy, waiting at the windowsill for Peter Pan.

"But you already know the way."

I give her a blank look.

"It's all around you," she says. "It's here." She touches her eyes, her ears. "And here." She moves her hand to her temple. "And here." She lays a hand upon her breast.

I look away. The sun's rising now and all the skyscrapers of midtown have a haloing glow, an aura of morning promise. A pair of crows lift from the roof of the pub and their blue-black wings have more color in them than I ever imagined would be possible. I watch them glide over the river, dip down, out of the sunlight, and become shadow shapes once more.

I feel something shift inside me. A lifting of . . . I'm not sure what. An unaccountable easing of tension—not in my neck, or shoulders, but in my spirit. As though I've just received what Colin Wilson calls "absurd good news."

When I turn back, my companion is gone. But I understand. The place where mystery lives doesn't necessarily have to make sense. It's not that it's nonsense, so much, as beyond sense.

My shadow is the parts of me I'd hidden away—some because they didn't fit who I thought I was supposed to be, some that I just didn't understand.

Her name is Mystery.

St. John of the Cross wrote, "If a man wants to be sure of his road he must close his eyes and walk in the dark."

Into his shadow.

Into mystery.

I think I can do that.

Or at least I can try.

I pause there a moment longer, breathing deep the morning air, drawing the sun's light down into my skin, then I turn, and head for home and Saskia. I think I have an answer for her now. She'll still be sleeping, but even asleep, I know she's waiting for me. Waiting for who I was to catch up with who I'll be. Waiting for me to remember who I am and all I've seen.

I think I'll take the plants off that board in the dining room and reclaim the desk it was.

I think I'll buy a sketchbook when the stores open and take one of those courses that Jilly teaches at the Newford School of Art. Maybe it's not too late.

I think I'll reacquaint myself with the animals that used to live in my chest.

I think I'll stop listening to that voice whispering "as if," and hold onto what I experience, no matter how far it strays from what's supposed to be.

I'm going to live here, in the Fields We Know, fully, but I'm not going to let myself forget how to visit the fields beyond these fields. I'll go there with words on the page, but without them, too. Because it's long past time to stop letting pen and ink be the experience, instead of merely recording it.